MODERN ENGLISH

RACHEL SPANGLER

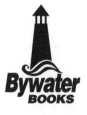

Ann Arbor
2021

Bywater Books

Copyright © 2021 Rachel Spangler

Print ISBN: 978-1-61294-213-1

Bywater Books First Edition: February 2021

Printed in the United States of America on acid-free paper.

Cover designer: Ann McMan, TreeHouse Studio

Bywater Books
PO Box 3671
Ann Arbor MI 48106-3671
www.bywaterbooks.com

To Susie, it's always your fault.

Acknowledgments

As I write this acknowledgment in the fall of 2020 it seems so odd to prepare to launch a travel romance into the world at a time when the world cannot travel. We are in the midst of a great global pandemic where people all around fight for their livelihoods, their health, and even their lives. I pray that by the time this book is read, we are on our way out of the darkest days, but in the meantime, I hope that instead of surrendering to the darkness, the fear, or even the fatigue, we will all find ways to look around at what we have lost and choose to appreciate what we still have. Even amid the horrors we have witnessed in 2020, I still believe the world is a great big marvelous place, and I know that no force anywhere in it is more powerful, healing, or transformational than love. Those core beliefs shape who I am and what I write, so while I cannot solve all the world's problems, I pray that in the pages ahead you will find a short respite from the fear along with replenishing doses of hope, faith, wonder, and most of all love.

I would like to start by thanking the readers for all the love they have shown me over the years, but especially after the release of *Full English* in 2019. I immediately began to hear from readers who wanted a story centered on Lady Victoria, and I made a promise that if more than half the reviews mentioned her, I would do my best to tell her story. When all was said and done, more than 90% of the reviews wanted more Lady Vic, so I got to work. Thank you to each and every person who took the time to email, reach out on social media, or write a public review. This book was a blessing to me at a time when I really needed it, and I'm not sure I would have written it without your encouragement. Please don't ever underestimate the effect a caring reader can have on the career path of a writer.

Next, I would like to thank the people who made my own months in England so fun to revisit. Kelly Smith, of course, made the whole thing possible. She also helped me work out some of the earliest ideas for this book as well, since she and Ann Shaw walked me through my first lessons in succession of peerage, along with some complex details around land and titles. Joanne, Barry, and Ethan helped us explore a beautiful castle and kept my family entertained (and fed) during my initial research visit for this spin-off. Jane, Hilary, Kristen, Max, and the entire Red Lion Friday Club welcomed us back and continued to serve as inspiration for the wonderful people Vic takes Sophia to meet at the pub. Our good friend Dr. Karen Randell served as my British proofreader, who caught all my embarrassing Americanisms. I also want to thank the tour staff at Alnwick, Warwick, and Warkworth castles, who took the time to explain so many details about castle walls, budgets, and land conservation, as well as who does what and when, and how much everything costs. I suspect they found me a rather suspicious character by the time I left, but they remained polite and engaging without ever once calling security, even when I took the same tour twice in a row.

Again, as was the case with *Full English*, while this book very much takes place in England, it is also half American, and the same goes for my creative team. Thank you to the entire Bywater crew, who continues to be top notch in every aspect of the business. Salem, Marianne, Elizabeth, Nancy, Kelly, and Ann McMan regularly put together the best books in the business, and they were incredibly kind and patient with me on this one. I especially want to thank Ann McMan for designing a cover that reflects the unique story I tried to tell, the region that inspired it, and its strong ties to *Full English*. Oh, and she made it a truly beautiful work of art as well. Thank you to Lynda Sandoval, who loved these characters as much as I did and treated both them and me with care. Thank you to Barb and Toni, my most trusted first readers, who always let me know when I'm on the right track. And of course, thank you to my awesome page proofers (Diane, Ann, Marci, and Melissa), because no matter how many professionals approve a book before typeset, they always manage to catch a few more mistakes before we send it off to the printer.

And now, if you will indulge an extra dose of sentimentality, this is where I admit this book is my first written fully since the passing of my dear friend Diane Gaidry. The pain of her loss knocked me flat and changed me in ways I found overwhelming and at times frightening. The grief had a profound effect on every part of my life, but perhaps most dramatically on my creative abilities. I didn't write at all for months, and when I did it was a challenge unlike any other I have faced in my career. I'm not at all sure I would have had the strength or the will to keep trying if not for the people around me who refused to let me fade into obscurity. Thank you first to Anna Burke, who reached out to me almost every day, to check in or sometimes just sit with me in the awfulness. Thank you to Nikki Smalls, who continued to poke me until I would answer, and then kept throwing ideas at me until some of them stuck. Thank you to Georgia Beers and Melissa Brayden, who insisted I belonged in their writerly conversations even when I didn't believe I had anything left to offer. Thank you to Alex and Jess for eating nachos and watching *Gentleman Jack* with me when it's all I had the mental space to do. And thank you to the Shibden After Dark crew for indulging the first wild ideas I'd had in ages. I still miss Diane every single day, and some days that still feels like more than I can handle, but thanks to the people listed above, I know I don't have to face it alone.

I also want to thank my therapist, Leah Eagan, who helped me finally begin to build the skills I needed to start pulling myself out of the pit. There is such a stigma around mental health in America, but if I can do my tiny part to combat that here, please let me. Your mental health matters. You matter. If you are struggling with grief, depression, anxiety, or any of the other number of complex issues that make you feel like you're in too deep or unable to cope on your own, please reach out. I know it's hard, I know it's scary, but trust me, it's worth it.

And finally, thank you to my amazing family. To Will, who got us to England together the first time and keeps calling us back each summer. I can't wait for us all to gather around a table at Latimer's. To Jackson, who is the best young traveler I have ever met, you inspire me to adventure. Your zest for new experiences, willingness to step outside your comfort zone, and ability to connect with people anywhere we go is a model for what we could all be if we stopped clinging to what we know and leaned into the extra-ordinary. And to Susie, how can I possibly find the words to thank the person who gives me everything all at once? You are both my roots and my wings, my freedom to roam and my safe place to call home. I know I have not made life easy for you, especially over the last year and a half. I have no romantic platitudes that can sufficiently convey my gratitude for the ways you have fought for me and for us. I only hope that you know how much I mean it when I say, I thank you, and I love you, come what may.

As always, none of these very long acknowledgements would be possible without the gift of grace from a loving creator, redeemer, and sanctifier.

Soli deo gloria.

Author's Note

Much like its predecessor *Full English*, this book is told from the point of view of two characters, one American and one British. And while I kept their vocabulary consistent with their nationalities, we ran into the same complications we faced last time, around spelling. While it's all fine and good to have an American say "truck" and a Brit say "lorry," it gets very disorienting to editors and readers alike to see the same words spelled differently, sometimes even on the same page. So, as I promised in the author's notes to *Full English*, this time those spellings are consistently British. That said, there were still a few instances where British formal spellings and British common spellings conflicted, and when that happened, we asked actual Brits what would feel most natural given the character's social class and geographical region. Obviously, language and dialect always carry a bit of subjectivity, so I hope you'll give the Northumbrians I leaned on the benefit of the doubt in this area.

Also, while the settings of this book are very much *inspired* by the places my family and I lived in and explored around Northern England, I had to take a few liberties with the towns and other locations that required I create a fictional village, dukedom, and castle. I hope those who know the area will still see the places and landmarks they love reflected in the story that follows, while understanding why the legalities of writing around them required me to change a few names of places. All similarities to people real or imagined are purely coincidental.

Chapter One

Vic changed gears on the Land Rover as she pulled off the motorway and started up the steep incline that marked her turn away from the sea. The road narrowed, and her chest tightened in anticipation. Winding first past a small orchard, and then along a brook that raced over stones, she sat a little taller as she neared the top of the familiar rise. A glint of sinking sun sparked the first flash of gold against white in the distance. A flag snapped back, then waved straight out as if the lion emblazoned on it had seen her coming. It was silly and sentimental to think her family standard might be eager to see her return, but she was the only person in the car, so what did a little sentiment hurt?

Atop the rise, her breath caught at the picturesque panorama before her. She slowed nearly to a stop. The valley spread out as far as the eye could see. Trees gave way to an expansive meadow rushing over hill and dale until it rose into a slope of green, moved not by nature but man. Steep earthworks rose sharply into the classically notched sandstone fortress of Penchant Castle.

From here she couldn't make out the cannons atop the battlements that looked low compared to the mammoth central keep they'd once protected from the threats of England's borderlands. Those dangers had faded from the landscape over the centuries, but little about the inward bailey had changed to reflect the reduced threat. Then again, maybe the threats hadn't vanished so much as morphed.

Vic shook her head and urged the car forward, picking up speed to match the rush of relief surging through her. As she drew closer, zipping over smaller hills and across a bridge barely big enough to accommodate her vehicle, the castle loomed steadily larger in her view. Strong, proud, imposing, comforting, and so many other things all rolled into one impressive package; she no longer tried to sort the myriad of emotions the expansive compound inspired in her. The complexities couldn't be separated from each other any more than they could be separated from her, and today she cared less about those conflicts than ones she'd left behind her to the north.

Vic slowed as she rolled through a bondgate marking the town that had sprung up under the historic protection of the Duke of Northland. Cobblestone streets rumbled under her tires, and the long, grey rowhouses threatened to obscure her destination, but Penchant Castle refused to be concealed. Down every side street and over every roof, its impenetrable walls and octagonal tower demanded their due. When she made the last slow turn onto a wide old military boulevard, she had her final unobstructed view of the grey stone, bathed in orange glow and showered in her own sentiment.

She was home.

Pushing a little button on her dashboard, she waited for the heavy iron gate to rise before her. Thankfully, it was too late in the day for tourists or summer staff to mill about the grounds or gawk at her with their discreet whispers and not nearly as discreet cameras. Still, she made a point to smile and nod her acknowledgment to the lone security officer stationed at the gate house. He returned the gesture with a slight bow of his head, and with that minor formality observed, she blew out the last of the tension she'd been holding.

Then, turning toward the inner bailey, she sucked the stale air right back into her lungs.

"What the ..." Hitting the brake hard enough to vent her surprise, she also managed to stall the engine. A large white lorry blocked the entire archway into the tightly enclosed courtyard, accompanied by the muffled voices of people doing God-only-knew-what inside.

Staring at the offending vehicle for several minutes, her sense of dread grew as each unreasonable possibility whirred through her mind. Surely no one would pull into a gated and guarded castle to rob them blind, but it was also prime tourist season, so no one would've scheduled anything major in the way of renovations or restorations either. If there had been a significant disaster via flood or fire, surely someone would've called her or her father before contracting for repairs. Her serenity evaporated at the realisation that no easy explanation met well with any logical one.

Climbing out and slamming the door to the Rover, she squeezed between the cargo compartment of the lorry and the stone walls into the courtyard. The smaller space was abuzz with activity. Men in Pickford polos hurried back and forth like ants carrying food toward their mound, only instead of leaves and berries, these little foot soldiers carried rugs, lamps, and her family's antique fainting couch.

"Pardon me," she called out. "What are you doing with that?"

"Loading." A man with a rough growth of dark facial hair stated the obvious.

"For what purpose?"

He shrugged and hoisted the low legs of the couch onto the bed of the enclosed compartment. "I don't ask questions. I lift, I move, I get paid."

Oh, to live with such a clear purpose. "Can you at least tell me on whose authority you do those things?"

He wrinkled his nose and furrowed his brow.

"There's a lady inside, Miss," the younger man holding the other end of the couch offered.

"Inside?" Her pulse accelerated a few more beats per minute. Of course, she'd known the furniture came from inside the residence, but the mental image of some strange woman giving orders to hired men in her own living room sent her stomach plummeting.

Vic jogged up the front steps and through the ceremonial

entryway, taking fleeting note that nothing there had been displaced before she turned toward the grand staircase. Another pair of men came toward her carrying an ornately carved end table she'd never been overly fond of, but she didn't have to like her mother's furniture to care that someone was making off with it. She practically sprang up the large marble stairs. As she approached the first-story landing, she passed another man who carried only a small statue of Athena.

"Where's your supervisor?" she barked, and he nodded over his shoulder.

She bounded up two more stairs and into a formal sitting room. Looking left, then right, she didn't see any more removal employees. She didn't see anyone at all. Childhood games of hide and seek had taught her one of the downsides to living in such a large estate was that one could end up running in circles all day without encountering the person they sought. The best course of action often involved staying put and, given that her family's belongings all seemed to be flowing down the stairs, this seemed as good a place as any to make a stand.

At least all the remaining furniture seemed in its place. Not that she would know for sure, as she didn't spend much time here. Mostly the room was set up for official tours. She certainly wouldn't want to sit on any of those fancy chairs, or . . . her gaze fell on an old umbrella rack in the corner. She didn't have to know the space well to know the walking stick standing upright in the bin didn't belong there. She picked up the staff and suffered an untimely bit of nostalgia. Her grandfather had carved the wood with a silver knife while she sat beside him and listened to her grandmother read.

Her grandmother.

Her eyes darted around the room until they fell on the bare patch of wall where her rapier should have hung. Her blood boiled. None of the furniture had been personal, and even the prospect of a stranger running roughshod over her home didn't compare with the rage she felt at the thought of anyone touching that sword.

4

Hide-and-seek strategy be damned, she was ready to release the proverbial hounds when she spun around and saw the tip of a metal hilt sticking out of a brown cardboard cylinder. It took her two steps to reach it, and in one grand flourish she unsheathed the blade.

God help whoever'd tried to make off with this. She gave a quick flick of her wrist and relished the whoosh the metal made as it slashed the air.

"Unhand the sword," a firm voice ordered from behind her.

Quite the opposite of the command, she whirled, arm at the ready until her eyes landed on the woman who'd issued the order.

Vic blinked a few times, as if trying to make sense of the strikingly beautiful body clad in traditional tan riding breaches that smoothly stretched from the top of tall leather equestrian boots, over smouldering curves of thighs and hips, and all the way up to a high, slender waist. From there, a gauzy white blouse flowed loosely everywhere but the bust. The woman's ample assets stressed the last button before the barest hint of exposed cleavage and collarbone. Vic stared at that meeting point only a second too long before the odd word choice finally seeped through her haze, and she snapped her attention to the woman's dark, defiant eyes.

Struck nearly speechless once more, she managed only to squeak out, "Unhand?"

The woman lifted her chin and stared down her nose at Vic. "Release it."

Instead of obeying, she stepped forward, tightening her grip on the hilt. Her anger flared at being spoken to with such disdain when it was *she* who had the right to make demands here.

To her credit the woman didn't back away even as Vic swung the blade more pointedly in her direction.

The intruder cut an imposing figure. Her boots made her only a smidge taller than Vic, but her bearing amplified her stature. Strong bone structure and dark hair pulled severely back from her smooth sienna face paired flawlessly with the haughty line of her lips. More impressively, her poise was so unfaltering that if the woman had commanded anything other than a symbolic severing of Vic's birthright, she might have complied.

"Look, I don't know who you think you are."

"Lady Regina Bronwyn Alistair."

Vic narrowed her eyes, unable to quite place the woman's posh accent. The name managed to sound both vaguely familiar and utterly contrived all at once. The resulting disconnect caused her guard to falter, and she lowered the tip of the rapier as she tried to place the name. The move proved poorly timed, because Lady Regina made use of the lapse to quickly sidestep the false edge of the sword and push well into Vic's personal space. Then in the same fluid motion, the woman placed a hand firmly around Vic's on the hilt, and pressed down, pinning the rapier between them.

"And who are *you*?"

Her mouth went dry, both at being so swiftly disarmed and the woman's sudden proximity. The chill emanating from the impressive body somehow managed to heat Vic to her core, as their eyes locked. "I'm Vic."

"Vic?"

"Toria." She sighed and collected herself. "Victoria. Victoria Charlotte Algernon Penchant, if you must."

Lady Regina arched an eyebrow coolly.

The lack of reception rubbed Vic raw once more. Why had she entered into a battle of wills and arousal with this stranger in her own home? Was her sense of self so weak?

She belonged here.

This woman did not.

Honestly, those were among the few things she knew for certain, and still her voice lacked conviction as she cleared her throat and added, "If you don't remove yourself from my living room immediately, I won't hesitate to contact the proper authorities."

A flash of something dark sparked in the woman's eyes, and the corner of her tight lips gave a little twitch. "Living room?"

Odd that she'd homed in on that word instead of, *immediately* or *authorities*. Still, Vic made use of the brief upper hand to attempt a withdrawal to a more suitable distance, but as she stepped back, the woman's hand tightened around her own, and, by extension, the rapier.

Vic's eyes flicked quickly to the place where strong fingers held hers captive, then back to the woman, and the last of her poise faltered. Her heart hammered in her chest as a fight-or-flight instinct took hold of her senses. The other woman must have seen it as well, because in the rush of fear, they both reacted in the same way.

"Security!" they called simultaneously, and with equal force, but before Vic could fully register the coincidence, several people ran in from opposing doorways.

To her right, and to her relief, a few familiar faces of her estate staff appeared, but behind the woman who'd yet to release her, another stranger sprinted into the room, followed by the house steward, James.

"Your Ladyship?" He lowered his head, then catching sight of the rapier, snapped his eyes up once more. "Are you quite all right, ma'am?"

"Yes," both she and Regina answered in unison again. They stared at each other for another long, tense second before the corner of Regina's pressed lips curled up slightly.

"For the love of God," the woman with James called out, in a distinctly American accent. "Cut. End scene. Break. Whatever the hell your safe word is, Sophia, I'm using it right now."

The woman snorted and cracked only the smuggest of smiles before she slowly released Vic's hand and stepped back. "Sophia?" Vic asked. It was the only thing she could manage to process amid the piles of mounting questions. "You introduced yourself as Regina."

"Oh, Sophia, you didn't." The woman with James stepped forward. "I apologize completely, for that and any other confusion we may have caused. I'm Talia Stamos, producer and screenwriter."

"And this," Talia gestured to the woman who still held Vic's attention, "is our lead actress, Sophia LeBlanc, who's currently flexing her method-acting muscles to prepare for playing the role of Princess Regina Alistair."

Vic fought the urge to step back or collapse as all the tension left her body. She'd not interrupted a robbery, but rather stepped into a film scene with a Hollywood powerhouse. Embarrassment came quickly on the edge of her relief, but if Sophia could play the role of princess convincingly, then Vic could certainly summon enough gravitas to greet her properly.

Giving a small, stately bow, she extended her hand to Sophia. "It's a pleasure to make your acquaintance, Madam LeBlanc."

Sophia raised an eyebrow before accepting Vic's hand with a half-hearted squeeze. "Likewise, I'm sure."

"Don't mind her," Talia cut in, practically shoving Sophia's arm out of the way and taking this Victoria woman's hand with a weak half-bow, half-curtsey.

Sophia rolled her eyes as her friend began to fawn, pouring on every ounce of properness her little middle-class heart could muster.

"Your Ladyship, there seems to have been an error on the contracts we signed for our on-location shoots at Penchant Castle." Talia tried again.

"Americans." The butler, or whoever he was, offered the entirety of his explanation and handed his boss a small stack of papers.

Victoria scanned them quickly, her brow furrowing in a way that made her appear older than she'd initially seemed. The woman had gone through a myriad of shifts over the last few moments, though, so Sophia didn't find her new, studious expression any more discordant than her entitlement as she'd demanded explanations, or her arousal as she'd surveyed Sophia like she might inspect one of the oil paintings on the walls all around them.

"We didn't mean any disrespect, Your Ladyship," Talia pressed. "We showed up on time, and we presented the contract to your staff, then went about our work as scheduled."

"They presented their contract to a summer staff member who didn't know any better, and he will be summarily fired upon reporting for work tomorrow," Mr. Butler-Man stated drolly.

Victoria didn't argue with the "off with their heads" proclamation as she flipped through to another page.

"We didn't know there was a difference between summer staff and full-time staff," Talia explained.

James shook his head as if he found this distasteful. "I was in the residence at the time, and before I even saw the removal van, they'd pulled into the courtyard and made off with several important pieces."

"We followed all the procedures outlined in the contract," Talia pointed out. "Local movers, no paintings, proper wrapping and padding of artifacts—"

"You're in the wrong room." James sniffed his disdain.

"We didn't know that," Talia pleaded.

"Hardly inspires confidence."

"Your people told us—"

Victoria raised a hand, causing both James and Talia to fall silent.

Sophia couldn't help but feel a little impressed. What she wouldn't give to silence her detractors with the flick of her wrist. And this woman managed to do so without wearing any of the ridiculous costumes Sophia would have to wear over the course of the film to convey that sort of authority. Victoria managed to speak quietly and dress like an Eddie Bauer catalogue model without undercutting her gravitas.

Then again, she wasn't playacting at authority. She'd been born into it, which of course was why Sophia wasn't taken in by her blue jeans and form-fitting cable knit sweater, or those clear blue eyes. She'd seen the full ferocity the others had only witnessed the tail end of. This castle dweller would've gladly run her through only moments ago.

Well, she smiled at the memory, *maybe not gladly*. Sophia made a living by understanding how people conveyed emotions, and Victoria had managed to convey quite a few of them during their brief interaction, most notably a healthy dose of attraction.

"You may be excused on all counts," Victoria finally said, handing the papers back to Talia. "Except you showed up three months too early."

"No, we didn't," Talia said quickly, then adjusted her tone. "I'm sorry, Your Ladyship, but I beg to differ."

Sophia rolled her eyes again at the forced formality. Talia Stamos was known as a bit of a ballbuster in the movie business, but she didn't act the part now, as she practically grovelled before this rich heiress. Though to be fair, the begging may have had less to do with the woman's station and more to do with the fact that Victoria held the keys to the literal castle.

"The contract states we're supposed to arrive on 7/10," Talia pressed.

"Exactly, October seventh."

"No, 7/10 is July tenth . . . unless . . . oh Lord, you all format your dates backwards over here."

Victoria straightened her shoulders. "Perhaps it's you who format your dates backwards. We are still in England, are we not?"

Talia raised her hands apologetically. "You're right, we are, and I want to be respectful, but the contract was written in Los Angeles."

"And signed here."

"But also, signed and filed legally in California."

"And yet, not to belabour the point," Victoria kept her tone even, "but, the document spells out legal terms for the use of English property."

Talia sighed heavily, and Sophia started to feel a little bad for her. She shouldn't even be the one having this conversation. It wasn't a screenwriter's or producer's job to run interference with local authorities, but Talia had been so much more than any one title could convey on this project. She'd fought for every detail of this film from long before even Sophia came on board. Now that she'd finally gotten on set, she should've been able to hand over the arguing to someone else, and yet here she was, having to basically fall to her knees before some blond-haired, blue-eyed, genetic poster girl for superior breeding.

Sophia's resentment rose in her again.

It was bad enough the two of them were even there instead of being able to trust the crew to get the pre-filming parts right. It was bad enough their interns couldn't get the dates right. It was worse that she'd spend the next few months of her life taking direction from a pretty boy, playboy, rich boy director who lacked any genuine artistic vision. She didn't need some pretty girl, play-girl, rich girl to make them grovel for the privilege of doing so.

And now that Victoria had regained her composure, she carried all the confidence she'd lacked when Sophia held her hand pinned to that silly sword. Then again, money could cut as sharply as any blade, and this woman was likely more comfortable wielding financial power anyway.

"The fact of the matter," Talia said calmly, "is we're here now. We've flown principal cast and quite a bit of equipment across the ocean."

"Then you can fly it back again in three months," Victoria said, not unkindly, but with no room for compromise.

"The seasons won't be right for the story, the cast has other commitments, the budget already spent, and I understand you don't see any of those things as your problem, but there has to be some other way to make this work," Talia pleaded. "Please, Emma has told me so many wonderful things about you."

"Emma?"

"Yes, Emma Volant and I have been friends for years."

Victoria's demeanour changed so quickly Sophia had to blink a few times to make sure she was still looking at the same woman. Her ladyship shed all pretense in a single second as she threw her head back and stared skyward, as if she could somehow see through the high-vaulted ceiling and straight into heaven. All the tension fell from her shoulders as she rolled out her neck and ran her fingers through long, blond hair. When she returned to them from wherever her mind had gone, even her facial features had transformed, lips, cheeks, eyes, all lifted on a smile so open Sophia's breath hitched in her throat.

It wasn't that she hadn't noticed the woman's beauty. She'd

have to be blind not to, but her affect had been forced, her appeal cool and detached in a business sort of way. The demeanour came from privilege and practice, and even Sophia could project similar bearing with the right makeup and lighting. As someone who had cultivated the look for herself, she generally had no trouble seeing through it in others, but for those transforming seconds, Vic shattered the façade and revealed something so perfectly genuine Sophia couldn't even breathe deeply.

She had the presence of mind to realize this strong a reaction was very, very bad, but not enough of her wits about her to look away as Vic's smile encompassed her once again.

"Emma is a dear friend," she said almost apologetically, but not fully managing to appear chagrined. "If you're friends of hers, I'd be remiss not to welcome you into my home."

"So, we can resume our prep work?" Talia asked optimistically.

"Kindly refrain from moving anything else this evening," Vic said quickly. "I give my word I'll do whatever's in my power to find a way to juggle your needs with those of the estate, but please understand this endeavour has become infinitely more complex than any of us originally planned for."

Then she turned back to Sophia, those blue eyes darker. "Ms. LeBlanc, I hope you'll understand those complications as well."

Sophia snorted softly, trying to regain some of the detachment that had dominated her emotions moments ago, but she couldn't bring herself to do anything further, because at her core she agreed very much with Victoria's assessment of the situation. Everything suddenly felt more much complicated than it had moments earlier.

Chapter Two

James followed the women out, but Victoria hadn't left the living room by the time he returned. She stood at the floor-to-ceiling windows, still holding the hilt of her grandmother's rapier loosely in her hand.

"Are you all right, Your Ladyship?"

She forced her standard business smile back into place as she turned to face him. "Yes. Thank you, James."

He nodded toward the weapon. "Would you like me to return that to its proper place?"

"You probably should. I don't think we'll face any more intruders this evening." She handed over the sword. "And even if we did, I'm sure it could be used as easily against me as for me."

He didn't even pretend he had more faith in her than she had in herself. "Perhaps when they return, your father should be present."

She swallowed a heavy sigh. "I'll make that suggestion when I speak with him this evening."

"Shall I ring him for you now?"

No rest for the weary, of course. She'd looked forward to a full night alone with her own thoughts. Now she would've gladly settled for ten minutes to herself, and yet even that small measure was apparently too much to ask.

"No, thank you, I'll do so immediately. Could I bother you to join me in the study, in about an hour?"

"Of course, ma'am. Would you like me to summon anyone else in the interim?"

The question suggested he thought she should, but her brain was full to the brim, and she had bigger questions to answer first. "Let's wait and see what conclusion my father and I arrive at."

"Very well." He nodded and took his leave. Vic wished she could do the same, but she'd just given herself a mere hour to formulate a course of action, get her father's approval, and figure out how to begin implementing details she'd yet to conceive.

She strode through the large dining room, down a wood-panelled corridor, and into her father's formal study. Unlike many other fathers, he'd never barred her from his sanctuary. Throughout the years he'd patiently explained a multitude of concepts, from lines of succession to land grants to resource conservation, in here. He'd never shied away from the complexities of their lives, always giving her a fair chance to understand what was at stake and form her own opinions. Now that their roles were slowly reversing, she owed him nothing less.

Dropping into his high-backed leather desk chair, she dialled his number by heart. It took only two rings before his gentle voice conveyed the smile she couldn't see. "Do you miss us already?"

"Always."

"Good, then you'll be back tomorrow?"

Vic sighed at the mix of emotions the questions inspired in her. She didn't relish the tasks that would now keep her at the castle much longer than expected, but she'd be lying to herself and to him if she said she wanted to rush back to Scotland.

"Uh-oh," he said. "Your silence is ominous. Let me find a quieter place to talk. Then you can tell me all about what's keeping you away."

She doubted she'd tell him all about it. She'd stick to business, as it was easier to understand than her mental state. It wasn't that she didn't love Scotland. She had such happy memories there. As a child she'd run free on their family's summer retreats. She'd climbed windswept rocks and run barefoot through fields. She'd never been expected to wear dresses or tie back her hair.

When had it all changed? It would be easy to associate that level of happiness with childhood, but not her childhood. The rules had always been different when in residence at the castle, or at boarding school, and anyway, Scotland continued its wildness well past her teenage years.

She'd learned to hold her whiskey in Scotland. She'd learned to hold Maggie Armstrong there, too. The two of them kissed atop crags and tangled together during days so long the twilight never seemed to fully fade. And even after those escapades also gave way to adulthood, she still cherished the memories of building a wee stick fort for her niece, Abigail. It hadn't been so long ago that she'd patrolled the perimeter of their imaginations playing the role of protector against the big bad wolf, played perhaps too convincingly by . . . Robert.

She sighed. There it was, suddenly, the moment of when the change had occurred shone crystal clear, though the events around that moment felt fractured. Perhaps crystal shards offered a more fitting allusion to that particular memory, both precious and sharp.

"Vic?" her father asked.

"Yes?"

"You've managed to sigh twice in the moment it took me to walk into the next room." His voice was gentle as always, and she experienced a new wave of guilt for what she was about to do. Summer offered their only prolonged chance to connect these days, but he more than anyone in the world would understand the responsibility weighing on her shoulders.

"We've had a mix-up with the filming crew for Emma Volant's movie."

"What sort of a mix-up?"

Vic told him about the paperwork, the furniture removal, and James's annoyance, leaving out only the part where a beautiful woman disarmed her in both the literal and figurative sense. She couldn't let her mind wander back to Sophia LeBlanc's imposing physical presence and cold indifference, or she'd never be able to maintain her focus.

"What do you think?" he asked, when she finished relaying the details.

She knew what she wanted to do, but she didn't want to overplay her hand and show her bias, so she first laid out the key arguments for sending the film crew back to Hollywood empty-handed. "This is our busiest time. We have our summer schedule set. Many families have already planned visits to the area, and local business owners who depend on the tourism traffic would bear an undue burden if we suffered unexpected closures."

"Certainly."

"And yet those same businesses would likely benefit a great deal from the influx accompanying a large film crew. Many of them were scheduled to stay at B&Bs around the castle, and surely they would eat and shop at local businesses. The studio also promised to hire locals for things like lights and carpentry, not to mention the extras for the film. Those things would undoubtedly benefit both the economy and community morale."

He made a slight noise of agreement.

"Additionally, we did sign the contract," she said with a little bit of chagrin. "I maintain they should've given thought as to how their filming locations would format dates, but seeing as how no one on our staff gave any consideration to where the contract originated, I'm not sure we have a much higher moral stand here, and our family name should stand for something when it appears on a legal document."

"Indeed."

She could picture him nodding.

"The contract was entered into in good faith, and intent should be upheld whenever possible. Our name is only as good as the honour behind it, but I suspect you'd already come to that conclusion?"

"Because I'm transparent?"

"No, because you're thoughtful. I suspect you didn't need my input here, but I believe that if a mix-up can be attributed to both staffs, then the burden for making amends should fall in the middle as well. What do you propose?"

"What makes you think I've formulated a grand plan?"

"You've had grand plans since you were old enough to talk." Some of the tension in her shoulders loosened at the humour in his voice. "I think I'll have to stay here and walk the tightrope between keeping the main tourism spaces as open as possible and protecting the sanctity of the family spaces from the invasion."

"That was our primary concern when you first broached the idea, if I remember correctly. Along with the standards of propriety the family must maintain."

"I intend to keep my word to you and mother as well," she said quickly, remembering the initial argument to grant access to the film crew at all. The family never allowed any other business interests into their private sanctuary, and even the formal tours operated under the strictest protocol for complex and varied reasons, ranging from basic safety to her mother's almost obsessive aversion to anything common enough to excite public perceptions. Her mother placed an exacting emphasis on timelessness, tradition, and transcendence. Vic, for her part, had often fallen short of her expectations in those areas, usually inspiring disappointment more than outright disagreement, but the former had stifled her enough over the last few weeks not to want to bear the brunt of them any further this summer.

"So, where will they film the movie if not in the public spaces or the family spaces?"

"That," she said emphatically, "is what I've got to navigate."

"Your mother won't like the vagueness of your new job description."

"Then perhaps it's best for her to remain in Scotland. Someone should convince her there's no need to disrupt her plans only to rush back into a stressful situation."

"Well thought," he said. "Then I suppose we both have our assignments. You're about to get much more involved in the movie business, and I'm to keep the rest of the family far from it."

She smiled at his summation. "Want to switch jobs?"

He chuckled softly. "No, we both know this setup plays to each of our strengths. Please phone me if anything changes."

17

She agreed and hung up with a wash of gratitude for his faith in her, but even with that vote of confidence and his offer to run interference on her behalf, she wasn't at all sure she was as up to her task as he was to his.

Sophia did her best not to roll her eyes at Brian Dawes as he sat on the small table inside her trailer. What was with these hipster guys' inability to use chairs like regular people? Or was the pose something he had seen in a movie about directors at some point? She never could quite shake the feeling that he wasn't so much a director as a little boy playing at one the way some children play soldier or house. To prove her point, he shook a few strands of golden curls from his forehead and held up his hands to mimic a camera lens.

"We could shoot from some obscure angles to make it look like we're inside the castle walls, when really we're outside them. Can't be any worse than the sound stages I grew up on."

"Yes, but not too obscure, because I was thinking I could look at the camera directly sometimes," her co-star, Tommy Malone, said from the front of the trailer where he was checking his own reflection in a makeup mirror.

"Yeah, yeah," Brian said dismissively, "like extreme close-ups."

"Close-ups work for me," Tommy said.

This time, Sophia didn't manage to keep from rolling her eyes. Thankfully the men were too self-absorbed to notice, but she caught Talia smiling at her.

They'd all reported to talk about their current quandary, but there wasn't much to say until they got their verdict from the lady of the house, so the last two hours had been spent trying to tame her annoyance amid the men's grandstanding and random visits from costumers or makeup artists.

"Have either of you even been outside the castle walls?" Talia asked. "Aside from your rooms at the B&B?"

"I went to a pub last night," Tommy said, in his authentic Scottish accent. "Good ales, better company."

Brian smiled lecherously. "Company, eh? Maybe that's what I'll do tonight. I was too jet-lagged yesterday."

Apparently, jet lag presented itself as hung over from the complimentary booze on his first-class flight the night before. Or maybe the complimentary Bloody Marys on his train down from Edinburgh, since Sophia and Talia had shared the same travel itinerary without similar effects. Then again, she'd nearly gotten into a sword fight with the owner of a castle, so perhaps she should try the jet lag excuse as well.

"Come on." Talia extended her hand to Sophia. "Let's get some fresh air."

She allowed herself to be pulled outside.

"Sorry," Talia said as soon as the door closed behind them. "The level of self-absorption in there was aggravating my allergies."

"You're allergic to rich, talentless, self-absorbed men?"

"Of course. Aren't you?"

"Come to think of it, that character trait does tend to carry rash-like symptoms for me. And not just in men."

"Right. I've gotten the same sort of under-my-skin itch around a starlet or two, but I've found it more common in the men of this business."

"I'm afraid our hostess is about to provide a counterpoint," she said. She recognised the form of Victoria Von Rich-and-Pretty striding toward them across the courtyard.

"Ah," Talia followed her gaze. "Here comes the judge and jury to deliver our verdict."

"Aren't you worried?"

"Only mildly."

"Because you called your mutual friend to exert her influence last night?" Sophia asked. No matter what she thought of Lady Victoria, she clearly had a soft spot for this Emma woman.

"I actually didn't feel the need to play that card." Talia's eyes never left Vic as she drew closer to them, stopping a time or two to greet staff members.

"Please don't tell me you left the entirety of this project up to *that* woman's better angels."

"I wanted to give her the benefit of the doubt before I pull in the big guns."

"I'd have thought she already had all the benefits a person could ever want handed to her at birth. Sometimes a bit of strong-arming is exactly what a woman like her needs."

Talia didn't disagree but said, "I've never been a firm hand when it comes to women. If we get to that point, I'll let you take the lead, but I'd like to go on record and say this one might surprise you."

Sophia was about to say it had been a long time since any human surprised her, but the comment died on her lips as Lady Victoria spotted them and raised a hand in greeting.

Talia returned the little gesture in a poor approximation of a royal wave, and mumbled, "Be nice."

"Good morning," Lady Victoria called as she crossed the cobblestones to meet them.

"Good morning." Talia made an awkward little half-bow; half-curtsey move that caused Vic to tilt her head to the side before turning to Sophia.

"Ms. LeBlanc."

"Have you come to hand down our verdict?" She cut right to the chase.

"I'd not quite thought of my visit that way," Vic said, with a polite smile.

"Of course not," Talia cut back in and banged on the door to the trailer. "We'd love to chat with you. Please, won't you join us inside?"

"I'd be delighted."

"You might want to reserve judgement on that one until you meet the others." Sophia's comment earned a sharp elbow to her ribs as Talia swung open the door and made quick introductions. Brian at least had the good sense to stand up, and Tommy offered a much smoother bow than Talia had pulled off.

"It's a pleasure to make your acquaintance, Your Ladyship," he said. "Could I get you a cup of tea? We've not got anything too posh, mind you."

"Not at all, please, have a seat, and tell me if that's a hint of Glaswegian I hear in your accent."

"Aye, well done."

"My family has an estate in Lanarkshire," Victoria said to the rest of the group as if that offered them any sort of meaningful explanation. "They're actually there for the summer, which leads me right into the main purpose of my visit. My family vacates this house during the summer months to allow tourist operations to run more smoothly. The income our summer guests bring is a major economic force, not for my own family, but for the area surrounding the castle and village. Any interruption to that schedule could have dire consequences for our local economy, so if we are to move forward with the filming schedule, there will need to be considerable concessions made."

Talia's eyes grew big. "For clarification, you're not here for the breakup talk, you're here for the 'let's work this out' talk?"

Victoria smiled brightly. "What a nice way to put it. Yes, and I do have faith that with a little compromise on both our parts, we'll find a middle path that does, in fact, work."

Half the room exhaled in a collective whoosh of relief, only it wasn't Sophia's half. Neither she nor Brian seemed to have been holding their breath in the first place. She felt a little twinge of annoyance to have even mentally aligned herself with that asshole, but she still didn't see what all the fuss was about. Of course, she wanted to make the film. She'd worked and prepped and compromised some of the standards around who she'd willingly accept direction from, all because she wanted to play the role so badly, which was all the more reason not to like the words *concessions* and *compromise* coming from some noblewoman who'd likely never worked a day in her life. She couldn't resist the opportunity to say so.

"I'm sorry. I don't mean to sound ungrateful, but if it's going to be such an ordeal for you, are we sure this is the right place for us? Aren't there a thousand other castles in England and Scotland?"

"There are a great many," Vic admitted.

"But none of the others have you in charge of them," Talia cut back in, "which is one of several reasons we'd very much like to stay here."

Sophia couldn't argue. This woman was a looker, and she'd mastered a commanding affability they must teach rich women at prep school. Certainly, other castles would come with other rich, entitled owners who weren't nearly as easy on the eyes in skinny jeans and soft, snug sweaters.

"If that's the case, we'll have to come to terms on a few new caveats."

Talia grabbed a nearby iPad and tapped the screen. "Lay them on me."

"Any filming done in tourist areas of the house will be done after 4 p.m., and the equipment used will need to be moved by ten o'clock the next morning."

Talia pressed her lips together, no doubt thinking of all the extra hours this would require for the crew.

"You can shoot outdoors any time of day or night, so long as it doesn't impede tourist traffic around the grounds."

"Wait, people will still be, like, hanging around in the background?" Brian finally engaged. "That'll wreck our sound all to shit."

Talia cleared her throat. "What he means to ask is, if we encourage people to watch us film, might we ask them to observe a few moments of quiet during the actual takes?"

"I'm sure some people would find it interesting to be part of that," Victoria agreed. "And we'll make reasonable accommodations to cordon off various parts of the grounds as needed. You can also shoot on the walkways atop the battlements as well as atop the outward towers."

"What about the big tower, in the middle?" Brian asked.

"Sadly, that's not feasible this time of year," Victoria said quickly, "both due to tourist traffic and the way large equipment like cameras and lights would alter the skyline of not only the castle, but also the village."

"Surely the village could handle a little bit of a blocked view for a few days," Brian pushed, and once again Sophia felt a bit peeved to find herself agreeing with him.

"I understand why you'd think so." Victoria maintained her politely firm tone. "But we actually have substantial photo tourism in the town, and a great many people book wedding shoots a full year in advance to try to get images with the castle in the background."

"Haven't they ever heard of photoshop?" Brian grumbled.

"I'm afraid this point is firm. I've already agreed to extra work for my people, extra inconvenience for our visitors, and extra hours for our security staff. Alienating photographers and brides alike would put a strain on our relationship with too many locals and tourists."

Victoria laid out her case in such a calm, measured, and amiable way Sophia almost caught herself agreeing with her. Certainly, when she framed the conversation the way she wanted, Lady Victoria came off as quite reasonable, even generous, but Sophia had yet to see her actually make any grand gestures. The woman owned a castle, for crying out loud. Surely it wouldn't be a hardship for her to lose a few tourist dollars. Then again, a woman from umpteen generations of history ruling over common folks probably wouldn't care about fleecing a few Hollywood producers either.

To be fair, Sophia didn't feel any sort of sadness for the poor movie moguls' dollars either. She did care a great deal about getting the shots she needed to make this movie a success, though, and some of her pivotal scenes were slated to be shot atop a high central tower with wide dramatic angles and sweeping cinematography.

"I can rework a couple scenes to reflect the use of a lower tower," Talia offered as she made a few notes.

A little muscle in Sophia's jaw twitched at the visual, but she bit her tongue waiting to see how the rest of the chips fell.

"Fine. Whatever." Brian slouched back in his seat again, as if the minuscule amount of artistic integrity he'd mustered, and then surrendered, had exhausted him.

"Would it be possible," Talia continued, "for us to make surface adaptations to places like the stables so long as they are in keeping with historical accuracy?"

Victoria tilted her head to the side as if considering the point. "I'm open to the idea. However, it would require considerable coordination to make sure your animals were cared for without damaging our facilities. We haven't kept horses on the castle grounds since the Second World War, as we do our own riding near our Blackstone Abbey preserve."

Sophia didn't manage to completely suppress her eye roll. This woman had multiple horse-storing facilities and also, apparently, an abbey, but she balked about space on set?

"Perhaps we could check out those facilities?" Talia asked.

"A visit could be arranged, and filming near the abbey would certainly give you more freedom, as it doesn't see as much tourism, but I need to stress every detail will have to be seen to with utmost care. Your staff will have to work closely with ours on that project."

"Of course," Talia agreed quickly.

"That's actually a salient point in most situations," Vic added. "I'm asking you to respect that this is our home. If one of my people asks you to desist from doing something or going somewhere, I need your word that you will."

"I'm not taking orders from some pimply kid who wants me to stand behind a yellow rope," Brian said with more force than he'd been able to muster earlier.

"Nor would I expect you to," Victoria said amiably. "I have several staff members who will liaise with your team to schedule the times and dates for filming various scenes, and a team of preservation specialists who'll work with you to make sure your needs are met while still protecting our possessions. And I'll be present to assure all the various stakeholders can move forward without issue."

"You personally?" Sophia finally spoke. She hadn't meant to. The words just sort of slipped out.

Victoria met the blue eyes boring into hers. "Certainly. Everything that happens here is ultimately my responsibility."

Sophia didn't break her gaze. "Yours? Not your father's? Not your man James's? Not your secretary's?"

Victoria's mouth twisted slightly, only for the barest of seconds, before she nodded, but Sophia saw it, and she leaned forward, looking more closely for any other soft spot in that armour.

"So, to be sure, if we have a conflict with any of your people at any point, we should contact . . ."

"Me." Victoria lifted her chin as if she heard a challenge in the question. "First and last."

"Not a problem at all," Talia cut back in before Sophia could push any more.

Out of respect for Talia, she took her cue to sit back, but she exchanged a glance with Tommy, whose green eyes reflected a hint of the surprise she felt at Victoria's little pronouncement. It wasn't uncommon for a filming location to assign someone to work with the film crew, but it was unusual for that person to be a rich, beautiful heiress of British nobility.

"Good." Victoria stood. "If we're in agreement, I'll have our people amend the contract and present it to you as soon as possible."

Talia rose and shook her hand. "I really appreciate this. The film is very important to me."

Victoria nodded seriously. "And to me as well."

Then she stepped out of the trailer, but before Talia had a chance to close the door behind her, Sophia jumped up and followed.

"Um, excuse me," she called. Not her strongest opening. "Ms., um, Your uh, Ladyship?"

Victoria turned around, her smile bright but polite. "Seeing as how we're to be colleagues, why don't you call me Vic?"

That seemed odd, but then again, so had every other encounter with this woman, and first names would at least give the appearance of a more level playing field. "Okay, Vic. Before you rush the contract off to your undoubtedly talented lawyers, could I press you to reconsider one of your restrictions on where we can film?"

25

"You may press, but I feel it only fair to warn you it may be a fool's errand."

"I'm familiar with those, trust me, but I have a lot at stake here. I need the film to be a success, which means we can't cut corners on cinematography. A smaller tower means smaller shots, and the loss of 360-degree panoramas. It'll constrict everything at precisely the moments when we need the views to feel endless."

Victoria raised an eyebrow. "I'll admit I don't know much about filmmaking, but isn't it unusual for a lead actress to concern herself with camera angles when the director didn't have any trouble making accommodations?"

"He's an idiot."

"That's less than inspiring to hear about a man to whom I granted a great deal of access. Maybe I need to rethink some tighter restrictions."

"Oh, come on." Sophia exploded. "Are you seriously going to extend your little power trip even further?"

Vic blinked in surprise, and for a second something akin to hurt flashed in her eyes before she regained the politely distant veneer all her social training had likely stamped onto her features. "I'm sorry you feel I came here in a power play, or anything other than sincerity."

Sophia didn't buy that, and her body language must've said so, because Victoria sighed heavily.

"Perhaps I failed to make my own personal stake here clear. I certainly understand that for most people, this place—" she gestured expansively to the castle behind her, "—feels like a movie set, but it's my home. I live here. My family lives here. My grandparents lived their entire lives here. The people I love have their fingerprints all over the place. Would you give a stranger, whom you yourself consider an idiot, carte blanche to trample all over your family's home and heirlooms?"

Sophia folded her arms across her chest. "I have no heirlooms, and my family home is quite often inhabited by idiots who ran roughshod over every part of my life for as long as I let them. If you're planning to gain sympathy with some family history argument, or an emotional connection to inherited wealth, then it's no surprise your appeal landed better with Brian, as he has plenty of both. I, on the other hand, have only ever had what I've been willing to fight for."

Victoria's smile faltered again, and this time it stayed that way, making her appear genuine for the first time all morning. "I'm sorry to hear that, but, the fact that you chased me down to go against the will of all your colleagues suggests you're long past the point where you'll accept less than you deserve."

"Touché." Sophia appreciated the quick turnaround of her sad story. "But now that you know that about me, I hope you also realize this isn't the last conversation we'll have on filming details."

"What makes you think we'll need multiple discussions?"

This time it was Sophia's turn to smile. "Because I'm beginning to suspect neither of us is the kind of woman who wilts under pressure."

Victoria's lips parted softly, and a myriad of emotions flashed across her beautiful features. Sophia couldn't read them all, much less understand what sparked them, but for the first time, a part of her wanted to.

Chapter Three

"Oh, my goodness," Emma exclaimed before Vic fully opened the door to her car for her. "It's finally happening."

She smiled at her friend's exuberance as Emma threw an arm around her waist and gave a little squeeze. The brief contact felt better than it should have, and she allowed herself a second to rest her head on Emma's shoulder, breathing in the soft lavender scent of her long blond hair, before stepping back and asking, "How's Brogan?"

"Ugh, she's swamped. The lifeboats got called out yesterday, and it set the sailing tours back, so she's offering extra runs today. Then, tonight she's promised a sleepover for all the nieces and nephews so her siblings can have time with their overtaxed spouses."

"So, in other words, she's still utterly perfect?"

"Basically." Emma's face radiated so much love Vic felt only the slightest pain at not having been the one to spark such a reaction. It wasn't that she still harboured any romantic intentions for her. They'd settled into such a lovely companionship filled with quiet understanding and heartfelt conversations, plus no one would deny Brogan made Emma happier than she ever could have, but the fear that she might never make someone so happy still left her sad sometimes.

"Have you met Talia yet?" Emma asked, oblivious to the path Vic's mind had wandered.

"I have, a few times actually. We had some minor details to hammer out."

"Uh-oh . . . is that why you're back from Scotland?"

"Not at all," she said honestly. "I came home before I knew the crew had arrived, but that's neither here nor there at this point. I'm sure you're eager to see your friend."

Emma beamed. "You'll come with me, right? I can't wait to have my best American friend and my best British friend in the same room. Don't you love it when worlds collide?"

"Indeed," she said, when what she really loved was hearing that she was Emma's best British friend. Such a silly little thing shouldn't have made her heart swell, but it did.

"Tal messaged and said she was in the guest hall. I know you're always busy, but let's go be movie stalkers for a little while."

She got swept up in Emma's excitement. "I suppose I could spare some time."

"Good." Emma bounded out of the courtyard, seeming so much brighter than when they'd first met. Her cheeks had taken on more colour these days, her clothes no longer hung limply from her slender fame, and her smile sparkled with ease. Love looked good on her.

Vic followed her out of the inner courtyard and across the grassy bailey before she remembered her way around her own home. "Um, the guest hall is over by the west garret."

Emma stopped, then laughed, the sound so light and airy. "Can you speak that in American?"

Vic pressed her lips together as she tried to translate things that came naturally to her but virtually no one else. "There's the Barbican, and the Ravine Tower, and . . . I'm not making this any better, am I?"

Emma shook her head, then grabbed her hand. "Show me."

Her breath caught at the contact, and she hoped she managed to act cool as she closed her fingers around Emma's and walked under a large stone archway into a more open parade ground. Only a few landscapers were present this early in the morning. The main gates wouldn't open for another hour, and many of the seasonal help wouldn't even recognise her, much less care if she held the hand of a beautiful and very-much-spoken-for American, but none of those facts stopped her from glancing over her shoulder as she passed a young man with a wheelbarrow full of sod.

They skirted an outer wall until it flared into a low building. She used her free hand to pull open the door, but she hadn't needed to worry about being the one to break contact because as soon as Emma saw Talia, she bolted across the room.

Talia, for her part, saw Emma coming and squealed as they collided into a massive, rocking, clutching hug. The embrace was so unrestrained, unencumbered, and seemingly endless that Vic looked away from such an American display of emotion. Only, when she did, she found herself staring straight into the dark eyes of Sophia LeBlanc.

She stood atop a pedestal only a few meters away, presumably in a costume fitting. Either that or she'd added another, much poofier layer to her character acting, as the period dress she wore swept down from her voluptuous hips in a flowing, ruffled, floor-length skirt and up into a much more form-fitting bodice. The entire ensemble was hued in a deep, shimmering maroon with black accents that clung to some of her finer features and revealed a few others.

Vic mentally chastised herself for allowing her eyes to linger, but Sophia's expression held no such decorum as an almost impish quality radiated from the upturned corners of her tightly pressed lips. Honestly, the hint of a smile did more to Vic's heart rate than the corset had.

Vic quickly turned back to find Talia and Emma talking excitedly as Emma practically skipped down a row of props.

"They're all perfect," Emma gushed over each jewelled hairbrush and pearl-handled mirror.

"I've been obsessive over every detail," Talia said with a firmness Vic didn't doubt. "Every piece is exactly how you wrote it in the book. I could see it all so clearly. I made Addie do hundreds of drawings, even though she's started art school now."

"I hope she doesn't flunk out of NYU over this film. I'd feel terrible."

Talia waived her hand. "Meh, there are worse ways for college students to make money, and I'd rather it go to her than someone's lackey nephew. Besides, if I hadn't insisted on the best, Sophia would have. She may be the only person I've worked with who's more of a stickler for detail than I am."

Vic fought the urge to turn back toward the actress, but Emma didn't share her sense of propriety. Her eyes lit up as she noticed Sophia in costume, and her mouth formed the most adorable *o* of awe.

"She's stunning," Emma effused. "Introduce us?"

"Of course." Talia led her to the actress. Vic suffered the sudden urge to excuse herself or maybe slip away quietly, but just as she started to back away, Emma spotted her and said, "Vic, come meet my Regina, er, Sophia. Isn't she perfect to play Regina though?"

Vic pulled on her most polite smile. "We've actually met, but yes, she's well-suited to the role."

Sophia's eyebrow arched slightly, but before she had a chance to respond, Emma cut back in to bury her in a pile of compliments. "Your face, your body type, the little look you just gave Vic, so haughty, but playful, too. You were born to play this role . . . and probably many other ones. Oh, by the way, I'm Emma Volant."

"Watch out," Talia warned, "I feel a hug coming on."

Sophia laughed lightly and opened her arms for Emma to jump in.

Vic stifled a prick of jealousy at their emotional freedom so in contrast to her own physical boundaries. Never in her life had she said or done anything so unguarded with someone she'd just met. Honestly, she couldn't even remember the last time she'd been openly affectionate, even with longtime friends or family members.

"I'm sorry," Emma said, stepping back, but she didn't sound sorry. "I'm not usually like this. I'm just so excited to have my first movie made here, with my friends. Talia and Vic are both the best. It means so much to have people I can trust on board."

Sophia cast Vic a bit of side-eye she couldn't quite interpret, but the smile she directed at Emma appeared genuine. "It's an honour to be part of your team."

Emma turned to smile at Vic.

"Likewise. I'm happy to help in any way I can."

"You already have," Talia said. "She's been much more than accommodating with the date snafu and all the schedule rearranging."

Emma frowned, making it clear this was new information for her.

"She didn't tell you?" Talia said. "Our contract writers used American dates and—"

"And it's all taken care of now." Vic cut her off, forcing an airiness into her voice she didn't feel.

Talia paused with a quizzical expression, and Vic willed her not to say anything else that might put a damper on this moment or Emma's uninhibited joy.

"We're all set now, and as I understand it, principal photography begins tomorrow," Vic asserted, bringing them back to business.

"Yes," Talia said slowly, seeming to pick up her tone. "We're on schedule, thanks to your friend here. We owe all the smooth sailing to her."

"Smooth," Emma laughed lightly. "That's our Vic."

She brushed off the compliment. "I can't promise there won't be complications along the way, some of which we probably need to address sooner rather than later. We'll need to know where you plan to shoot some of your early scenes, so we can have our archivist catalogue any pieces that need to be relocated."

"Maybe we could do that with Emma here," Talia offered. "No one will have a better vision for the rooms in the book than her."

She nodded. "Should we also bring along your director?"

Talia made a slight grimace. "He was supposed to be here this morning, but I gather he's a bit . . . indisposed."

He's an idiot. Sophia's comment echoed through Vic's ears as she read between the lines. She turned back to the actress and raised an eyebrow of her own this time. "Ms. LeBlanc, since you seem to have stronger opinions on the subject than he does, would you care to accompany us in his stead?"

A tinge of pink coloured Sophia's cheek, or maybe Vic merely imagined the hint of pleasure at the invitation. As it quickly faded behind a more neutral mask, she said. "I suppose I'd probably better."

"This main circuit through the official state rooms will be off limits from ten till four-thirty every day, but I gather you will have significant outdoor filming to do when you have the natural light." Vic glanced toward Talia, who nodded, but Sophia hung back and reserved her judgement on these updates to their filming regimen.

There were times she felt certain she had this woman pegged. For instance, the way she threw around terms like "governess quarters" and "garrets" with the casualness Sophia might use to say "station wagon" or "front yard" spoke of an almost mundane regard for the extravagant. Yet, at other times she seemed so walled off and carefully controlled, the very opposite of opulent.

"And Talia said they can film outdoors even when the tourists are here?" Emma asked.

"My staff agrees the filming could serve as a draw for locals to see a real movie in production, but I was under the impression there were still a few details to be made out around sound?"

"We can certainly make tourist presence work on several days," Talia said. "The script calls for places where the instrumental score would more than cover, and also a montage where no one has any lines to deliver, so our sound mixers wouldn't have to differentiate between actors' voices and crowd noise, if we do decide to admit a crowd."

Vic nodded resolutely, but as she turned to Emma, her smile grew warm. "Then that's what we'll do."

She started walking again, then stopped, causing the rest of them to bunch up behind her. "Actually, if you're going to admit locals to observe filming, would it be possible to give preference to young arts students, either from the upper school or nearby universities?"

Talia shrugged. "I don't see why not."

"Good," Vic said resolutely. "Let's see if we can inspire a new generation of Northlandian filmmakers."

Emma beamed at her, and Talia once again seemed impressed. Sophia would grant, it was a nice touch for her to consider the peasants as she paraded around her castle, but she'd yet to see anything in Vic to inspire the devotion the other two women had clearly developed for her. It wasn't as if she walked on water. Though she did walk fast once she got going, and backwards, like some tour guide on speed.

"This wing of the estate was built in the early thirteen hundreds and refortified after a siege during the Wars of the Roses. With your movie taking place in the late eighteen hundreds, it would've all been decorated differently, mind you, but actually"— she backed quickly through a doorway she couldn't have possibly seen unless she had eyes on the back of her head—"the wallpaper in here is authentic Victorian."

A startled man glanced up from a large table where he stood polishing a silver tea tray.

"Oh, hello Lawrence," Victoria greeted. "Sorry to barge in."

"Not at all, Miss." He grabbed his rag and started to shuffle past them, but Vic didn't budge.

Instead she met his eyes. "How'd the cricket go this weekend?"

"Very well, Miss." He grinned, a crack in his formality. "A good bunch of youngsters on the pitch."

"My father will be thrilled to hear it," she said warmly, then turned on a heel. "Moving on."

Sophia had to scamper to keep up with her. She was wearing flats instead of the high-heeled boots her full costume called for, but the lower stance may have actually made the large skirt more unwieldy, as the hem now dragged on the ground.

"Morning, Hannah," Victoria called out to another member of the staff as she passed an open door.

"Miss?" A surprised woman perked up as Sophia bustled by.

"And over here"—Vic gestured to her right— "is the family library. You're welcome to use it at will, as the family will likely be away for the duration of your stay."

"Wonderful," Emma said. Then turning to Sophia and Talia, she added, "It's my favourite room in the whole place."

"And while the furniture in there is modern, the structure, including the windows and the ceiling, are all original to the 4th Duke of Northland, which would've made it relatively new during the time in which your film is set."

Sophia was impressed; Vic didn't have to search for that information any more than she needed to watch where she was going as she kept her tone steady in a politely efficient register. Then again Vic was on her home turf, or rather, as she'd pointed out yesterday, in her actual home.

"What about the dining room?" Emma asked.

"Right," Vic said. "I can show you the space, but I have to warn you certain pieces are too fragile to be moved."

The phrase struck Sophia, and she wondered if the same held true for the woman herself. At times she did seem almost fragile, then again, other moments, not so much, though she came across as equally unmoveable in both states.

She barely had time to process the question, much less come to any conclusion before they set off again. This time they strode through another sitting room and down a long hall in the general direction from which they'd come, and yet they passed through different places, leaving Sophia disoriented.

As if reading her mind, Victoria stopped to peek into another room, this one with lavish tapestries and a mammoth stone fireplace. "There's the formal state living room we came through earlier, also where you and I met."

"Hmm," Sophia mused. "I hadn't even noticed the fireplace, what with being distracted by the tip of your sword."

Emma came up behind them. "Sword?"

Vic flushed and pressed her lips together, her blue eyes flashing brilliantly as they met Sophia's. "Have I adequately apologised for my behaviour preceding our formal introduction?"

Sophia laughed outright. "I wouldn't think it would occur to you to apologise to me, or anyone else who trespassed into your space."

"Then I've given you the wrong impression," Vic said solemnly, "both of my character, and my hospitality. You are a guest in my home, and I should've afforded you the courtesy inherent in that position."

"Don't you love it when she talks like that?" Emma said, her tone light and teasing.

"It's impressive," Talia admitted. "It would've taken me ten minutes to construct a sentence that formal and gracious. Maybe you should take some lessons from her, Sophia."

She rolled her eyes. "Thankfully, I've never felt compelled to offer an apology like that to anyone."

"Come on, really?" Talia nudged her. "You don't feel any need to say sorry for whatever happened before I barged in on you two?"

Her memory flashed back to that moment, Vic's body pressed close, the rise and fall of her chest, the fire in her eyes, and the strength of her long, elegant fingers tightening around the hilt of the sword. She merely gritted her teeth and shook her head. "I never apologise . . . to anyone."

"Movie stars." Talia rolled her eyes. "I don't care what she says. I'm committing 'You are a guest in my home, and I should have afforded you the courtesy inherent in that position' to memory so I can put it in a movie someday."

Vic smiled weakly. "How would you have phrased it?"

Emma shrugged. "Something more common or American."

"Like—" Vic affected a higher register, "you guys are visiting me and I shoulda, I don't know, been *nicer* to ya."

Talia and Emma both immediately burst out laughing, and even Sophia relaxed a little. The move, the voice, the playfulness of Vic's posture all caught her off guard. She wouldn't have thought her capable of something so silly or self-deprecating.

"That was the worst mixing of American accents I've ever heard," Emma pronounced. "You went from the Bronx to Wisconsin in like four words. By the end I expected you to offer us some cheese curds."

"Cheese curds?"

"Don't ask." Emma nudged her forward. "We were headed for the dining room?"

"Right." Vic shifted back to business in a snap. "There's a shortcut."

She ducked around a corner into a narrow hallway and sped off again, leaving Sophia to catch up both physically and emotionally. She had to gather her skirts to fit through the slim corridor, which was clearly designed for servants. The floors here weren't polished, but grooved by centuries of passage from busy feet. How had a woman like Victoria learned to navigate this route as effortlessly as the more grandiose spaces where she belonged?

She was pondering the thought along with the inconsistencies Vic had shown over the last few moments when they came to a short but steep set of stairs. She barely had time to even process how tricky they would be to navigate in her awful death trap of a dress when a hand appeared in front of her lowered gaze.

For a second the gesture felt so out of context she could only stare at the slender fingers and smooth palm before glancing up at the woman it belonged to. Even after meeting those eyes and taking in Vic's expectantly upturned lips, she still needed a few more seconds to comprehend the offer.

Vic wanted Sophia to take her hand. She wanted to assist her up the shallow wooden steps. She wanted to steady her.

She stepped back and eyed Vic almost suspiciously.

"I didn't mean to offend any feminist sensibilities," Vic said, her voice low. "I merely have personal experience tripping on these steps, and many others, while wearing dresses like that. The combo has been treacherous for women for centuries."

Then the woman smiled, an easy, almost conspiratorial expression, and Sophia finally saw it. She suddenly understood exactly why Talia and Emma practically swooned for her, and it wasn't just the titles or the trappings, or even her impeccable skin and flawless social graces. In that moment, close, kind, confident, and considerate, Vic was the living, breathing image of a magnanimous millionaire, the stuff of fantasy and legend, like unicorns.

It took everything Sophia had to remind herself no such creature actually existed.

"What are you two doing down there?" Emma called, breaking Vic from the trance of Sophia's eyes.

"Yeah, Sophia. You're going to want to see this," Talia said, oblivious to whatever was happening between them. Then again, Vic felt more than a little oblivious herself. She'd only meant to offer a hand, and yet Sophia looked at her like she might be a unicorn.

She glanced over her shoulder and was about to withdraw when she felt smooth skin slide against her palm as Sophia propelled herself up the stairs and right on past her. She didn't even have time to revel in the brief contact before it was broken, but the heat of Sophia's body in close proximity brought with it the scent of summer, or maybe impending rain. The woman carried something ethereal or even elemental that left Vic a little wind-whipped as she followed the others into the grand dining room.

Thankfully, Emma and Talia didn't even register her presence as they spoke excitedly about the potential of the space.

"It's too bad there's never any real reason to get Tommy in this room," Emma said. "He'd look so out of place it would give a stark contrast."

"Maybe we could rearrange something, or instead of Regina sneaking him up to the tower, she could sneak him in here. That would actually solve two problems at once."

Their conversation flowed quickly and naturally, leaving Vic entirely too free to watch Sophia move quietly around the room. She touched nothing, but her gaze was so intent she might as well have been mentally rearranging Vic's furniture. No detail escaped her inspection.

"What about candlelight, Vic?" Emma asked.

She blinked at the sound of her name, "Pardon?"

"Could we light candles in this room?"

She gave a half shrug. "As I said, the wallpaper is from the court of Victoria and Albert . . ."

Sophia turned to give her another one of those pointed looks that suggested she was barely containing an eye roll. It shouldn't bother her that someone she didn't know thought her a little silly, but for some reason she heard herself adding, "I suppose as long as it's done carefully, candlelight would be nice."

The corners of Sophia's lips twitched again, as if she understood the effect she'd had on her.

"And we can have this room any time after 4:30 p.m. so long as we clear out by ten the next morning?" Talia asked.

She nodded.

"Perfect," Talia said, then added to Emma, "I told you, she's been a lifesaver."

"And I told you, I wouldn't expect anything less from her." Emma piled on, but this time their praise didn't cause even the slightest hint of blush to heat her cheeks as she waited for the final opinion to fall.

Sophia stood by one of the floor-to-ceiling windows, a slight crease between her high, elegantly curved eyebrows. What did she see that the others didn't?

Vic couldn't stand the silence. "And what's your verdict, Madam LeBlanc? Does this space meet your elevated standards?"

"It certainly fits the scenes, and there's ample room for multiple camera angles."

She didn't seem nearly as happy about those things as Vic would have liked. "And yet?"

Sophia sighed. "I'm not sure if the filming schedule will cause conflicts, as the natural lighting here seems like it will be best in the late afternoon, and there's little room to anchor artificial lighting, assuming you don't want us to hang them from your very Victorian ceiling."

Vic must have blanched at the suggestion because Sophia continued. "So, with dark windows and stand lighting forcing the cameras closer to the actors, I worry the space will seem considerably less grand, which defeats the purpose of the scene they're crafting."

"I don't know," Talia started, but Sophia didn't even glance at her. Those dark eyes stayed firmly pinned to Vic, driving home the point that even the most cavernous rooms could be made to feel claustrophobic under the right conditions.

Not that Vic was complaining. On the contrary, she felt anything other than constrained. A sense of something she hadn't experienced in ages rose in her chest, something she wasn't even sure she could feel anymore. She stood a little straighter to meet the challenge in Sophia's stare. "How shall we test your fears?"

Sophia arched an eyebrow as if she hadn't expected the response.

Bolstered by the realisation that she'd been the one to surprise for once, Vic fought the urge to plant her tongue in her cheek as she said, "I know. You'll dine with me tonight to see for yourself."

"Excuse me?" Sophia asked, finally glancing at the others.

"You're both welcome to join as well," Vic said as an afterthought.

Emma shook her head. "Sorry, I can't leave Brogan all alone on the boat with a horde of nieces and nephews."

"And she invited me to join them," Talia said sheepishly. "I was promised a dinner out of the deal, too."

"Far be it from me to stand between anyone and Brogan's boat or culinary skills," Vic said, not displeased as she turned her focus to where she wanted it. "Ms. LeBlanc, I'd be happy to accommodate your questions, and any guests you choose, either in the name of professionalism or pleasure. Shall we say eight?"

Sophia pressed her lips together for a moment as if she didn't quite like the corner she'd found herself painted into, but slowly she nodded. "This evening works as well as any."

Vic managed to nod politely rather than doing a happy little victory jig, because it very much felt like she'd won a contest and scored a dinner date at the same time.

"But if I'm going to free up my evening, I'd better get back to my costume fitting," Sophia added.

Talia glanced at her watch. "Crap, me too."

Victoria took her cue to get out while she was ahead and showed them back to the main tourist entrance, careful not to actually come in contact with any tourists or their ever-present cameras. But as she bade the women goodbye, Emma did as well, choosing to stay beside her instead of following her friends.

Once the other two Americans were out of sight, Emma turned to her with both eyebrows raised.

"Yes?"

Emma's smile turned almost shy as she whispered, "You're smitten with Sophia LeBlanc."

Her face warmed, slightly. "I don't know what you're talking about."

"You asked her out on a date."

"I offered to assuage her concerns on a project in which we have a mutual stake."

"Yes, as a cover to get her to have dinner with you."

She forced a scoff even as her heart hammered. Had she really been so transparent? Emma clocked her straight away. What if Sophia had, too? Then again, she'd said yes, so maybe she should be thrilled she'd accepted what was apparently an obvious date.

"Do you have any idea who that woman is?" Emma asked.

She shrugged. "I read her bio."

"Have you seen any of her movies?"

"I haven't had the chance yet, but I know she won some prestigious award for supporting actress in something called *Vigilant*. I assume the film is about being prepared for anything."

Emma burst out laughing.

"What?"

"It was the biggest blockbuster of last summer. It's a gritty, dark, lesbian vigilante film. Talia wrote it. Sophia played a sexually and morally ambiguous villain who traps the antihero in an erotic—"

Some of the blood must have drained from her face, because Emma came up short.

"I'm sorry. You don't need the full recap, and believe me, I'm

41

not trying to warn you off women." She took Vic's hand in her own. "I'm glad you're reaching out. I don't even know why you're not in Scotland right now, but whatever it is, I hate the idea of you facing everything alone."

Vic looked away, not trusting herself to meet Emma's soft, searching eyes.

"It's okay." Emma squeezed her fingers. "You don't have to tell me, but I care about you. I want you to have fun. I want you to have a torrid affair if that's what you need, but I don't want you to get eaten alive."

"I'm a grown woman." She bristled. "I'm having a business dinner with a woman who interests me as a person. I'm not pulling her onto any balconies to introduce her to the dukedom."

Emma grinned. "Good, then enjoy your evening. Just keep it casual."

"Casual?" she asked playfully. "I am the epitome of casual."

Emma laughed heartily again. "I think you mixed up the meaning of the words *epitome* and *opposite*."

"Low blow to insult my vocabulary, Volant. Maybe you haven't had the opportunity to see me in my casual date settings?"

"Haven't I?" Emma asked. "I seem to recall we went on one pseudo-date, and you spent much of it telling me all the reasons you'd be a terrible person to marry."

Her heart clenched at the memory, but she couldn't dispute the charge. "That might not have been my finest moment."

Emma's expression softened. "I wouldn't go that far. You were beautiful and earnest and open. Anyone who's genuine and honest with themselves would find you utterly endearing. I just worry Sophia is world-wearier and more suspicious than either one of us is used to. I don't want to see you get your heart broken."

Vic chuckled even though her chest still constricted. "I appreciate the sentiment, but it's misplaced. For what it's worth, I share your assessment of Ms. LeBlanc's calibre, and I highly doubt a woman like her would ever give me any reason to indulge silly romantic fantasies long enough to endanger my heart."

"Okay. I trust you. I'll stop, but for clarity's sake, I don't think there's anything wrong with indulging silly romantic fantasies, so long as you share them with the right person."

Vic sighed and stepped back, breaking the contact between them at the reminder inherent in that statement. "Speaking of which, do you need to get home to Brogan?"

Chapter Four

"Have fun on your date," Talia called as she hopped into a cab driven by a young man with a shock of bright red hair.

"Ha." Sophia laughed as she tucked her room key into the pocket of her slacks. "Your evening with a brood of other people's children will likely be infinitely more engaging than my company tonight."

Talia fixed her with a stern glare. "If it is, you're doing something wrong."

Then she closed the door before Sophia could respond.

Not that Sophia had anything witty to add. Talia was obviously a little taken with the lady of the castle, and nothing Sophia said would change her opinion. She wasn't even sure she wanted to. Just because she didn't believe in Santa Claus anymore didn't mean she had to ruin it for the other kids. At times she might even envy the simple pleasure that came from the naiveté of believing in the best in people. Then again, other times she felt a prickling sort of anger at the privilege of holding such a worldview.

Thankfully, tonight she didn't have the luxury of the time needed to vacillate between those two positions as she was staying directly across the street from the castle. She had barely stepped across the cobblestone street before a guard threw open an ornate gate. "Her Ladyship is waiting in the inner courtyard. Would you like someone to accompany you, ma'am?"

She blinked a few times and fought the urge to glance over her shoulder to confirm he hadn't spoken those words to someone behind her.

"No." She affected a demeanour closer to the woman she'd begin to play in earnest tomorrow. "I know my way around the castle."

With a nod he stepped back into a little guard hut, and she strode on along the path she'd walked earlier in the day. Keeping her chin high, she didn't even survey her surroundings. She was already bored with them. Feeling that way made it much easier to not be intimidated. Not that dinner alone with the beautiful daughter of a duke should intimidate her. Being a movie star meant she could be anyone she wanted.

Well, maybe not anyone just yet, but she was working on it, and if she kept her head and her focus, she'd be where she wanted soon. The reminder galvanised her resolve right up to the point where she turned into the central stone courtyard to find her host leaning casually against a pillar. A brilliant shock of warmth and colour amid the cold, grey confines, Vic wore a bright blue blouse with a white collar and pinstripes. Her blond hair fell free past her shoulders, and even at the distance of several yards her eyes sparked an almost luminous shade of cerulean.

"Good evening," Vic said in a tone slightly lower than her business register, and Sophia's mouth went so dry she nearly forgot her line.

"Same to you."

"Shall we?" Vic nodded toward what Sophia had come to think of as the front door of the castle.

She stepped through into, well, she wasn't sure. There was probably some formal name for the large entryway lined with ancient swords and suits of armour, but as far as she was concerned, once you'd seen one shiny helmet, you'd seen them all.

"May I take your jacket?" Vic asked, with her ever-impeccable manners, and suddenly Sophia couldn't stifle the urge to shake up the script a bit.

45

"Only if you promise to toss it somewhere casual and not hang it neatly in some coat check you people use for guests of state."

Victoria's smile quirked, but in response she only extended her hand, as if upping the ante.

She slipped off the light summer jacket and handed it over, amused when Vic accepted the garment and immediately draped it over the shield of the closest suit of armour. "There. Chuck will hold it for you."

"Chuck?"

"Unofficial name of course," Vic confided as they started toward the stairs. "There's Hank and Buck, and there at the end is Sal. She's a woman but a bit of a tomboy, and we're all for letting our knights self-identify here."

She smiled. She couldn't help it. Not only had Vic accepted her subtle challenge to silliness, she'd taken the game a step further.

"My little sister, Lizzie, had a real thing for Hank when she was about 11," Vic continued as they ascended to the second floor, "but I suspect Sal was my mind's earliest inkling of something amiss."

"Did you want to be Sal, or date her?"

She sighed dramatically. "That's the million-dollar question. I'll let you know if I ever find a definitive answer."

The little hint of something wistful and almost tired undercut the playfulness of the comment, but before she got the chance to pry, Vic turned another corner and gestured for Sophia to precede her into the formal dining room she'd nearly forgotten she was here to inspect.

Vic pulled out a chair, because of course she did, and assured Sophia she'd return shortly.

Then she disappeared, which seemed odd given her usual state of constant attentiveness. Still, it gave Sophia a chance to survey the room more fully. That afternoon she'd noted things like the size and scope of the windows, and the space between the walls and the table, but between her eye for camera angles and the unsettling aspects of Vic's proximity, she'd failed to notice the finer details. For instance, the high-back chairs appeared hand carved, and each ornate place setting had about twelve utensils and several glasses. That is to say every place setting except for two, the one in front of her and the one at the corner to her left. Those were each set with a single plate and fork atop a plain, white linen napkin.

She had to give it to Victoria. She knew how to tone down in a way that made a person feel seen while still making it clear she didn't have to. What kind of energy did it take to always be one step ahead of the common folk? Or did such behaviour come naturally after a lifetime of practice?

Victoria returned, carrying a plate in each hand, a bottle of wine under her arm, and a corkscrew between her teeth, causing Sophia to wonder if she'd overestimated her grace.

"Sorry," Vic mumbled around the corkscrew and lowered the plates onto the table. Juggling the wine, she began to open it before adding, "I hope you like French reds, because I'd rather not run to the cellar again."

"Depends on the vintage."

Vic froze and squinted at the label. "This one is, ah, it says 2005, and Gran Vin, which I think means it's a first edition basically, and *mis en bouteille . . . bouteille*? Blimey, that's um, oh, 'bottle.'"

Sophia laughed. "You're bad at French?"

"I wouldn't say bad."

"That wasn't great."

"I wasn't expecting to be put on the spot. I didn't know you were a wine connoisseur. I would've brushed up."

"I know nothing about wine," Sophia admitted.

"Then why the comment about the vintage?"

She shrugged. "Probably to be difficult, or maybe to see if you really would run back downstairs again, but dinner would get cold, and what's the fun there?"

Vic raised an eyebrow but returned to opening the bottle.

"I'm surprised you don't know more about wine, though. I would've thought it would be one of those skills women like you just possessed."

"I'm more of a gin woman." Vic leaned across Sophia to grab her wineglass. When she did, it was impossible not to notice her shirt was open one button past professional, offering a quick peek of smooth skin covering distinctive collar bones. Had she done that purposely? Sophia certainly had experience opening an extra button or two when she needed to make an impression, but for some reason she liked the idea of Victoria slipping into something slightly more comfortable for their dinner. Besides, women like Victoria didn't have to rely on sex appeal, so making the choice to do so anyway proved much more intriguing.

Vic generously filled two glasses and eased into the chair at the corner adjacent to Sophia, so they managed to be simultaneously close and able to look directly at one another. "I hope you like salmon. I admit I took some liberties here, but we can absolutely stuff it and call for takeaway if I missed the mark on the menu."

"No, this smells amazing." She speared a bit of fish that flaked beautifully under a fragrant crème sauce, then fought the urge to moan as she placed it in her mouth. "Wow, actually it's perfect."

Victoria seemed only mildly relieved as she began to eat her own serving.

"Seriously. This is much better than anything I've eaten on a movie set . . . ever. Please give my compliments to the chef."

Victoria practically flushed. "It's good to know I'm not total rubbish when it comes to domestic arts."

She froze, another bite mere inches from her lips. "And now you're teasing me?"

"What? No."

Sophia stared at her, then back down at the immaculately plated meal of salmon, sauce, parsnips, carrots, and asparagus. "You made this? All of it?"

"I didn't pick the tarragon or anything, but yes, I mixed everything up and applied heat. Is that a problem?"

"No." She drew out the word. "More of a surprise. I would've thought you had people to cook for you."

"My family does have a chef, but they are all in Scotland for the summer."

"And you've just got the one?"

Vic managed to look almost embarrassed. "Full time, yes. We of course have event staff, but I hate to break it to you, nobility doesn't come with the same perks it used to."

Sophia let her eyes make a slow, pointed sweep around the grand dining room. "Oh yes, please forgive the assumption. I can see you're practically living in shambles here."

Vic's laugh was genuine. "Well-played. I didn't mean to imply the need for sympathy."

"Sure, sure. I know how your type is. Always fishing for compliments."

"It's true." Vic affected a serious tone. "I'm absurdly needy, always in desperate ploys for affirmation. It's sad really, the lengths I have to go to in order to get women to dine with me. For instance, once I even invited a movie star over to quote-unquote check out my lighting."

Sophia pressed her lips together, trying not to give in to the charms of this woman's sense of humor. Honestly, she found Victoria's self-deprecation even more unexpected than her ability to cook for herself.

"So, don't leave me hanging, Ms. LeBlanc. Is my dining room suitable for your movie scenes?"

Funny for Vic to bring up the topic, as Sophia hadn't even thought to check yet, but it didn't take any more than a glance at the floor-to-ceiling windows to realise they still had full daylight behind them. She frowned. Not only was the sun still visible, it didn't even appear precariously close to the horizon, with its orange hue still low and full above the castle's outer walls. "What time does the sun set in this country?"

Victoria cradled her wineglass close to her lips, turning it slowly as if she needed time to ponder the question "This far north? Around ten o'clock, but you won't have total darkness until nearly eleven."

Sophia sat back as the answer sparked two realisations. One, she'd have a lot more shooting time than she'd initially planned, and two, if she wanted to see full darkness, she'd be spending almost three hours with Vic tonight. She wasn't sure which one of those things should take priority because all she could focus on was the fact that any remaining doubts she'd held about whether or not this was a date had just vanished.

"So, does anyone call you Sophie?" Vic asked, sipping her second glass of wine.

"Does anyone call you Vickie?"

She wrinkled her nose.

"Exactly," Sophia concluded. "It's like a shoe that doesn't fit."

"Oh, I know all about those, both literally and figuratively," Vic admitted, no longer drinking the wine so much as inhaling the bouquet and soaking in Sophia's presence. The latter had a much stronger effect on her senses. "But aren't actresses supposed to be chameleons of sorts?"

"Chameleons, not contortionists. I can certainly mimic any behaviours or affects I can observe, but I can't change myself into something else entirely. I don't believe any human can."

"Change?" She leaned forward. "Do you honestly believe we're all static creatures?"

"Maybe we change in small ways, habits, preferences, tastes, but not on any fundamental level. I may learn a thing or two about myself with each project, but I don't become more villainous when I play a villain any more than I'll become an actual princess by playing one for the next few months."

"Hmm."

"You disagree?"

"Maybe not about the title—those are hard to come by these days—but I've always hoped that if you played a part long enough it would eventually become second nature."

Sophia's dark eyes narrowed as if trying to see some small detail inside Vic. Had she caught the hint of wistfulness in the statement? Vic didn't find the prospect frightening. She wouldn't mind being truly seen by a woman of Sophia's calibre, but years of experience told her not to expect that level of interest from the women she spent time with. Only Emma had ever come close, and Emma had warned her not to hope for too much tonight. In an attempt to heed that warning she forced her voice to remain casual as she added, "I mean, don't some roles help define whole careers?"

"They can." Sophia accepted the slight redirect. "And this movie has the potential to be one of those for me. I've made no secret about that fact. I went after this role hard precisely because it could change my life by earning my entry pass into a mostly pedigreed class."

"How so? Aren't you already well established?"

"Not in the way I want to be."

"But you've got awards, and money, and some clout. You must have done something well."

"I've played villains and best friends to much acclaim," Sophia admitted, as if the idea bored her. "I get recognised on the street almost daily back in LA, which is a good first step."

"Is it?" The thought made her palms sweat. "I most often strive not to be recognised in public."

Sophia raised an eyebrow. "How does that work for you?"

"My face is vaguely familiar to a lot of people." She shrugged, not wanting to let herself dwell on that idea too long. "But if I move quickly, with a sense of purpose, and avoid eye contact, away from the castle most people's brains don't work fast enough to put together where they know me from."

"Then we're in the same boat, but rowing in different directions," Sophia said. "For me to do the kind of work I got into this business to do, I need to become a household name, not 'Hey there's the woman from that one movie with Cobie Galloway.'"

"And Emma's movie can give you that sort of star power?"

"Emma's movie," Sophia echoed the phrase as if she found it amusing, "is my first chance to carry a narrative almost alone, and it's a period piece, which breaks the moulds people typecast me into. No slinky costumes, no action scenes, or even any overly graphic sex scenes, just me and every ounce of nuance I can squeeze out of a strong, multifaceted female lead."

"You seem to relish the challenge."

"There's nothing I relish more than a challenge." Sophia delivered the line with enough bravado to send a little shiver along Vic's skin.

"I harbour no illusions about being an Oscar contender here," Sophia continued. "It's not the most earth-shattering story, and it's got some sappy romantic moments that will likely be written off as too feminised for serious filmmaking."

Vic felt a little prick of indignance that someone would write off Emma's story for having a romance amid a sweeping saga about class, power, and the constraints society places on women of marrying age. Still, she had no desire to interrupt Sophia, who had grown more animated, going as far as to gesture with her wineglass so emphatically a little drop spilled down over the rim and onto the white tablecloth.

"The sentimentality is a small price to pay for finally getting to play someone so far out of my own experiences that the critics won't be able to write off a compelling portrayal as being too close to who I am as a person."

"Have people really done so in the past?"

Sophia's jaw tightened, and Vic flashed back to Emma's comments about Sophia's last role as a sexually and morally ambiguous villain.

Her stomach tightened at the comparison. "I'm sorry."

"It's fine." Sophia sipped her wine, holding it in her mouth before seeming to find the strength to swallow something that likely tasted more bitter than it had moments earlier. "I opened the topic. You're not wrong to ask."

"I wasn't apologising for asking," she clarified. "I was apologising for the answer I saw on your face. I'm sorry people have underestimated you. I'm sorry for the pain and frustration of having one's genuine best efforts written off. I'm sorry for a culture that discredits a woman's talents as stemming from baser instincts."

Sophia waved her off.

"I mean it."

She scoffed. "Even if I believed that, you'd have no qualifications to apologise for other people's behaviour."

"My advisors would disagree with you." Vic stared down at her own wine, which had undoubtedly also turned bitter in her glass.

"Don't expect me to apologise for them either," Sophia said emphatically.

"Of course not." She forced a smile. "My position comes with higher standards of behaviour and codes of conduct. I accept the responsibility—"

"No." Sophia cut her off sharply. "That's not what I meant."

Vic waited for some sort of explanation, but the woman in front of her seemed to take a moment to compose herself with a deep breath.

Still, when Sophia spoke again, her voice held a hint of steel that hadn't been there earlier. "These so-called advisors of yours are clearly wrong. It's not your responsibility to apologize for anyone else's actions, much less their thoughts. Apologies are silly and too often sexist. I never give them. I do what I do, and I say what I say, and I stand by those things. If my mind changes later, I deal with that later. I don't owe anyone anything, especially apologies."

Vic stared, flushed and little breathless at the speech and the feelings it stirred in her.

She had never wanted to kiss anyone so much as she did in that moment.

Her head swam as the implications of those thoughts swirled. She could almost get drunk on the prospect of a life without guilt, without shame, without apologies. The idea felt infinitely more foreign than any movie character she'd ever seen on screen. Could a woman actually live the way Sophia had just described? Nothing in her experience suggested so, and yet from the fire in Sophia's voice, Vic didn't dare doubt her.

£ £ £

53

Sophia lifted her wineglass to her lips once more, only to find it empty. The bottle on the table between her and Vic had somehow ended up in the same state. Glancing around for the first time in she didn't know how long, she noted the sun that had seemed unnaturally high earlier now only appeared as a saffron sliver on the horizon.

Hours had clearly passed more quickly than expected, and she found that more than a little disorienting. Vic was a deft conversationalist, managing to be engaging, open, and most shockingly, relatable. Whatever charm school she'd attended had certainly done a stellar job. Sophia wouldn't have thought it possible for her to forget where she was and who she was speaking to, but a time or two, she almost did.

The thought must have caused her to frown, but thankfully her hostess misread the root of her expression.

"There are actual barrels of wine in the cellar. If you'd like, I could fetch some."

"From a barrel in your cellar?" She shook her head, once again hyperaware of her surroundings. "No, thank you."

"We don't keep alcohol on this floor during tourist season," Vic said. "Too many people were too keen to nick a bottle of gin from the duke in the past, but it'd be no trouble to bring some up."

"No, honestly, I don't often drink while filming, and we start principal photography tomorrow." She stated another fact that should've occurred to her sooner.

"So, what you're saying is you're about to become infinitely busier?"

"That's an understated way of putting it. Honestly, this night has been lovely, but . . ."

"It's not likely to happen again," Vic finished for her. "I understand."

Sophia bit her lip, not sure she really did. She hadn't come here intending to enjoy a social evening. Of course, she'd never been blind to Victoria's interest or her physical appeal, but rich, beautiful women were nothing new in her sphere, at least not over the last few years. The combination of sizzle and sparkle was the stuff Hollywood was built on, but it rarely came with any substance behind the special effects. She hadn't expected Vic to pose any more of a distraction than any of the others.

"If you need to take your leave now, I understand that as well," Vic offered.

"Do you?"

"Of course. Far be it from me to keep an artist from her work. I only hope you were able to get enough of a feel for the lighting in this room to satisfy your earlier concerns."

For a second the words didn't even make sense, and Sophia had to make a conscious effort not to let it show while she processed the statement.

She snuck a quick glance at the large, elaborate chandelier overhead, then another out the window at the now fully sunken sun. That's why she'd come and why she'd stayed. Her chest tightened so swiftly she had to draw in an extra breath to expand it again. It was one thing to be pleasantly surprised by someone's ability to kill time comfortably. It was another to get so distracted she'd forgotten her reason for needing to kill time in the first place.

Vic raised her eyebrows as if waiting for an answer to the initial question. Clearing her mind the way she might before shooting a pivotal scene, Sophia surveyed the room once more, but it wasn't completely dark yet.

She needed more time in the space to know for sure, and yet more time with this woman might also be the exact opposite of what she needed. When conflicted between her personal life and her goals, she always chose her long-term plans. Only, in the moment, the two had intertwined, and she needed to untangle them as quickly and clearly as possible. "I do think I should stay a bit longer."

Vic's smile spread in a way that suggested she'd read exactly what Sophia hadn't wanted to convey. "As you wish."

"I mentioned earlier how much this film means to me, not just in the moment, but for the future I've been working toward my whole life. These scenes have to be flawless. I don't have any room for error, or even distraction." She wasn't sure if she'd made the statement for Vic's benefit or her own, but she searched the blue eyes before her for any hint that her meaning registered with at least one of them.

"I admire your dedication to detail," Vic said seriously, then with a lighter tone added, "And if our first encounter was any indication of the dedication you have to your craft, I've no doubt you'll slay the role."

The reminder of their first meeting cracked some of the wall Sophia had been trying to build between them. She worked to reinforce it quickly. "I was merely trying on the voice for the character. I assumed you were another employee come to harass us. I wanted to see if I had what it took to convince someone I belonged in the place."

"Oh, it was a compelling performance," Vic confirmed. "Were I to rate us both in that exchange, I'd say you actually appeared more convincing as a haughty castle dweller than I."

Sophia shook her head, trying not to be too pleased.

"I do believe at one point you nearly had me questioning my right to be in my own home, which is quite a skill."

Warmth spread through Sophia, both at the compliment and the earnestness with which Vic delivered it. Why did she have to be so disarming?

"Will you be character acting through the whole film?" Vic added a playful grimace. "I'm asking only to know whether or not I should hide all the swords and pistols in the armour room after you leave tonight."

Sunlight began to stream through Sophia's shoddy defences as she lowered her guard. "No need to fear for your limbs or my sanity. I'm not like that all the time. I promise not to remove anything from the walls and wield it against you."

Vic's brows knit together as if she still found her vow a little dubious.

"I'm serious. From here on in I'll slip out of diva mode and fully into professional lead actress mentality. I honestly arrived early attempting to prepare more thoroughly. This character, this setting, the language, it's so far from my own experiences. I worried about my ability to pull it off."

"Does the accent scare you?"

She shook her head. "I have a coach who runs lines with me. I worry more about the intangibles associated with a life of privilege I've never lived. Wealth and power come with a whole different worldview. It affects the way a person walks, holds their head, takes up space. I don't want to turn this character into a parody of royalty, but I also don't want to come across as Louisiana trailer trash pretending to be a princess."

Vic grimaced. "I'd hardly use those words to describe you."

"Only because you don't know me," Sophia answered quickly and without an ounce of shame. "Those words absolutely describe where I come from and how many people still see me. I don't sugarcoat any of my past, but I don't dwell there, either. I'm too focused on the present and using it to create a future of my own choosing. As far as I'm concerned, I came from nothing and nowhere."

"Believe it or not," Vic said softly, "I envy that in a strange way. Not the poverty part, I'm not one of those members of the upper class who harbours petty illusions about the quaintness of being poor. I only mean the idea of not having a past worth feeling any sort of responsibility to."

"You should try it some time," Sophia said dryly.

"It's not easy to do when people insist on introducing you as Lady Victoria Charlotte Algernon Penchant. There's no escaping the past inherent in a name like mine."

Sophia nodded thoughtfully, unable to argue that point, but not exactly feeling sorry for her either. She'd spent so many of her younger years wishing she possessed a name that would open doors, and then so many more trying desperately to make one for herself.

"Then again," Vic pushed on with a little more playfulness in her voice, "surely a name like Sophia LeBlanc has some sort of backstory. It's too interesting to have actually come from nothing and nowhere."

"That's a polite way to ask for information I didn't offer," Sophia said, but she didn't feel pressured, either. She wasn't sure how much she wanted to say, but to her surprise she started talking anyway. "Most people think it's a stage name, but I've never hidden anything about myself. My mom is straight up Italian, only first-generation American. My dad's roots run deep in eastern Texas and western Louisiana with a little bit of Spanish, some Mexican, Cajun, and French Canadian to his DNA. It's all a bit muddled in me. I'm every bit the genetic mutt my name implies."

"Yeah, I know what you mean," Vic said conversationally. "I've got a little bit of everything in me, too . . . Both Anglo and Saxon."

Sophia stared at her, not sure she'd actually just said that. "Seriously?"

Vic laughed. "No. I'm just Anglo. I'm quite dry and boring, actually. My family tree barely forked for almost a hundred years in the Middle Ages. Don't worry, we've dealt with the inbreeding over the last two centuries . . . mostly."

Sophia burst out laughing. She didn't know what else to do. Vic could say the most astoundingly aristocratic thing one moment, then follow it up with a sarcastic crack at her own expense without ever shifting her tone in the slightest.

"I didn't mean to make light of your upbringing though," she added. "It actually sounds fascinating to me."

"Sure," Sophia said. "This from the woman who casually mentioned where her people were during the Wars of the Roses earlier today."

"My upbringing is as second nature to me as yours is to you."

"I wish yours was a little more second nature to me, if only for this role."

"What do you want to know?" Vic asked.

She shook her head. "Nothing in particular . . . yet. I'll let you know if that changes."

"You can, you know? I'm right here."

"Thank you," she said, though she had no intention of accepting the offer. She reminded herself she was here only until evening fell fully. Then she planned to put a healthy distance between herself and Vic's disarming appeal. "I'm sure I'll figure it out, and if not, I can always have Talia ask Emma for advice."

Vic's smile turned a little sly or maybe almost shy. The expression was new, and Sophia couldn't constrain her curiosity. "Why do you look so . . . satisfied?"

"Nothing, no reason, I don't." She bit her lip for a second before going on. "Emma's info is as good a source as any. She had impeccable research methodologies. It's not easy to get into the mind of a woman bound by title and tradition who has to choose between love and honour while sitting high atop her ancient castle, but Emma did so beautifully."

Maybe it was the blunt summary of the plot, the wistfulness in her voice, or the faraway gleam in Vic's eyes as she stared out the windows into the darkness gathering over the grounds. Which ever way it was, in that instant everything connected and slammed into Sophia like a jolt of electricity she couldn't believe she hadn't felt until this moment.

"It's you."

Vic blinked a few times. "Pardon?"

God, why hadn't she seen this before? Vic's breeding, her demeanour, her close friendship with Emma, the way she protected her home, all of her comments about taking care of locals first. Sophia shook her head.

"What?"

None of the hoops and red tape Vic had thrown up around this production had ever been about her money. It was always about her sense of responsibility conflicting with her own relationships. She was a walking, talking, beautiful conflict of interest. In other words, she embodied all the things that drew Sophia to this role. "I'm playing you."

Vic blushed profusely as she denied the charge. "I fear I've over-served you from our wine cellar. How will you be able to properly discern the light of this room in your altered state?"

She glanced at the windows to see the darkness outside had done little to dim the glow around them. "The light is fine, and

I'm not going to let you change the subject this time, Your Lady-ship. Do you know how important it could be for me to be able to actually talk to the person my life-altering character is based on?"

Victoria looked nearly stricken as she rose from the table. "I've already offered to be on set and available personally, but it's gotten awfully late. Now that your lighting issues are resolved, shall we adjourn for the evening?" She didn't wait for an answer, turning toward the door and leaving Sophia to follow her.

"Vic, come on," Sophia called as she rushed to keep up. "Why are you being weird about this? Are you afraid I'm going to tell someone? I won't, but who wouldn't love to have people know they were the basis for one of the most admired female literary leads of the last ten years?"

"I suppose most people would enjoy that sort of notoriety." Vic kept walking right on down the stairs. "I'm not most people, but even if I were, this character is not me, and I would be uncomfortable with the comparisons."

Vic reached the front door and collected the coat off of Chuck's shield as Sophia caught up.

"Which comparisons could you find unflattering?"

Her expression turned polite and distant once more as she lifted the jacket for Sophia to slip into. She accepted the gesture, but as she put her back to Vic, she stepped closer, so their bodies brushed together. Turning her head so her cheek was close enough to be kissed, she lowered her voice and said, "Please tell me, which part of me playing you do you find unappealing?"

Vic took a deep breath as if trying to steel herself, or perhaps restrain herself, but as she slowly released it, warm and steady against the back of Sophia's neck, she pulled away. Side-stepping Sophia completely, she opened the heavy wooden door, then took Sophia's hand.

"It has been a pleasure to share your company tonight. To answer your question, I find absolutely nothing unappealing about you, the idea of your playing me, or even the idea of your playing *with* me, as you appear to be doing now."

Sophia opened her mouth to protest, then closed it again, seeing no reason to deny what Vic obviously recognised.

"The only issue I have is that you seem to be harbouring some illusions about who I am. If you think I'm the stuff of romance novels or feature films, it would be dishonourable for me to continue under false pretences."

"I don't understand."

She smiled sadly. "If you must know all the ways I fall short of the character you're trying to conjure, I'm not nearly as royal, nor am I as rich or powerful or pampered."

Vic paused, then lifting the back of Sophia's hand to her lips, she kissed it gently. Stepping back, she met Sophia's eyes with a melancholy sort of finality. "And perhaps most importantly, there's no blacksmith coming to sweep me off my feet and away from the responsibilities of my life."

Sophia's breath caught in a little hitch. She had so many questions, and yet she couldn't give voice to any one of them. A chill much colder than the air outside surrounded her as Vic gently closed the door behind her. She had the urge to pound it, to beg her to open it again and explain, but at the same time, she wasn't sure she wanted to know what caused the sadness she'd seen in those seconds before Victoria's lips had caressed the back of her hand.

Chapter Five

The camera was so close to Sophia's face that Victoria's body gave a little sympathy shiver. How could any person stand stock-still under such scrutiny? Was it some deep-seated confidence or pure defiance? Perhaps Sophia knew on some fundamental level how commanding she was as she stared out the window, unblinking, as the photographer hovered so close his breath stirred the little wisps of dark curls along the nape of her neck. Either Sophia was the most talented actress in the world, or she simply carried a level of self-possession Vic could only fantasise about.

She turned away under the guise of checking a few knick-knacks they had moved onto an end table to unclutter the shot. She hadn't meant to use the words *Sophia* and *fantasise* in the same thought, but that's what she'd done over and over for several days. She picked up a porcelain thimble and placed it over her thumb just to have something to do with her hands other than wring them together, which is what she'd done ever since she closed the door on Sophia and their ill-conceived date.

So much for casual.

She set the thimble down and picked up the refrain she'd carried around in her brain for days. She'd done the right thing that night. She'd said the right things. She'd been honest and extracted herself quickly as soon as she realised they'd crossed a line into a place she didn't want to go. More importantly, she'd stayed away ever since. Thankfully, Sophia hadn't pushed, which allowed both of them to focus on their work, but there was no escaping the fact that their work now threw them in each other's path frequently. One of them seemed to be handling the new roles much better than the other, and spoiler alert, it wasn't Vic.

She'd been a ball of tension bouncing back and forth between regret, and sadness at feeling that way. She should have been stronger or cooler. She would have even settled for resigned. She had plenty of practice with all of the above. Instead, she was full of nervous, fidgeting energy. The contrast of Sophia's fortitude under professional pressure only reaffirmed why Vic had been right to step back.

She wasn't Sophia. She didn't get to exist without apologies or explanations. Her life didn't hold up under scrutiny, and never had that been clearer than when Sophia connected her to the character she was playing. The two women couldn't be more different, and the reasons Vic had listed only scratched the surface. She just wished the underlying concerns didn't cut so deep. Perhaps if Sophia had shown any real interest in her sooner, or maybe if she only wanted help with things like her accent, Vic could have convinced herself there was no harm in following that path a little further, but that's not what had happened.

Sophia had been easy to talk to, with her wit and sardonic humour. Time passed quickly in her company, and she seemed to enjoy herself as well at times, but her eyes never sparked with any overwhelming passion until she connected Vic to the character she saw as life-changing. She only wanted Vic when she thought of her as some sort of inspiration for Regina. Even now a sense of cold spiralled through her at the memory, and all the others that preceded it in her life. She couldn't pretend to be someone she wasn't, or rather, she could, she had, and she still did, but not with a romantic interest. Not ever again.

"Whoa," James called, shaking her from her musing. "Ma'am!"

She spun to see a handle from one of the cameras pressed flat against an oil painting of Henry the Hearty, her tenth great-grandfather. Her heart hammered against her already tight chest. "Whoa indeed."

The cameraman turned to stare at her, then back at the director, clearly uncertain who to take his cues from.

"Don't step back any further," Brian said dismissively.

"Actually, I need you to step forward," she corrected quickly.

"He's not hurting it," Brian argued.

"Any contact with the canvas is unacceptable."

Brian rolled his eyes. "Fine. Move the painting."

She shook her head. "You're not qualified to move it. If you'd like it relocated, I'll contact one of our preservationists to make sure it's handled in accordance with its value."

"We don't have time."

"I understand it seems tedious, but I can't compromise on this."

"And I can't compromise on my shot," Brian growled.

"The camera has a certain depth of field," the cameraman offered, still literally trapped in the middle.

"Then perhaps you should use a different one."

"Hey, now," the director snapped. "Don't tell my men what camera to use. Do you have any idea what that piece of equipment is worth?"

"I don't," Victoria admitted, "but I'm sure you can tell me."

Brian blinked a few times and shrugged.

Sophia snorted, the first indication she'd even been following the conversation. Vic fought the urge to look at her. She didn't trust herself not to begin fidgeting nervously if she did.

"The camera and the lenses together cost about fifty thousand dollars," the camera operator said. "That's not to mention what we paid to get them here."

"I'm not immune to budgetary issues," she continued in her most reasonable tone. Sympathetic but firm, or at least that's how she hoped she sounded. It was one she'd cultivated in years of land dealings. "And believe me, I understand that's a considerable price tag, but I'm asking you to acknowledge that the painting you've backed into doesn't have a price tag. Its worth can hardly be calculated in any meaningful way, because it cannot possibly be replaced."

She stopped to stare up at the face of her ancestor, feeling the weight of their lineage press down on her. "There's no CGI, there's no alternate angle on this one. That portrait was commissioned to commemorate the end of the Wars of the Roses, which this dukedom ended up fighting on both sides of, costing—" She turned back to see both men's expressions had glazed over. "I'm sorry, I don't know why I'm trying to explain all that. The point is, if you so much as nick the portrait, your insurance would go utterly bankrupt trying to make amends."

Brian stared at her for a long couple of seconds before throwing up his hands and sighing so dramatically she wondered why he wasn't in front of the camera instead of behind it. "Fine. Swap out the cameras. Everybody take ten. I need a smoke anyway."

She nodded, equally grateful for the break, but as she turned to leave, a hand landed gently on her shoulder.

The touch was so wholly unexpected she didn't have to wonder who it was. No one on her staff would touch her, and certainly none of the men would dare to after the way she'd just spoken to them. A touch like that came only from a woman, and she closed her eyes against the rush of emotions it caused.

"I'm sorry about your lost shot," she finally managed without trusting herself to turn around.

"I'm not," Sophia said, her voice low and close. "You were right. Brian was being lazy and self-indulgent."

"I didn't mean to imply his motives were—"

"You didn't," Sophia said. "You were looking out for what's yours. I ascribed motives because you apologised worthlessly again. You really should stop that."

She finally turned, struggling to keep her expression neutral in such close proximity. "Force of habit."

Sophia arched an eyebrow. "I wouldn't think someone of your status would be forced into any habits she didn't choose."

"Then you would think wrong," Vic snapped, then caught herself. "I'm sorry. That was . . . well, worthy of another apology, but I assume you don't want it."

"I'd rather have an explanation."

"Why? For you or your character?"

Sophia's eyes softened. "What about for you?"

A lump formed in her throat before she had time to put her walls back up. She managed to swallow it, but her voice still sounded a little strangled as she said, "Neither of us has time."

She turned to go, but Sophia touched her arm, freezing her in her tracks. God, if this woman didn't learn some physical boundaries, Vic might not survive the next two months.

"I can make time. It's one of the benefits of being rich and famous."

Vic smiled in spite of herself. "Then it turns out, I am neither of those things, but if I remember correctly, I've already made this point."

Sophia's fingers tightened around Victoria's forearm as she opened her mouth to speak, but before the words came out, Talia jogged into the room.

"Hey Soph—" she said before she registered the tension surrounding them and skidded to a stop.

"Talia," Vic said politely as Sophia dropped her hand. "How lovely to see you again. I was beginning to suspect Emma and Brogan kidnapped you, or perhaps they'd just shown you enough of their lovely little village to make you want to stay there forever."

Talia glanced from one of them to the other, clearly not fully sold by the quick conversation opener Vic was currently clinging to.

"Oh, yes, um, Amberwick really is as pretty as Emma made it out to be."

"Indeed. And I won't even ask what you thought of Brogan, as anyone who doesn't immediately like her must be lacking in some way. So how was your sailing voyage?"

Talia's cheeks flushed, either with pleasure or confusion or both, but the longer Vic kept making conversation, the more in control she felt, and the less chance Sophia had to pull them back onto uncomfortable topics.

"The sailing and Brogan were both wonderful, but I didn't mean to interrupt."

"Not at all." Vic waved a hand. "Ms. LeBlanc and I were finished."

Sophia pressed her lips together as if she disagreed but didn't say so.

"Please." Vic stepped back and motioned for Talia to take her place. "The show must go on, and I must check on a few things of my own."

Then she turned and fled as calmly and deliberately as possible.

The camera was back in Sophia's face. She barely noticed it anymore. They'd switched to a steady cam mounted on the operator's chest. It was a better option for a multitude of reasons, but it also meant more people in her personal space. She didn't care, though. Her personal space had never been all that personal, and the lens was a mere extension of the eyes she'd worked hard to have fixed on her. She did nothing to adapt her movements for any of them once she slipped into character. They'd work around her the same way the peripheral characters in the film would shift around her character.

Honestly though, that part of the character wasn't particularly challenging. She barely acknowledged anyone else's gaze most days. She might as well have been in the room alone if not for one particular set of eyes on her now.

She felt more than saw Vic reenter the room after they resumed shooting. She stood back near the doorway away from the crew, and even farther from her manservant, James, and yet she felt so much closer.

"Now stand over the book," Brian said. His vague direction might have annoyed her earlier in her career, but now she understood what she needed to do. The ancient-looking ledger on the desk in front of her would appear at several points in the film, always telling her something she didn't want to hear, either about finances, or a line of succession. She frowned as the thought reminded her of Victoria's comments about not being rich or famous enough, even when all evidence pointed to the contrary.

"Yes. Perfect." Brian startled her simply by still being there. "Now hold the same expression, but tilt your face up."

When she followed his direction, she met Vic's eyes. Her breath caught in the second before the other woman looked away. Those blue irises were swirling again, and they'd been focused intently on her. There was so much emotion there that didn't make sense. Hunger, certainly, just like the men who'd tried to woo her in the past, but instead of drawing closer when given the chance, Vic pulled away.

Sophia possessed enough self-confidence not to question her own appeal. Besides, Vic's body language told her the attraction hadn't faded so much as it had been complicated by something she hadn't fully given voice to yet. Sophia shouldn't care what was going on under Vic's professional exterior, but she did, and that sent up a red flag.

Everyone had their own life, and she didn't make a habit of getting involved in anyone else's simply because they shared a movie set. Of course, Vic was much easier to look at than any of the men who'd come before her on various sets over the last few years. She was also more enjoyable to chat with. The dinner they'd shared had been the most enjoyable work-adjacent function Sophia had attended in a long time. Still, she was work adjacent, as evidenced by Victoria's presence currently distracting her in front of a camera. Another red flag. And despite the woman's beautiful body and sharp mind, she was also mind-numbingly wealthy and steeped in completely unearned privilege, which should have been red flag number three, and the ultimate deal-breaker.

"Okay, now turn to face us," Brian said, "And maybe put your hands on your hips."

It was a dumb request, and she suspected he was merely talking because he liked the sound of his own voice, but the position gave her the chance to stare at Victoria without pretense for much longer than any social situation would allow. Vic, for her part, looked everywhere but at her. Damned if she wasn't growing more intrigued by this woman with each moment.

They'd reversed roles so many times in the week since they'd met, and while Vic had been compelling in each of the personas she'd affected, she'd been much easier to write off when she'd presented as haughty and commanding. Her appeal improved with her improving mood, or glimpses of a genuine sense of humour, and even the hand kiss when they'd parted ways the other night had been sort of endearing. Sophia would've thought she'd find something so chaste and chivalrous silly, but when paired with the almost frantic emotions emanating off of Vic, her restraint seemed almost beautifully tortured. Something had clearly been clawing at the woman from inside her pristine façade, and yet, in an instant of near panic, she'd summoned the restraint to brush her lips lightly over Sophia's hand.

That's what ultimately did her in. The contrast of light and dark, the proper up against the raw, made Sophia want to peel back the layers and inspect them more fully. She would've liked to pretend the impulse stemmed completely from artistic integrity, but the way her heart beat a little faster as Victoria's gaze fell on her once more suggested otherwise.

"We're done," Sophia said quickly, refusing to let another opportunity slip through her fingers.

"What?" Brian asked.

"You got the shots you need. Well done."

He scratched the stubble on his chin, not sure what to do with her stepping into his territory in the form of a compliment. "Thanks?"

"You're welcome. Shall we send the frames over and let you get to that pint you earned?"

He nodded slowly, seeming to enjoy this idea more with each moment. "Yeah, that's a wrap."

Talia looked from one of them to the other before shrugging. "Call time's 6 a.m. tomorrow in the stables by the abbey with Tommy. Then Sophia's in at eight o'clock."

They had assistants to make these sorts of announcements, but Sophia suspected Talia had already realised Brian didn't listen to assistants. If she wanted to take on the role of cat herder in addition to screenwriter and producer, that was probably for the best, but Sophia was interested in herding only one person right now. She quickly sidestepped several crew members in an attempt to intercept Victoria, who was already headed toward the door.

"Your Ladyship," she called just before she got away.

"Ms. LeBlanc." Vic returned the formal greeting.

"I hoped to speak with you about a few things regarding my character motivation."

"Right now?"

"If you're free, or perhaps over dinner again this evening? You wouldn't have to cook. I could have something delivered, either to my trailer or to my room."

Vic's smile faltered. "Today isn't good for me. Perhaps we could meet at the stable tomorrow morning and discuss your concerns before filming commences."

That wouldn't be nearly private enough for the conversation she wanted to have, and she suspected Vic knew as much. Sophia had offered many similar redirects over the years, but she'd rarely needed to circumvent one. She had no backup plan and felt more than a little caught off guard by needing one. "If that's all you've got to give me."

A little muscle in Vic's jaw twitched, but she gave a curt nod.

Then she bolted around the corner, and from the sound of her footsteps, she hightailed it all the way to another wing of the castle.

"You're playing with fire."

She turned to find Talia leaning against a camera dolly, arms folded across her chest.

"Whatever do you mean?"

"Don't go all Scarlett O'Hara on me. I've worked with you before. You never showed a lick of interest in anyone else on the set."

"You're the one who told me to enjoy my date the other night. What if I merely heeded your advice?"

"You're not looking at our host like someone who's developed a little crush. You're eyeing her like a hyena might size up a wounded gazelle."

"Oh Tal, this is why you're the writer and I merely read the lines."

"Flattery is much appreciated, but not enough to redirect me. Whatever you're after with Vic, it's not going to end well."

"How do you know?"

"Because she's a good person, and you're . . ."

"Not?" The implication stung, and Talia must've seen it.

"I didn't mean that. I was going to say, 'up to no good,' but I paused because I honestly haven't figured out what you're up to. One day you've got nothing nice to say about her, and now you're practically chasing her out of rooms. You can't blame the woman for going all deer-in-the-headlights on you."

Her smile spread. "I think you're underestimating her."

"I think you are," Talia shot back

"Care to make a little wager?"

"Absolutely not."

"Do you even want to hear what I have in mind?"

"Not really," Talia said.

"I'm gonna break her." She hadn't formulated the plan until it came out of her mouth, but it felt good once she'd said it. A challenge, a risk, a chance to test a few limits, in other words, all her favourite things.

Talia threw up her hands. "Why? Just because you can?"

She paused to ponder the question. She didn't think that was an inherently bad reason for doing something that sparked her interest, but she didn't think that was her sole motivation, either.

"She's not like the women and men we're used to running circles around." Talia pressed. "She's got something more under the shell than she shows people."

"Maybe you're right. Maybe I've misread her. I doubt it, but I'm willing to admit something new and authentically amazing could exist in the world." Sophia wouldn't argue a point Talia had clearly made up her mind on. "But isn't that all the more reason to break her open and see? Wouldn't it be nice to test her mettle and find silver instead of ash? If she's living in a cage of some sort, wouldn't I be doing her a favour by bending the bars a bit?"

"I don't believe you're in this for doing favours. I think you want to see what will happen if you open the flood gates."

"Cages, gates, façades, you're only making my point. They hide things, they restrain them, they pin them in."

"Except we're not talking about a thing. We're talking about a woman. Let's not be like the men in this business who constantly act like they know what's best for us, and instead trust her to tell us what she needs."

"What if she doesn't know what she needs?"

"What makes you think you do?"

She shrugged. "I might not, but I'd like to find out."

"And I'd like to go on record as saying you're playing a dangerous game. Walls are usually put up for a reason, and if you start pulling out bricks, the whole thing is liable to come crashing down in ways you don't expect."

"Point taken," Sophia said solemnly, but Talia had only reaffirmed that neither of them knew who Lady Vic would be when those walls fell, and that was more than enough intrigue for Sophia to want to blow them up.

Vic sat at her father's desk, breathing in the scent of worn leather and furniture polish. They were two of the three smells she associated most strongly with her childhood. Now if only his cologne were added to the mix, she might begin to actually relax. Then again, if he were home, she likely wouldn't be in here. She had her own office, in another part of the estate, but it was modern and bright and filled with other people most of the day. She generally enjoyed being around them, working with a common purpose, never having too much time to get lost in abstract thoughts. Only she wasn't supposed to be in the land office this month either. She was supposed to be in Scotland with her whole family. Which brought her mind right back to why she'd returned, seeking sanctuary in the very room where she now sat, still feeling unsettled, as unsettled as she had been under the constant shadow of her mother's persistent disappointment.

She'd begun to suspect there were no more uncomplicated spaces for her when a little clinking sound stirred her from her musing.

At first, she wasn't sure she'd actually heard anything at all, but when the sound came again, distant and small, she turned her ear. The cleaning staff had already been in this area during the day, and there shouldn't be anyone clinking glasses in the dining room or kitchen, but when the sound came again, she realised that's exactly what it was, clinking glass.

She slowly spun the chair to face the windows behind her. The sun was hidden behind clouds that had threatened to break open all evening. They cast an unseasonably gloomy pall over the grounds, but even in the dim light, she caught sight of a tiny flash of something hitting the glass pane the next time she heard the sound. Rising, she walked over to stare down into the courtyard just as another item, clearly a little pebble this time, plinked against the window, and there at the bottom of its trajectory stood Sophia LeBlanc.

Throwing open the sash, she rested her hands on the sill and said, "May I help you?" only her voice sounded much more amused than she'd intended.

"Why, yes, yes you can." Sophia stared up at her with a Cheshire grin. "I need your help killing something."

"Excuse me? What are you suggesting we kill?"

Sophia held open one side of her jacket to show a hidden parcel. "This bottle of gin."

She shook her head. This couldn't be happening. She'd lived a charmed life in a lot of ways, and she'd been schooled in a myriad of social graces, but nothing had prepared her for such a brazen push into her personal spaces.

"Come on, Vic," Sophia called up. "You told me you were a gin woman. Let me inside and prove it."

She braced her hands on the windowsill so tightly her knuckles went white. She should call security. Sophia had broken in and thrown rocks at a three-hundred-year-old window, and yet she'd done so because she'd remembered a small and trivial detail about what Vic liked. "Things like this don't happen in my life."

"They do now."

She shook her head. She shouldn't let that be true, but her brain couldn't formulate the words to send her away when she had so many other questions. "How did you even get in here?"

"I never left when everyone else did. I've been lying in wait all evening, watching from the staging area for a light to come on and stay on in that castle of yours."

"Then where did you get the gin?"

Sophia laughed. "I actually got the idea from you. Remember how you said you had to keep the liquor out of the tourist areas because people liked to nick bottles from the duke? Well, we weren't filming in the tourist areas today, were we?"

"You didn't."

She shrugged in a way that made it quite clear that's exactly what she'd done.

This couldn't be real. None of this could be real. "Things like this happen only in movies."

Sophia laughed. "Lucky for you, I'm in the movies. Now are you going to let me in the front door, or would you rather lower your hair and have me climb up?"

She couldn't help but give her hair a playful little shake, but it only fell just past her shoulders.

"Okay, the front door it is," Sophia called, then jogged off toward the Norman gateway, and without thinking Vic ran off to meet her.

"This isn't the best idea," she said as she pulled open the heavy wooden door.

"Of course it isn't, darling." Sophia shed her jacket and tossed it over Hank's arm. "That's what makes it so tempting."

She couldn't argue. If Sophia had merely tried to schedule an official appointment via their assistants, Vic wouldn't have spent more than a minute wiggling her way out of it. The fact that Sophia's approach was so very improper and ill-advised was exactly what prevented her from saying no. Well, that, and her thin maroon shirt with the deep V-neck that showed off Sophia's throat, and chest, and . . . *eyes up, Vic.*

Sophia caught her staring, again. She smirked. "Thirsty?"

She shook her head.

"Sure you are." Sophia gave her hand a little tug. "Where are we drinking?"

"I don't know if—"

"We should do this. I know." Sophia cut her off. "Can we go ahead and enter into the record of the evening that you protested valiantly while I used my well-documented charm and evil influences to overcome your better angels? That way we can skip the hemming and hawing and get down to the good parts."

Vic smiled. No one had ever spoken to her that way. As far as she was concerned, this already was the good part, but she didn't want to explain that to Sophia. She didn't want to explain anything to anyone right now. "Okay, we've got the library, and the, well, you've seen the dining room, or . . . do you want to go upstairs to the residence?"

Sophia raised an eyebrow, and the deal was done.

Vic didn't even know how they got into her personal suite of rooms. She must have moved on autopilot or in some sort of dream state, because the next time she was aware of even breathing, she was seated on a settee in her dressing room while Sophia poured an inordinate amount of gin-to-tonic ratio into a highball glass.

She accepted the drink without the slightest bit of apprehension. The gin might be the only thing in the room she felt certain she could handle, so it might be as good a place as any to try to regain her footing. "You know I've been drinking these things since I was fourteen."

"Are you trying to establish your credibility as a rebel?" Sophia asked, pouring herself a decidedly lighter dose.

"No. I'm merely sharing my honest hope that you didn't come here with the intent of getting me inebriated," she explained. "I'd hate to disappoint you again."

Sophia turned to face her, then glancing around the room, seemed to forgo the chair set at a more appropriate distance in favour of the much closer and smaller open end of the settee. "What do you mean, again? When did you disappoint me the first time?"

"When things ended in our first, well, our last evening together."

"First date?"

Her heart gave a little kick to her stomach. "If you will. I merely meant to say I know you weren't pleased with my abrupt withdrawal, and I apologise for not being in a position to offer you more. I apologise for not being the person you hoped I could be."

Sophia shifted her weight, settling herself into the space between them so the distance felt even smaller. "Apologies, apologies. Please tell me, Your Ladyship, what's with you and apologies?"

Her face warmed. "I don't have a thing with apologies. It's just habit for me to make them."

Sophia pressed her lips together as she pondered the answer. Then she raised her glass with a new little twinkle in her eye. "Habits are meant to be broken."

Vic wasn't at all sure she understood the full impact of the statement, but as she clinked her glass against Sophia's, she had to admit she liked the way it sounded.

Chapter Six

The gin was so much smoother than anything Sophia remembered drinking in her youth. Then again, the gin warming her throat right now was likely infinitely higher quality than anything she'd stolen in her teenage years. The thought annoyed her, but she hid it by glancing at the seal on the bottle. "So, does your dad have his own gin distillery?"

"What?" Vic asked, her eyes still a little far off and dreamy.

"The stamp on the bottle has his mark on it. I've seen the lion crest all over the castle and the contracts."

"Well caught. But no, he doesn't own the plant, only the land it's built on."

"How does that work?"

"Those contracts are actually part of my office. Land, conservation and development, both divisions technically fall under my purview, but I mostly have my fingerprints on the development side."

"I have no idea what that means." Sophia didn't have any real interest in the details, but Vic seemed more at ease with the topic, and getting her to talk comfortably constituted a good step.

"The duke owns over 150,000 acres of land that has to be managed or developed in some way, farms, businesses, nature preserves. I oversee all of those operations though I lean heavily toward the real estate market."

"And by 'the duke,' you mean your father?"

"Yes and no. It's complicated. The land and the title have always been in conjunction, which has never allowed for any real test of ownership, but maybe it belongs to my father, and maybe it belongs to the dukedom."

"I'm confused. You mean, if your dad just decided to up and abdicate his dukeship or whatever, he wouldn't get to keep the land?"

"Traditionally the land would pass to whoever became the next duke, as he would take over the associated responsibilities."

"And that's hereditary?"

Vic sipped her gin calmly. "Also complicated."

"What's the short version?"

"My father doesn't have a male heir or even a close male relative. When he dies, which is still hopefully a very long time in the future, no one is quite sure what happens."

"Well, that's some *Downton Abbey* bullshit."

Vic laughed harder than the comment warranted. "You're not the first person to ever draw the connection, but I do believe you might be the first person to put it so succinctly."

"Why do I get the idea not many people call bullshit around you?"

"Oh, they do," Victoria said seriously, "but they usually phrase it differently, snide comments, backhanded compliments, or anonymous statements to the press. I actually prefer your direct approach."

"You might be the first person to ever tell me that."

"And you're certainly the first person to ever throw rocks at my window, so maybe we're even."

"Not even close, sister," Sophia said quickly. "I wanna know the rest of this inheritance saga. What happens if your dad were to die tomorrow?"

Vic grimaced. "Like I said, he's impressively healthy. I have the utmost hope and even a relatively reasonable expectation that he lives to be a hundred."

"Not trying to be morbid about your pop, but you know what I mean, right?"

"I do. And I'd love to give you some definitive answer. Honestly, I might be willing to murder another human right here, right now if that would provide some certainty on the future of inheritance laws and my life."

"How very Macbeth of you," Sophia said, totally loving the darkness of that comment.

"The Thane of Cawdor has nothing on me. At least he knew what his succession of peerage was."

"Come again?" Sophia asked, finding she actually did want to understand the answer.

"The laws governing how titles get passed down are called the 'succession of peerage.' My father was the only son of an only son, and his closest great uncle had no children who survived long enough to procreate. It's possible the government could find someone way back in my family tree to oust me from the estate along with my younger sister, but they'd have a hard time making a definitive claim."

"What if they can't do it?"

"Then it's possible the government could oust my sister and me from the estate and reclaim everything, either to dissolve the title and sell the land, which has happened a few times, or hand it over to some royal nephew or something, which has happened many times."

"Wait, either way you're homeless?"

"We'd not be cast into the streets or anything. We have other properties in private holdings."

Of course you do, Sophia thought, but managed not to say so.

"But to say we'd be out of the only home our family has known for centuries would be accurate."

"All because you were born with lady parts instead of a penis?" A familiar tick of indignance rose inside her.

"To put it bluntly."

"And until it happens, your very existence is just . . . what? A walking legal time-bomb?"

"I try not to think of it that way, but yes, it's my reality. Every time the phone rings in the middle of the night, I steel myself for the news that my mere biology has brought an end to eight hundred years of history." She lifted her glass again in mock salute.

"Damn." Sophia hated to give Talia's comment about under-estimating this woman any credence, but she hadn't seen the one-dead-dad-away-from-losing-it-all angle coming.

"That's the aristocracy for you."

"It's sexism for you," Sophia shot back. "Look, I can't believe I of all people am about to get irate about inheritance laws, but what the actual hell? It's not like you're living in ancient times. No matter what enragingly nepotistic class system you're working under, the rules should at least be the same for men and women."

Vic shrugged. "We've had female monarchs and prime ministers. We have plenty of non-discrimination laws in business and schools."

"So why can't you fight for the same thing with the titles?"

"There was a push some years ago to start making major changes, but it keeps stalling in Parliament, and then the session ends and everything must be completely restarted over and over again." Victoria swallowed another solid sip of her drink. "Maybe eventually new laws will get passed, but obviously there aren't a ton of people in my position, so I can't imagine Parliament will feel a sense of urgency until some high-profile case slaps them in the face."

"Holy crap, that could be you." Sophia started to feel excited about the prospect. "You could, like, bring some landmark law-suit. You could set a precedent and change this for every woman who comes after you."

"Once upon a time, maybe." Vic shook her head as a flash of sadness shadowed her features. Then she sat up a little straighter and forced her expression back to neutral. "Anyway, you didn't break into a castle to talk about lines of peerage and titles."

"You don't know what I broke in here for."

"True." Victoria crossed one leg over the other, angling toward Sophia in a graceful way that effortlessly indicated interest. "Care to tell me?"

"Oh, that was smooth!" Sophia raised her glass in a salute. "You know, I often try to pull off that move."

"Move?" Vic played innocent, but Sophia didn't buy it.

"The subtle shift to signal enough-talking-about-this-thing-I-don't-want-to-talk-about by making it seem like you're way more interested in the other person."

"I did no such thing, and I'm genuinely more interested in you."

"Well, I'm more interested in you."

Vic's cheeks flushed a slight shade of pink. "You've already heard the most interesting bit about me, and incidentally it has virtually nothing to do with who I am as a person. It's a fact of my birth, a genetic lottery of sorts."

"No." Sophia waved her off. "I'm interested in hearing about this 'once upon a time' you mentioned before changing the subject."

"Oh, you caught that?" Victoria gave a little grimace that managed to make her look sheepish, which seemed both discordant and adorable on a woman who spoke about the aristocracy in completely neutral tones.

"Yes, and I know all the moves people use to deflect. I'm professional grade on both sides of the equation, so you should surrender the information now and save me the trouble of dragging it out of you with some morally suspect method."

This time Victoria didn't shy away from the suggestiveness of the remark. "What if I suspect I wouldn't hate some of your methods?"

"Seeing as how my sex appeal fell short last time—"

"It didn't," Victoria said flatly. "Your sex appeal has never been lost on me."

The boldness of the comment caught Sophia off guard, and she took another sip of gin to try to buy time. "Then why did I end up standing on the other side of your big, heavy door?"

"Because you wanted something I couldn't give."

"Couldn't or wouldn't?"

"Couldn't," Vic affirmed in a gentle voice. "Believe me, if you'd

81

pressed up against me and asked for anything within my power to give, it would've been yours."

Apparently, it was Sophia's turn to open her mouth wordlessly. It wasn't that she didn't thrill at the thought of holding such power over such a beautiful woman, but the soft melancholy in Vic's voice also triggered other emotions she didn't want to examine.

"But you asked me to be someone I'm not, and you used the possibility of a personal relationship as a sort of bait or reward to entice me into betraying my sense of self. I can't trade who I know myself to be in order to be with someone else."

"So much for welcoming morally suspect methods."

Vic shook her head. "I wish my position were borne of some high-minded principles, but I meant what I said about the difference between *can't* and *won't*. I'm not that pure." Vic lifted her eyes and met Sophia's. "I'm merely incapable of keeping up a charade of that level. I've tried. I failed."

"Hmm." Sophia hummed like the electricity surging through her, from Vic's defiant gaze, from her intimate tone, from the openness she'd wilfully revealed. "You know I'm not leaving until I hear this story now."

Vic's smile spread as if she didn't hate that idea. "Then perhaps I should pour us another drink?"

Sophia was no longer sure if Vic was falling into line with her plans or if perhaps it was the other way around, but either way she handed over her glass. "Make it a double, Your Ladyship."

Vic accepted the glass as if it were a life preserver and hopped up off the settee. Her hands trembled as she tried to pour the gin, but she turned her back to Sophia in the hopes she wouldn't see. Then again, Sophia seemed to see everything. Vic could have stripped naked and stood in front of a wall of mirrors and felt less exposed than she felt sitting next to Sophia moments ago.

She couldn't remember the last time another person had stared into her eyes so intently. Much like the touching Sophia had used liberally earlier in the day, her prolonged eye contact carried an informality Vic was unaccustomed to. She never consciously worked to build or enforce those barriers, but people in her employ rarely dared to look too closely. At times the disconnect left her lonely, but she'd never stopped to think about how the opposite approach could have a similar effect. Having Sophia see her in her weakness, her openness, her shortcomings made Vic feel smaller and more vulnerable than she had in ages.

"Don't skimp on the liquid courage now," Sophia called playfully from behind her. "How will I ever get you to tell me those dark secrets you keep alluding to if you're not sufficiently plied with gin?"

She laughed in spite of the fact that Sophia had laid her cards on the table and revealed the real reason for her visit. "I told you, I've been drinking this stuff for nearly two decades. Trust me when I say you didn't steal nearly enough gin to make me tell you about Robert tonight."

"Robert?"

She didn't even have to turn around to know Sophia's eyebrows were raised and her mouth was curled up in one of those tight-lipped smiles.

"Who's Robert?"

She braced herself with both hands on the glass top of the bar cart and hung her head as shame washed over her.

"You can't keep dropping these little teases and then leaving me hanging," Sophia prodded.

She was probably right. It was unfair, and yet Vic hadn't meant to let his name slip out. His name hadn't slipped out in years, not unintentionally. Nothing about Robert would ever be unintentional again, or easy. And yet, it just had been. She'd mentioned him as casually to Sophia as she might allude to a school friend.

But that's what he'd been, hadn't he? Long before everything spiralled so out of control, he'd been so much more than he became, and then again, he'd become so much more than she'd ever let herself fear. Her breath grew shallow at the thoughts

83

she'd held at bay for so very long. Had the talk about her history, her future, her position brought them too close to the surface, or had Sophia broken down the defences with her refusal to keep a respectful distance the way all the others did?

"Come on," Sophia whispered, much closer now.

She shook her head and swallowed the bile rising in her throat.

Sophia picked up a glass and took a sip before extending it to Vic.

"I haven't added the tonic yet."

"Oh, you're not going to find the tonic you need in a bottle tonight." Sophia wrapped an arm around her waist. "Come back and sit with me."

It took everything Vic had not to melt into her. Only her fear of never being able to let go kept her from clinging to Sophia. Instead she lifted her chin and blew out a stiff breath. "I'm fine."

"Of course you are, darling," Sophia practically purred in her ear. "Come on."

She allowed herself to be led back to the settee, and Sophia pressed the glass into her hand. She stared down at the faint imprint of Sophia's lipstick on the rim and her heart beat a little faster. She snorted softly at the immaturity of finding a thrill in such a thing. She wasn't some silly schoolgirl with her first crush. She was a grown woman with a past and a near crushing sense of decorum. As if to prove her point she said, "Robert is my ex-husband."

Sophia nodded thoughtfully. "And here I was, assuming that the way you undressed me with your eyes the first time we met was a solid indicator of your lesbianism."

She shook her head at the perfectly disarming response to the hardest thing she'd had to say in ages. How did this woman keep managing to shake her equilibrium enough to make her feel off balance without quite letting her fall?

"So, are you bisexual? Pansexual? A generalised sort of queer?"

"I wish. Things would be so much easier in so many ways."

"How so?"

"If men were an option for me, physically I would have taken hold of it by now, but it's not in my nature, no matter how hard I've tried."

"And Robert is the evidence of how hard you tried?"

She shook her head. "No, I knew before I married him that I'd never share a physical attraction with him. We both did."

"Hmm." Sophia reached for the glass and took another sip, while making a rolling motion with her hand. "Keep going."

"I already told you. Everything about my future will likely hinge on a legal battle, but it's not only my future or my sister's or even the castle's. This estate is the biggest employer in the region. The entire economy of Northland depends on the tourism, the farming, the businesses propped up by the dukedom. If that disappeared it would destabilise the entire region. Thousands of people would face unemployment and thousands of acres of conservation land could be subject to development. Corporate ownership of . . . well, everything. A lot of people around here don't always agree with how my family handles land and contracts, but they can petition us. We serve them. No multinational business based in Stockholm or Bejing would—"

"Right, right," Sophia cut in. "You have a well-established sense of responsibility. Can you skip to the part about what all that has to do with you marrying a man you didn't love?"

The words hit her like a punch to the stomach, and she sucked in a sharp breath.

"There." Sophia snapped her fingers. "That reaction. Where does that come from?"

"I did love him," Victoria said with more fervour. "I might not have been in love with him, but I trusted him. I shared my dreams and fears and insecurities with him, and he stood beside me. He promised to fight for me, and with me. I loved him deeply for his loyalty."

"Sounds like a great friend, but marriage is a big leap."

"Too big, apparently," she admitted, the prick of sadness overtaking the shame once more. "I was naïve. I believed friendship, understanding, and a shared sense of purpose could overcome a lack of passion. We could meet all of each other's needs but one."

"Let me guess. That one particular need undid all the others?"

She nodded and took the glass back again. She didn't even taste the gin anymore, but she longed for its warmth.

"So, you had an arrangement? You both got what you needed on the side and—"

She shook her head quickly. "Not both of us. I made vows in a church, in front of my family, in front of our entire community. I never once broke those. Not in body or even spirit. I didn't look at a woman for three years."

Sophia blew out a long, slow breath. "Wow, I thought I was goal-oriented. That's impressive. Let me guess. Ol' Robby didn't have your fortitude?"

She shook her head again, this time more slowly as the tabloid headlines flashed through her memory in rapid succession. "And every time it hurt a little more. Not the infidelities so much as the betrayal of everything we'd worked for. We were supposed to be a picture-perfect couple, the standard-bearers of modern nobility, the perfect legal precedent people would trust and want to follow into a new era: self-sacrificing, service oriented, steady. Instead, my best friend became the worst of every generation before us."

"That's some Prince Charles and Camilla what's-her-name level scandal there."

She snorted. "Not quite, but close enough for people to whisper that we're all the same. Enough for the local rumours to attract greater scrutiny. Enough for a major reporter to take Robert to a private room in a gentleman's club one night."

"Oh shit." Sophia grimaced. "He wasn't even classy about it. What did he say when he got caught?"

Vic didn't even try to hide the tremor in her hand as she lifted the glass to her lips and drained it. Then meeting Sophia's eyes once more, she said, "He told the whole world it wasn't his fault because his wife was a lesbian."

"Fuck," Sophia didn't know what else to say. She'd done what she considered to be an admirable job of staying emotionally distant and sarcastic during much of the Poor-Little-Rich-Girl might lose castle portion of the story. As much as she was starting to appreciate Vic's complexities, it was still hard to relate to her life circumstances, but the idea of a woman giving up a vast part of herself for some perceived greater good only to have a pecker-headed asshole rob her of everything she'd worked for *and* her right to self-determination just to save his own stripper-screwing self . . . She hopped up and began to pace. "This is not okay."

Vic watched her stalk around the room. "I didn't condone his actions."

"I'm not talking about him," Sophia said quickly. "He's irredeemable."

"He had many good qualities. He was—"

"He was a worthless, spineless coward who rode your coattails and was prepared to become a duke on your back while betraying you and all your sacrifices. No amount of being good with kids or helping out around the house is enough to redeem someone like that."

Vic tilted her head to the side as she seemed to ponder that for the first time.

"What I'm upset about now is this." She gestured back and forth between the two of them. "You're making me feel all outraged on your behalf, because cheating on people is wrong, sexist double standards are wrong, and outing people is so fucking wrong. I don't want to feel sorry for someone like you who had every opportunity to make good on every advantage that people like me have never been afforded, but damn."

"I understand," Vic said in that maddeningly reasonable tone with which she accepted so much criticism. "I made my own choices."

"Yeah, and that's messed up, too." Sophia crashed back onto the couch, so close their legs touched this time. "God, Vic, you were just going to not be with another woman ever again? For what? The regional economy? Do you realise how insane that is?"

Vic bristled. "It's hard for people outside my circumstance to grasp the weight of responsibility that comes from having people depend on a position I didn't ask for and might not be able to hold, but I owe it to everyone—"

"What about what you owe to *you*?"

"Excuse me?"

"You keep talking about what you owe everyone else, your family, the government, your employees, the woman working on a farm down the street, but you're a person, too. You're a woman who has needs of her own. I mean, I get you have this whole stiff-upper-lip-and-icy-nobility vibe, but have you seen yourself?"

She shook her head.

"You should." Sophia laughed and grabbed her face, cupping her jaw and cheeks between both of her palms. "This face, those eyes, the way you look at me like you could eat me for dinner and then again for dessert."

Vic's face warmed under her fingers, only managing to prove Sophia's point.

"You're a red-blooded lesbian. You have dreams and desires, and every one of them is a power source. How could you bury them or drown them like they're something to be ashamed of?"

Vic tried to turn her head, but Sophia held her steady and firm. "You have no idea, do you?"

"What?" Vic whispered.

"You don't even understand what you could be if you weren't so afraid of yourself, if you stopped choking off the best parts of you."

"The best parts of myself are my honour, my dignity, my sense of purpose."

"Do you think the rest of us don't have those things? You think they come with your title, or could be taken away as easily?" Sophia asked. "You think loving women makes you less worthy of your position than if you'd stayed married to a man who betrayed you in every possible way? That's not honour. That's cowardice."

Victoria jerked away. "Don't you dare speak to me about cowardice."

"Well, well, well." Sophia sat back, her smile slow. "Did that barb get under your armour?"

"No, I simply won't be spoken to like that in my own room."

"Oh, really?" Sophia enjoyed seeing a little bit of fire in her. "Because I think that might be exactly what you need."

"Don't presume to know me or my needs."

"No, we wouldn't want a woman to do that now, would we? Might mess with the neat little boxes you keep trying to cram yourself into." Her tone carried a hint of mocking, but she'd come here to push buttons and get answers. She had no intention of letting up on either front. "Tell me Your Ladyship, when was the last time anyone dared speak to you with something other than deference?"

Vic scoffed. "About two weeks ago."

"Pray tell me who?"

Vic pressed her lips together and glanced away.

"Come on," Sophia needled. "Don't lose your momentum now. Who had the gall to chastise you?"

Vic sighed. "My mother."

Sophia actually did laugh for real this time. "I suppose you managed to find the one woman around here who outranks you. Must be a short list. I'll wager she didn't get the axe for her transgression."

Vic shook her head.

"You just took it, didn't you?"

"No, I left Scotland."

Sophia sneered. "Must be nice to have a second castle to run to when your mommy's mean to you. But please, tell me more about how none of your decisions have been based on cowardice."

"Okay." Vic stood. "I think it's time for you to leave."

"What if I don't?" She kicked one leg out along the length of the couch, crossed the other over the top of it and settled in. "Will you call security? Or will you run away again?"

"Don't be childish. It's beneath you."

"You have no idea what's beneath me . . . honestly, the list is about as short as the one of people above you."

"Am I supposed to respect that? Does it make you a better person? Cooler? Sexier? I married my best friend for honour and that makes me a coward? You've done . . . what?"

"You can't even begin to imagine the things I've done."

"To what end?" Vic asked.

She shrugged. "To get ahead."

Vic wheeled on her, eyes blazing now. "To build a life of wealth and power? To bank some social or professional cachet? For the ability to call your own shots? Oh wait, you don't get to do that either. You're still taking cues from idiot directors and studio executives you disdain. You're still jumping through hoops to please a fickle public. Wow, why does that sound familiar?"

Sophia seethed as her vision tinged red at that horrible little summary of her current reality delivered by someone who'd never understand what it took to claw her way up to it. "We are not the same."

"Why not?" Vic pushed a step closer until she towered over Sophia's still seated form.

She clenched her jaw. "I earned what's mine."

"And I have paid for mine," Vic shouted, her voice full of the emotion and strength it lacked before. "I paid for it over and over and over, with my name, with my body, my privacy, with my past and my future. I am well aware of my privilege, but what's unearned was also unchosen. I didn't get to pick my job, my studies, my own partner. Things the people who work in our kitchens or landscape our gardens take for granted are denied to me."

Sophia made a show of looking bored, but she wondered if her considerable training managed to come through her voice as she fought to remain neutral in the face of such a stunning outburst. "Do you want my sympathy?"

Vic's shoulders fell. "I'd never even dare to wish for that."

"What then?"

Vic shrugged.

"No, don't do that." Sophia stood and pushed into Vic's space, desperate now not to let her extinguish the fire. "Don't go on another one of your little rants about what you can't have and then refuse to say what you want."

Victoria bit her lower lip, and her gaze became hazy.

"If you don't want sympathy, what do you want?"

"I want . . ." She shook her head as if trying to dislodge a thought she couldn't shake free.

Sophia's chest tightened in anticipation of the words Victoria didn't seem able to say. Had it been so long that this woman didn't even know her own desires, or did she merely need the right motivation to overcome years of self-imposed restraint? She leaned close, so close she felt the heat radiating off Vic as she whispered, "Say it."

"I don't want to disappoint anyone," Vic said softly.

"That's still making what you want about what someone else wants."

"I don't want to be alone," Vic whispered.

"That's what you *don't* want," Sophia pushed. "It's not the same thing as what you *do.*"

"I want . . ." Vic's eyes flicked lower, as if unable to focus on anything but Sophia's lips until she closed her eyes. "I want to be irresponsible."

"Hmm." Sophia hummed at the hint of pleasure the phrase sent up her spine. "Better. Keep going."

"I want to act on my impulses."

"Tell me about them," she whispered directly in her ear.

Vic bit her lip a so hard the deep red went white.

"They aren't impulses if you have to think that hard about them," Sophia goaded.

Vic opened her eyes and turned her head only slightly, so close. "I want to kiss you."

The corner of Sophia's mouth curled up slightly. Pleasure? Amusement? The hint of a challenge? Vic felt helpless to interpret the expression, and absent enthusiastic consent, she remained rooted in her responsibility and being ripped apart by her own desire. Mercifully, Sophia didn't seem nearly as frozen or conflicted. Cupping Vic's cheek in the smooth palm of her hand she asked, "Is that all?"

Vic melted into the touch, so tender, so evocative. "It feels like quite a bit."

Sophia ran her thumb over Vic's lower lip. "It's a start."

Then she pulled Vic forward and pressed her own mouth to the spot she'd caressed. To say the sparks were immediate would've been an egregious understatement. Sophia's lips were soft yet insistent as they moved against her own. God, how long had it been since she kissed someone? She couldn't remember. She couldn't remember any other kisses or any other someones with Sophia pressed against her.

Parting her lips slightly, she welcomed more contact, but Sophia took her time. Light touches, little brushes, not teasing but drawing her forward, drawing her deeper, she stoked the fire she'd been building all night. The patience and poise were wholly unnecessary now though. Something had broken in Vic the moment she'd given voice to her own desires, as if the speaking of them had been more transgressive than the act itself. With that threshold crossed, she had no reason or restraint left to prevent herself from tipping fully forward into the flames.

She cupped Sophia's face in one hand and wrapped her other arm around her waist, pulling them steadily closer together. She would know every inch of this woman. She decided it with the same ease and clarity with which one might order an entrée off a menu, but at no point did she forget Sophia was full, complex, and vibrant. She could not be commanded or cowed, and Vic wanted nothing of the sort. She did, however, want to kiss those lips that were so often pressed into a tight line. She wanted to explore the corners with her tongue so the next time they turned up in such a coy smile, she would know them on a deeper level. She wanted to kiss along the strong jaw, to feel the muscle go slack beneath her caress. She wanted to breathe in the summery scent of Sophia's intoxicating perfume and breathe out a contented sigh next to her ear.

And she did. All that and more. Not an impulse passed through her mind unheeded. Time bent or suspended as hours may have passed in minutes, and yet no amount of stated desires did anything to quench the thirst continuing to build in her. Before long, the kiss that seemed so great a leap felt small compared to the realm of possibility opening between them.

Sophia, too, opened. Parting her lips, she encouraged Vic's tongue, exploring, tracing, testing boundaries that no longer existed. Slowly their hands picked up the theme, first exploring over arms, backs, tangling hair, then clothes before slipping beneath them. Sophia's hand on the small of Vic's back made her gasp. This woman had never shown any respect for her personal space, and Vic had never been more thrilled by that disregard than she was in the moment when her shirt was pushed up over her head.

Exposed now in one of the ways she'd feared, she felt none of the shame so many others tried to instil in her. The shudder that coursed through her body was borne of something else, something more primal than even pleasure. She stepped back barely far enough to check the consent of the only other person who mattered. Holding Sophia's dark, dangerous gaze as their chests rose on heavy breaths, she watched those eyes as she unclasped the button on Sophia's jeans. Refusing to break the contact between them, she slowly drew down the zipper, its sound raw and harsh in the silent room.

Then, sliding her hands back over Sophia's hips, she eased into the waistband and urged the trousers downward until they reached the point where gravity overcame resistance.

"That escalated quickly," Sophia said with one of her wry smiles as she kicked off her shoes and stepped free.

"Indeed." Vic pulled her close and kissed her soundly once more, but this time as their tongues slid against one another, her explorations were no longer aimless. Instincts, long buried, had not been eradicated. They roared back as she grabbed hold of Sophia's waist and directed them back toward the door to her bedroom.

Sophia, for her part, was an apt dance partner, accepting her direction and exuding grace despite moving backward with her eyes closed. Along the way she added a few of her own steps for flare, shedding her shirt before burying her face in Vic's neck. What started as a sexy nuzzle turned into a kiss, then a bite along her throat.

She would have loved to see where that particular path led, but before they had a chance to fully follow it Sophia's back bumped against the bedroom door, and from the little gasp that escaped between their lips, it must have been chilly.

Smiling into the kiss, Vic freed one hand and opened the door. Then with her arm snug around Sophia's waist, she orchestrated a little spin move that set them on a direct collision course with the large, four-poster canopy bed.

Tugging back the comforter with her free arm, she eased Sophia onto the crisp white sheets. She stood for a few glorious seconds imprinting that image on her mind, then crawling up next to her, dipped down to kiss Sophia once more, only deep enough for their mouths to meet, but nothing else.

Sophia worked one hand into Vic's hair, using steady pressure on the back of her neck to urge her down, but she resisted. Breaking the kiss, she thrilled at the little whimper that escaped Sophia.

"Don't tease."

Vic smiled down at her. "It would only be fair after everything you've put me through, but clearly I have neither the inclination nor the fortitude to withhold anything from you."

Then taking her hand, she interlocked their fingers even as she scooted farther away.

"Wait." Sophia laughed. "What happened to not teasing? Get your body back here."

"No." Vic eased down the bed as far as their joined hands would allow. "I want the first thing you feel against you to be my mouth."

Sophia sucked in another sharp breath, and this time Vic suspected it had nothing to do with the cold.

Leaning lower once more, she kissed a path up Sophia's left leg. Slowly, steadily she worked her way upward with varied strokes of her lips and tongue, until reaching the apex. She paused, partially in wonder and partially out of a desire to make this exquisiteness last. Sophia seemingly had no such sentimentality. Relaxing her fingers from Vic's hands, she eased it back into her hair and lifted her hips in a seductive circle. The movement was enough to utterly undo Vic. She bowed, not to the pressure, but to the unstated request. She wanted to meet Sophia's needs as much as her own. The two were as intertwined as their bodies.

She wasn't sure which one of them moaned as she closed her mouth around the centre of Sophia's need. Either way, they moved in concert, the hand on the back of her head encouraging rather than pushing, not that she needed further inspiration. The response of Sophia's body tugged at her core, rising and falling, writhing, yielding, and surging to meet her once more.

She couldn't remember the last time she'd done something she desperately desired and managed to do so well, but judging from the sounds coming from Sophia, she was doing this very well. The realisation only amplified her own arousal. She had reduced a woman to pure, primal incoherence, and not just any woman, a sharp, stunning powerhouse who didn't take anything less than what she desired from any given interaction. And tonight, she desired *her*.

Vic's stomach clenched as Sophia called out and clutched her shoulder. Long, strong, fingers dug into the muscles on her upper back. The clawing of Sophia's nails matched the piercing sensations ripping Vic apart. She needed more in a way that would've frightened her if she'd had her wits about her, but Sophia's body twisting underneath her turned her world upside down until logic seemed a folly, and abandon posed the most perfectly reasonable option.

Sophia's muscles gave one more lurch and then went slack along with the pressure on her back, but instead of using the natural resting place, Vic merely used the opportunity to reorient herself. Easing back only far enough to replace her mouth with her hands, she stared up at Sophia's lavish body in all its prone glory. Then she pushed slowly inside and warmth enveloped her.

Easing forward, she slid the length of her body along the woman beneath her. She groaned at the pure, hedonistic gratification of bare breasts pressed flush against her own. Her hips began to rock as they settled between the thighs she'd kissed and caressed.

Wordlessly they picked up a slow rotation. Up and down, in and out, breath, hands, chests. Her pleasure came in giving, and a sense of strength surged in her as she stared down at Sophia. She had the most expressive features. Her brows would furrow with each withdrawal and then relax on every return. Her lips, slightly swollen, parted softly with laboured breathing. Her eyes, darker for their expanded pupils, served as reflecting pools, allowing Vic to see her own desire shining back up at her.

Their movements picked up speed as Sophia tightened around her, but she refused to break their combined gaze. Vic pressed her forehead to Sophia's, anchoring them to each other for as long as possible. Sophia threw back her head, exposing herself in one final way for Victoria to seize, and she did, dropping her mouth to the pulse point in her neck. She kissed and sucked as she rode the disintegrating rhythm between them, until the body beneath her collapsed, spent and languid.

Even then Victoria took her time on the withdrawal, more for her own benefit than Sophia's. If she were being honest, and she saw no reason not to be, the entirety of this experience had likely benefitted her infinitely more than Sophia. Despite the fact that only one of them had been reduced to mush, Vic suspected the emotional aspects of laying claim to those physical desires would have a much more expansive effect on her mental state. She already felt different, more powerful, more confident, more . . . everything.

"Wow," Sophia murmured.

"Wow?" She eased back only enough to look down at the mirth beginning to curl that beautiful mouth once more.

"I suspected there was something more to the lady-in-waiting demeanour you had working for you, but honestly, I had no idea all of *that* existed underneath your polite veneer." Sophia gave her hips a little thrust, but not hard enough to unseat Vic from atop her. "You've been holding out on me."

Vic smiled, only a hint of sadness poking through her new confidence. "I've been holding out on me, too."

Sophia pushed a strand of hair from Vic's eyes and tucked it behind her ear before trailing it slowly down her jawline. "If you're looking for an opportunity to make up for lost time, I'm free until at least dawn."

She laughed at the extravagant idea of spending all night trying to exhaust this woman from her system. The challenge lit every nerve ending of her body. "We'd better get to it then. Dawn comes early around here."

Then she kissed Sophia again, this time with both entitlement and understanding. The hours left in the night wouldn't be enough, but that wouldn't prevent her from trying to make the most of them.

Chapter Seven

"What the hell happened to you?" Talia asked as Sophia climbed slowly out of the van into what appeared to be some sort of forest preserve.

"That's a great question." One she'd been trying to answer ever since it started. The only conclusion she'd come to was that she'd lit a fuse on what she'd thought to be a firecracker, only to find out too late that it was actually dynamite.

Not that she was complaining. Not exactly.

But the explosion, or rather explosions, as there had been way more than one of them last night, left her more than a little unsteady, and she'd had virtually no time to reflect. Vic hadn't been wrong about the early Northlandian dawn, or her ability to adequately fill the hours in between. Sophia finally found the strength and wherewithal to crawl from the lush, four-poster bed shortly after five in the morning, and yet her walk of shame had been fully lit for all the security staff to see.

Not that she felt any shame. She felt plenty of things, but shame was not on her docket, ever, and especially for a night like that with a woman like Vic. For her ladyship's part, she'd lived up to the chivalry of her nature by offering breakfast followed by a car to the set. What Sophia really needed, though, was sleep followed by caffeine, and she'd found both in short supply. From Talia's shocked stare, their absence must've been blatantly obvious.

"Do you have coffee?"

Talia nodded. "They apparently don't use creamer in this country, though, so how would you like to take it?"

"Preferably in an IV. But I'd drink it black as my soul if need be."

Talia snorted. "Okay, I'll go drum some up for you, but when I get back, I'm going to hear this story."

"As soon as we have time."

"We have time." Talia rolled her eyes. "In a shock to no one, Tommy's shoot is running behind."

She pinched the bridge of her nose. "Coffee first, then murder."

"Got it." Talia scooted off, and Sophia went to lean against a nearby stone structure. She was probably violating some sort of historical landmark rules and wrinkling her dress at the same time, but she couldn't bring herself to care. At least this outfit wasn't as puffy as some of the others. The square-cut bodice still showed more than would have been historically prudent, but the sleeves were straight, and the skirt hung loosely without too many ruffles, which was damn lucky, as she wasn't sure she could handle a sex hangover and a hoop skirt simultaneously. Still, it felt nearly ridiculous to be wearing such an elaborate and heavy get-up after how free and exposed she'd been hours ago.

The thought sent a vivid flash of memories through her mind's eye, and it must've shown because Talia gave a low whistle as she approached with a steaming cup in her outstretched hand.

"You better make this story as dreamy as the expression on your face, because if it's not earth-shattering, I'm going to send out a missing person's report on my most cynical and aloof friend."

"Oh, the cynic is very much still here, but yes, I'll admit, this story is really that good."

"Spill," Talia ordered. "Well, drink, then spill."

She lifted the coffee to her lips, fully intending to heed those directions, but before she'd managed even two full swallows, the sound of hoofbeats pounding the ground caused every head to turn.

Her first thought was that someone had lost control of an animal, and her senses surged into high alert, but as a stunning

99

white horse burst into view between the trees ahead, it became instantly clear that not only was its rider still astride it, she was one hundred percent in command.

Victoria was upon them in seconds, wheeling her ride to a halt and practically vaulting from its back. She turned first to pat her mount's muzzle, which gave Sophia the chance to get a full look at her riding breaches and knee-high leather boots. Victoria handed the reins to a man who'd apparently been waiting for them. Then she unclasped her black riding helmet and snapped off her leather gloves, before handing them to the assistant as well. As if that little display weren't enough, she ran her hands through her long blond hair, shaking out the locks and straining her form-fitting white shirt like some literal lesbian wet dream.

The move looked like something out of a movie, and it took Sophia a second to realise they were actually supposed to be shooting a movie here, only Vic wasn't in it, which now seemed like a vast oversight since Sophia's brain felt like it was on actual fire. It wasn't lost on her that Vic's outfit nearly matched the one Sophia wore during their first encounter, but for her it wasn't a costume. She was born to wear the attire, and it showed right down to the way she moved with grace and confidence. If the cameras had been on this moment, Sophia would've been utterly lost because she could barely remember her own name, much less her lines as Victoria strode toward them like she owned the damn forest, which come to think of it, she did.

"Good morning, Ms. Stamos, Ms. LeBlanc." She gave a playful little bow.

"Good morning, indeed," Talia marvelled.

"Your Ladyship." Sophia hugged her coffee a little closer for moral support.

"Sorry I'm late," Vic said, apparently the only one oblivious to the sex appeal she oozed. "The morning was too glorious to let pass without a ride."

"No apology needed," Talia said as she regained her composure. "We're actually running a bit behind."

"I hope not on my account."

"Not at all. It seems our male lead is fond of having the camera on him."

"You have a male lead?" Vic winked playfully. "Seems a waste to divert valuable screen time away from a thespian of Ms. LeBlanc's calibre and appeal, but I suppose not every one of your viewers will share my particular and impeccable aesthetic."

"Yes, unfortunately, a great many women actually enjoy having men in their movies," Talia said sadly.

"What's the saying? There's no accounting for taste? But Tommy's self-indulgence at least grants me a few moments in superior company." Vic smiled brightly. "If you'll allow me a moment or two to see to my mount, I'd happily grant you a little tour of our stable."

"Please take all the time you need," Talia said. "I have a feeling we'll be here awhile."

"Very well." Vic gave them another quick nod before striding briskly into the building behind them.

She'd barely made it out of earshot before Talia spun on Sophia. "What the fuck and hell did you do to her?" She shook her head slowly, "Seriously, when you said you were going to break her open and find out what was under that polite shell, I didn't expect you to unearth some lesbian superhero version of Mr. Darcy."

Sophia held up her hand. "Stop."

"Did you see her? She winked at you. The daughter of an English duke winked at you and suggested we chuck Tommy off script to hand you the entire film."

"That actually is a legitimate suggestion." Sophia allowed a little smile.

"I'm not disagreeing, but the question remains, what did you do to her?"

"I wish I could parse it out myself. At one point I had her backed into a corner conversationally, and the next thing I knew, she had me backed against her bedroom door, quite literally."

"That's delicious on multiple levels. You went in there to break her, and she broke you."

"She didn't break me." Sophia swallowed a few key memories. "At least not in any lasting way."

"She certainly flipped your script."

Sophia pressed her lips together, unable to deny the charge.

"What are you going to do now?"

"Nothing" she said. "I'm going to get back to work."

Talia threw back her head and laughed so loud several other people turned to stare.

"Shh." Sophia shoved her. "Stop that. And what's so funny anyway?"

"If you could've only seen yourself when she jumped off the horse. I thought you might pass out from all the blood rushing out of your face to places farther south."

"I wasn't any worse than you were."

"No, you totally were. If you'd been wearing pants, you would've dropped them."

"I would not have."

Talia laughed again.

"No. I'm serious. She caught me off guard last night. I'll cop to being unprepared for her ... her ..."

"Skills? Charms? Passion? Smoking hot body? Her ability to rock your world and leave you a mere wisp of your former self?"

"Enough," she snapped, when in reality she could just as easily have answered *all of the above.*

"She's formidable in a lot of ways I didn't predict, but I've got a job to do here. I don't have the time or inclination to lose focus over some sexy noblewoman in sexy-ass boots and sexier breeches."

"So sexy." Talia made a knee-buckling motion.

"Then you're free to swoon all you want, but last night was a one-time thing . . . or maybe a four-times-in-one-night sort of thing, but it won't carry over onto the set. I'm here, one hundred percent."

"Good, because so is she."

"What?"

"Incoming," Talia whispered and plastered a polite smile on her face that clearly indicated Vic was approaching.

"I'm sorry to have kept you waiting. Shall we start the afore-promised tour now?"

"Actually, I've been called to a different part of the set." Talia's bold-faced lie came out of her mouth so quickly Sophia didn't have time to process, much less call bullshit before Tal added, "Please, show Sophia around, and I'll make sure she gives me a *full* report later."

"Ah, I do hope there's no crisis on your end, but Ms. LeBlanc and I will carry on in your stead."

"I don't doubt it," Talia said, seemingly unable to keep a little laugh from escaping as she wandered away.

Sophia shook her head and turned to Vic, trying to convey her most unamused facial expression. "She did that on purpose."

"Then I'll offer my profound thanks at the first opportunity, but in the meantime, you and I still have a serious job to do. I promised you a tour of the stables, and I think if I've proven myself to be anything thus far, it's thorough."

Sophia rolled her eyes in an attempt to hide the shiver that little comment sent down her spine. She didn't know what do with the new, more brazenly confident Vic any more than she'd known what to do with sexually aggressive Vic the night before. Well, at least last night she had some very compelling reasons to simply lie back and enjoy what she'd unleashed, but it wasn't like her to let herself be led around in broad daylight, and on her own movie set, no less.

Now was probably time to assert herself. There was no legitimate reason why a lead actress needed a location tour of some stables. They paid people for that sort of thing. It was time to find one of them and put her foot down on this whole charade.

"I hope you'll find these stables authentic to your cause," Vic said.

Sophia opened her mouth to tell her *no*, but before she even formed the word, Vic lowered her voice and added, "They're also quite private."

The involuntary tightening of her chest expelled a little rush of air from her lungs.

Vic took the non-answer as acceptance, and with a sideways tilt of her head, motioned for Sophia to follow her.

And she did. Which annoyed her. It hadn't even been a proper request, just a mere motion, a silent indication of her will, and Sophia trailed along like some well-trained puppy. This was no longer merely getting out of hand. It was fully there.

"As you can see, despite the age of the building, there's great potential for natural light, both from the large doors at either end and the access points to the haylofts. Additionally, these stable stalls were outfitted for draft horses originally, so they're much larger than the ones at the castle."

"Vic," she managed.

"Oh wait, I haven't shown you the best part." She swung open a wooden door and flipped on a light illuminating a small room stacked neatly with what Sophia could only assume was a wide array of horse equipment.

She stared from all the horse stuff back to Vic's smiling face, wondering if their vast class difference had reasserted itself. She had no idea what she was supposed to feel . . . Surprised? Impressed? Pleased? And she was too exhausted to try to figure it out. "Those are very nice horse accessories, I'm sure, but I think we need to set some—"

Vic's laugh derailed her train of thought. "I hadn't intended the room's content to be the focus, so much as the room itself . . . or perhaps the door to the room, which happens to have a lock."

"A lock?"

"If you step inside, I'll demonstrate."

The connection snapped into place, and her whole body warmed with a mix of embarrassment that it had taken her so long to understand, and arousal at any number of possibilities in store for her if she allowed Vic to flip that lock.

No, she internally scolded herself. She was a professional, she needed to start acting like one. "Damn it, Vic, this is my place of work."

Vic grinned. "What a twist of fortune. It happens to be mine as well."

"I don't mix business with pleasure."

"Nor have I . . . yet."

Sophia stared at her. Who was this woman, and more importantly, why couldn't she bring herself to walk away? She'd never had any trouble calling Vic on her entitlement. Then again, it had never come with such blatant sex appeal before now. "We need to talk about boundaries."

"Shall we talk about them inside? Or out here, where any member of your cast or crew could leak the details to the press?"

"Fuck," she muttered. The press, the crew, of course Vic would be aware of those things, and honestly, she usually was, too. She stepped inside quickly while Vic both closed and locked the door behind her.

Then Vic's mouth was on hers. She didn't have time to think or brace herself, not that either of those things could've helped her process a kiss like that. There was only one response to having Vic's mouth pressed against her own, and that was to lean into it. They were up against the door, the shelves, the saddles, as they clutched each other and stumbled about. She had her hands in Vic hair and her teeth on Vic's lower lip. Where had all this energy been moments ago when she'd barely been able to form a complete sentence? Now she felt like she could run a marathon if only Vic would never stop kissing her.

And yet, that's exactly what happened.

As quickly as it had begun, Vic stepped back and with a cocky grin said, "So, you wanted to talk about boundaries?"

Sophia gaped at her, too shocked and winded to speak.

"Sorry." Vic didn't sound sorry at all. "I didn't mean to undercut the seriousness of the conversation, but we were both so hazy and hurried this morning I didn't get to give you a proper kiss goodbye."

"That was not a kiss goodbye."

"Oh?" Vic shrugged. "I'm quite out of practice. What kind of kiss was that? A hello kiss?"

She shook her head.

"A good morning kiss?"

"Try again."

"A thank you for a lovely evening kiss?"

Sophia snorted. "How about an, I'm-going-to-ravish-you-until-the-walls-crumble-to-dust kiss?"

"If that's the case, then I'm sorry to have come up short." She made a show of glancing at the walls. Then stopping to pick something up off the ground she added, "We didn't manage to disintegrate any stone. We merely knocked some riding crops off the shelves. Shall we try again?"

Vic leaned forward, but Sophia held up a hand quickly. "I'm not saying 'no,' but I am saying 'not right now.' I have to be on camera any minute, and you weren't wrong about the possibility of someone leaking to the press if they catch us together."

That stopped Vic in her tracks. She even went so far as to step back. *Interesting.*

"Maybe we could take a rain cheque?"

"Tonight? Dinner, my place?" Vic suggested quickly.

She should say no. Two nights in a row could set a pattern, and she needed sleep, but one long look at Vic in those tight breeches and boots and … who was she kidding? She'd never been one to deny herself when it came to women who looked like Vic, or possessed her particular set of skills, and what's more, she'd rarely found a woman who fit both categories.

"Shall we say eight o'clock?" Vic asked.

"That depends."

"On?"

"Will you still be wearing that outfit at eight?"

"It could be arranged," Vic said, a hint of her cocky grin returning. "Will you still be wearing that dress?"

She glanced down at the ridiculous costume. "Absolutely not."

Vic threw back her head and laughed.

The deep, throaty sound made Sophia's stomach tighten.

"I'm sure whatever you wear will suffice through dinner, and then I have an ardent hope it'll become immaterial."

She shook her head. If she didn't get out of here now, she feared the clothes might become immaterial well before dinner. As if reading her mind, Vic stepped forward and kissed her quickly and full on the mouth, then turned and unlocked the door.

"Eight o'clock, Ms. LeBlanc. Do you have any request for the menu?"

"Not specifically, but I suspect both protein and carbs may be in order."

"Duly noted."

Vic reached up to hang the crop back on a rack as Sophia headed for the doorway, but when she reached it a flash of mischief struck, or perhaps Vic's case had been contagious, because she couldn't resist saying, "Oh Vic, you might want to keep the crop with you . . . for tonight."

Vic's eyes went wide and her mouth dropped open, giving Sophia her first uninhibited smile of the morning. She walked away knowing she might not have scored as many points as she would've liked in that interaction, but she'd certainly scored the last one.

"Kneel," Sophia commanded smoothly.

"Pardon me?" Vic arched an eyebrow as a little shiver of anticipation worked its way under her skin.

"I said, *kneel*," Sophia reiterated, her tone low and unwavering.

Vic gritted her teeth against a major case of restraint fatigue, and not just from keeping her hands to herself through dinner, but also from the years of self-denial and discipline. She had thought she was past the fits of passion that plagued her youth. She'd prided herself on abstaining now, even, from the rough, fast abandon that marked the two or three trysts that immediately followed her divorce and stirred up a coinciding fervour in the press. In the last two years she'd gone on fewer than five dates and invited zero women into her bed, but apparently she'd deluded herself into thinking she had what it took to live that existence, if not interminably, at least until she found the right woman to complement her goals and dreams.

As Sophia picked up the riding crop from the chair beside her

107

and circled Vic with a dark sort of lust smouldering in her eyes, Vic pushed away from the table and dropped to one knee before her.

Sophia gave a little purr of pleasure or amusement. "God, you didn't even flinch. Do they teach you that at charm school, or are there some special classes for nobility on social hierarchies?"

"We're tutored on how to properly present ourselves to a queen," Vic admitted. "But it's traditional to curtsey rather than kneel."

"Where's the fun in that?" Sophia asked. "A curtsey seems too fleeting. Besides, you can do so much more for me on your knees."

Her face flamed, but not from shame. "Then I am at your command."

Sophia laughed. "Where was this submissive streak last night when you pinned me against the door?"

"You pinned me in your own ways. I've merely been responding on instinct ever since you broke in last night."

Sophia cupped Vic's chin in her strong fingers and tilted it up until their eyes met. "Your instincts are phenomenal. You should follow them more often."

Vic took her cue to claim this woman she'd ached for every minute since their lips had parted this morning, but as she went to stand, Sophia pressed the crop to her shoulder.

"Not so fast, Your Ladyship. Who said you could rise?"

"You told me to trust my instincts."

"I said you should trust them more often. I didn't mean to imply you'd get to act on them tonight."

A little whimper escaped her throat, and she dropped her head. What they'd done last night carried no promises or even implications for a future, but when Sophia had showed up in a little black dress that showed the most delicious expanse of her smooth shoulders, she'd hoped that offered at least favourable inferences for the night ahead. Now a sinking suspicion that Sophia had returned to toying with her seeped through her libido-laden haze. "I seem to remember mentioning after our last dinner together that I'm not fond of games."

"And your message was received. But you caught me off guard with your commanding performance last night. Don't get me wrong. That little display of prowess and power you carried right on through to this morning did not go unappreciated." Sophia sank her fingers into Vic's hair, and this time tilted her head back far enough to expose her jugular. "But deep down nobody wants to be in charge all the time, and you've been in charge entirely too long, darling."

She didn't know where this was going. One minute it seemed as though she could have whatever she wanted from Sophia, a feeling she found intoxicating, then other times it felt as if the world had tilted under her feet. She had enough wherewithal to understand those shifts should make her nervous enough to flee. Instead, she stayed still and silent in anticipation of whatever Sophia would declare next.

"Tonight, I'm in charge, and your only job is to let go."

"Let go?" Vic asked.

"Of your responsibility, of your title, of your deep, noble sensibility." She gave her hair another little tug. "For tonight, you're pledged only to your own pleasure."

Her breath came fast and shallow as blood roared in her brain.

Sophia leaned down so low the open buttons on her silk shirt offered Vic a flash preview of where her pleasure might lead her first, but the sharp nip of teeth on her earlobe stole her attention once more. "Do we have an understanding?"

"Yes." It was the only word she could muster, but it must have been enough, because Sophia released her and stood back, playfully tapping each one of her shoulders with the riding crop as if she'd conferred some sort of sexual knighthood upon her.

"You may rise," Sophia said with her subtle smile, "and then claim your reward."

Vic was on her feet in one fluid movement, pinning Sophia to the table as she kissed her fully. Finesse gave way to the ferocity of her need. In the space of a minute, she'd lifted Sophia onto the edge and moved into the space between her knees. Elaborate place settings rattled as she thrust her hips forward, spreading

Sophia's legs wide enough to push the dress to its limits around her bare thighs.

She ravished her throat and neck with her mouth and slid her hand up long legs, massaging as she went. She wanted to take her time, to caress every inch of skin, at least in theory, but she also wanted to push into Sophia hard and fast. She wanted to be enveloped by her body and lose herself in the raw physicality of it all. She'd spent years trying to cultivate restraint, but tonight Sophia had freed her. More than the freedom, she'd pledged them to their baser impulses.

Wasting no time in living up to that promise, she pushed inside Sophia with one strong, steady stoke. She refused to let her knees buckle at the pure eroticism of that tantalising body tightening around her. Never in her life had she felt so good about doing something that felt so good.

Sophia wrapped her legs around Vic's waist, pulling her closer, deeper. Urging her on, she worked her hands up Vic's shirt and around her back, clutching her so close the friction of their clothes created heat second only to the fire inside her, because Vic burned for this woman. No matter what she offered, Sophia accepted it and more. The fact that Sophia had never been intimidated by her title and its accompanying trappings put her in a rare class, but tonight it became increasingly clear Sophia didn't fear Vic's animal instincts either. She'd seen both sides and met them with the same mix of irreverence and attraction.

As if to prove that point, she tightened her grip on every part of Vic and hissed a single "yes" against her ear before throwing back her head in one beautiful moment of abandon as her body contracted.

Vic marvelled at the sight of her suspended on a wave of decadent gratification, unashamed and unencumbered. Vic had promised to surrender to herself, and in return Sophia had surrendered as well, offering herself as the perfect inspiration, role model, and recipient all wrapped up in the most brutally beautiful package.

Vic could barely breathe as the full impact of perfection slammed into her.

She'd always had to choose between her wants and her needs. Tonight, Sophia had given her the ultimate gift in merging the two.

"You're fucking amazing." Sophia bit the back of Vic's shoulder, hard, as she used her body weight to pin Vic to the tall headboard of her four-poster bed. Spread knees sank into the lush mattress as they both kneeled, torsos upright and exposed in flickering candlelight.

The dining room table had only been the beginning of their adventures. The preservationists on Vic's staff would've fainted if they had any idea how many ways the two of them found to defile priceless antiques once they returned to Vic's suite of rooms.

She pressed her bare breasts against Vic's back, a thin sheen of sweat making every inch of them slick. Then wrapping an arm around the magnificent curve of Vic's waist, she sank her fingers into wet folds. She didn't even have to search for the centre of Vic's desire. Both the hardness begging for attention and the way Vic's hips jerked when she made contact told Sophia everything about where she was most needed and how close Vic had gotten to coming apart in her hands.

Part of her still couldn't believe how utterly amazing Vic had been again and again. Every time they collapsed, Sophia barely had the time to catch her breath before Vic would rev her up once more. She'd encouraged Vic to take what she wanted, and it thrilled her endlessly that what Vic wanted most of all was her. Still, Sophia had her own mix of pride and desire to contend with. She couldn't have a body of this calibre in her grasp and not at least attempt to put it through its paces. For her part, Vic received every bit as good as she'd given, proving herself open and present in ways Sophia wouldn't have thought possible, but damned if it wasn't sexy as hell.

She continued to suck on the sheen of salt along Vic's shoulder as she timed each circle of her fingers with the thrust of their bodies. She kept a strong, steady pace until the muscles of Vic's jaw tensed, and Sophia growled.

"Don't you dare hold back." She accentuated her point with a push forward that caused Vic to gasp. "No restraint. You promised to let go tonight."

And miraculously, she did. As easy as that, Vic allowed her head to fall back against Sophia's shoulder as the first wave of release shook them both. Sophia braced herself, using the last of her functioning muscles to keep them from collapsing under the strain of Vic's orgasm, until neither of them could stand it any longer and they eased themselves to the bed with what little grace they could muster.

Vic rolled onto her back with a dreamy sigh, and Sophia's heart gave a silly little flip-flop. She should chastise herself for allowing any room for sentimentality after the raw ravishing they'd given each other. She wasn't entirely sure what she was doing in a canopy bed in a castle with the daughter of a duke, but it clearly had to be about the sex. Lord knew there was nowhere else for this to go, but Vic was so beautiful in her bare and relaxed state that not even the most ardent cynic could fault Sophia for being captivated. Which of course was why she shouldn't sink any deeper into the feather pillow.

The muscles in her arms and back protested, but she pushed herself to sitting position and swung her legs off the bed. She took a deep breath and stood, but before she even got both feet on the cool floor, a strong arm caught her around the waist and hauled her back into bed.

She made a weak effort to wrestle herself away, but Vic was deceptively agile for someone who'd been curled in a limp pile only seconds earlier. She threw one long leg over Sophia's hips and caught both of her hands in one.

"Where do you think you're going?"

Sophia laughed. "Home . . . or my hotel room."

"In the middle of the night?"

"That is when people usually go to bed."

"You're in a bed."

"Your bed, not mine."

"And what can you do in a hotel bed that you cannot do in mine?"

"Sleep, apparently. Something I desperately need before filming tomorrow."

"You can sleep here," Vic said. "I'll relent for a few hours."

She laughed again. "Even if I believed that, what makes you think I share your level of restraint and good sense? I lack all your breeding and high ideals. My only hope is to flee when I have the chance."

"And what? Slink across the castle grounds in the dark? Security would be all over you before you cleared the inner bailey."

"I'd rather take my chances with them tonight than try to sneak out in broad daylight again."

Vic kissed her temple and snuggled closer. "Then it's settled, no sneaking out at all. You'll stay the night. On my honour I'll see to it we both sleep, and in the morning I'll make sure you're well fed before we face the day."

Sophia tried to squirm away once more, not at all liking the sound of that. It was too clear, too up front, too level-headed. She didn't want to be level-headed about what was happening between them. The things she felt for Vic were wild and unreasonable, and she didn't want to examine any of them more deeply. "I'm not a stay-all-night kind of woman."

"And I'm not a dirty-little-secret kind of woman." Vic sighed and sat up. "So, we seem to have reached an impasse."

"Oh Vic." She cupped her face in her hands. "Do we have to have this conversation so soon?"

"What conversation?"

"The one where you try to put a label on things, and I have to tell you I don't want that, then you insert your sense of honour, and I have to explain that I'm not the kind of girl you bring home to your parents and—"

"I had not intended on having that particular conversation,"

Vic said, a little crease forming in her brow, "for all of your reasons and a hundred more of my own."

"Oh." Sophia didn't know whether to be relieved or offended.

"I merely meant to say sneaking around in the dark or slinking out of here at first light is neither practical nor appropriate for women of our respective positions. It's beneath our dignity, it'll arouse suspicion, and most importantly, it implies a level of shame I refuse to feel about what we're doing here."

She noticed Vic made no attempt to put a label on what they were doing.

"After my divorce"—the word seemed to catch in her throat, but she pushed on—"I had a few *interactions* with women. The press caught on. Some of their characterisations were wretchedly unfair, and perhaps some others weren't, but the ordeal was horrible for me, for my whole family, and for the women involved. I swore I'd never get caught off guard again, and I would never allow anyone else to define my relationships. I also swore I'd never again be made to feel ashamed of any woman worthy of my company."

Sophia's heart sank, both at the idea of how added press scrutiny could take away from her own narrative and the pain undercutting Vic's calm, reasonable tone. "How has the proclamation worked out for you?"

"In all honesty, you're the first woman I've shared my bed or my body with since then."

She sank back into the mattress, wishing she'd known that sooner, or perhaps feeling glad she hadn't. She sort of wished she could unknow it now. She didn't want to feel responsible for this woman's first shame-free encounter, and yet she'd blown through every stop sign Vic had thrown up between them, so she had only herself to blame.

"Hey," Vic whispered, "nothing has to change, at least nothing momentous. I'm not eager to make any big statements, and I claim no ownership of your time. We both have important work to do, and while I can't speak for you, I also want to keep open the possibility of more nights like this when the impulse arises."

She nodded. It would be easier to pretend they could stop now, but she wasn't one to lie to herself or anyone else about her tendency to take what she wanted. "I agree on all counts, but I don't see a way."

"Move into the castle."

"What?" She scooted to the edge of the bed once more. "Seriously? You have this big speech about not wanting too much and being reasonable and professional all as a lead-up to asking me to move in with you after two nights of fucking?"

Vic's eyes went wide, and her cheeks red. "I hadn't thought of it that way."

"Which part?"

"Any of it." She shook her head slowly. "Let me start again. I propose you move into your own suite of rooms here at the castle. A space to sleep, a space to dress, a space for you to relax after work. A space that also happens to be close to mine should the desire arise to spend more time together."

She pursed her lips to keep from reacting rashly, but she didn't hate the idea. The sexy daughter of a duke had offered her a taste of castle living while allowing her to maintain her autonomy and privacy. What was to hate about that?

"And it makes sense from a work perspective," Vic continued. "The plan provides you with a retreat between takes to quickly change or adjust your elaborate wardrobe without having to go all the way back to costuming."

"And it would offer an amazing opportunity to stay in character or study up on what it feels like to truly inhabit a castle."

"Which makes it easy to explain as artistic integrity to anyone who questions."

Sophia eased back onto the bed. "Why does everything you say always sound reasonable?"

"When your very existence functions like mine, you get a lot of practice making the absurd feel logical. Trust me, in the grand scheme of modern nobility, you staying here during filming barely ranks on the scale of absurdities I navigate daily."

Sophia laughed, both at Vic's skill for self-deprecation, and the entire situation she'd managed to land herself in. "Okay, let's do it."

"Good. I'll have your rooms prepared first thing in the morning and inform the staff that you're to be treated as a distinguished guest with all the associated privileges."

"I do like the sound of that, but what will the servants think?"

Vic chuckled. "They'll likely find you more suited to the role than I."

Sophia shook her head.

"I'm serious. I'm much too informal for their tastes, and I lack the command that should be requisite in my position. Perhaps you'll teach me a few things in your new role, because you, my dear, were born to rule."

"There's no need to lay it on so thick. I already agreed to stay."

"You wound my honour, but I want to be a good hostess, so I'll refrain from further flattery. What's more, in the interest of chivalry, I'll adjourn to the settee in my dressing room and allow you to sleep in peace."

With another quick kiss she rose, but before she even made it to the door, Sophia sat up again. "Hey Vic?"

She turned and stared, so stunning and attentive. "Yes?"

"Sleep and peace are both overrated. Come back to bed."

Chapter Eight

"Wow." Vic bit her lip to hold in an all-out laugh when Sophia stepped into the sitting room wearing her full set costume for the day's shooting schedule. "That's so . . . wow."

Sophia pursed her lips and gave her a stern look, which only made the whole picture infinitely more amusing. It wasn't Sophia's fault. She still had a killer stare, and two weeks of sleeping together regularly had done little to lessen its overall effect on Vic, but it was almost impossible to find someone intimidating in a pink and purple plaid dress with sleeves bulbous enough to serve as floatation devices. Then again, at least the sleeves kept the viewer's eyes off the immense skirt of ruffles that protruded on a series of hoops cascading out into a tent large enough to camp under.

"Not another word," Sophia warned.

She held up her hands as if to show she had no weapons to wield, but she couldn't stop one tiny giggle from escaping.

Sophia rolled her eyes dramatically. "I know I'm dressed like a clown, okay?"

"No. I was going to say you look exactly like an oil painting we have of my grandmother."

"Exactly what a woman wants to hear from her lover."

Victoria's breath caught at the term. It was the first label either of them had used in the time they'd been sleeping together or sharing space, and while she'd worked hard to hold her own fears at bay about where they could be headed, she did thrill at the idea of them at least being something to each other in this moment. "I didn't mean you looked old or matronly, just the style, and the way you carry yourself reminds me of—"

"Your grandmother?" Sophia rolled her eyes. "You walked right back into that one."

"Authentic!" Vic tried again. "I meant to compliment your authenticity. It was a compliment to make you feel better about the constraints of the role."

"You're terrible at compliments," Sophia said, though her smile suggested otherwise.

"Fine, but for the record, my grandmother was a badass."

"Oh yes, by all means, keep talking about your grandmother with the only five minutes we're likely to get alone together today."

Vic laughed. "I'm sorry. I don't know what else to do."

"You didn't seem to have any such trouble last night."

Vic warmed at the memory and the jolt of confidence it gave her. "I'd gladly shoot for a repeat performance, but I suspect you'd have to redo your makeup, and I'm not sure I'd be able to get my hands under all those skirts and petticoats in the allotted time."

"I have faith in your ability with the skirt," Sophia said quickly. "You've proven yourself quite dextrous, but you're probably right about the makeup. If we have to go back to square one on that front, we'll be here all night."

"And that would be a travesty, because I had plans for the evening that involve a rather ostentatious soaking tub and a bottle of wine."

"I assume 'ostentatious' means there's room for two in this tub?"

"Ample," she confirmed, "but I wouldn't presume to make plans for you, especially after twelve hours on set."

"No, you've been ever so accommodating in your respect for my personal space." Sophia gave her a subtle nod of gratitude. "But personal space wasn't a concept made for soaking tubs."

"Point well taken. I'll amend my plans to include one tub, one bottle of wine, and two bathrobes. Will that be enough to atone for my wanting you to stay the course and get this afternoon's scenes done in as few takes as possible?"

"That depends, do you have more stories to tell me about your grandmother in the meantime?"

Vic started to laugh, but another thought hit her. "Actually, I do. Follow me."

She held open the door for Sophia to squeeze her hoop skirts through and then led her around the residence and back toward the public areas of the castle.

"I was being sarcastic," Sophia muttered as they wandered down a back passage. They turned a corner to see two of the house staff rearranging a few pieces of furniture.

"Good morning, Sarah," Vic called.

"Good morning, Hannah," Sophia said at the same time.

Both women glanced up and smiled.

"Thank you for rerouting the school group yesterday," Vic said.

"And for not killing Brian when he barged into the library during your speech to the antiquities collectors last night," Sophia added as they kept walking.

They turned another corner, and Vic glanced over her shoulder, smiling at the easy way Sophia had eased into life in the residence. Not that she wanted to overstate anything. Sophia was clearly still on some sort of a cross between character study and castle holiday, but her presence hadn't been a disruption. She was kind and confident with the staff, and respectful of the boundaries inherent in residing in a living museum. She moved deliberately and fluidly between one space and the next, not as if she owned either of them, but as if she certainly belonged in them. Victoria had hosted enough guests over a lifetime to recognise that delicate balance. People generally allowed the setting to intimidate them or embolden them in problematic ways. Sophia merely adapted to her surroundings.

They entered the main receiving room where they'd first met, and Victoria snagged the rapier off the wall.

"Whoa there, Tiger." Sophia stepped back. "Not this again."

She laughed and gave the blade a quick flourish before holding it up in both hands for Sophia to inspect. "I promise I won't run you through this time."

"Good to know, but why are we back to sword play after how far we've come, or rather how many times we've . . . never mind. You were saying?"

Vic's face warmed a little bit at the innuendo, but she was too happy to stumble through this story. "This was my grandmother's. My grandfather had it sent over to her from France immediately after the liberation of Paris in World War II."

"The spoils of war?"

"Maybe for him, but for her it came to symbolise her power and her new position. She was a young bride even by the standards of the day, and they'd been married mere months when he left in service to king and country. Suddenly, she was the lady of the house and manager of an entire estate."

"She wasn't born to such things?"

"She was not poor, not by any means, but she definitely married up. My grandfather's mother had already passed away, so there wasn't anyone here to show her the ropes. His father was distant and often away for months at a time tending to government business. She had staff, of course, but most of the men had gone off to the war. The place was being run largely by women. They were making it up as they went along. She took to carrying the sword, first when riding or walking the orchards, and then apparently around the grounds, and sometimes the house as well."

"And no one dared to question her authority then," Sophia said.

"They probably thought twice about it, but more importantly it helped her stop questioning herself. She was the first truly modern duchess in my line, a ruling partner, a shrewd businesswoman, stoic and sensible, but with a flair for inspiring confidence."

"So, it runs in your DNA?" Sophia said playfully. "Here I was crediting charm school all this time."

Vic's smile faltered as she took the rapier back and turned it around in her hands a time or two.

"What is it?"

"What? Nothing." She shook her head and put the sword back into its hook on the wall. "I thought you might appreciate the story, given the role you're playing."

"I do appreciate it, but more because of what it tells me about you. The first time I saw that sword in your hand, I thought you were just a privileged rich girl who didn't like the riff-raff touching her stuff."

"No, you thought I was a servant."

Sophia laughed. "Only for a moment. Your bearing made your rank known relatively quickly. Was it the sword that gave you the power of fiery women from generations past?"

"Something like that," she said with a little twinge in the pit of her stomach.

"Wielding her weapon must—"

"*My* weapon," Vic corrected.

Sophia raised her eyebrows just a tick.

"She gave the rapier to me on her deathbed."

"A passing of the torch?"

Vic shrugged. "She told me to remember where I came from when it was my turn to assume the title."

"But she knew you couldn't inherit on your own."

"She believed I'd be the next modern duchess. She thought I could . . . It doesn't matter. I hadn't come out yet. She didn't know the real me."

"Vic, she knew you." Sophia cupped her chin in her hand and turned her face away from the sword until their eyes met. "She knew your character when she handed you that sword. It's your birthright, and you have every right to use it against anyone who tries to take it from you."

She managed a strangled laugh around the lump of emotion forming in her throat. "You tried to take it from me."

Sophia's expression turned coy once more. "And I learned my lesson. I swear on a stack of Bibles never to come between you and that sword or anything it implies ever again."

Her mouth went dry and her head swam at the myriad of

implications in that statement, but before she could pick any single one to try to parse out, the door to the library opened, and a page stuck her head out.

"Ms. LeBlanc, we're ready for you."

Sophia's smile turned to a grimace.

"Go," Vic said, her voice soft but clearer than she feared. "I'll be right in."

"Vic?"

"You heard the woman. They're ready for you." Vic regained enough of her composure to be convincing before silently adding that she couldn't yet claim the same.

"That's a wrap." The words still echoed through Sophia's ears with the same emotions they'd sparked nearly an hour ago. Relief at being done with Brian and his bullshit angles and condescending notes mingled with the burn of knowing deep down that he hadn't gotten the right shot. Would he even notice, in which case she'd be right back in that cripplingly heavy dress tomorrow, or would he simply run with a substandard cut? Neither option offered her anything to feel good about, and as much as she'd been looking forward to the bubble bath Vic promised, she wanted to slip into those suds with a clear mind and conscience.

Instead she'd stewed all the way through their post-production meeting, and the scheduling meeting, and the long, arduous process of stripping off her elaborate wardrobe and heavy makeup. The shift lifted the physical burden from her skin and shoulders but did nothing to lift the mental weight she carried back into the residence with her.

She pushed open the door to her sitting room and immediately spied the lush white bathrobe hung over her settee. Then her eyes fell on the fresh flowers in a vase by the window. Did all castle guests get these little touches, or had Vic ordered them for her? She wasn't sure she wanted to know the answer.

She didn't want to get too comfortable in this place. She walked through to her bedroom, noting her perfectly made bed.

She didn't pretend she'd arranged the mountain of pillows so neatly. Surely the staff noticed the times they had to fix them corresponded more often with midday naps than long nights of restful sleep, since she spent most of her evenings in Vic's bed, further evidence that the castle wasn't the only thing she shouldn't let herself get used to.

And yet, wasn't that exactly what she was doing? Never mind the fact that she'd already come to think of this as her room, her settee, her bed. She'd also come to think of Vic as her evening plans, her object of desire, her easy conversation at the end of a complicated day. Of course, they'd yet to give voice to any of these things, but she'd be lying to herself if she tried to pretend an unspoken routine hadn't taken root between them. And she never lied to herself.

At some point she needed to dial things back, but while focus had always been her strong suit, self-denial was a shaky virtue in her world. Passing up a bubble bath with a beautiful, sexy woman might be a bridge too far, especially given her lingering frustration.

She changed out of her clothes and shrugged on the soft warmth of the robe. She had to give Victoria another nod of approval. This woman never flaunted her wealth, choosing a more subtly graceful sense of style, but that didn't make her any less luxurious. And that kind of luxury, lacking in flash but dripping in class, kept Sophia on her toes. It was one thing to acquire wealth. She'd managed to do so with relative ease, but she knew enough about how the world worked to understand acquiring class was another matter entirely.

With that thought butting up against her already frayed nerves, she wandered down the hallway to find the door to Vic's suite slightly ajar. She followed the sound of classical music playing softly through the sitting room, but instead of turning toward the bedroom, she turned through what she'd been told was a dressing room, though she'd never seen Vic dress there, then what appeared to be an office of sorts, before pushing open the door to a bathroom with stone floors and stone walls. The space itself wasn't cavernous, but the pristine, white soaking tub was. Thick, rich, bubbles bobbed across the entire surface, and in the middle sat Victoria, her honey-blond hair pinned up, exposing her neck and the tops of her bare shoulders. Her eyes remained closed, but the slightest trace of a smile played across her lips before she said, "How was your day, dear?"

Sophia sighed at the dreamy, intimate tone undercut by only a hint of humour. "Dreadful, but how did you know I was here?"

"I could feel your eyes on me."

"How did you know they were my eyes?"

"Hmm." Victoria made a happy little noise. "I'm used to having people's eyes on me. Only yours have ever made me feel seen."

Her breath caught as warning bells sounded. She didn't want that responsibility, but god help her, she did want to be up against this woman right now. She sidestepped the seriousness the comment inspired and moved closer to the tub. "You started without me."

"I was informed when you finished with wardrobe."

"Keeping tabs on my whereabouts?"

"Always." Vic finally opened her eyes, a brilliant flash of blue in the otherwise white and grey palette of the room. "But also, I get updates when various contingents of the film crew vacate each area of the castle, so they can be cleaned, reset, and secured as needed."

"I'd think you'd have people to do that."

"What's the saying Talia keeps repeating when things go off schedule, something about monkeys?"

"Not my circus, not my monkeys."

"Right, well this estate is my circus and all the people working here are ultimately my monkeys." Vic smiled up at her. "Now, why are you still dry?"

"I'm not entirely," Sophia shot back in a low voice, enjoying the split second of confusion on Vic's beautiful features before the innuendo landed and her cheeks coloured. Then Sophia slowly untied the thick rope holding the robe to her body and shrugged it to the floor.

The blue of Vic's irises receded around her widening pupils, and Sophia thrilled at the knowledge she still held a physical sort of power over her. Then easing into the warm water, she realised Vic wouldn't be the only one in a bit of a stupor for long. "Bless us oh Lord for these thy gifts, which I am currently receiving."

"I didn't know you were religious."

"Neither did I." Sophia sank lower and kicked her legs out with ample room to spare. "My Italian grandmother was Catholic. Maybe it's in the bloodline, but don't you just feel like hot baths are a religious experience?"

"I'm Anglican."

"Of course you are."

Vic laughed lightly. She wrapped one underwater arm around Sophia's waist, pulling her back until she settled into the space between her legs, so they reclined, back to front, slick and submerged. A deep moan escaped her throat as she sank into the position, completely ensconced with woman and water. Then when she thought nothing could improve upon the perfection of her current situation, Vic reached over and lifted a glass of red wine from a table next to the tub, brought it around Sophia's body, and placed it neatly in her hand.

"I could die right here and not mind."

Victoria nipped at her ear. "Please don't."

"Would you miss me?"

"Terribly; also, it would be an utter shit storm in the press."

A little bubble of laugher escaped her lips. She'd spent nearly two week's worth of nights with this woman and still had not come to expect those irreverent asides.

"How was Brian today?"

"The worst." She shook her head. "I don't know how he keeps getting work. I mean, I do know how he got work at first."

"Explain it to me please, because I haven't figured it out."

"His father's a three-time Oscar winner who sits on the board of multiple film festivals and grant-funding organisations, which makes Brian one of the most pedigreed trust fund babies in Hollywood."

"Ah." Vic nodded. "Trust fund babies are the worst."

Sophia snorted. "Present company excluded, of course."

125

"The jury's still out on that one, but please continue."

"Anyway, Brian's last name opened a lot of doors for him, but this is his tenth film. Shouldn't his utter mediocrity have become painfully obvious to everyone by now?"

"I've found mediocrity to be a rather high bar for many white, upper-class males. Our government is full of them."

"Ours, too," Sophia admitted, "but we're not talking about trivial things like ruling countries. We're supposed to be artists, and Brian can barely paint by number."

"Is he hurting the production?"

"Like actually hurting?" She blew out a slow breath. "I don't know, but he's not doing anything to elevate it. He lacks vision. His camera shots are so flat and static we might as well be shooting a '70s sitcom. I don't know why he booked a full arsenal of Steadicams when he insists on laying down tracks and tripods at a respectable distance. And I can only do so much to overcompensate for lacklustre . . . ugh. Do you even want to hear this?"

"Of course," Vic said quickly. "I understand only about half of the words you're using, but it sounds important."

"Most people find it dull and technical," Sophia said, "but it all boils down to how cameras move, and he's using a concrete approach, but it's safe and distant, and it does nothing to convey the subtlety I'm busting my ass to portray."

"What option should he have chosen?"

"There are a million choices to be made, but an easy shift to make would be a Steadicam in a harness on someone's chest. We could get much closer and convey a more intimate feel. I don't want the audience to watch me. I want them to merge with me, to inhabit this castle, to experience the emotions I'm projecting. They can't do that from a respectful distance. I want the camera so close I can tell what its operator ate for lunch."

Vic shuddered. "I'd rather have needles under my fingernails."

"Oh, come on. You're great with people, and the camera must love you."

She shook her head as much as she could without jostling them both. "I'm terrible. I never manage to get across any message

I really want to convey. I never manage to project the right amount of poise or grace."

"Seriously, have you ever met you?"

"Have you ever met my mother?"

"No, and I don't want to talk about her."

"Let's not," Vic agreed. "Please go back to talking about the film. I want to hear more about connecting with your audience across miles and pixels and screens. It's quite amazing you can have such a powerful effect on people."

"It doesn't happen magically. It takes work and attention to detail and craft. You can't rush or cut corners on greatness. You have to always remember there'll eventually be other people viewing you through the camera lens, and you have to be absolutely dedicated to delivering for them, because otherwise, what's the point?"

Vic kissed her cheek.

"What was that for?"

"Because you're dedicated to delivering, because that *is* the point for you. That's why you're doing this."

"Well . . . that's the end game, anyway. The acting is a way to get me there."

"What do you mean?"

"I know it's such a cliché in Hollywood for stars to get a few movies under their belts and suddenly decide they can direct, but that's what I wanted from day one."

"You *never* wanted to be an actress?"

"I wouldn't say 'never.' When I was little and I started watching movies, I wanted to be in them. They seemed magical, and everyone led interesting lives, but as I got older and realised those weren't real people living real lives, I started to unpack the magic. As soon as I learned the director was the person who pulled it all together, the cameras, the actors, the final cuts, that's what I wanted to be more than anything."

"Then why aren't you directing?"

She laughed humourlessly, her muscles tensing as if for a fight. "We'll both be pruney and cold before we reach the end of that list."

"We'll top off the hot water, and I quite like prunes."

"You would," Sophia said, but she settled back, noting how easily all the tension slipped away as Vic's hand came to rest on her stomach. "I guess it's not really that long of a list if you break it down to the roots."

"Which are?"

"Sexism. Classism. Nepotism. Lack of educational access, which I guess throws us back to the first things on the list." She sipped her wine. "Poor girls from Louisiana don't have expensive cameras or editing software lying about. We don't have the leisure time or money to play around or develop a style. Our high schools don't have film studies courses. We don't have what we need to apply to high-end film schools, much less pay for them. And I don't have a last name like Eastwood or Coppola to open doors for me."

"Which is why you had to find another way to make a name for yourself in the business," Vic surmised.

"Pretty much."

"And also, why you hated me the first few times we met."

She rolled her head to the side and kissed her cheek. "What, you mean your wealth, your unearned position, the über-long and fancy family name you dropped at our first meeting?"

"To be fair, you dropped yours first."

"I dropped the name of the character I was playing to try to gain access to the world you were born into. I know, I know, your birth is no more your responsibility than mine is."

"Thank you," Vic said. "But I also know firsthand the absurdity of those systems and believe it or not I have my own disdain for being judged on anything other than my merits."

"I know that now, but at first you looked like another one of the people who held power over me without earning it."

"And now?"

She sat up, creating a few waves as she turned to face Vic, taking in her eyes, the pink of her cheeks, the rise of her breasts near the water's surface. "Now you have a different kind of power over me, one you earned."

Vic pushed off the back of the tub and pulled Sophia, legs spread, onto her lap. "You know we're equals in that area, right?" Sophia kissed her soulfully, liking the idea of equals very much. Of course, she hadn't lost sight of their vastly different circumstances, but she couldn't deny the unexpected ways they fit, and not just physically. Though, as their wet chests slid up against each other, there was no denying they fit in that area as well. In fact, they fit so well, she couldn't prevent a little groan when Vic eased back slightly.

"So, will this movie allow you to direct in the future?"

Of course, Vic had found the one topic that could distract her from sex right now. "I don't know. It'll put me closer, though. Every movie I've ever done brought me closer and trust me when I say I've done some terrible films. Still they were always chosen to move me one step closer to the kind of people and experiences I'm after in the long run. This one should earn me some mainstream recognition, as long as Brian doesn't fuck it up with his lack of vision."

"Is that hard for you? I mean of course it is, but at first I thought you were just a controlling sort, the prototypical Hollywood diva."

"I can be that, too."

"But you're also more." Vic pushed. "You're like a musician who hears a sharp note, or a race car driver who hears a novice grind the gears. It's more painful to be part of a lackluster movie when you can see what it could've been, what it should have been, and to know that opportunity has been denied to you, not because of any factor of your own making, but due to constraints of a world you didn't build or choose."

Sophia stared at her, no longer capable of some quick comeback, barely even able to draw a full breath.

"Isn't every day, every scene, every take, an act of restraint not to snap and smash cameras that men like Brian don't even know how to use to your standards?"

How had Vic just understood that and summed it up so beautifully? How had she managed to see on a fundamental level what Sophia fought against every day?

Vic's smile spread slowly. "Sorry, did I get a little carried away?"

Sophia shook her head. "No. Or maybe I like it when you get carried away. You're this totally put-together woman who knows all the right things, and does all the right things, and says all the right things because you're dedicated to playing the long game, but deep down you're also a woman who's equally capable of burning the whole thing to the ground."

Vic threw back her head and laughed that low, rumbling sound of an unguarded moment. "Why do you think I keep those matches in the table beside my bed? They aren't for the candles."

"Will you use them if they deny you the title?"

Vic's expression turned wistful. "Wouldn't it be nice to think I could simply strike a match and let it fall without my hands even trembling?"

The sentiment sparked something powerful inside Sophia. She would hate to see either of them go up in flames after everything they'd worked for, but the thrill of this deeper connection building between them did feel like a fire of another sort. "I won't be able to get the image out of my mind as you light those candles tonight."

"If you're looking to incinerate something . . ." Vic leaned so close their foreheads touched, and Sophia's pulse accelerated. "Why wait until tonight?"

"I can't even believe I can walk after that," Sophia said as she tightened the rope on her robe.

"I can't believe either of us has been able to function at all for the last two weeks." Vic opened the door to the bathroom and gave a quick glance around to make sure none of the staff had slipped in to clean or drop off the clothes she'd sent off to be pressed. Once certain the coast was clear, she nodded for Sophia to follow her through the office. "We really should congratulate ourselves on our physical fitness and stamina."

"And here I was thinking I'd let myself go after my last role."

"You've got to be joking."

"Not in the least. You wouldn't believe the diet and exercise regimen I had to maintain in order to keep up with Cobie Galloway while we were filming *Vigilant*. God, that woman was nonstop."

Vic couldn't quite decipher Sophia's tone. Exasperation? Admiration? Annoyance? "Do we hate her?"

Sophia laughed. "No one hates Cobie Galloway. She's, well, she's actually a lot like you."

"How so?"

"Perfect all the damn time."

Vic felt a rush of pride that Sophia would associate her with perfection after all this time.

"She's just so unabashedly good at being a colleague, an actress, hell, at being a human, so actually maybe I do hate her a little bit."

"Wait, you said she was like me. Where does that comparison end?"

"Well . . ." Sophia drew out the word with a hint of teasing that made Vic's breath catch. "I suppose it's a little easier to be irked by someone's perfection when they aren't using it to turn your muscles to mush multiple times a day."

"In that case," Vic started toward her, "I'd better keep up my pace so as not to fall into the same category as this Galloway woman."

"I think you're safe." Sophia backed toward a different door than the one they'd come through. "No need to demonstrate again."

"I don't know. You said multiple times a day, and I've only proven myself once in the last hour."

Sophia backed away, but the smirk on her still-swollen lips said anything but stop. "We should at least eat first. Aren't you hungry?"

"Famished," Vic admitted in a tone that sounded wolfish even to her own ears.

"Don't you want to eat something?"

Vic closed the distance and pinned Sophia to the door with the weight of her body, relishing the way they melded together. Leaning close to Sophia's ear, she practically growled. "I fully intend to eat something."

A sharp gasp escaped Sophia as her hips jerked forward. "Your Ladyship, I had no idea you even had such vulgarity in you."

"Then I'll have to redouble my efforts." She bit Sophia's ear a little harder than usual.

"You're scandalising me. What would your people think?"

Vic fought off a little grimace as she scraped her teeth along a pronounced shoulder muscle. She should probably worry about that very question at some point. Then again, she probably should have thought about it many times before now. Why make this moment any different?

Shifting her weight, she dropped a hand to Sophia's thigh and grabbed a handful of robe before slowly working upward over smooth skin. Then, while moving her other hand to balance against the door, she nicked the brass handle. She processed the click of the latch only as the door gave way and sent them both tumbling into the corridor.

It took every bit of the skill and athleticism they'd been congratulating themselves on a moment earlier not to sprawl across the floor, but as she manged to catch hold of Sophia and tangle their bodies together, she couldn't quite manage to miss the imposing figure standing just to the side of the doorway.

She straightened as quickly as she could and stepped in front of Sophia in a vain attempt to shield her should there need to be any robe adjustments for the sake of propriety. The move proved futile, as James had already seen everything he needed to see and now stared straight ahead with his chin lifted, lips pressed tightly together.

"Sorry, James," she said automatically.

"I should say," he huffed.

"Are you all right?"

"Quite." He raised his nose a little higher.

"Was there something you needed?" she asked, as her surprise faded and confusion set in. "I'd expected you to have finished in the residence by this time of night."

"Obviously," he said. "I heard noises coming from the office, and since no one is supposed to be in those quarters, it raised concerns."

"Ah," she said, though the explanation still didn't cover why he'd been close enough to notice anything amiss. "Very well then."

"Is it, Your Ladyship?" He didn't turn his head, but his eyes flicked sideways to where Sophia stood in his periphery.

Her cheeks warmed. "Yes. Thank you, James."

He hesitated a second before nodding sharply.

And then he walked away, shoulders stiff and back straight, but without another glance in her direction. Vic stood rooted to the spot until he turned the corner. Then she burst out laughing.

"Vic?"

She turned toward Sophia but could barely see her through the tears forming there.

"Are you okay?"

She tried to nod, but her head fell to her chest as her shoulders shook with giggles so strong they nearly strangled her.

"This is funny?"

"Yes," she finally managed between gasps of laughter. "I know, I know it shouldn't be, but oh, poor James, he's quite scandalised right now."

Sophia finally cracked a smile. "He did an admirable job of hiding it."

"No." She shook her head forcefully. "You just don't know him very well."

"I'm not sorry about that, honestly. Does he always speak to you that way?"

"What way?"

"Like you're . . . you're, I don't even know."

"A disappointment? Beneath him? An utter dead end to a once mighty lineage?"

133

"Yes."

"Then yes, yes he does."

"Why do you allow it? Doesn't he work for you?"

"He works for my father, technically, but honestly he's much more closely aligned with my mother. He's never aligned with me even in the moments when he reports to me."

"Okay, fine, and trust me, I can't believe I'm about to try to make a noblewoman snobbier, but he does report to you right now?"

"I suppose."

"And he just spoke to you like you were a distasteful nuisance?"

She cupped Sophia's face in her hands. "Can I say how much I adore how confusing you find this?"

Sophia rolled her eyes.

"That sort of disdain is a simple fact of my life. We've already covered that my title may cease to exist, and many people want that for good reasons around class and power. Others want my home taken from me because they see it as a way for them to make money. Then there's another set of people who want it taken from me because they find me unworthy of holding it."

"Because you're a woman, or because you're a lesbian?"

"Both, yes, but there's another subset of the population who believe I lack the poise or gravitas or all-out superiority they've dedicated their life to cultivating and maintaining. I suspect James falls there, though he'd never say so." She tried to shrug off the tension creeping back into her recently relaxed shoulders. None of this was new. "The point is, for every person who thinks I should be cast out because I'm outdated and out of touch with my average countryman, there's someone to the other side of the scale who thinks I should be thrown out because I'm too irreverent and graceless for the duties of my station."

"At least you can say you bring people together across the spectrum."

She laughed again. "Maybe I should put that on tourism brochures. 'Victoria doesn't belong here: one thing we can all agree on.'"

"I wouldn't say 'all.'" Sophia stepped into her personal space once more.

"No? Have I yet to disappoint you, Ms. LeBlanc?"

"I wouldn't go that far." Sophia smiled slowly and hooked a finger through the belt of Vic's robe. "I find it a little disappointing you've not once shouted 'off with his head' when James gives me some side-eye."

"Ah yes, that disappoints me occasionally as well. Alas, James does work for my father, and beheadings are quite messy. Is there any other way I've managed to let you down? Perhaps some way I could remedy? Someone else I could have guillotined?"

"Maybe not guillotined, but there's certainly something bothering me that you could possibly have removed from the premises."

Vic tensed. "I swear, you are a guest in my home and if someone is upsetting you—"

"Not someone." Sophia cut her off. "Some *thing*."

Vic frowned.

Sophia gave the rope to her robe a sharper tug. "I'm personally finding this robe offensive, and I'd like to see it removed . . . immediately."

"Hmm." She wrapped an arm around Sophia's waist, pulling her close as she backed toward the still-open door. "That could be arranged."

Chapter Nine

Something was happening. Sophia could sense the emotional shift around her before she saw any evidence of what caused it. Everything had seemed fine when she'd arrived on the set in the morning. Better than fine, even. She'd arrived early for the day's scenes recharged, recommitted, and actually excited to dive back into her role, which, given how she'd left things with Brian the day before, spoke volumes about the restorative powers of a good bath and an exceptional lover.

That combo had been particularly potent in her case because she'd slayed every single take all day long no matter who stood opposite her, and that had been a revolving door for hours. The next few days called for a series of scenes that included the full royal ensemble cast. Thankfully, the actors playing the king and queen were old professionals who showed up prepped and ready to work without extraneous drama. Brian, on the other hand, had shown himself even less adept than usual when accounting for shot scenarios featuring more than two people. At one point she'd even had to tell him bluntly that he'd reversed their positions from the previous shot without having either of them move on camera. That wasn't even a rookie mistake, it was sheer stupidity.

And still, she hadn't once harboured any elaborate murder fantasies where he played the role of corpse. Each time her frustration rose to a threatening level, her eyes found Victoria's. Blue.

Confident. Steady. The timing always seemed fortuitous, or maybe she'd started to seek Vic subconsciously. She chose not to dwell too much on the why and instead focused on how the move affected her. All Sophia's animosity evaporated as quickly as Vic appeared in her periphery.

She'd actually been marvelling over that fact during one of their many resets when she first noticed the sound of softly shuffling feet from a nearby servants' passage. She'd initially written them off as the product of sensible staff trying to thread the needle between the movie crew and the tourists two rooms over, but a few minutes later she heard hushed whispers outside the door, and what the voices lacked in volume they more than made up for in their frantic tone.

She managed a few more solid takes deep in character, yelling at the King about the injustice of patriarchal power structures before someone interrupted them outright by opening one of the heavy wood-panelled doors.

"Bloody hell," Brian shouted in a way that made it clear he was merely trying out the local lingo.

James didn't show the slightest chagrin. In fact, she wasn't sure James had ever broadcast any emotion other than disappointment, distaste, or disdain, but he did manage to convey the latter two simultaneously as he approached Vic and Talia, who'd both been watching from a distance. The three of them had a quick discussion, which consisted of him talking and Vic doing her best to hide her emotions behind her most professional façade.

First her eyes went wider, followed by a tensing of her shoulders so subtle it would likely have gone unnoticed by someone who hadn't spent part of last night sinking her teeth into those very muscles. In the next second a wall dropped over her alluring features.

Sophia shivered at the chill radiating off Vic from all the way across the library.

"Reset," Brian called, causing her to flinch.

She pinched the bridge of her nose. For a moment she'd forgotten he was even there, and she at least had the awareness to sense the red flag in that disconnect. She didn't forget her place on a set. Not ever. She didn't slip out of character. Not for illness or injury, not for inopportune working conditions or idiot directors. Certainly not for a woman who was more than capable of dealing with anything that arose on her own damn estate.

She returned to her mark, and when Brian called action, she began to shout. "Do you have any idea what it's like to be born a woman in a world where your only job is to marry and mate?"

"I'd imagine that sort of mandate would make your choices rather easy," the man standing beside her said, his voice as dismissive as the side-eye James had taken to giving her.

"Choices?" she scoffed. "Where's my choice? You pick the marriage. The man will decide when and how to mate. Is there a choice for me? The choice of what to wear while playing the part of chattel?"

"Would you prefer something weightier? The choice between financial ruin and military ruin? The choice of taxing your subjects into starvation or cutting the forces who protect them from invasion?"

"Is that really what you're doing here, Father?" She lowered her voice without softening it. "Is it the weight of your responsibility, or the weight of your pride?"

For some reason the recitation of this line brought to mind James, the way he'd spoken to Vic, the way she accepted it, the way she accepted the opinions of so many wholly unqualified people. All for a system she hadn't chosen and for people's misplaced sense of ownership or abhorrence.

"The fact that you think those two things could be separated shows how unqualified you are to make decisions for your kingdom, how little you understand the mantel of divine rights and absolute sovereignty." He slammed his fist on the table with a thunderous crash that caused her to startle and jump back.

"Cut!" Brian shouted. "Brilliant. Well done, Your Majesty."

The king nodded his agreement. Sophia blinked and looked back and forth between them. Had the compliment been directed at her?

138

"The way you shrank slowly, turning inward, only to be shaken back out was a nice touch," the man playing her father added.

She forced a smile. The emotions she conveyed might have fit the scene, but they hadn't been intentional.

She'd lapsed.

She'd gone somewhere else, become someone other than the person she'd meant to be. Getting away with it this time did little to assuage the panic trying to work its way up in her. This wasn't how this was supposed to go.

Honestly, she couldn't remember how any of this was supposed to go. She remembered throwing rocks at a window. She remembered pushing into Vic's personal space, yes, but she hadn't intended to push into her life, into her psyche, into her sense of self any further than research required. Of course, there had been moments along the way when she had some concerns about the wisdom of sleeping with someone close to the film, but until this moment she'd thought those initial doubts unfounded.

Ever since the morning after their first sex fest weeks ago, Vic rose to every challenge inherent in their positions. She'd been respectful, confident, and compelling. She hadn't been a distraction, or a detraction. If anything, their connection and the passion it inspired raised Sophia's romantic acting level.

No, she couldn't blame Vic for commandeering head space. Honestly, Vic had done a better job of keeping her head than Sophia, and that was saying a lot.

The realization might have upset her more if it didn't impress the hell out of her. But it also piqued her interest again. She glanced around the room to see Vic hadn't returned. Something didn't seem right. This woman handled everything from sex to security to social situations with aplomb. What could possibly shake her?

"We got what we needed there," Brian called as he set aside his camera. "Let's take ten and get the queen back in here."

Sophia dodged the makeup artist and a page, then ducked around a wheeled dolly, not quite sure where she intended to go, other than in the same general direction Vic had taken.

She pushed open the door, then held her hand back behind her to keep it from slamming in her wake as hushed voices whispered, then fell silent. She felt the stares on her before she even saw them, and when she turned around, she immediately recognised the faces of the two people she'd never met.

The Duke and Duchess of Northland stood close to Vic, whose cheeks flushed all the way over her tight jaw. The rigid body language and electric silence told Sophia everything she needed to know about the tenor of the conversation she'd interrupted, and if she'd had any opportunity to back away unnoticed, she would've gladly shrunk into the shadows, but it was too late.

Vic turned to her, not quite hiding the panic in her eyes, and Sophia couldn't help but go to her any more than she could've chosen to stop breathing.

"Ms. LeBlanc." Vic recovered, with only a slight tremor in her voice. "May I have the honour of making introductions?"

She nodded slowly and tried to force a politely neutral expression to mirror Vic's.

"Mother, Father, this is Ms. Sophia LeBlanc, the lead actress of the film they're shooting in the library. Sophia, these are my parents, His Grace and Her Ladyship, the Duke and Duchess of Northland."

Sophia froze, unsure how to respond. Should she bow, curtsey, genuflect? As if it weren't awkward enough to meet your lover's parents unexpectedly under normal circumstances. It didn't escape her notice that Victoria chose to use their formal titles the way she might in a business setting rather than calling them by name or *Mom* and *Dad*.

Thankfully, the duke seemed to register her indecision and took mercy on her, extending his hand. "Ms. LeBlanc, such a pleasure to meet you."

She accepted the gesture, surprised to find his hand soft and slight. She'd expected someone more commanding from his position, but then again, the rest of his appearance did match. He wasn't an imposing man in stature, but he managed to strike the impression of easy elegance, while his fair hair and complexion had clearly been the dominant genes in Vic's colouring.

"We had no intention of interrupting your work, but you must forgive us for not quite being able to stay away from our daughter and the excitement of her latest endeavours."

"I understand," Sophia said without being fully certain she did. "I'm sorry we've kept her from vacationing with the family this year, but she's been indispensable to our efforts here. We've all marvelled at her ability to juggle so many responsibilities at once. I don't know that we could've made any of this work without her."

His smile took on a more genuine quality. "That's our Victoria."

"Don't sell yourself short, dear," the duchess cut in, her voice every bit as cool and refined as her pale skin and highly manicured brows might imply. "You've no doubt played a central role in keeping this project afloat as well."

Sophia eyed her more closely, searching for the same type of resemblance to Vic that had put her at ease with the duke. She found little to cling to. The duchess undoubtedly possessed a commanding type of beauty, but willowy and graceful with long dark locks pulled tightly back from her face. Her dark eyes carried no sparkle to match her husband's and daughter's. Then again, perhaps they simply didn't sparkle for her. Instead, her gaze held a more serious scrutiny as she scanned Sophia the way one might appraise a fine diamond, appreciation without affection.

Still, after a blatant examination that left Sophia wishing she wasn't in a hoop skirt and heels, the duchess stepped forward and clasped her hand. "You must tell me all about the movie business."

The comment was so unexpected, so gracious, and laced with something akin to real interest, Sophia almost found herself wanting to accept.

Almost.

The tension radiating off Vic, who'd yet to meet her eyes, told her there was more to this conversation than she could possibly understand. "I'd love to, but unfortunately we've only been given a ten-minute break in filming."

"Of course," the duke agreed quickly, "and we have to get settled into the residence. We have no intention of interrupting
your plans, or Victoria's, for that matter."

"Yes, we must freshen up, but I look forward to some quality
time with my daughter this evening. Perhaps you'll join us? I
would relish the chance to get to know the woman who's been
captivating the castle in our absence."

Sophia used the same airy laugh she'd used on set over the last
few days, finding it easier to slip into a more practiced persona
than to try to parse out a power structure she didn't fully understand. "You give me entirely too much credit. My job has merely
been to reflect this beautiful setting and a very compelling
script."

"Modesty is overrated, my dear." The duchess gave a little dismissive wave as her voice fell only slightly. "From what I hear,
you've been so much more than either the set or script could've
dictated."

The hair on the back of her neck stood on end at both the
comment and the knowing way in which the woman delivered
it. Thankfully, she didn't have to decide how to respond because
the duke stepped back in. "Perhaps then you'll join our family for
an evening meal?"

"That's kind of you." She tried to edge away. "But I have a long
day scheduled, and I'm afraid I wouldn't be very animated company."

"Right, and we've been traveling," the duchess offered. For a
second Sophia thought she might let her off the hook. "Why
don't we try something less formal? Shall we say drinks and a
movie in the library whenever your film crew clears out for the
evening?"

She felt the snare closing in as the duchess negated her excuses
around scheduling, space, and formality in one fell swoop. To turn
down the offer now would make it clear Sophia simply didn't
want to accept. Normally, she wouldn't mind saying so bluntly, but
these weren't some rich producers or fans. They were the nobility
whose home she was both working and living in. She had a

professional and social obligation to them on both counts, even without factoring in their relationship to Vic. And yet, the pull toward Vic tugged on her more than all the others combined.

She turned to her now, searching her for some cue as to what she'd have her do; only the face she'd come to use as an anchor or touchstone had transformed into an impenetrable wall.

Sophia suffered a pang of loneliness at the loss of Vic's open, easy assurance. Then a surge of frustration welled up in her. She hated feeling out of place. She hated feeling lost. She'd worked and fought and climbed too hard and too far to awkwardly await cues from anyone. She was a strong, confident woman, and Vic had never done anything but affirm that belief. Whatever was happening between them now, Sophia had no intention of letting herself feel any less worthy of Vic's company because of it.

"Sure." She forced a smile. "I don't see what harm could come of a movie night with three gracious hosts."

The duke's smile was genuine, but Vic's shoulders fell slightly. It was only a small movement, but that combined with the slow curl of the duchess's lips told her quite clearly that she'd just walked into a trap.

Vic's stomach roiled as she fought to keep from pacing in front of the library doors. Even the sound of the ice rattling around her mother's cocktail glass made her want to crawl out of her skin. The waiting might drive her to the brink of insanity before the other shoe ever had a chance to crush her, but she didn't delude herself into thinking this would be the worst part of the evening.

"I must admit, the crew did a lovely job of clearing out quickly this evening," her mother said from near the window. "You do seem to have held them in check thus far."

"They haven't been a problem." Vic kept her voice neutral. "The scheduling continues to be a nightmare, but never the people."

"I find that to be true in a great many situations," her father said, rounding the corner. He'd changed into khakis and a blue dress shirt, left open at the collar. It was as dressed down as he generally got in the evenings. "What are you drinking tonight, Vic?"

"She's not yet," her mother cut in. "Curious, no?"

"I was merely waiting for Father to arrive. I've missed his gin and tonics. No one else makes them to his standards."

"It's good to know my Eton education still serves its purposes in some areas." He smiled broadly, but her mother merely glanced at her watch.

Did she think Sophia was running late? Should Vic offer to escort her? No, that would give too much away. She needed to appear calm and casual, almost indifferent, but not to the point of being rude. If she overplayed her hand, her mother would pick up on that immediately. She needed to behave exactly how she would if any other house guest had been invited to a family evening. Only that didn't happen. Not unless they'd known the family for ages. For her mother to extend such an invitation to Sophia was such an utter breach of protocol, it meant there was no established way for Vic to respond. She suspected that was the point, to keep her off balance. Either that, or her mother was making a point about how Vic had already blurred those public and private spaces.

If only she could've warned Sophia. She'd tried, through a series of furtive glances and subtle head nods, but she'd had few opportunities to actually speak with her, and none of them offered any chance to be alone. The conversation she desperately wanted to have could no longer happen around any member of the film crew or the house staff, and perhaps they never should have. She strongly suspected that's what landed them in this situation to begin with. She'd trusted too much in her own authority and the privacy of her own home, something she'd been kicking herself over all afternoon.

The last few weeks had been too beautiful, too perfect, too easy to be her real life. She should have checked every lock, every window, and every passageway. She should have looked over her shoulder more often. She'd been so certain none of the staff would talk to the press that she completely failed to consider the possibility that one of them might alert her parents. Not just any one of them, either. Clearly James led the betrayal.

There was no other real suspect. He'd probably had his suspicions since the day he found her and Sophia together, sword out and eyes blazing. Then when Sophia moved into the castle, he'd likely been lying in wait. Old James never missed anything, but last night she'd given him more than the evidence he'd needed to fire the shot he'd dreamed of for years.

She blew out a frustrated breath. Part of her wanted to rage and scream, but she had only herself to blame. She'd told Sophia point blank that James didn't work for her. She'd always known where his loyalties lay, but instead of bracing for impact, she'd laughed and let down her guard even further. She'd allowed herself to grow content and comfortable with a woman who was undoubtedly about to be eviscerated for it.

Footsteps fell on the main stairway, and Vic rose to meet Sophia as she entered the library. She parted her lips, not sure if she intended to shout *it's a trap*, or perhaps kiss her one last time before everything changed, but her breath caught at the mere sight of her.

Sophia had obviously showered after work. All her makeup was gone, and the ends of her dark hair were damp and down over her shoulders. She wore jeans that hugged the delicious curve where hip met waist, and the loose white blouse offered the most alluring contrast to her deep skin tone.

"Ms. LeBlanc." Her father stepped into the void left by Vic's transfixion.

"Your Grace." Sophia took in his attire and glanced over his shoulder at the duchess, who still wore a classic black skirt and grey blouse. "I'm afraid I've underdressed for the occasion."

"Not at all," he said in a tone Vic recognised as genuine. "We've both come directly from dinner."

"Yes." Vic's mother cut in. "I envy your ability to leave your work at work. I've never had the luxury of compartmentalising my responsibilities or my attire."

145

And so it begins, Vic thought, but before she could even sigh, Sophia laughed.

"I'd offer to let you borrow some of my lounge clothes, but I fear they'd swallow you. You must tell me your secret to still being able to stand in heels this late in the evening, though."

Vic's mother waved off the redirect. "There's no talent to it, merely submission to the mores of my position along with a great deal of practice."

"In that case," Sophia said, "perhaps I'll be more judicious in choosing my next project. Maybe a Western? Or something that films on a beach."

"Well thought." Her father cut back in jovially. "What are you drinking?"

"What are you pouring?"

"Do you like gin and tonic?"

"That depends." Sophia arched one of her expressive eyebrows. "Are you the one who taught your daughter to mix them?"

He brightened considerably and straightened his shoulders. "I am indeed."

"Then I'm forever in your debt, and I'll have one of those, please."

"A woman of exquisite taste." He clapped his hands together and headed for the bar as Vic waited for her mother to argue. Instead she merely pressed her lips together and nodded briefly.

Vic released a slow breath at the reprieve and even felt a small prick of pride in the woman who'd done an admirable job of winning over her father.

Sophia was so much more than beautiful. She carried a social grace and an ability to read a room that Vic envied. Surely, she had to feel at least a little intimidated when walking into this room with these people tonight, but she didn't show it, and Vic fell a little harder for her. If only Vic could have given her hand a squeeze, she might even have been able to bolster her own confidence as well. As it was, she would have to content herself with the fact that Sophia seemed to have won the first volley.

Still, Vic understood too much history, both of the country and of her own life, to delude herself into thinking one skirmish could sway the outcome of a much larger war.

"I hope you don't mind, but I took the liberty of choosing a few film options," the duchess said as Sophia settled onto the couch next to Vic. She wished the two of them could sit a little closer, but she still sensed the tension radiating off the woman to her right. She didn't know what exactly Vic was afraid of, but the subtle changes in her demeanour spoke to something much larger than the awkwardness of having a lover meet her parents. The warm, open, confident woman she'd grown used to spending her evenings with had vanished, and in her place sat someone she hadn't seen in weeks. This version of Vic, the one with the sharp shoulders and tight jaw, had a smile that barely managed to push past her stiff upper lip. Her expression seemed permanently stamped into a politely neutral setting, making it impossible to read any nuance there. Only her eyes conveyed any emotions, but they were too mixed for Sophia to pick out a dominant one.

"I will admit, I'm woefully behind on all things popular culture," the duchess continued. "I'm not sure I've seen a blockbuster in years. You'll probably find me quite a bore."

"Not at all," Sophia said, "and I'm a student of form and technique. If you'd rather watch a documentary or art house film, I'd be thrilled."

"Not you, too." Vic's dad groaned. Funny how she'd come to think of him through his relationship to Vic, and still thought of the duchess according to her formal title.

"My husband was hoping that in present company he'd get to watch something a little more mainstream."

"Here, here." He leaned forward conspiratorially. "Every event I go to, people try to impress me with how proper they are. No one lets me see car chases or explosions unless they're in some black and white war reels from the Forties. Please don't tell me you're into silent films or those dreary think pieces."

147

She laughed. "In that case, don't let my personal affinity for cinematography stop you. What would you like to watch?"

He turned to his wife. "You heard our guest. Please present us with our choices."

The duchess's smile was small but satisfied. "Very well. I actually had James select three of Ms. LeBlanc's films for us to choose from."

Sophia blinked, then squinted at the options that flashed on the TV screen a few feet away. "My films?"

"Yes." A hint of genuine joy sounded in the duchess's otherwise cool voice. "There's one called *Vigilant*. One called *Star Killer*. And one I believe, oh yes, it's titled *Casting Couch*."

The superiority in the duchess's tone as she listed the last one told Sophia everything she needed to know. She'd picked three of the most sexually explicit roles in Sophia's film list. So that was her game. She'd brought her here tonight to show the others what sort of skeletons Sophia had in her closet, or perhaps she'd done it to let Sophia know what she knew.

"Which one would you recommend, Sophia?" the duke asked, clearly not in on the game. "Or is that like asking a parent to choose their favourite child?"

Sophia kept her gaze and her voice level and directed toward the duchess. "I'm proud of every movie I've ever made for one reason or another, but I like to think I've grown considerably as an actress over the years. If you want to see my most representative work, I'd start with the newest."

"Very well." The duchess moved the cursor over to click on *Vigilant* and then paused. "Wait, shouldn't that be the other way around? Shouldn't we see where you started in order to appreciate your progression?"

Vic shifted on the other end of the couch as if she'd just figured out where this might be headed, but Sophia refused to turn to her for help. She wouldn't be intimidated, and she wouldn't be shamed, not by her own choices, and not by a woman who would use Sophia to hurt her own daughter. "You can watch them in whatever order you want, but I don't think any of us have time to watch all three tonight, so whatever one you choose will be what you get."

The duchess raised an eyebrow as if she heard the undertones of the comment.

"Didn't you win some big award for *Vigilant*?" Vic asked, then undercut the casualness of her question by adding, "Besides, Mother, maybe Ms. LeBlanc doesn't want to spend her only free time all day dissecting her own work."

"Is that true?" the duchess asked. "I'd merely thought it would be enjoyable to watch a film with the star in our midst. We don't often get actresses here. Politicians, state visits, royalty even, but never anyone of your unique class. I hope I didn't make a faux pas in bringing up your body of work?"

"Not at all." Sophia lifted her chin the way she'd seen Vic do so many times, trying to channel some of that noble bearing the woman beside her had mustered when she'd talked about her family or her detractors, or were the two one and the same? "I'm not one of those artists who hates to look at their own work."

"Good, then let's start at the beginning." The duchess eyed her for a long minute as if waiting for an objection in some sort of game of chicken.

Sophia refused to give her the satisfaction. Instead she upped the ante by saying, "You don't have the very beginning available. My earliest work is utterly unfit for most video rental services, but I do believe *The Casting Couch* will give you a more than accurate picture of what you're looking for."

Vic cleared her throat, but Sophia merely smiled at her, trying to reassure her as best she could in the seconds before the duchess dimmed the lights and pressed play.

This was about to get awkward. There was no way around it, but not in the way the duchess expected. Then again, she didn't pretend to know the full extent of this woman's aim. Clearly, she wanted to embarrass Sophia, but honestly, what they were about to watch barely ranked on the scale of embarrassing things she'd done to get ahead. If anything, it would only reaffirm for her how far she'd come in the last ten years, and she'd done so only by making films one after another like rungs on a ladder. If she'd missed one of the rungs, she would've inhibited her climb, and she had made peace with that long ago. Frankly, she suspected that what was about to happen would be infinitely more uncomfortable for the others in the room.

Maybe that was the point. Perhaps shaming her only served the purpose of shaming Vic, a bank-shot betrayal.

The thought made her stomach twist. She didn't know what bothered her more. The idea of her past being used against Vic, or the idea that Vic might be weak enough to be hurt by something as superficial as a D-list movie made a decade before they met.

She supposed the latter would serve her right for getting involved with an heiress in the first place. She'd always suspected this whole thing had the potential to end badly, and while it had slipped her mind a time or two, the prospect had never disappeared completely. Still, she hadn't intended to get in deep enough to feel a responsibility to the woman beside her. It irked her a little bit now that she had.

The opening credits rolled over a cheap jazz synthesiser, and her own name flashed across the screen in a cheap font.

"Ah, there you are," the duke said excitedly. "Top billing."

She liked him all the more for his cluelessness. Too bad she'd probably never speak to him again after tonight. They might have enjoyed each other's company, at least in small doses, but unlike him she knew exactly what this movie was about, and she didn't need to offer any spoilers because the opening scene would make the gist of the plot abundantly clear.

Her face filled the frame, young and eager, and she didn't feel anything but affinity. She couldn't help comparing her physique of ten years ago to the dailies she'd watched of her work today as her younger self walked into a casting agency. She hadn't aged poorly. She'd even grown into her more angular features a bit over the years.

"*I'm Candy Mickles. Here to see Mr. Jacobs.*" She delivered the line in a voice a little higher than her current register. "*I have an appointment.*"

Vic shifted on the couch beside her, and Sophia took the risk of sliding her hand across the cushion to brush her fingers softly. She hoped the move was comforting, reassuring even, but as the screen switched to a sweaty, balding man with a bad comb-over, she had to admit this part wasn't going to be easy on someone with Vic's exacting moral standards.

Still, she sat upright, her legs crossed and one hand draped loosely atop her knee. She would not flinch. Not as the man playing the casting agent leered at her younger self. Not when he explained what a tough business movies could be. Not when he asked Candy to demonstrate what she was capable of to secure a part.

She even managed a hint of amusement as her character launched into a not-half-bad monologue she intended to use for auditions.

The duke, bless his heart, cracked first, clearing his throat as the casting agent cut off poor little Candy's monologue to explain that wasn't the type of demonstration he'd been hoping for. Because of course it hadn't been, and the only two people who'd ever misinterpreted the request had been Candy . . . and now the Duke of Northland.

Under other circumstances it might have been comical how things devolved. If only the scene hadn't actually depicted something close to actual offers Sophia had received over the years. If only the scene hadn't been shared out of malice. If only the duchess wasn't sitting in a high-backed armchair a few feet away, stewing in her own superiority, Sophia might have laughed at the terrible dialogue as the casting director used every heinous euphemism in the book to describe his own dick.

Vic shifted again, this time more dramatically. At the same time ice in the duke's glass rattled loudly, betraying a tremor in his hand. Which one of them would break first and put an end to this little exercise? Or would their stiff British nobility doom them to politely sit through the entire film? Was the duchess placing her own internal bets on the subject? Too bad she hadn't let Sophia in on the game. They could've added a side bet, maybe an over/under wager on how many minutes of simulated fellatio

151

her family could stomach watching together in the same room, because any woman who was eager to host a public viewing of this movie obviously had a sick sense of humour.

The only thing Sophia knew was that she wouldn't be the one to call *uncle*. She had two advantages over the others. One, she already knew the full plot of this movie, and two, she had a lifetime of practice in not apologising, or even caring about making other people uncomfortable with her life choices.

She settled back deeper in the lush couch cushions as her poor young character settled onto her knees under the casting director's rusty metal desk.

The shot wasn't nearly as graphic as it could've been. The camera focused much more on the actor playing the agent. What was his name? Mike? Matt? He was a bit over the top with all his grunts and twisted facial expressions. At times she wasn't even sure if her character was doing a really good job or a pretty bad one. The thought might've been funny if not for the tension practically pulsing off the people around her.

The duke crossed one leg over the other, and then uncrossed them as if trying not to appear uncomfortable, or maybe he didn't want to appear aroused. That would make an already awkward situation infinitely more terrible. Vic certainly had no such mixed reaction. In a particularly well-lit moment on screen, Sophia could clearly see her face had lost all its practiced neutrality. Anger beset something else. Pain? Repulsion?

Humiliation.

For the first time some of Sophia's defiance wavered. Was Vic upset that her mother had clearly chosen this film to hurt her, or was she actually embarrassed on Sophia's behalf? The former she could get behind; the latter was a more complicated matter. She didn't even consider the worst option, the one that involved Vic being embarrassed *by* her.

Her face warmed at the fear she tried to hold at bay. Surely Vic wasn't so prudish, not after all the things they'd done to each other over the last few weeks. She certainly hadn't held anything back when either of them had been on their knees with each other. Surely, she didn't think they had invented the position, and while no one wanted those memories sparked around their parents, the awkwardness was something a person should be able to laugh off and move on from.

Wasn't it? Or did rich people pretend they'd never had sex or an embarrassing job, which ultimately was what they were watching. She hadn't actually slept with Matt or Mark or whatever his name was. It was a D-list film, not a sex tape. Hadn't any of these people ever done a college play or worked in a—

She came up short on that question. The answer was no. None of the people in this room had ever done a damn thing that offended their sensibilities. Not to climb a ladder, not to make money, not to get their foot in any doors. They'd all been born with every single door wide open to them. A wave of nausea caused sweat to prick the back of her neck.

"All right," Vic snapped, grabbing the remote from her mother and turning off the television completely.

The whole room went mercifully dark. Sophia took the opportunity to school her expression into something that wouldn't show her disappointment. She wouldn't want any of the others to misinterpret the emotion. She wouldn't give them the satisfaction of thinking she felt any sort of sadness or shame. On the contrary, the defiant sort of pride stirring inside her now overruled even her anger at the duchess. Sophia had worked, she'd sacrificed, she'd been smart and talented and cunning. She'd earned everything she'd ever had, and no one else in the room could say the same.

She never expected the duchess to respect that about her. She hadn't even expected her to understand, and if the duke had been the one to pull the plug, she could've convinced herself the move was chivalrous at best, or outdated modesty at worst. But Vic . . . she shook her head. Why did it have to be Vic?

Vic snapped on the lights, her eyes blazing hotter than the overhead bulbs, and Sophia couldn't ignore the pink tint to her cheeks or the seethe in her voice as she wheeled on her mother. "May I please speak with you . . . privately?"

153

"Privately?" The chill in the duchess's voice dropped the temperature in the room several degrees. "I thought we were in one of the private areas of my home. Or did you unilaterally change the designations this family has employed for centuries?"

Vic didn't bite, but her eyes betrayed her as they flashed quickly to Sophia, making it clear she didn't want her to hear what was about to be said. It was the final break. She didn't know exactly what Vic thought or felt, but all the affection had drained from her gaze, and now she wouldn't even air her concerns in front of Sophia. Not only couldn't she bear the shame of watching her onscreen, she could no longer find the strength to defend her in person.

Vic turned back to her mother. "I'd like to speak to you in the corridor. Now."

The move could've been construed as polite, but they'd long since left the realm of good manners. Withdrawing now felt weak, and Sophia couldn't stomach weakness.

Vic's blood ran hot and her skin burned as she stormed out the door to the library, then slammed it behind her mother.

"Victoria, I'm appalled by your behaviour. Stomping around and slamming doors like a petulant teenager is beneath both your age and your station."

She refused to engage in a discussion of manners after what her mother had done in there. "If you had a problem, you owed it to me to air that grievance to me."

"Whatever do you mean?"

"Sophia is a guest in our home."

"Oh, now it's our home? I worried you'd forgotten that fact. Maybe it slipped your mind when you invited an entire film crew into our family space, or maybe you had a momentary lapse when you moved that woman into the residence, but surely you have to have had some pause when you decided to parade around half-dressed in front of our staff?"

There it was. Honestly, her mother could have dragged it out much longer before showing her cards. She didn't know if that meant she was more or less angry than usual. Honestly, she didn't care anymore. Nothing in her mother's range of emotions could match Vic's rage.

"I know decorum has never been your strong suit, but honestly, if you were going to lower your standards so drastically again, you could've at least done so discreetly."

The remark hit her like a slap. She couldn't even parse it out with the blood roaring through her ears.

"Don't look at me like I'm some sort of monster. I've made my peace with the gay thing, and I even understood your dating pool would be smaller, but surely you could've found someone with a touch of class."

"Sophia has class." She sputtered her weak defence. "Just because she's not from our social status doesn't mean she's common."

"That's exactly what it means."

"She's smart and driven. She's commanding and compelling. She's worked harder than anyone I know to get where she is, and she's more comfortable in her skin than I have ever been."

Her mother rolled her eyes. "Even if that were true, and even if there were any nobility in any of those qualities, she more than squandered it by baring that skin she's so comfortable in, repeatedly, publicly, and in the most repugnant ways."

"She's an actress, Mother, not a prostitute."

The duchess raised an eyebrow. "Are you sure there's a distinction when it comes to the types of films she's made? Because, believe me, what you saw in there was merely the tip of the iceberg. She said herself she's made several movies unfit to be rented through normal channels."

"I refuse to stand here and let you imply what you're implying."

"Wouldn't you rather I imply it here, in private, before you do something egregious? The press won't be half as tactful or genteel in their assessment."

"Sophia has been vetted by the press more than you and I could even imagine, and that's saying a lot."

"She's been vetted as a sex symbol, not as a partner for the heir-apparent to the Duke of Northland, England." Her mother sighed. "Do either of you want that type of scrutiny? If what we saw in there is the first thing reporters find on a mere surface-level search, what else do you think they'll unearth when they dig deeper?"

Vic's temperature rose, this time from something other than anger, at the thought of the press that had hounded her relentlessly after Robert's betrayal turning their ire on Sophia. "They will find a strong, beautiful woman with an iron will and immeasurable talent."

Her mother gave an uncharacteristic snort of derision. "I'll do us both a favour and not question which one of those immeasurable talents ensnared you so completely, but at least ask yourself honestly if you think the tabloids will focus on her artistic abilities with so many of her other ample assets clearly on display."

Vic wanted to shoot back, she wanted her anger to make her fast and sharp in the face of such offensive commentary, but she'd barely opened her mouth when her mother moved in for the kill.

"You, of all people, Victoria, should know by now not to rely on anyone's better angels, but then character judgment has never been your strong suit, has it?"

All the air left her lungs and the unspoken hit her as hard as the spoken.

Her mother, never one to relent until she'd twisted the knife, leaned in close and said, "Perhaps you're prepared to make the same mistakes again, but can't you think of something other than your basest needs for a moment? After everything you've already risked over the last few years, haven't you put your family through enough?"

Vic lost all her fight. The anger, the offence, the righteous indignation, every one of them failed her as she used every bit of energy she had left to simply stand under the last strains of her mother's scrutiny.

The duchess waited, no doubt searching for any ember of the flame that had flared moments earlier. Seeing none, she eventually nodded and swung open the door to the library.

"Ms. LeBlanc," she declared, her voice strong and clear. "You'll have to pardon us, but it appears as though we need to cut this whole thing short."

Sophia made no response Vic could hear as she rose, but as she reached the door, the duchess stopped her. "I presume we'll meet again under other circumstances?"

"Indeed," Sophia agreed, but her eyes were already on Vic.

Vic's face burned once more, but not for the same reasons as earlier. This time she had only herself to blame, and she had neither the time nor the space to explain herself. Instead she managed only to meet Sophia's dark eyes long enough to whisper, "I'm sorry."

Sophia's smile was small and tight. "You know how I feel about apologies."

Then she walked away.

Chapter Ten

"Lay on the ground and shoot up," Brian suggested, flippantly.

"What?" both Sophia and the cameraman asked in unison.

"I said," Brian pinched the bridge of his nose as if trying to stem the headache accompanying his perpetual hangover, "shoot from the ground with the Steadicam. Follow Tommy's hand closely as he takes hold of her leg and work upward."

"That's not what the script calls for," Sophia said sharply. They were shooting in the stable this morning, and the space was a little tight, but not enough to warrant upskirting her. "The note specifically called for the camera to focus on my face."

"The audience won't know what he's doing with his hands if we focus on your face."

Sophia snorted. "Trust me, if we're to assume he's doing it correctly, the audience should definitely be able to tell by watching my face."

The cameraman snorted to swallow his laugh.

"Besides," Talia offered, stepping forward and using her most soothing voice, "he's not supposed to actually touch her leg today, just push up the skirt and the petticoat. If we're going up higher, we may want to call in someone to—"

"If I wanted an intimacy coordinator, I would've hired one," Brian snapped.

"Maybe we should have." Tommy sounded a little uneasy. For all his self-aggrandizing antics, he wasn't a brute. Quite the opposite actually. Sophia had had to work hard not to overpower him in their previous scenes.

"Oh my god, are we seriously living in a world where we have to call an intimacy coordinator over a fucking camera angle?" Brian's tone went from annoyed to something more bitter, and Sophia clearly wasn't the only one who heard his disdain.

"What's an intimacy coordinator?" Vic stepped out from behind the closest row of camera equipment. Sophia's heart rate accelerated at the sight of her in a pencil skirt that showed off her legs and the pale blue silk shell that accentuated her eyes. The killer combination almost overcame her anger for a moment.

Almost.

They'd just spent their first night apart in weeks, and as much as Sophia hated to admit it, she'd missed her. The thought irked her as much now as it had every moment of their separation.

"Seriously?" Brian threw his hands up in the air. "Why are you still here?"

Talia held up a hand to him as she addressed Vic. "An intimacy coordinator is a person who helps plan scenes that might put our actors in sensitive positions. They keep everyone safe and comfortable as well as protect the production from even the appearance of impropriety."

"And you think we need one here now?" Vic asked, her voice serious and her brows furrowed.

"I hadn't thought so, not as the script read," Talia said, "but if Brian insists on—"

"No," Sophia said firmly. "We don't need one because we're not going to shoot up my skirt."

"You don't get to tell me how I'm going to shoot." Brian pushed back into the conversation and into her personal space. "I'm the director here, and I'm sick of you acting like you are."

"Fine," she said, refusing to step back. "You call any shot you can justify."

"What's that supposed to mean?"

"Just what I said. Tell me why you need this angle. What's my motivation, oh great director? And more importantly, how would

159

you like me to convey that emotion with my knees? Because he's not going any higher than that."

Brian frowned, but didn't seem any more eager to give in. "First of all, we're in cramped quarters, and I have to convey that. I need us to feel Tommy close the distance his character has respected until this moment."

"Great," Sophia said, mildly impressed he'd managed to articulate something at least close to awareness, but still not seeing any valid justification for shoving a camera between her legs. "Start farther back and close in until the camera's on his shoulder, not up my skirt. Problem solved."

"Why are you suddenly growing a sense of decorum on this film?" Brian sneered, then glanced pointedly at Victoria. "Trying to do a little social climbing?"

"Brian," Talia warned.

"No, seriously." He blew through her stop sign this time. "Half the B-list has-been actors in Hollywood have been up her skirt, and a few of the women, too. Does all this Me Too, women's libber bullshit really extend to women like her?"

"Enough!" Victoria snapped with all the commanding presence she had baked into her DNA. Even Sophia stood a little straighter in deference.

"I don't care who you are or what role you have with this film," Vic continued, seeming to grow taller with each word if only for the privilege of looking down her nose at him. "No one will be allowed to browbeat anyone into a sensitive situation on my estate. If the women on this set have concerns, they will be thoroughly and respectfully addressed before you move forward."

"Or what?" Brian asked through clenched teeth.

Vic blinked. "Pardon?"

"You said you won't allow me to control my actors as I see fit, but what will you do to me if I don't bow to your highness?"

"Your Ladyship," Vic corrected, lifting her chin, "and if you continue down this path, you'll be forced to cease production of Ms. Volant's film."

"Who the fuck is Ms. Volant?"

"The writer," Talia supplied.

"I thought you were the writer." He shook his head. "Never mind, I don't have time for this. It's my movie now, and I'll direct it how I see fit."

Then he turned to the cameraman. "Get on the ground. Tommy, get your hand up her skirt, and Sophia, act like you like it . . . or don't. No one cares."

Sophia's face flamed and her blood simmered as every eye on set fixed on her. It had been a long time since anyone dared speak to her like that, and she'd long passed the point in her life when she had to take it, a fact that everyone but Brian seemed to understand. Everyone awaited their next cue, not from him, or from Vic, but from her. A surge of power blended with her anger. She could end this all right now. If she stormed out, they would follow, and she drew a sort of satisfaction from knowing that, but she'd spent years swallowing a myriad of emotions. She wasn't about to surrender to them now. Not when she'd come so close to getting what she'd worked so hard for.

She nodded, prepared to swallow her pride one more time when Vic raised her hand and called, "Halt!"

If the others hadn't been frozen already, that would've done the job, and no one dared move now as Vic fixed an imperious glare on Brian. "Out."

"What?"

"Get out."

He laughed. "You can't throw me off my own set."

"In the name of the Duke of Northland," Vic stated in a low, dangerous tone Sophia had never heard from her before, "and the power vested by my lineage, I order you off this land immediately, and effective until such time as you make a formal apology and the appropriate behavioural adjustments."

"You can't be serious." He turned to Talia, his face purple with impotent rage. "She can't do this, can she?"

Talia shrugged. "She'd know better than me what she can do on her ancestral land, and that sounded pretty official to me."

He stared at her long and hard, but Vic refused to so much as blink. Everyone else refused to breathe, including Sophia, whose mind screamed at her to stop this, but as much as the rush of emotion threatened to carry her away, she found she wasn't any more immune to Vic's commanding presence than anyone else.

Damn her stupid libido. She could only stare in horror as Brian threw his hands in the air and stomped off, bringing the entire production to a screeching stop.

Once he climbed into a transport van and rolled away, everyone turned to Vic, as if she'd somehow become their default leader. Camera operators, crew, actors, even Talia. Then Vic sighed, and the spell was broken. Maybe not enough for everyone, but enough for Sophia to recognise the woman behind the official façade.

"Everyone take thirty," Sophia called, stepping into the role she had every right to play on this set. "Talia, you're going to have to make some calls."

"So many calls," Talia agreed, her face pale and emotionless.

"And I'd like a word with you, Your Ladyship." She turned to Vic. "Alone."

The others seemed all too eager to escape the awkwardness and cleared the space quickly. One of them even went so far as to leave a rather expensive piece of camera equipment sitting atop a bale of hay. But Sophia waited until every one of them was completely out of sight before stepping into the tack room.

She didn't wait to see if Vic would follow. She'd learned enough about her to realise that little outburst had likely cost her a great deal of energy and adrenaline. She might've even felt sorry for Vic if not for the myriad of things the temper tantrum had cost the rest of them as well.

She waited until she heard the latch close behind her before turning slowly. "How dare you?"

"What?" Vic's eyes went wide.

"How dare you overrule my authority around my own body, and in front of my colleagues, in front of my crew, in front of my boss?"

Vic shook her head. "I took your side."

162

"No, you took my agency."

"You said you didn't want to do what he was pressuring you to do. He said awful things to you. I defended you. I fought for you."

"I don't need you to fight my battles for me."

"Then for the love of god fight them for yourself." Vic found some of her fire again. "How can you let a man like that degrade you?"

"Men like that have been trying to degrade me my whole life."

"And you just take it? You would've let him tell you what someone else is allowed to do to your body without fighting him tooth and nail?"

"Probably." Sophia shrugged, refusing to admit that the condemnation in Vic's question stung.

"Why?"

"Because when you're fighting a war, you can't win every battle. And this little pissing contest with Brian wasn't even a skirmish in the grand scheme of things. He's not wrong. I've done much worse with much less at stake."

"But he's an idiot. You said so yourself."

"Yeah, he certainly didn't get where he is because of his merits, which should set off a big red flag for you, because it means he's shockingly well-connected."

"Not as well-connected as I am," Vic shot back.

"Lovely for you, Your Ladyship." Sophia's voice dripped with sarcasm. "Would you like me to curtsey? Genuflect? Lick your boot?"

"No."

"I would if I had to." Sophia bit back a seething kind of anger she hadn't felt in ages. "Because I'm *not* well-connected. Even after years in this business, I struggle daily for the chance to be judged on my work ethic, on my talent, on who I am as a professional, and you took that opportunity away from me."

Vic's face fell. "I didn't mean to make things harder for you."

"But you did!" she snapped. "With one outburst, you undercut all my authority. You made me look like some damsel in distress.

163

You gave me the reputation of a diva who stops production when she doesn't get her way."

"You didn't throw him out."

"No, my lover did, which is even worse. Do you know what a reputation like that could mean for my ability to secure future roles? I've always been the person who shows up early, shows up ready, shows up to *work*. Never in my entire career have I let my personal life affect my job. My priority has always been my career, my goals, and the films that move me closer to them. In one fell swoop, you shattered that reputation."

Vic hung her head. "I'm sorry."

"I'm sick of hearing apologies out of you. I don't pretend to understand what's going on with you and your mother, who, by the way, I've begun to think of as the Wicked Witch of Northland."

Vic managed a weak smile.

"But whatever it is," Sophia continued, "you need to fucking deal with it without letting it spill over onto me again, because as awkward as last night was, I still came to work this morning with my game face on, and you didn't. That's not okay. This set is my place of work. This is my whole life. Do you understand that?"

"Yes. And I am genuinely—"

"Don't." Sophia raised a hand. "Don't you dare say you're sorry one more time."

"But I am sorry. For this morning and for last night. I knew my mother wasn't happy, but I had no idea she intended to . . ." Vic stumbled, seemingly unable to even find words for what she'd seen onscreen. "I was mortified."

"I got that much." Sophia laughed bitterly. "What was less clear was whether you were mortified by your mother's behaviour or mine."

"What? Why would I be ashamed of yours?"

"Oh, I don't know, the way you snapped off the television last night might've suggested you didn't particularly feel comfortable with my work. Then you went and snapped on the entire production

164

of this film the first time you saw a man touch me on set. Seems like there might be a connection between me doing sex scenes and you losing your shit."

"No," Vic said quickly. "I don't have a problem with you doing . . . your job."

"Really?" Sophia pushed. "You didn't feel any little twinge of embarrassment while watching the scene last night?"

Vic shifted from one foot to the other.

"Yeah," she scoffed, "that's what I thought."

"It may have taken me aback," Vic admitted. "I wasn't prepared for the reality of your work, and I should have been, but you have to admit, even if I were totally comfortable with your making those movies, it can still be unsettling to watch my . . . someone I've slept with simulate, well, similar acts on someone else with my parents in the room."

She laughed in spite of her anger. "Now that's quite a summary."

Vic sighed. "I should have handled all of this better, but I was on edge from the moment Mother's eyes landed on you. I've seen her predatory look before. I know what she's capable of, the way she can eviscerate a person without ever breaking her smile. I didn't want her to do it to you."

Sophia's anger faded at the unspoken aspects of that last comment. "The way she does to you?"

Vic shrugged, but a little muscle near her jaw twitched, revealing more than she probably wanted. "It's too late for me. I wanted to protect you."

"And what if I went in there knowing full well it was a trap but wanted to protect you?"

Vic's mouth opened, then closed as colour rose in her cheeks.

"Seriously?" Sophia asked. "It never occurred to you that I was smart enough to read the room?"

"No," Vic squeaked.

The word landed like an ice pick to her chest. "Thanks."

"No." Vic shook her head, and then reached out to her for the first time since everything went to hell. Taking Sophia's hand, she gently intertwined their fingers. "I meant it never occurred to me that someone like you would endure my family to protect me. No one else ever has."

"Oh."

Vic's smile was slow and almost bashful. "I didn't recognise what was happening because it was a totally foreign experience for me."

"Yeah, well." She squeezed Vic's hand as another new emotion welled up between them. "Maybe I could've conveyed it better, I guess. Perhaps it was a new experience for me, too. The urge to protect someone, I mean."

Vic rested her forehead on Sophia's shoulder, shrouding them in the intoxicating mix of her expensive perfume and the hints of honey in her shampoo. "I made a pretty big mess of things."

"You really did." Sophia kissed her temple. "I'm still a little mad at you."

"But not a lot mad at me?" Vic asked, her voice soft and hopeful.

Sophia sighed. "Not as mad as I should be."

"And does that bother you?"

"A little," she admitted. "It's annoying, really."

Vic looked up, not appearing as chagrined as she should have. "But not so annoying that you won't let me make it up to you tonight?"

Sophia snorted. "I'm not sure your mother and James will allow any more sleepovers."

Vic grinned. "Lucky for you, I've had about twenty years of getting around those two when I know they are coming. Just leave it to me, okay?"

Sophia pursed her lips together. The idea of sneaking around like a pair of guilty teenagers didn't appeal to her. Then again, the idea of sneaking around with Victoria Penchant . . . she shook her head, then grinned in spite of her better judgement. "Okay, Your Ladyship, you've got one more shot. Show me what you've got."

£ £ £

Vic sneaked down the backstairs and through the kitchen, where two young women glanced up from the dinner dishes she and her parents had dirtied. Lifting a finger to her lips, she gave them a little wink. The younger of the two grinned conspiratorially, but both of them immediately resumed their work, and she made a note to praise their diligence to the housekeeper when things died down, if things ever died down.

No, she wouldn't let her mind go there. If there was anything, she'd learned through all her trials it was that everything in her life had an expiration date. She may not know when or how, but good or bad, nothing lasted forever. Not even a dynasty. One might think a person whose family had lived in the same place for hundreds of years might take some certainties for granted, but she'd never had the luxury of indulging fantasies of permanence. Her parents would return to Scotland, the filming would wrap up, Sophia would fly back to America. Someday even her title and all the responsibilities inherent in it would disappear, one way or another, eventually. Wasn't that all the more reason to steal her moments when she could get them?

She skirted the edge of the courtyard and around a low wall as the relative warmth of the day began to fade. She'd left Sophia in the stables an eternity ago, and the rest of the day had been a long string of one obligation after another, including one rather unpleasant meeting with Talia and several legal representatives from the film studio followed by an equally tense cocktail hour with her parents. Neither event had fully resolved anything, and she was eager to put both of them in herrear-view mirror, literally.

As she reached the other side of a small courtyard, she strolled as casually as possible through her mother's elaborate gardens. In her olive-green cargo pants and lightweight black sweater, she hoped she looked more the part of tourist than heiress. The gardens stayed open later than the castle grounds, which gave her a cover she didn't technically need. Still, she paused to sniff a few roses, not wanting to seem in a hurry, or even on too direct a path to the high hedgerow maze.

She took one cautionary glance over her shoulder to make sure none of the groundskeepers were still about that part of the gardens as she entered the maze between two thick, tall rows of yew hedges marking the entrance. Then, as if guided by some sort of autopilot system installed in her unruly youth, she turned right then left and left again, right into a dead end. Then she stepped right through the yew branches.

She grabbed a door handle before she even saw the fence in front of her and slipped a key from her pocket, using the tips of her fingers to feel for the lock. Thankfully it hadn't rusted in the years of neglect. Then again, her younger sister, Lizzie, also had a key, so maybe she'd used it a time or two before she settled down. She smiled as she stepped through the gate into a deserted car park.

The thrill of freedom buzzed through her body, only to be completely subsumed by a low thrum of arousal at the sight of Sophia leaning against the only vehicle in the lot.

Vic allowed herself the time and space to stare at her. Her skintight jeans showed off endless legs and most of the curve of her sumptuous hips before they were covered by a supple red leather jacket open to reveal a flimsy white undershirt. The ensemble was all at once effortlessly informal and over-the-top chic, much like the woman underneath it all.

Sophia's smirk was slow and knowing as she stood steady under Vic's blatant appraisal. "Did you escape through the wardrobe like all the other British prep-school children?"

Vic shot one last parting look at the door behind her as she kicked it shut hard enough to hear it latch. "Something like that. You're not carrying any Turkish delight, are you?"

"Oh honey, I'm way more dangerous than that."

Vic's mouth went dry, both at the truth of the statement and the rush of heat it sent sizzling through her. She closed the distance between them in an instant and had to grind her teeth against the impulse to push Sophia against the side of the Land Rover and ravish her right there. It would be easy to slide a knee between Sophia's legs and work one hand down the front of those painted-on jeans.

The images flashed through her mind with frightening clarity, and the strength of the urges behind them tore at her insides like a beast clawing for release. She closed her eyes and clenched her jaw in an attempt to hold them at bay, less out of a sense of decorum and more out of a sense that, once she surrendered control, she might never get it back again.

When she regained enough composure to open her eyes, Sophia's expression held both sympathy and satisfaction.

"Shall we?" Vic managed to ask.

Sophia laughed. "Shall we what? Do you have a plan for this evening, other than fucking me in the back of your Land Rover, because right now that seems to be where we're headed."

"An undoubtedly tempting option." Her cheeks warmed at both the colourful description and the accuracy of Sophia's assessment. "But, no. When I voiced my willingness to sneak around like teenagers, I didn't quite mean that far. I'm taking you out to dinner."

Sophia grimaced. "'Out' as in 'out of the castle grounds'? Might not be such a good idea."

"Yes, but unfortunately staying inside the castle grounds has considerable drawbacks as well."

"Right. I met your mother last night, but the problem is that while I'm not quite a household name yet, the local press does know we're filming here." Sophia said the words *local press* with exactly the level of fear and disdain the term inspired in Victoria. "Several websites have already shared pictures of Tommy in pubs, and he's not nearly as famous as I am. If we show up somewhere public together, we'll be mobbed within half an hour."

Vic fought down a wave of nausea at the prospect, but it wasn't as if the idea hadn't already occurred to her. It had weighed on her mind all day, giving her ample time to calculate and mitigate the risks in what she had planned. "I fully understand and share your concern. However, I'm asking you to trust me."

Sophia pursed her lips and scanned Vic up and down slowly. "Why do I get the feeling this isn't your first rodeo?"

She frowned. "Actually, I can assure you I've never attended a rodeo, but if that phrase is a euphemism to express my ample experience at evading both the press and my parents, then yes, you can rest equally assured that I'm professional grade."

Sophia rolled her eyes playfully. "You might have sounded a little more rebellious without that twenty-dollar vocabulary of yours, but then again, you had me at 'trust,' because ultimately, I do."

Vic's chest filled with some emotion that made her feel both warmer and lighter as she opened the car door for Sophia. She didn't want to put a name on the feeling, but she didn't want to lose it, either.

Once Sophia's mind adjusted to sitting on the wrong side of the car and driving on the wrong side of the road, she found herself captivated by the most beautifully rolling countryside. She hadn't been outside Newpeth since her initial arrival, and she hadn't left the estate grounds in weeks. She'd never been one to sightsee on location, and it had taken all her focus and fortitude to adjust to living and working in a castle. She hadn't even considered the fact that she wasn't just in a foreign environment, but also a foreign country.

"This area is stunning," she finally said as they curved along a winding road between pastures lined with low stone walls. "It's like something out of an old storybook, or—"

"Movie?" Vic supplied with a little smile.

"Yes, I walked right into that one, didn't I?"

"I'm glad you did." Vic took her hand as they passed a small school and field filled with children playing some sport.

"Is that cricket?"

"Indeed." Vic's face lit up. "Several nights a week, the young lads and lasses of Northland meet at the pitch. My father keeps tabs on the promising players in the area. I think he'd like to have a winning team someday."

"It didn't escape my notice that your family crest is on the entrance to the field, and the school, and the farm we passed with all the sheep. You've got a hand in all of it, haven't you?"

"Yes. I know I've talked a lot about the weight of responsibility in my title, and the complications of my family, but I'd be remiss if I didn't also express my genuine affection for this country, its beauty, its people." Vic's expression softened as her voice grew more wistful. "This is my home, and I'm proud of that. I wouldn't want to live anywhere else."

Sophia gave her fingers a little squeeze. She didn't understand that kind of responsibility. She'd made her way in the world by saving herself, but her chest tightened as she listened to the mix of emotions thickening Vic's voice. What would it be like to be so anchored to who you were and where you belonged?

They drove across a stone bridge above the point where a lazy stream broadened into a picturesque estuary filled with sailboats, and a quaint town began to rise up around them. Stone buildings lined narrow streets, and in the breaks between them, she caught her first real glimpse of the sea. They made a wide sweep around the edge of an open field, and the water spread out before them, shimmering silver and orange in the low glow of evening.

"Wow."

"Yeah, that's no hardship to look at."

"I never thought of England as having beautiful beaches. I've only ever been in London."

"Then you don't know what you've been missing." Vic's voice took on a playful lilt as they swung wide, back toward the river and the heart of the town. "The village of Amberwick is one of the most impressive jewels in the crown of Northland, but it's not the only one. I wish we had time to make a progress through the country. I know I'm biased, but this whole area is breath-taking. I wish more people knew about what we had to offer up here."

"Sounds like you need better PR and marketing."

"That's where you come in, isn't it? Your movie might just put us on the map. Soon people will pilgrimage from near and far to see the place where Sophia LeBlanc made a name for herself."

Sophia bit her tongue to say that would only happen if they actually got back to work tomorrow, something she wasn't at all sure of yet, but if Vic could take a night off, so could she. Thankfully, Vic offered a nice distraction from the questions trying to bubble up inside her by pulling into the driveway of a small white cottage.

"Oh my god, do you have, like, a secret little sex escape?"

Vic blanched. "A what?"

"I don't know what you call it here, like a sex shed, but nicer?" Sophia glanced back at the house. "You know, a place to take your lovers so your wife—or, in your case, your mother and her flying monkeys—don't know."

Vic looked from her to the cottage and back again before she burst out laughing. "That's Emma's house, and we're only parking here so we can walk to the pub."

"Oh, that's a much more mundane explanation."

"Sorry to disappoint you with my lack of secret sex sheds." Vic still sounded mildly amused by the idea. "It never occurred to me to secure an entire home specifically for the purpose of an illicit rendezvous."

"Really?" Sophia asked. "Most of the men I know in Hollywood have them, and a great many of the women as well."

Vic stiffened slightly as she twisted a single silver ring on her right hand. "I suppose it might be prudent if one were to do that sort of thing often, and I certainly wouldn't cast judgement on anyone who did, but—"

Sophia's chest tightened, not at what she'd inadvertently implied, but at how Vic seemed to have taken it. She hooked a finger under Vic's chin and turned it until their eyes met. "I don't have one, Vic."

"Oh." She blew out a shaky breath and her smile returned. "Not that it would be any purview of mine to have an opinion on whom you associate with when we're not together."

"No, it's really not," Sophia said, still cupping Vic's chin in her smooth palm. "The same way it's not my place to feel jealous at the thought of who will come after me for you, but feelings are a funny thing, aren't they?"

172

Vic stared into her eyes, so many questions hanging unspoken between them. "They aren't exactly logical."

Sophia gave a little hum of agreement. "Not at all. But we're both grown women who have understood what we're doing from the beginning. And we're both fully aware that when one makes the choice to play with fire, there's a high probability of getting burned."

It was the closest they'd come to discussing the realities of their inevitable end, and honestly as close as she wanted to get to the topic. She could add it to the growing list of things she didn't want to acknowledge on their first, and possibly only, night out together. There was no use dwelling on what everyone knew, and it was silly to pretend she wasn't already in deep enough for that knowledge to sting. Still, talking about the hurt before it occurred wouldn't do anything to diminish it. She'd said goodbye enough times to know the memories could be either a balm or a burr, and she hoped that what they did tonight would eventually fall into only the former category.

Vic seemed to come to the same conclusion as she gave her another little squeeze before pulling back into herself. "Come on, let's go eat some of the finest pub fare Northland has to offer."

They strolled with forced casualness down the half block of long rowhouses until they reached a stone archway, and Vic nodded for Sophia to follow her into what looked like a cobblestone alley. The whole thing might have felt a little seedy if not for the light at the end of the tunnel giving way to a large patio, and beyond it that beautiful estuary they'd passed on the way into town. Still, she couldn't tell where they were headed until Vic turned toward a low, unassuming door in the wall to their right.

"So, this is the Raven. It's not much in the way of frills. No Michelin stars to brag of."

"Are you trying to tell me we're going slumming?"

Vic laughed again, and Sophia realised how much she'd missed that easy sound over the last two days. "Not hardly. I'm just saying you might need to brace yourself because, well, maybe it's not what you're expecting."

Sophia arched an eyebrow. "I'm intrigued, but please don't keep me in suspense."

A wave of nervousness flashed across Vic's features, but she nodded and swung open the door. She didn't barge right through like she did around the castle. Instead, she stood in the entryway, so Sophia had to peek around her to get her first view of the place.

It took several seconds for her eyes to adjust to the dim light, low ceilings, and dark wood interior of the room. A long bar stretched across much of the opposite wall, and two stone fireplaces bookended the room. Every other available space sported small tables or low-backed booths with varying degrees of upholstery. She didn't even notice the cluster of people sitting in the far

corner until a cry of recognition went up among them.

"Vic!" they all called in unison.

"Good evening," Vic said with a smile in her voice.

"We didn't know you were coming by tonight," a male voice called.

"Officially, we're not," Vic said. "We're hoping to keep a low profile."

"Of course, dear," a woman said with a little chuckle. "You've come to the right place, but who is this 'we' you speak of?"

Vic glanced over her shoulder and gave Sophia an expression that contained equal parts smile, grimace, and apology. Then she stepped aside.

A few gasps and a mumbled comment or two passed among the group gathered in the corner.

"It's that woman from the movie with Cobie Galloway?" one of the women asked.

"Sophia," another one stage-whispered. "Sophia something or other. She's starring in Emma's movie."

One of the men grinned broadly and scooted over. "Pull up a chair right here."

Sophia braced for the phone cameras that would undoubtedly materialise next, before turning back to Vic. "So much for privacy."

"No, no," another woman's voice called, and she turned to see a redhead enter from another room and make straight for the bar. "Don't let them bombard you. I already cleared out the tourists, and I'll drive that lot out, too, if they can't mind their manners."

Vic laughed again. "No worries about Friday Club."

"I mean it," the woman warned, drawing herself up to her full height as she grabbed a pint glass and began to fill it with amber liquid. She moved with ease and spoke with an accent much less polished than Vic's or even Tommy's. To her untrained ear, Sophia might have placed it as almost Scottish or Irish, but not quite. The woman slid the glass across the bar toward Vic before turning to her. "What'll you have, Ms. LeBlanc?"

She warmed both at the easy way the bartender pegged her and the comfort with which she handled the encounter. If not for Vic standing so close and wreaking havoc on her senses, this woman would've pinged a few alarms of arousal.

"Seeing as how I have no idea where I am and what I'm in for, I guess I'll have what Vic's having."

The woman nodded. "Another Thatcher's cider coming right up, and for what it's worth, you're in the Raven. As to what you're in for, that's over my pay grade."

The woman slid the second glass over, along with two menus. "The table in the corner's all yours if you'll have it."

"Thank you, Brogan." Vic's tone suggested her gratitude encompassed more than the drinks.

"No worries. I'll call my wife, and then I'll be round for your orders."

Vic lifted her glass in acknowledgement, then turned so the gesture encompassed the others still watching them intently from the other side of the room. "I hope you'll not find us rude if we—"

"Not at all, dear," one of the women said knowingly before Vic could even finish. "We'll all be over here doing our best to act natural while we eavesdrop on the both of you."

"I'd expect nothing less, Esther," Vic said as she motioned for Sophia to slide into the booth the bartender indicated. "I'm not supposed to play favourites when it comes to local businesses, but between you and me, I do. And this is it."

"You do seem to have a following here." Sophia arched an eyebrow over her drink. "I have to admit, when you mentioned sneaking around, I didn't anticipate a public pub where we'd be recognized before we even got through the door."

Vic reached across the table and covered Sophia's hand with her own. "I'm sorry if I made you uncomfortable. Perhaps I should've explained earlier."

Sophia's tension melted, both at the touch and the sincerity in those blue eyes. "It's fine, I just…I guess we'll deal with the fallout, whatever it may be, when it occurs."

Vic shook her head. "There won't be any fallout, at least not from anyone in this room."

"I never pegged you for having lax standards around privacy."

"I don't," Vic said seriously. "I've simply come to understand privacy as a complex proposition, and when given the choice between trying to achieve it through isolation or trust, I'd rather have the latter."

Sophia glanced over her shoulder at the woman who'd openly admitted her intent to eavesdrop on their conversation. "And you trust these people?"

Vic didn't even pause. "Unreservedly."

Chapter Eleven

"No. The book I'm writing now is a modern romance, and it's just dreadful not to have all the frills of a period piece to hide behind," Emma explained in a self-deprecating tone, but her blue eyes shone with a lightness that belied the good-natured gripe about her current writing project. "It's about a famous musician who escapes to the country hoping to hide out after a press scandal, but all the locals are busybodies who interfere in her business and drag her into small-town life. Of course, there's also a romance."

"A bit autobiographical, then?" Vic asked, looking over Emma's shoulder to see much of the Friday Club crew still firmly planted in their usual booth. She'd meant what she'd told Sophia. She trusted that none of them would ever admit to the press that the two of them had ever been in town, not even under the threat of torture, but that didn't mean they wouldn't discuss it at length among themselves.

Emma rolled her eyes. "I wouldn't go that far."

"But it is a romantic comedy with a British travel backdrop?" Sophia leaned forward over her now-empty plate. Vic might have worried about her mussing up her alluring white undershirt if Sophia hadn't licked the dish clean of any remnant of Brogan's chicken bacon pie.

"Yes," Emma exclaimed. "Exactly that, sort of like a Hallmark movie with an international flair. Hopefully I can capture the charm of those great, down-home, fish-out-of-water stories, but with a less familiar setting than abstract Americana."

"I like where you're going." Sophia nodded thoughtfully and ran one finger along her lower lip.

She seemed part story scholar, part circling shark, and Vic enjoyed both immensely. It wasn't hard to see how Sophia became a force in Hollywood, not just on the acting side of the equation, but through carefully calculated career risks as well.

"You're combining something familiar with something more exotic to keep it from being stale," Sophia continued. "Adding a real sense of place gives the story a deeper anchor, and if you filmed in this area, you'd have so much to work with. Sweeping vistas, crooked cobblestone streets, windswept coastline, I mean, have you even seen the beach out back?"

Emma laughed. "Every morning from my conservatory, and I'm still not immune to it, but I'm a long way from thinking about film rights."

"Why?" Sophia asked.

"I haven't even written the full first draft yet!"

"So, what you're saying is, I still have time."

"Time for what?"

"To get a solid directorial debut under my belt." Sophia sat back, somehow managing to appear both energised and relaxed all at once.

Vic envied her that ability, along with so many others. She had a way of commanding a room or a conversation that felt totally authentic, probably because it was. The ease with which Sophia slipped into meaningful conversation with Emma made Vic a little wistful. Even in the place where she felt most comfortable, with the people she most enjoyed, she'd never quite reached a level of unguardedness Sophia could apparently summon at will.

"I didn't know you wanted to direct." Emma's own interest ratcheted up another notch. "Is that common?"

Sophia waved her off. "A lot of actors dabble."

"But for you it's more than a hobby, right?" Vic asked, hoping to spark more of the fire she'd seen in Sophia the last time the topic had arisen. She wanted to stand close to that flame, and perhaps, in some place deep she didn't want to examine too closely, she also enjoyed showing off this captivating woman to a small part of her own circle of people.

"Correct." Sophia gave her an indulgent smile. "Directing is my endgame, and this movie of yours we're filming right now should help me get one step closer. Which means, it's only fair that I should get to call dibs on your next screenplay as well."

Emma's cheeks flushed pink with pleasure, and Vic's heart swelled at how thoroughly Sophia was managing to win over her closest friend. She'd never let herself harbour any illusion that Sophia might become her girlfriend. The title simply wasn't available to either of them, but surely if one were to entertain such fantasies, winning over one's friends would be a very good attribute to have.

"I really am the biggest fan of *Vigilant*," Emma continued to gush. "From Talia's first draft of the book, I fell in love with everything about the story, the characters, the gritty details. I've always been impressed with people who capture the darkest elements of human nature without making them seem monstrous. Talia did that on the page, and you brought that element to life perfectly on the screen."

"It's easy to do when you have an amazing script and such dedicated professionals in charge of every aspect of the project." Sophia tried to brush off the compliment, but Vic recognised the low undercurrent of pleasure in her voice. She'd heard it before, and the memories of when and why sent a tingle across her nerve endings. She took a drink in order to soothe the dry heat building in the back of her throat.

"But how do you do it?" Emma pressed. "How do you step into a character like that, with all their moral and ethical flaws, and make her so powerfully compelling?"

"I took lessons from Vic's mother."

Vic snorted and nearly coughed up some of the cider she'd just swallowed.

Emma looked from one of them to the other, eyes wide in surprise.

"Sophia met the duchess last night," Vic offered by way of explanation. "It went as well as one might expect. Or rather, even worse than that."

Emma grimaced. "I've had the pleasure only a time or two in official settings, but I've heard the stories. No beheadings, though?"

"Everyone left with their heads attached to their shoulders." Vic tried to play off the wash of anger-tinged embarrassment. "Much to my mother's chagrin, she no longer has the authority to order executions. So, at least there's one vote for modernising the nobility."

"Which reminds me," Emma said more seriously, "I saw Parliament adjourned without even discussing the Downton Abbey bill. I can't remember the real name—about the successions."

"Succession of peerage," Vic offered dryly. "You may be the only person I know who thought they might consider it this session."

"They're going to have to eventually," Emma said with a certainty Vic didn't share. Perhaps it was her American optimism, or the relative newness of her wealth, but Emma seemed to think anything could be resolved any day now if only one had faith and good will.

"They've managed to keep putting off the matter since, well, the *Magna Carta*. I don't see why they'd find any sense of urgency around the issue now." Vic turned to encompass Sophia within the summary, though she would've rather changed the subject. "With more austerity measures on the horizon and cuts to the NHS, half the country thinks people like me should be guillotined, and the other half is so conservative they're infinitely more likely to see queer women as an impediment to our former glory than the saviour of it."

Emma shook her head. "You know, it's no knock on your father, but a lot of people might see you as a hopeful middle ground toward a more modern future."

"By 'a lot of people,' are you talking about yourself and the rest of Friday Club?"

"No. Archie is always impressed with your ideas and insights. Mind you, he won't tell us what they are, for confidentiality reasons, but I'm fairly certain he'd follow you into any sort of corporate or legal battle you chose."

"Archie is Brogan's older brother," Vic explained to Sophia. "He works with me in the land office, and he's a good sort. Anyone would be lucky to have him on their team."

"Oh, blimey," Brogan said, joining them again. "Please don't ever say that in front of him. He's insufferable enough as it is."

"I'll do my best to navigate the McKay family politics with tact and discretion." Vic laughed, happy for the diversion and the extra company. Brogan could always be counted on to keep the conversation on an amiable track. "Speaking of which, can you add Charlie's next few drinks to my tab?"

Brogan groaned. "You two weren't betting on the cricket again, were you?"

"Not at all," Vic said. "Young Charles is in much deeper than that, I'm afraid. He sneaked my Land Rover out of the main entrance tonight and left it round back of the gardens so we could make our escape undetected."

"Then maybe I should open up a tab for him as well," Sophia cut in.

"I've no doubt he took his reward in the form of a little joy ride before leaving the Rover for you," Brogan said. "Did you check to make sure he hadn't drained it of petrol?"

"Now that you mention it—"

"Who is this guy?" Sophia asked. "I feel like we'd be great friends."

"Charlie is Brogan's younger brother. He works at the castle and the gardens. He's also my go-to for inside jobs because he works quickly and accepts payment in ale instead of cash."

"Well, well, well, a bit of a bootleg economy, I may have underestimated your network of back channels." Sophia winked at Vic, then turned to Brogan. "I may actually be in the market for similar skills throughout the rest of this shoot. I have a good line on the duke's finest gin. Do you have any other siblings?"

The other three people at the table all burst out laughing, while Sophia seemed to realise she'd stepped into something. "What?"

"There are a few more of us to choose from." Brogan's tone made Sophia suspect she had a gift for understatement. "But you'll be hard pressed to find many of them who aren't already in her employ, at least tangentially."

"I'm starting to see a trend here." Sophia sipped her cider and regarded Vic over the rim of her glass. "She's not been overplaying this communal responsibility business, has she?"

"Not particularly," Brogan said.

Emma leaned in conspiratorially. "They've both got this British modesty and stiff-upper-lip thing, but most families the size of Brogan's have people working for the duke or his estate in one way or another."

"And they've all got very mixed feelings about that," Vic cautioned. "Don't paint an overly idyllic picture for her. My lineage hasn't always been benevolent landowners, and a great many people would much rather we not own the land at all."

"What would they rather see instead?" Sophia asked.

"I suspect most of them haven't thought that far, but those who have may envision the land going to the National Trust or other conservation groups."

"Is that a likely outcome if you get overthrown?" Sophia asked, seeming less irritated and more curious than she had when the topic had previously arisen.

"It's not impossible." Vic sipped her drink.

Emma shook her head. "She didn't ask about impossibility. She asked about likelihood."

Vic shifted in her seat. "It's unlikely a majority of the land or its contracts would be protected long-term. Mind you, this is all wildly speculative, as there's little modern precedent for trying to separate a title from an estate, but if we failed to do so, the land would likely go first to some sort of governmental entity. Then some of it could be set aside as publicly owned parks or historic sites, but we're talking about thousands of acres of farms, pastures, and forest in addition to the land already leased to corporations, schools, and public ventures. Most legal experts assume the majority of it would be auctioned off to the highest bidder."

"They'd log much of the forests." Brogan sat down beside Emma. The few locals left in the pub seemed content to nurse their drinks. "Charlie said some of those forests you own contain old growth trees that would go for a king's ransom."

Vic nodded. She couldn't reveal what several corporations had already offered for the land around the stables where Sophia's crew had been filming, but the figure was substantial enough that few agencies in the country could have turned it down without pause.

"And they'd want to develop much of the coast," Emma added with a little shiver.

Brogan wrapped an arm protectively around her wife's shoulders and pulled her closer. "That's the last thing we need, condos on our beaches."

Vic snorted. "My family hasn't stayed out of the real estate development business. We've not exactly been charitable in our efforts to balance affordable housing and income properties either, as I've been told often."

Brogan grimaced, causing Vic to laugh.

"What did I miss?" Sophia asked.

"There've been some controversial building projects over the last few years. And by controversial, I mean there may have been calls to have my father and me drawn and quartered."

Sophia's elegant eyebrows shot up. "If they were that unpopular, then why go forward?"

"The same reason no one else tries to sell their homes or land for a loss, either. Financial responsibility."

"I wouldn't have thought your family needed to worry on that front."

"No one ever does." Vic sat back. "I can't go into details, obviously, but the castle is more money than it's worth most years. The tourism over the summer doesn't make enough to cover the upkeep. Honestly, it would be a considerable financial boon to our family to let it go to ruins like so many others around here or sell it. It's not as though we haven't had plenty of offers from entertainment or amusement companies."

Brogan and Emma both groaned.

"What?" Sophia glanced from them back to Vic. "What do you all care who owns the castle so long as it stays open?"

"The places where those big conglomerates take over turn into total circuses, and the towns around them become bloody side-shows," Brogan explained. "Cheap labour, transient populations, garish medieval-themed attractions, low-end lodging, it's all a mess with zero local oversight."

"They aren't wrong," Vic said, "but few people ever think that far ahead. They see all our wealth and land and rightfully say no single family should own such a sizable share of space, money, or power."

"And those people aren't wrong?" Sophia pushed back.

"No, they aren't," Vic said emphatically, noting once again how much she enjoyed that Sophia didn't hold back.

Brogan tipped her glass in Vic's direction. "Glad you said it instead of me."

"Listen," Emma cut back in, "I never expected a kid from sub-urban New York would be the biggest monarchist at this particular table, but I've done a lot of research for my last few books, and the problem most people run into when they say things like, 'there's got to be a better way' is that the better way they envision involves them getting richer, when in reality, there's a possibility the entire region gets a lot poorer."

"Archie and Charlie would certainly be worse off," Brogan said, "and honestly I suppose we'd have less tourism as well if the castle or the beaches fell into the wrong hands, which would hurt the whole village."

Vic nodded solemnly. "You know that's not what I want, right?"

"Of course," Emma said quickly.

"But it's not within my control." Her voice sounded strained even to her own ears. "No one ever asked my opinion on any of this, and if I could snap my fingers and just magically have every-thing I owned put into a community trust or some iron-clad conservation status where everyone kept their jobs, I would with-out a moment's hesitation or regret."

"No one's asking you to do the impossible," Brogan said.

Vic laughed, trying not to let any tension or bitterness seep in. "That's the first time you've been wrong all night, my friend, but I'll forgive it if you provide us with some of your famous sticky toffee pudding."

"Fair." Brogan rose from her seat and placed a kiss atop Emma's fair hair. "But for what it's worth, I think you'd likely find a way to serve the area as well as anyone could."

"Hear, hear," Emma echoed as her wife headed for the kitchen. "I just wish more people around here could get to know you better, because I think they'd definitely rather have you at the helm than some random land-grabber."

"Thank you for your vote of confidence." Vic forced a smile. "I appreciate the sentiment even if I don't agree with your assertions. Either way, though, it's not my decision to make, and no one will make it tonight."

"Fair enough." Emma sat back. "Besides, I think I've been polite long enough. I'm ready to hear the story of how you two went from fighting over a sword to . . . whatever it is you're doing here tonight."

Vic turned to Sophia, who met her gaze with a spark of mischief in her eyes and a little smirk across her beautiful mouth. Warmth spread through her, causing the tension to dissipate. "Shall we tell her?"

"Oh please." Sophia ran her finger lazily around the rim of her pint glass. "And while you're at it, maybe you can explain it to me, because the last thing I remember clearly is a bottle of gin, and rocks against a windowpane. Everything after that's been a bit of a blur."

Emma gave an excited little squeak and tapped her index finger against the table. "Details, I want all the details right now."

This time Vic's smile was genuine. Many people might have cringed at the invasion into their private life, but she much preferred that topic to the weight of responsibility pressing on her chest moments before.

For the first time in her life she was in a relaxed space with friends who knew her well enough to pry and a beautiful woman, with a story to tell. For tonight she wanted to luxuriate in experiences the rest of the world took for granted.

Sophia didn't even know what time it was anymore. She wasn't wearing a watch, and she didn't want to check her phone for fear the outside world might try to creep into this perfect evening. She couldn't remember the last time she'd had an uninterrupted meal in a public place. She couldn't remember the last time she'd had a casual outing at all. Two days ago, she wouldn't have thought it possible, even on her own, much less with someone of Vic's status and profile. And yet even the last of the Friday Club had given up trying to eavesdrop and one by one headed out. Their polite and staggered goodbyes left her, Vic, and Emma plenty of time and space to get several drinks and many conversations into the night. She needed to stop soon, on both counts, but for once her sense of professionalism finished a distant second to her enjoyment of the moment.

Still, even the thought of why she needed to head back to the castle soon made her jaw tighten once more. Either Talia had brokered a deal with Brian and the production company and she'd return to a much more fraught set tomorrow, or no deal had been secured and she'd have to take it on herself to make some concessions to get the production back on track. Her stomach turned at what those concessions might entail. She squeezed a fist tightly under the table and shook the thoughts from her mind.

Those were problems of the previous day that would spill into many days to come, but they wouldn't steal tonight from her. She'd become an expert at compartmentalising every aspect of her life, and tonight she had already managed to lock away her knowledge of how all things would end. Tonight, she would stay here as long as she could stand. Tonight, she would revel in every detail of this little pub, in her typical British meal, and in the company of good people. There was an exuberance to the everyday aspects of it all.

Only, even here, nothing about Vic seemed mundane.

She was so beautifully relaxed tonight, as she laughed again at some story Emma relayed about her niece, or maybe Brogan's niece. Sophia couldn't follow all the relationships, but that didn't keep her from taking this chance to watch Vic's features shift in their unguarded state. She wouldn't have thought it possible for Vic to be any more attractive than she was in her full commanding mode, or in those sexually confident moments where she'd pinned Sophia to the wall and ravished her, but seeing her here with these friends she trusted and in a place she could relax stirred a new, deeper emotion.

Her thoughts were interrupted by Brogan rejoining them as she declared, "That's it. Kitchen's closed for the night."

Vic scooted over under the guise of letting Emma sit next to her wife, and Sophia thanked the gods of chivalry for putting Vic within arm's reach.

"And, if you want anything else from the bar, you'll have to pour it yourself, because I'm off the clock," Brogan declared.

"An open bar?" Vic raised her eyebrows. "What a treat."

Emma shook her head. "It's not like you don't have one of those in every room of your house."

Brogan grinned. "Don't you love how she's taken to calling your castle a 'house'?"

"It's social class, darling." Emma affected a snooty tone. "When you're as rich as she is, it's not a limo, just a car. Same goes for castles."

"Emma, my dear." Vic played along, accent shifting into something more closely resembling a BBC commentator. "Let's not share all the secrets with the peasants. We must maintain our position through an air of superiority, only throwing out enough crumbs to the masses as to prevent them from constructing guillotines."

"Right. Right." Emma tried to stay in character but cracked a smile. "I still forget about the guillotines."

Vic sniffed the air. "It's the scent of all your new money that clouds your thinking."

"How do you know it's not *my* new money?" Sophia asked, wanting to get in on some of the humour. She'd seen Vic tense so many times about her wealth or responsibility, it felt good to poke a little fun at themselves.

"I know it's not mine," Brogan said amiably.

"Now, now, I saw a young woman tip you rather handsomely last time I was in here," Vic teased. "Maybe if you rolled up your sleeves and showed off those sailor's biceps you have—"

"No," Emma cut in. "Those are for me, and me only."

"Sad. They are rather impressive," Vic mused with a playful wink at Sophia.

"It hardly seems fair that everyone else has seen them but me," Sophia pouted, but she snuggled a little closer to Vic, resting her head on her shoulder.

"Maybe you'll have to stick around long enough to go sailing with us sometime," Emma offered. "Brogan has a 'sun's out, guns out' policy."

"What's with you Americans and your gun references?" Brogan asked.

Emma pointed across the table. "Vic has more guns than any American I know."

"Yes, but we keep the majority of our arsenal in the armoury."

They all stared at her as if waiting for her to realise that wasn't exactly a logical explanation or even a thing normal people said.

"What?" she asked, and the rest of them finally fell into a fit of giggles.

God, it felt good to laugh. Not just for a second, or at a single joke, but as an extended state of mind.

Was Vic always this way with these people, or had the anger and urgency of the last two days precipitated a sort of break in her? Perhaps it was both. Sophia couldn't help but wonder if this evening had been more than a simple date on the sly.

As Vic casually draped an arm around her shoulders, she got the sense that tonight was a coming out of sorts, or maybe something akin to introducing Sophia to her true family. She certainly understood the importance of a family of choice, at least theoretically, though she'd yet to establish one of her own. On some level that made it feel all the more important that Vic included Sophia in hers, at least for one evening.

She settled into the crook of Vic's arm as the three locals argued good-naturedly about the best place to get scones.

"It's got to be Warkworth," Emma said. "I've done exhaustive research on the subject, and nothing has beaten them."

"You might have an emotional attachment clouding your judgement," Brogan said, then for Sophia's benefit added, "That's where I took her on one of our first dates."

"Then where would you vote for?" Emma asked.

"I think yours are the best in town." Brogan punctuated her answer with a quick kiss on Emma's cheek.

Emma rolled her eyes without actually managing to seem exasperated. "You're a terrible liar."

"No biases there." Vic piled on.

"Then who would you say does them best?" Brogan asked Vic.
"Your mum."

Both Emma and Brogan's mouths dropped as they stared at her for a few seconds before dissolving into laughter again.

"Did you just make a 'your mom' joke?" Sophia asked, craning her neck up to stare at Vic.

"Your Ladyship," Emma gasped in mock horror. "I never knew you had such common vulgarity in you."

"I did." Sophia laughed.

Vic's cheeks turned a bright shade of red. "I didn't . . . I wasn't . . . bloody hell, I was dead serious. Brogan's mother, who's a fine and upstanding member of the community, also happens to make some of the best scones I've ever eaten anywhere."

The others were still laughing too hard to care about the defence, but Sophia shrugged. "I liked it better when I thought you were being—"

Their conversation was interrupted by a jarring blare coming from somewhere on Brogan's body.

"Aw, shite." Brogan jumped up and patted along her pants.

Emma groaned but managed to extract a phone from her wife's back pocket.

Brogan took one look at the screen, and her shoulders fell. "Duty calls."

"Go," Emma said firmly, though her face had gone a little pale. "I'll lock up."

Brogan leaned down to stare into her eyes. "I'm sorry, love."

Emma swallowed whatever words might have been pushing up and kissed her so soundly Sophia looked away until she heard her say, "No apologies. Just come home."

"I love you," Brogan said.

"And I love you."

"What's happening?" Sophia stage-whispered as curiosity finally overtook her.

"Lifeboats—" Brogan started. "I have to cut our evening short. It was a pleasure to meet you, Sophia."

"Lifeboats?" she homed in on the part that made the least sense.

"I'll explain," Vic said, then turning to Brogan, added a sincere and serious, "Thank you."

"Aye." Brogan nodded. "And you."

Then Brogan bolted out the door.

The three of them sat in silence for a long, heavy moment before Emma finally pushed back from the table. "I could use another drink. Would anyone care to join me?"

Vic nodded, and turned to Sophia, who still had no idea what was happening, but she got the sense it warranted more alcohol. "Sure, top me off."

Emma collected their glasses and headed around the bar.

"Are you going to tell me what the hell just happened?" Sophia sat up and searched Vic's eyes. "'Cause it feels like someone died."

"Someone may have. At the very least someone is in grave danger, and Brogan has gone to help," Vic explained solemnly.

"She's like a volunteer firefighter or something?"

"No, she mans the lifeboats."

"And we're back to the part that needs more explaining."

"Most of coastal England has these sort of lifeboat brigades," Emma said as she returned with their drinks. "You're not far off with the volunteer firefighter comparison, but this is like a volunteer Coast Guard, and they take emergency calls all along this section of the North Sea."

"What kind of calls?"

"Could be anything from a disabled fishing trawler to someone swept up in a current. This time of year and time of night, it's likely to be some tourist who got out too far and couldn't get back."

"Or maybe a bachelor party on a boat where someone's had too much to drink and done something dangerous," Vic suggested. "Actually, either way, someone's done something dangerous. You don't call out the lifeboats for anything a first aid kit could fix."

"And when someone does something dangerous on the water around here, it invariably puts people like Brogan in danger." Emma sipped from her glass, and her hand trembled as she set it back down, but her voice remained steady. "She knows these waters better than anyone, and thanks to Vic she's got the safest, most modern lifeboat on the market."

"It's the least I could do," Vic said, her cheeks a little pink, either from embarrassment or maybe the alcohol, as she was taking heavier swigs than she had earlier. "I wish I could go with them."

"I know." Emma's expression tightened. "We all know."

Vic shook her head. "No one else knows. They all see me as sitting up on my throne throwing a little money at a problem, so I don't have to actually care."

"You did more than throw a little cash around," Emma said firmly, then turning to Sophia added, "Our fundraising efforts came up short two years in a row, and the government slashed the budget again, but Vic came through for us and provided the funds to buy not only one, but two new lifeboats."

"Wow. That's generous of the estate," Sophia said, "especially given what you told us about the castle barely breaking even on upkeep these days."

"It would've been a sizeable gift from the duke," Emma admitted, "but it wasn't from the duke or the estate. The money came from Vic's personal trust, the one she'll have to live on if she loses her title."

"Vic," Sophia started, then stopped, not sure where she intended to go. Was she really about to tell a rich woman she shouldn't donate money to save people's lives? She didn't get the chance to decide before Vic waved her off.

"What's the use of having money if I can't use it to help the people who matter? It's all worthless if you don't do something worthwhile with it."

"You know I agree with you on that point," Emma said. "I only meant to point out that you matter, too. You do a lot of good."

"Not enough." Vic's jaw tightened. "Not as much as people like Brogan who put their lives on the line in frigid seas to save strangers. Not nearly as much as I would like to do if I could."

"You can't get on the boats, Vic." Emma's tone made Sophia suspect they'd had this talk before.

"No one moves as quickly or speaks as freely when I'm around," Vic explained. "I'd only slow them down."

"And so would I," Emma said. "Brogan is so appreciative of what you—"

"No," Vic cut her off. "I don't need anyone's appreciation, and I didn't do it for Brogan."

"You didn't?" Sophia asked.

"Well, not completely for her. Brogan is my friend, and that matters, but there are a lot of other people on those boats tonight, and there are people in the water, and people waiting up, praying for their safe return, and they are all my people. I bear a responsibility to every one of them."

Sophia took her hand, wanting desperately to soothe the anguish in her voice.

"I'm fine," Vic said quickly. "I'm sorry I snapped. Emma, forgive me?"

"There's nothing to forgive. You're entitled to your emotions."

Vic snorted softly. "Never mind my emotions, how are you doing?"

Emma smiled faintly. "I'm getting used to this. It's part and parcel of the woman I married. A part of me will always hate it when she does these things, but a much bigger part of me loves her for being the kind of person who does."

Vic stared into her glass. "I could not love thee dear, so much, loved I not honour more."

Sophia stared at her, trying to process the statement, and who it referred to. She turned to Emma for some clarity, but she only shrugged.

"Richard Lovelace," Vic finally said.

"The poet?" Emma laughed.

"Because of what you said about hating that Brogan has to go but loving that she is the kind of person who—" she looked around as if waiting for someone else to finish. "She loves honour more than anything, and if she didn't, she wouldn't be the person worth loving as much as you—god, what do they teach you all in American schools?"

They both burst out laughing again.

"Sorry," Emma said without sounding sorry. "We didn't go to prep schools, and you don't hold your alcohol as well as you think you do if you're drunk-quoting cavalier poets. Sophia, I think it's time you get her to bed."

"It would be my pleasure," Sophia admitted, not sure if she wanted to kiss Vic sweetly on the forehead for that little bit of sentimentality, or thrash her for being the kind of person who spent her own nest egg because she felt survivor's guilt over not being on a lifeboat herself. "Sadly, I'm totally unfit to drive a Land Rover on the left side of country roads, even when completely sober, which I no longer am."

"No worries." Emma rose from the table and carried their glasses back to the bar. Then reaching up, she grabbed a key. "Vic already reserved a room upstairs for tonight."

"She did?" Sophia turned to Vic. "You did?"

Vic nodded. "I'd intended it to be more romantic than you pouring me into bed."

Sophia smiled slowly as her heart rate shifted from sweet-kiss territory and began to beat a little faster. "Don't worry, Your Ladyship. Apparently, we've got all night."

"I'm honestly not inebriated," Vic said as they pushed open the door to their room. Surveying the cosy little attic charm of sloped roofs and pitched dormers lined in exposed Edwardian beams, she couldn't deny the reasons why the Raven served as a favourite getaway for so many city dwellers from London to Edinburgh. The sense of being ensconced in a warm and protective sanctuary offered a stark contrast to her own home.

"I know you're not." Sophia kissed her on the mouth as she kicked the door closed behind them. "If you can handle your father's G&T's you aren't going to fall prey to four hard ciders over the course of five hours."

"Then why did you feel the need to help me up the stairs?"

"Maybe I wanted an excuse to touch you a little sooner." Sophia illustrated her point by sliding her hands from Vic's hips up and over her chest.

"You needn't have waited. Surely you know by now you can have me anywhere and anytime you wish."

Sophia's tone turned pensive. "Sure, let's pretend that's true for one more night."

Vic opened her mouth, but Sophia silenced her with another kiss, this one deeper, more soulful. Running her hands up over her shoulders, she tangled skilled fingers in Vic's long hair, and used her tender strength to hold them together.

Vic luxuriated in the desire building between them. The fire burned as hot as ever, but without the explosion of their earlier encounters she found herself able to better appreciate the warm glow of heat spreading through her.

They broke apart once more to smile at each other, almost

bashful in the awareness of their familiarity. So many times over the last few weeks they'd collided in blind lust, but tonight she wanted to see Sophia clearly. "You're beautiful."

Sophia's eyes ran over her body in response before her gaze flicked over her shoulder. Vic turned to follow the direction, surveying the large bed draped in a feather-down duvet.

Then Sophia's hands were on her face, pulling her back, staring into her eyes just one extra second before bringing their mouths together with that gentle, insistent pressure. Vic felt it to her core, the need pulling at them now. She slid her fingers under Sophia's jacket, easing it back slowly, teasing the sides of her breasts through the thin cotton undershirt before continuing up to caress two strong shoulders. She dug her nails into the exposed skin, enjoying the yield of those tight muscles as she slid the leather down Sophia's arms.

She tried to drape the jacket neatly over a chair back, but at that moment Sophia swept her tongue along Vic's in the most deliciously possessive way, causing her knees to buckle. Sophia took the opportunity to ease her back onto the bed.

Vic accepted the new position gratefully and reached down to unzip her boots.

"Let me," Sophia whispered, catching Vic's foot in her hand.

Vic had to lean back to accommodate Sophia's height as she remained standing. She ran both hands down Vic's leg until she reached the point where black suede met mid-calf.

"Have I mentioned how much I like this relaxed appeal you're exuding tonight?" Sophia asked as she pulled the zipper slowly.

Vic shook her head, mesmerised by her darkening pupils, her knowing touch, the low timbre of her voice.

"I should have." Sophia tipped up the heel of the low boot with one hand and caught Vic's foot with the other as it slipped free. She massaged the arch with deliberate circles before removing her sock and massaging a little more. "I didn't think I could find anything more attractive than those moments when you turn on your commanding persona with all your regal glory, but it turns out I was wrong."

Vic arched an eyebrow. "I'm sorry. I must have misheard. I thought you admitted to being wrong."

The right side of Sophia's mouth curled up. "Maybe *unaware* would be a more apt descriptor."

She gently lowered Vic's foot before releasing it.

Vic let out a little groan at the loss of contact. The disappointment dissipated, though, as Sophia sank rather gracefully to her knees. Vic watched, transfixed, as Sophia brought her other shoe to her chest. Then she kneaded her way up Vic's leg before working back down her thigh and calf once more.

"You see," Sophia continued, "how am I supposed to know how alluring I find a side of you I've never seen before?"

Vic struggled to keep up with the conversation through her increasingly insistent hum of arousal.

"Thank you for bringing me here tonight." Sophia took a more direct approach. "Thank you for trusting me with the people you trust."

A new emotion spread through Vic's chest, or maybe it was a deeper level of an emotion that had been building in her for a long time.

"I would say you're a different person when you're relaxed and open, but you're not. You're the same person I've been attracted to all along, only more so."

"More so?"

She unzipped Vic's remaining boot, pulling it and the sock off, but instead of rising to her feet, she rubbed one hand up each of Vic's legs. "More than I thought possible, which is saying a lot. You're very sexy in that total package kind of way."

She reached the apex of Vic's thighs, running her index finger along the inseam of her pants, before meeting her eyes. Vic could barely breathe, but that didn't stop her from lowering her head to catch Sophia's mouth with her own.

They kissed more fervently this time, and she caught hold of Sophia's shirt, pulling up and toward her, but instead of coming with it, Sophia merely lifted her arms enough for Vic to pull it free. Then she settled back between her legs as the kiss broke.

Vic groaned. "Please. I need you against me."

"Soon," Sophia whispered.

Vic closed her eyes against the urge to slip onto the floor and smother Sophia's body with her own. She did believe patience was a virtue. She'd spent her life waiting, and she liked to think herself better than most at such practices, but at the moment she couldn't remember why.

"Look at me, Victoria." Sophia gave the command softly but seriously. "Early on, I made you kneel before me."

"I remember." Her voice cracked, thick with desire and something weightier.

"It's time for me to repay the favour."

"I don't need that." She shook her head. "I've never asked that of you."

"No." Sophia smiled again. "I get the feeling you've never asked it of anyone, even when you had every right to, and that's why you've earned it."

"Sophia—"

She lifted her finger to her lips, and Vic heeded the unspoken instruction.

"You're special, and not because of where you were born, or what you were born into. In fact, I couldn't even see it fully until you got us away from all the trappings of your life." Sophia flicked open the button atop Vic's waistband and pulled down her zipper. Then urging her hips off the bed, she stripped her legs completely bare. "You've got so much pressing in on you, and you bear it all beautifully."

Vic shook her head again, but this time it felt heavy and uncoordinated to the point she had to fight to keep it from lolling back. Only the sight of Sophia on her knees kept her upright.

"You do. I've grown more than fond of watching you command a room, or a set, or a conversation. I love stoking your anger and your arousal in equal measure. But tonight, seeing you relaxed and unguarded made me realise I've missed out on the pleasure of helping you shed the burdens." Sophia gave a sexy little sigh. "I've seen you worked up, and pent up, controlling

197

and controlled, empowered and wrecked. Tonight, I want to see you undone."

She leaned so close Vic registered the warmth of her breath even amid all the other heat of her need.

"Actually, I don't just want to see it," Sophia corrected. "I want to cause you to come undone."

And then she did.

Her mouth closed on Vic, and everything went silent. Not just the voices in the room, but also the ones inside Vic's head. The whispers of insecurity, the echoes of shouts, even the subtle hum of trauma fell into blissful silence. For once there was no inner monologue, there was nothing but Sophia.

It wasn't the first time her body had overtaken her brain, but never before had the transformation been so complete, and never had her heart stayed steady in the transfer.

All the best sensations surged through her as every sense heightened, but she hadn't tipped into the usual oblivion Sophia inspired. She remained fully present as Sophia worked one hand up underneath her sweater. Could Sophia feel her rapid heartbeat? Did she know it beat for her? Not only for the wonders she was working with her mouth, but for everything she'd been tonight, for everything they could be together.

Sophia eased her other hand between the intersection of their bodies and slipped inside her. Vic lifted her hips, her body acting on some primal recognition of where this woman belonged, indeed where so much of her had already taken up residence. She sighed with her whole being as the visceral reactions cresting in her melded with the emotions she'd worked all night not to call into the light. Now there was nothing but light. More than a warm glow, or a raging blaze, this kind touched everything, revealed everything, illuminated everything, and still continued to spread.

Breathing became a secondary concern as the pressure in her chest dwarfed the pressure coiling at her core. She sank her hands into the dark swirls of Sophia's silken locks as they spilled across her trembling thighs. She clung to her for so many reasons now: stability, need, fear of falling in ways that transcended the physical. But the rush didn't overwhelm her or sweep her away. It built from her toes, from the tips of her fingers and the top of her scalp. It gathered, spreading, crawling from one nerve ending to the next with a steady certainty, a realisation sweeping forward on the waves of her impending release.

Sophia continued to open her, to push her, to seep into her as Vic's awareness grew, like a thousand pinpricks in a dark sky opening rapidly, each one showing her a little more. The vast vulnerability of it all might have caused her to cave in on herself if not for the woman holding her upright and urging her forward.

Undone.

That's what Sophia had asked for. To take the weight off, not to drop it, or let it drop in a fallen moment, but to knowingly, willingly, deliberately lay it down before her. Sophia could bear it. She was strong enough and sure enough to catch them both. Vic knew those things with the same certainty she knew the other thing, the bigger thing burning through her now. The two certainties were inseparable.

She gasped as her heart gave a little jump that radiated through her core and out along her limbs.

Sophia remained relentless in her attention. Her mouth, her hands, they beckoned Vic forward, higher, closer to the place she hadn't intended to go but no longer tried to run from.

Then with one more push, one more sweep of Sophia's tongue, one more knowing caress, Vic surrendered and splintered. All the pieces of her resistance crumbled in one sharp, sobbing cry. She hung suspended in that moment without any successive waves or diminishing returns. She existed purely as pleasure, purely vulnerable, purely safe, and purely sated.

There was nothing left but the absolute. Maybe that's why this time felt so different, without the wind down or even the gentle easing back to earth.

She wasn't falling anymore because she had already fallen, thoroughly and completely, for Sophia.

Chapter Twelve

The shrill ring of a phone jolted Sophia awake. She sat up in a strange bed, which wasn't at all unusual given her work and travel schedule, but she usually needed a few minutes to orient herself. This morning, however, the warm body next to her provided an anchor, both physically and mentally. She took a second to stare at the stunning, sleeping form, classically beautiful and heart-achingly unguarded.

"Vic." Sophia placed a hand on the subtle indent at the small of her back. She fought against the urge to push the comforter lower and seek a little comfort of her own. Only the bright slant of light through the dormer window and another teeth-rattling ring stopped her. "Your phone is ringing."

"I don't have a phone with me." Vic rolled over, all golden and glorious in her bare-chested grogginess. "It's yours."

The sharp sound struck again, and Sophia pressed her thumb to the bridge of her nose. "I wouldn't choose that ringtone even if someone held a gun to my head."

Vic sat up, eyes still squinting against the light as she swivelled her head to survey the room. The ring sounded again, and her face went pale. "It's the room phone. Oh god, Brogan."

Vic sprang from the bed and snatched the receiver. "Hello?"

"Oh shite, it's you, you're okay." Vic sighed heavily. "Yes, but after last night I feared . . . never mind. Are you offering room service?"

The slight smile that had started to curl her lips faded, and Sophia scooted to the edge of the bed, trying to hear what Brogan said.

"Right, well." Vic grimaced. "Archie? The castle? We can . . . Oh blimey, the gardens too?"

Sophia's stomach tightened. Whatever it was wasn't great. All the tension she'd drained from Vic's beautiful shoulders last night returned.

"I'm sorry you've all been—" Vic rubbed a hand over her face. "No, I'm sure they'll do. We'll be right down."

Vic dropped the phone back onto its cradle and turned to face Sophia, her expression tight.

"What is it?"

She shook her head and sat back on the edge of the bed. "Let's try this again. Good morning."

"Good morning," Sophia managed as the buzz of tension hovered around them.

"You were amazing last night." Vic kissed her softly on the mouth. "You are always amazing, but last night was something I will cherish always. I hope you—"

"Vic, you're scaring me," Sophia interrupted. As much as she agreed with her assessment of the previous night, something felt horribly off this morning, and she didn't want anything sugarcoated for her. "What's going on? Who was on the phone?"

"Brogan," Vic said calmly. "She made it safely home last night, as did the rest of the lifeboat crew, but she was awoken after what I can only imagine felt like a very short hour of sleep by a call from her brother."

"Which one? Doesn't she have, like, seventeen of them?"

Vic managed a weak smile. "Archie first, and then Charlie."

"Oh good," Sophia said sarcastically as the two names stood out in her mind. "The two who work for your family."

"Unfortunately, yes. It seems the castle is surrounded by reporters. Apparently poor Archie got a slew of inappropriate questions about you when he arrived at work a few hours early this morning."

"About me? I've never met the man."

"No, but apparently the reporters are eager enough to pounce on anything out of the ordinary, and a lone man in a suit arriving at the castle, briefcase in hand, shortly after dawn, set them off. Perhaps they mistook him for a lawyer or a public relations person. I'm not certain, but apparently they suspected he'd been brought in to extinguish a fire."

"Did they get word of what happened on set yesterday?"

"I don't know what they know, but something's made them think there's a scandal brewing, so Archie called Brogan, afraid there might be a problem with Emma's movie. Emma, having a more complete picture, immediately called Charlie about moving my car, but he didn't have the keys anymore. He went back to the castle intending to sneak in through the back way only to find the garden entrance completely surrounded as well."

"So, Brogan called you about the keys?"

"I wish." Vic kissed her forehead this time. "Archie may've been the first person to draw a connection to Emma, but he wasn't the last."

The tension knotting Sophia's stomach ratcheted up another level. "They went to Emma's and found your car?"

Vic nodded. "The town's overrun with snooping press, but the Friday Club has managed to gather downstairs, and as we speak, they're no doubt hatching cloak-and-dagger plans to smuggle us out of here."

Sophia groaned. "Just what we need, amateur sleuths fighting amateur paparazzi. What a clusterfuck."

"My sentiments exactly, even if I've never used that particular term before, but at this point I fear amateur help might be better than no help at all. Plus, Brogan's making coffee."

"I hate that we've dragged your friends into the crossfire after they were so wonderful to us last night, but you may be right. Friends who hold off the press and brew you coffee are the best kind of friends to have."

"Indeed." Vic rose resolutely and began to gather her clothes from the night before. Sophia followed suit, hating the sense of

202

dread that chilled her more than the early morning air. Vic pulled on her pants and shirt, then turned back to Sophia as she did the same. "You know I'm going to protect you, right?"

Sophia's chest tightened at both the words and the sincerity in which they were spoken. No one had ever said such a thing to her, at least not anyone who meant it, and the fact that Vic had infinitely more to lose in this situation only made the offer more meaningful. It was also why she couldn't allow Vic to make any such promises. "Your chivalry is endlessly endearing, but I can take care of myself."

Vic smiled brightly for the first time all morning. "I never doubted that you could. I only meant to let you know that this time you don't have to do so alone."

Then Vic kissed her again, quickly enough to forestall any argument, but not deeply enough to burn away the sense of gravity building around them now.

"Good morning," Vic called cheerfully as they reached the bottom of the stairway that led from their room to the bar area below. She needed only a cursory glance to see all the usual suspects had come to her aid. Brogan stood behind the bar with a pot of coffee in one hand and a tea kettle in the other. Emma sat with the rest of the Friday Club in their usual booth. Diane, Esther, Tom, and Will had all greeted her warmly, as if she'd casually dropped in. Despite the bright light of morning and the fear building in her core, she found their constancy comforting. "You all remember my friend, Sophia."

"Aye," a few voices said, and Diane patted the seat next to her. "Come join us, my dears. I brought scones."

"Coffee or tea?" Brogan asked as they passed by.

"Coffee, please Jesus the strong kind, as black as my soul?" Sophia asked.

Brogan grinned as she poured.

"Tea for me, please." The last thing she needed was something to make her jittery. She'd done an admirable job of remaining calm upstairs, but it hadn't felt quite as real when they'd been barricaded in their little sanctuary. Now, in this place, with these people, she was faced with the reality of how none of this was just about her. If a scandal touched this town, it would touch every one of them. Already Emma's relative anonymity had been shattered. Despite her success in the literary world, she'd never been one to do major tours or television interviews, which afforded her a certain ability to move about the area largely unrecognised. If she had her face splashed across tabloids and celebrity gossip shows, she'd no doubt see changes for the worse in her quietly introverted existence.

And what of Brogan, would they hound her as well? Would she be able to go about her various jobs with the same casual confidence she'd always carried with her? How many headaches would she face if cameras and callous reporters pushed into her space? And the other locals, would they still want to gather in places overrun with gossip-seekers and gawkers?

Vic took a seat and then accepted one of the scones Esther pushed across the table toward her, but she didn't have much of an appetite. She'd had a hard enough time trying to figure out how she'd protect Sophia, and now she had even more people to worry about.

"We've got some rough ideas," Brogan said, coming around the bar and setting their drinks on the table.

"It seems easy enough to explain one of you being here all night," Emma said calmly. "Vic, everyone knows we socialise, and Sophia, they seem to have drawn an easy connection between your acting and my script."

"Yes, and they do seem to be searching more for Sophia," Esther said, then blushed. "May I call you Sophia?"

"Of course. I'm generally called much worse."

Tom snorted as if he'd heard a few of those things but knew enough not to mention any at the moment.

"The way we figure it," Will started, in his slow easy cadence, "is the only way the press has something substantial to chew on is if they know you were here together, and we've yet to find anything to suggest they do."

Vic blew out a heavy breath. They weren't caught yet, at least not fully. She could still offer Sophia some shelter.

"They have traced the Land Rover back to the castle," Emma said. "We'll need a cover story if we say Sophia drove out by herself."

"Say she borrowed it from the castle," Diane offered. "She can drive it back in like nothing's amiss. It's not as if the duke doesn't have enough cars to go lending them out to his guests."

"The only problem with that story is she doesn't know how to drive it, and as soon as she tries to back out of our place, they'll know something's up."

"You can't drive a manual transmission?" Tom asked.

Sophia grimaced. "I haven't for over ten years, and never on the left side of the road. I could probably pick it up quickly if I had time, but it doesn't sound like I have time."

The others all frowned and seemed to think on this a bit.

"I've got the boat," Brogan offered. "The press is all camped out down by our house. We could sneak you out the back way, through the beer garden, and down some side streets to the estuary. From there we'd get you below decks and sail up the coast, then bring you ashore someplace remote."

"And I could drive out and meet you all in my car," Esther offered. "No one would follow me anywhere."

"But you'd still have to get them back to the castle somehow, and if they roll up together . . ."

"I'll take one of them in my car," Diane said. "We'd space out their arrivals."

"Actually, I could go to the stables." Sophia seemed to warm to the plan. "That's where we're supposed to be shooting, and I doubt the press is waiting there, but if they are, I'd just walk into work like I do every morning. Nothing out of the ordinary."

"But surely if you and Vic were both out all night, they'll put two and two together?"

"They may try," Sophia admitted, "but they won't be able to prove anything, and it's a hard sell if they placed Vic here all night and me on set miles away without anyone seeing me leave here. Besides, I've made my living playing cool and manipulative characters. I know how to shut people down. Go ahead—try me."

Esther and Diane giggled at each other as Sophia schooled her expression into something resembling dry and distant.

"Ms. LeBlanc," Diane tested, "did you spend the night at the Raven with Victoria?"

Sophia gave her a disdainful stare and bored sigh. "Victoria who?"

The dead tone, or perhaps the emptiness in Sophia's eyes sent a cold wind straight to Vic's core, and she pushed back from the table.

Emma regarded her with sympathy. Did she see the old wound opening again, or did she simply understand the choices that lay ahead? None of them would be easy, and none of them offered any real comfort. And while Vic had known that all along, nothing in her distant or recent past prepared her to hear those words from Sophia's mouth. They might not have something lasting, or even something worth fighting for, but they were something to each other. They had something together. She would never be able to pretend they didn't, and it hurt that Sophia could.

"No." She rose to her feet.

Everyone turned to stare at her.

"I won't lie," she finally croaked out.

Sophia reached for her hand, but she stepped back.

"I won't," she said again, trying to force the frantic edge from her voice. "So far, the press hasn't linked us together, and I'll do nothing to help them along in those equations. The duke, his family, and his staff do not comment on the personal affairs of anyone in our household or our guests. That's the official line, and I'll have no problem delivering it, but I will not lie."

"Vic," Sophia whispered.

She shook her head. "I spent years lying about who I was, and it almost killed me. You may craft your stories and plot your escape. I want you to make your choices based on what you need, but I'm going to walk out of here right now, go pick up my car, and drive back to my house."

Brogan eyed her with a measured amount of respect. "They'll pounce before you get halfway down the block."

"I'll give them all the truth that's mine to give and nothing more," Vic said gravely. "I'll say I spent last night in the company of my friends, which I did. I consumed alcohol in moderation. When the lifeboats were called out from the local station, I took a room, where I spent the night, and had breakfast with the same friends before returning home. If they have any further questions about any other guests at the inn or at my home, I will suggest they address them to the proper staff, though I'd expect they won't get far."

Then she turned toward Sophia. "I may not share your talents for subterfuge, but please don't harbour any doubts about my appreciation for them. I fully endorse your use of any means you find appropriate to protect your career or your honour."

Sophia gave a bitter laugh, but Vic pressed on.

"My departure will undoubtedly offer you more and better options, and I trust you'll chose one that affords you both safety and anonymity until we have the chance to speak again."

Sophia seemed to recognise her resolve because even though her eyes burned with unspoken argument, she merely pursed her lips.

Then Vic expanded her attention to include the others, seeing on their faces a mix of fear, confusion, and admiration. "You all have shown me a great loyalty this morning, a loyalty I've never been afforded even by members of my own family. To say I am at your service and in your debt would be both an understatement and overly formal, but I do hope you know how proud I am to have friends of your calibre."

"You'd do the same for any one of us, love," Diane said.

Vic smiled at the truth of the statement. "I only hope I'm in a position to do so in the future."

"I'll walk with you." Emma scooted out from the booth. "It's my house those vultures are gathered around, and me strolling up with you will add credibility to your story."

Her heart ached a little more at the offer, knowing full well that facing a horde of reporters unprepared was Emma's actual nightmare, and yet she hadn't hesitated to do so for her.

"Thank you, but first may I have a private word with Ms. LeBlanc?"

"Of course, take all the time you need."

Sophia rose quietly and followed her into a hallway leading toward the kitchen. Once they were out of earshot of the others, Vic stopped and faced her. She didn't even get a chance to open her mouth before Sophia tore into her.

"If you think I'm about to come back here and make out with you before you fall on your sword for me, you are wildly mistaken."

"I beg your pardon?"

"Cut the upper crust bullshit. I'm not impressed with your manners or your vocabulary anymore."

"Not at all?"

"Stop being charming. I didn't ask you to protect me, and if you think I'm going to reward that kind of over-the-top nobility, you're wrong because it's crazy and honestly a little patronising. I'm a grown-ass woman who made her own decisions last night, and I can damn well make them this morning. And another thing—"

Vic burst out laughing.

Sophia placed a hand on each hip and directed her most caustic stare at her. "You think this is some kind of a joke?"

"Not at all. I'm just happy."

"Happy?"

"Yes." She risked both life and limb by stepping closer and wrapping an arm around Sophia's waist. "I'm happy you think me chivalrous and not dumb or cowardly."

"You might be those things, too."

"I may indeed—" Vic touched her forehead to Sophia's, "—but I promise you, I'm not doing this to protect you. I'm doing it to protect myself. I've dealt with a great many things and faced a great many losses in my life, but none of them would wound me as badly as pretending I don't know you."

Sophia sighed and melted into her embrace. "I hate this, and I hate how fucking good you are."

"I'm not good. I'm terribly selfish and entitled." Vic kissed her temple, breathing in her scent deeply as if it might be her last chance. "I simply don't want to have to keep secrets in order to keep you."

"You know this can't continue much—"

"I know nothing except I intend to see you this evening at the castle. If you need to impart any more hard truths, perhaps you'll do me the courtesy of waiting until I'm in a safe place with a stiff drink in my hand."

"You can't keep buying time indefinitely."

Vic smiled against her cheek. "We don't know that for sure. I'm very rich."

"Rich enough to bend the rules of time, space, and celebrity gossip?"

She kissed Sophia quickly one last time. "Rich enough to try."

Chapter Thirteen

"Thank you again for the lift and the scones." Sophia tapped the top of the foil bundle Esther and Diane had loaded full of pastries. She glanced around the nearly deserted entrance to the nature preserve. "I think you managed to get me here undetected. I don't know how I'll ever repay you."

"Tickets to your next premiere?" Diane asked.

"An introduction to that handsome Scotsman playing opposite you?" Esther suggested.

"Deal." She would've gladly paid a lot more not to have to deal with reporters this morning.

"We're only teasing, dear," Esther said, probably reading the exhaustion on her face. "We're only too happy to help a friend."

"Yes," Diane added, "getting to play chauffeur to the stars is merely a bonus."

"Bless you," Sophia said sincerely.

"Take care of yourself."

"Get some rest."

"And eat something!"

She waved as they backed out of the nature preserve shouting various bits of motherly advice.

"New fans?" a voice asked from behind her.

She turned to find Talia leaning against the stone wall of the stable. "They might be new friends."

"Lucky you," Talia said drolly. "You're going to need as many of those as you can get around here."

"That bad?"

Talia shrugged. "Come on inside and pull up a hay bale."

Sophia sighed, wishing she could go back and follow all of Diane and Esther's advice. Instead she followed Talia into the stable, taking a seat beside her on one block of straw, and setting the package of scones on one in front of them. "I brought breakfast."

Talia grabbed one greedily. "It's the least you can do after the last twenty-four hours of shit storm you've put me through."

"I didn't exactly start it."

"You didn't exactly end it," Talia said without any real bite to the comment. "I might've strangled you on sight if I didn't have a pretty good suspicion of where you've been all night."

"How'd you know I'd end up here?"

"Criminals always return to the scene of the crime," Talia mumbled around a mouthful of scone, then swallowed. "Also, this is flipping delicious. Are they angel cakes from heaven?"

"Scones, from my new friends."

"You get new friends and a new food source while I get a sleepless night of fielding calls from studio execs, press coordinators, and one smarmy reporter who somehow got hold of my personal number."

Sophia grimaced. "I hate that, I really do, but if you're waiting for me to apologise for something Brian screwed up, you're going to be here a long time."

"No, I'm actually on Team Sophia on that particular front." She cradled the scone in her hands like a precious treasure. "I didn't appreciate your lover/landlord pulling rank on my film schedule, but if Brian can't stick to the screenplay as I freaking wrote it, then we absolutely need an intimacy coordinator."

"For what it's worth, I would've shot it exactly how you wrote it. We don't need any more male gaze on this story of female empowerment."

211

"Thank you, and the studio came down on our side. They want to send an intimacy coordinator up from London this afternoon."

"That's great. We can get back to work."

"If only." Talia sighed heavily. "Last I heard from Brian he was still refusing, and now he's not even answering his phone, which makes me worry he's gone on a bender."

Sophia pinched the bridge of her nose. "This morning keeps getting better and better."

"No joke." Talia shoved the remainder of the scone in her mouth and picked up another one, leaving Sophia to suspect she might be starting a bender of her own, only with carbs instead of booze. "Right? Like it wasn't bad enough juggling the estate reps and the studio reps, but then about 4 a.m., I started to get calls and texts from the PR reps saying they were fielding reports about you having gone on a date with a local woman."

Sophia swore under her breath. "So, someone did see us?"

"Yeah, that was my first thought, but something didn't quite add up because no one mentioned Vic. Only you."

"Emma actually said the same thing this morning. Even though they found Vic's car at her house, the press kept asking about me."

"I didn't realise they found Vic's car. How did you two get back? No, wait, the less I know the better, but surely if they were looking for you and found her, someone is going to do the math."

Sophia felt a little woozy. "But you don't think they've figured it out yet?"

Talia shook her head. "No, that's actually one of the weirdest parts in an overwhelmingly off-kilter couple of days. All the requests for comments or confirmation were almost stupidly vague. Things like you went on a date, or you were spotted leaving the castle with someone, or maybe you spent the night some-where away from the set."

"That hardly seems newsworthy, given my history and the public perception."

"I agree. So, the last time I got a call I pushed back a little, and it turns out the lead was so shallow it probably wouldn't have gotten any traction at all if not for the credibility of its origin point."

The dull ache at the base of Sophia's skull suggested she wasn't going to like this part at all. "Brian called the press as some sort of payback?"

Talia shook her head. "That would make sense given how mad Vic made him, but he would've thrown you both under the bus, and I'm not sure the locals would've given him the time of day."

Sophia's jaw tightened "Who then?"

"Apparently," Talia gave a little shiver, "the call came from inside the castle."

Sophia's blood rushed through her ears to the point where she had to strain to hear Talia's next comment.

"And I get the sense from the way everyone around here snapped to attention that the tip didn't come from some random groundskeeper or scullery maid. I may be wrong, but the way these reporters are dancing around, I suspect the leak came from someone high up on staff, or even a member of the family."

"Or a member of staff working on the orders of a member of the household." She ground her teeth. This had James's finger-prints all over it, and James worked for the duchess. So much for not commenting on the personal affairs of castle guests. Had it pained him a little bit to break long-standing protocol, or had he been all too happy to heed that order from the lady of the house? She'd have to ask when she pinned his uptight ass to the wall.

She stood and took two steps before Talia caught her by the wrist and pulled her back. "Calm down."

"Oh, I'm calm. Dead calm."

"Okay, then you need to get to alive calm before you fly off the handle."

"I make no promises about keeping anyone alive."

"I'll lock you in this stable if I have to, because as much as I'd love to see you knock a few snooty bastards down a peg, the

213

production is in a precarious position, and don't think I didn't notice all of our problems started when the Ice Queen-Mother waltzed into the castle."

Sophia folded her arms across her chest and stewed.

"We still have a job to do," Talia pushed. "The filming schedule is at a standstill, the studio is already forking out extra time and resources, our director's gone AWOL, and hey, no judgement here, but you also seem to be sleeping with the daughter of the people who own our set. The duchess is holding a lot of cards here, and we're sitting on a pair of twos. Do you really want to call her bluff?"

She wasn't wrong. As much as Sophia's insides screamed in frustration, nothing Talia had said fell flat. And honestly, Sophia had swallowed more with less at stake over the years. There wasn't any real reason she shouldn't do the same right now. The duchess may have the upper hand with the press and procedures, but Sophia could at least pull the movie back on track.

She could go to Brian and apologise. She could bury her pride and get the scenes on film. She could get the job done and get the hell out of here before anything else had a chance to blow up. The duchess would disappear if Sophia would only stay away from Vic for the duration of her time here. All she'd have to do was keep her head down, her eyes on the target, and her hands to herself. She'd made a career out of the former two skills, and while she'd never been a fan of abstinence, she'd also never let any woman get in the way of what she'd set out to do with her life.

Why was she even debating her options when the choice before her had a clear answer supported by an abundance of arguments in its favour?

Vic.

Vic was the reason she hadn't surrendered yet. Vic, with her beautiful eyes and her idealistic morals. Vic, who kept doing the right thing even when it was also the absurd thing. Vic, who cared so damn much for so many people and still looked at Sophia as if she were more treasured than the whole lot of them. Vic, who would go back to getting pushed around by her mother and her title until they ground her into dust. "Who does that to her own daughter?"

"What?" Talia tilted her head as if trying to make sense of the non-sequitur.

"The duchess called the press on me knowing full well I was with her daughter. She knows what getting caught would do to Vic's life, to her sense of self, to her prospects for the future. She knows how much Vic has sacrificed and hidden and been hurt by people she trusted. She knows how awful it was the last time someone dragged her daughter through a public scandal, how much it broke Vic's spirit, and she risked the exact same devastation again. Who does that to her own kid?"

"Someone who doesn't cede power easily." Talia's eyes filled with sympathy. "Look, this movie we're making is a fictional representation, but you've known all along what the stakes were for your character, and you got into the role by drawing from Vic. Surely you saw the similarities. You get people, you understand their darkness better than anyone I've ever worked with, and you've had the script for this play from the beginning. How did you expect this to end?"

"I didn't think about what I was doing with Vic as part of some larger machinations or Macbeth cosplay. I didn't think about anything at all."

"Maybe you should start thinking, because Vic's family isn't going to let her go easily."

Sophia shook her head. "Why do you assume they'd have to let her go?"

"Because either they will, or you will." Talia stood up. "Those are the only two ways this ends, and you might want to think about which way you want this to go before you decide to storm the castle."

"Your Ladyship. Your Ladyship!" Reporters still shouted from outside the gate, and tourists turned to stare as she handed off the keys to the Land Rover to a pocked-faced young man with a stereotypical deer-in-the-headlights sort of expression.

A camera flashed to her right. She turned to stare down the perpetrator, who quickly jammed a phone in his pocket and scuttled back into the crowd. Archie and Charlie hadn't been wrong about the throngs of reporters, first at Emma's and then at the castle. Honestly, she hadn't known there were enough reporters in the entire region to create such a stir, but then again, she'd seen a crew from Edinburgh on her way through Newpeth, so maybe this wasn't just a local story anymore.

Her stomach lurched for about the tenth time in as many minutes, but she kept her chin up and her eyes forward as she marched into the courtyard and through the main hall. She'd managed a short interview back in Amberwick, giving the assembled press the official line on her night out. She'd kept her cool and hoped she'd managed to appear bemused by all the attention. Sadly, she'd had plenty of practice at handling unwanted and unwarranted ambushes after Robert outed her a few years ago, but the prospect of returning to that sort of vigilance as a way of life made her stomach do another somersault.

Weaving between staff and visitors alike, she bounded up the stairs and made a sharp turn toward the residence. A security guard nodded his recognition and stepped aside but had the good sense not to say anything. Surely everyone on staff knew what was happening, at least on the outside, but none of them could know about the battle ripping apart her insides, and she preferred to keep it that way.

She'd held herself together in front of Sophia and Emma and the reporters, but with each step another tiny part of her resolve cracked. Her feet fell heavy on stone floors, and each strike of her heel served as a drumbeat for her breakdown chant. "Oh god, oh god, oh god."

She didn't even know where she was going until she skidded to a stop at the half-open door to the family chapel. She stared at the room she hadn't entered in months. Suddenly, now felt like as good a time as any to call on a higher power.

Jaw clenched, fists balled, she stepped inside. Her eyes adjusted slowly to the muted light filtered through stained glass. She trained her gaze on the large cross hanging above the altar.

"Oh God," she said more pointedly. "Please do not do this to me . . . again."

She sank into the closest pew and hung her head. Her shoulders shook as the tension she'd carried there drained from her body.

"Please," she muttered again, then glanced up. "Don't make me choose. I'm not strong enough to do this again."

Someone cleared their throat behind her, and she jumped up, wheeling around frantically to find her father standing in the doorway.

"Sorry to startle you," he said, his tone soft and sad. "I'll admit, I didn't know how to announce my presence amid such piety. Anglicans aren't generally prone to such passionate displays of faith."

She rolled her eyes.

"I didn't mean to make light," he said gently. "I envy your faith right now. It'll serve you well if you hold onto it as you step into your future roles."

She sank back into the pew. "I think what you meant to say was these little outbursts make me *less* fitted to my future roles."

"No. I may not be the most passionate or powerful speaker, but I'm a man who chooses his words carefully." He nodded to the pew. "May I join you?"

She shrugged and slid over to make space for him.

"I gather you've had a complex morning."

"That's a delicate way to describe my current state."

"What would be a more apt description?"

"I don't know." A million incomplete thoughts flooded her brain. "I don't know so many things, but especially how to spin my personal life into something palatable to the masses, which serves as yet another reminder of how ill-suited I am to the mantle on my shoulders."

He frowned, then smiled. "Good."

"Good?"

"The role you're facing is a great paradox," he said in the same patrician tone he'd used to try to explain advanced concepts like fishing treaties or deeded land rights when she'd been a little too young to fully understand them. "Those who feel entitled to assume the position and the responsibilities therein are generally the ones who least deserve it, whereas those who have most protested their worth tend to wear the responsibility best."

She met his eyes, only a shade or two paler than her own. "Not you. You've been both worthy and have worn it well."

"I'm glad you think so," he said, a weariness seeping into his voice. "It reflects well on a man to have his children see him in an idealistic light, but I fear for your sake I must draw back the veil a bit, because I most certainly did not wear my title well for the first few years of my inheritance."

She started to protest, but the sadness in his smile drew her up short.

"Your grandfather was a stern man with strong opinions."

She chuckled. "I remember."

"You remember him as a grandfather, and that's quite enough for you, but as a son I always wilted in his shadow. He seemed so much larger than life, and I never quite lived up to his model of leadership. I was too much in my head, too much in my books. I wasn't quick or decisive. I took time to ponder, to weigh, to measure."

"All the things I don't do?"

"All the things *he* didn't do. It made me feel rather inadequate by comparison, and when he passed, I felt so unprepared to assume his place that I gave serious thought to abdication."

"No."

"I did," he said plainly. "I met with three different solicitors, which is why I know how muddy your own inheritance situation is."

"I assumed you'd done the research on my behalf."

"Perhaps a better father would have, and even I would have eventually, but at first I couldn't see past my own fear. Even after

I learned how hard it would be to separate our family from the title, or the title from our ownings, I still may've tossed it all and run if not for your mother's steady hand."

Victoria's stomach clenched at the mention of her mother, but her father continued in his soothing voice.

"She took to her role much better than I. She had even less preparation, but she possessed an iron will and a determination to learn. She made some early blunders, and the press was unrelenting in their criticism, but she refused to be cowed by it. She merely rededicated herself time and time again. She became an expert hostess and studied everything from state protocol to land management laws. Mostly, though, she studied people. She could examine situations I'd taken for granted my whole life and immediately discern all the hidden power dynamics."

"That's not surprising," Vic said dryly.

"She became my confidante and my most trusted advisor. She challenged me to be better without making me feel incompetent. Slowly we developed a partnership that spoke to each of our strengths and public images."

There was the whole public image concept again to pile on her current state of crisis. There was no getting around how essential the concept was to their way of life.

"Because of her I never actually had to learn how to be a duke in my own right, at least not as a stand-alone. From the day I ascended to the title I was merely half of the Duke and Duchess of Northland. I was part of a pair, a unit, indivisible. Looking back now, I realise the only real decision I ever had to make on my own was the one to marry your mother."

Her chest ached again. "You were very lucky to be able to make that decision for yourself."

He frowned. "You've had a much harder road than I in that area, but the world is changing quickly. You've still got time to find the person who will best help you settle in and bear the burden of your inheritance."

Sophia's face jumped into her memory, those dark eyes staring into hers last night as if seeing her for the first time. The image left her feeling anything but settled. Still, it did make her feel something powerful, something transformational.

"But what if my person, the one who challenges me to be better without ever making me feel lacking is . . . I don't know, is there more to the partnership than social acumen?" She shook her head. She couldn't keep dancing around the issue any longer, not here in a chapel beside the only person in the world who understood the stakes. "Are you in love with Mother?"

He stiffened beside her, and she glanced up to see an aggrieved expression on his face. "I won't pretend it doesn't hurt a little that you had to ask, but yes, I am. I am not an overly demonstrative man, and maybe I don't wear my feelings on my sleeve the way others do—"

"No," she said quickly, "I didn't mean to imply you were somehow deficient. Of course you show love. My question, I only meant . . . Mother can be, well—"

"Ah." He relaxed a little more into the pew as his expression softened. "Your mother is not an easy woman, but that's all the more reason to admire her. She's strong and complex, and she's of her own mind. A weaker woman would've wilted under the kind of scrutiny this life carries; a weaker woman would've allowed me to surrender to my own weaknesses as well. I never wanted an ornamental rose to rest on my arm. I fell in love with your mother not in spite of her strong personality, but because of it." He turned to her and smiled. "And I'm glad I did, because I see so much of her best qualities in you."

She rolled her eyes.

"Don't." He placed a hand atop hers. "Don't let your conflicts blind you to her best qualities. If you do, it'll be harder for you to respect those same traits in yourself."

"I'm nothing like her."

"She is strong-willed and principled, but also graceful and gifted at reading people."

She snorted. "You must be in love to see those things. I've never once considered her a people-person."

He laughed softly. "Understanding what drives people and letting them control you are very different things. Learning the difference isn't easy, but it's an invaluable skill."

His words wiggled their way into her brain. "Even if I turn around and use it against her?"

He kissed her forehead gently. "Especially then."

Sophia crossed one leg over the other as she relaxed onto the settee in Vic's sitting room. She hadn't turned on the lights, but the cleaning staff had drawn back the curtains to offer a view of the courtyard and the evening sun hanging low above the castle walls. She could've gotten used to this vista. In fact, a part of her had grown accustomed to it without meaning to. She felt a little pinprick of annoyance at the fact that she'd even felt comfortable letting herself into this room, or anywhere in a castle, compounded by another quick shot of embarrassment that her comfort level hadn't sent up red flags sooner. It wasn't as if she hadn't had fleeting moments of awareness along the way. Maybe if she'd let herself dwell on how little she belonged in this place instead of always pushing those thoughts away or quelling them with her raw appetite for Vic, she might have saved everyone from what had to be done next. Then again, how could she ever have expected to develop the type of feelings she'd felt for Vic last night and this morning? Would she have undone them if she could?

No. Regrets carried no more appeal than apologies, which left her with little to do now but wait. Thankfully, the duchess's social graces lent her to punctuality if nothing else.

She pushed open the door to the sitting room exactly as the large clock down the hallway struck eight o'clock.

Sophia didn't rise as the duchess entered the room. She didn't move at all, taking the moment before her presence was noticed to look past the dark pantsuit and imperial posture to survey the woman's profile. She wore her hair back from her pale face with a severity that accentuated her high brow. Her chin and nose, though, weren't as angular as they'd seemed head on. In fact, she had Vic's chin, or perhaps it was the other way around. The way she lifted it and squared her shoulders when she realised she was being watched also reminded Sophia of Vic. Was that where she'd learned the move? Was it meant to project strength outward, or offer a form of self-protection? With Vic, she'd always suspected the latter. How many times had she needed to protect herself from this woman?

"Your Grace." Sophia finally rose. "Thank you for joining me."

The duchess arched an already high eyebrow. "Ms. LeBlanc. I merely received a message that my presence was requested in my daughter's private quarters."

"And you didn't expect to find me here?" Sophia smiled coyly. "Why ever not?"

A hint of fire sparked in Lady Penchant's dark eyes.

"I thought that perhaps since it's just the two of us tonight, we could move past the pretense. How about we start by not pretending we aren't both aware how many nights I've spent in here." Sophia gestured toward the settee. "Please, have a seat."

She didn't move. "Where's Victoria?"

"Working," Sophia said. "Undoubtedly trying to find a way to put out the fire you and James set with your phone calls this morning."

The duchess pursed her lips.

"Did you not know we'd put that together? Surely someone was meant to, right? You didn't give anyone enough information to actually catch Vic and me together, so I suspect that wasn't the point. Maybe you wanted to remind us you had the power, and that's why you made little attempt to hide your tracks. Or perhaps you're not used to needing to hide them. Everyone around here jumps when you snap. Speaking of which, would you like a drink?"

"No." The duchess's eyes narrowed as her surprise faded back into a detached sort of disdain. "I don't think I'll be staying long enough to enjoy one."

"Just as well," Sophia shrugged. "I'll admit I'm not much of a bartender. I'm used to having my drinks poured for me. Maybe that's one of the few things you and I have in common. We both expect a certain amount of deference in our dealings. Is that what offended you deeply enough to wound your own daughter? That I didn't scurry away when you fired the first shot across my bow?"

"Oh dear, did you think that had to do with you?" The duchess laughed lightly. "One must get used to being the centre of attention in your line of work, but I'm afraid you'll find me much less prone to fits of passion."

"That's certainly not the impression you've given over the last few days, what with your dramatic re-entry, the passive-aggressive movie night, and the paparazzi chase you orchestrated. I have to admit I'm a little disappointed, though."

"It would seem to me that someone of your background would have such low standards you'd have a hard time being let down."

Sophia grinned at the little zinger. "That's better. So far everything you've levelled at me has been so basic, I'd begun to worry you didn't have it in you to really get your hands dirty."

"I generally leave the dirt to the cleaning staff." She gave a bored sigh. "Which might be why you feel experienced enough to speak about such things, but again, I apologise if I gave you the wrong impression. In fact, I never intended to give you any impression at all, much less a personal one."

"Then you do a poor job conveying your intentions."

"Perhaps my lack of concern for you led to the misunderstanding. I hold you in no more contempt than I would any other inconvenient house guest, and I assure you, there have been many of them over the years," the duchess continued airily. "They've always left on their own. I've no reason to believe you won't do the same. Then we'll all breathe a sigh of relief before moving on without ever thinking of you again."

She had to admit, the duchess was good at the whole ice-queen routine. In fact, if Sophia had been a dispassionate observer, she would probably believe the woman held no stake in this discussion at all. It would certainly make Sophia's life easier if that were true, but unfortunately this wasn't just about her life. She could still see the sad resolve in Vic's eyes as she left to face the press head-on this morning. Vic hadn't wanted to choose between Sophia and her birthright. She shouldn't have had to. She wouldn't have had to if not for the woman talking down to Sophia now.

"I imagine it's easy to overestimate your influence when you don't know your place on the larger stage of events. You have money, a modicum of fame, a certain amount of power in your small circle. I can admire, at least in theory, that you made it all yourself, but you'll also undoubtedly squander it all yourself, which again matters little to me because it's your concern." She paused for the ice in her voice to register fully as she said, "My daughter, however, is very much my concern."

"Oh, I see." Sophia smiled.

"I doubt you do."

"You're worried I'll lessen the influence you have over her."

The duchess laughed again, and disturbingly enough, the sound seemed genuine this time. "The fact that you think so shows how little you understand."

"Enlighten me."

"Impossible. Your worldview is so small it cannot conceive of something outside your own control, but trust me, Victoria can. Her life has never been her own, and it never will be. I thought she'd learned those lessons, but apparently she's forgotten them for the moment."

"So you decided to remind her?"

A little muscle in the duchess's jaw twitched. "I tried to do so privately, and I'll admit I was surprised by her reaction."

"You underestimate her strength."

"You and I have a different understanding of strength." The duchess eyed her more closely, then wrinkled her nose. "You must have some skills I don't even want to imagine in order to get your hooks in deeply enough for her to overlook your distasteful past and continued poor judgement."

Sophia's face flamed, not at the mention of her past, but at the implication that the only connection between her and Vic must be blind lust.

"But ultimately, you and I both know you'll be gone in a matter of weeks, or even sooner if you allow your professional life to spin out of control like you have over the last few days."

Sophia's jaw tightened.

"Oh, did you not know I knew about your problems at work?" The duchess threw Sophia's own echo back at her. "You're not the only one with a finger on the pulse of what's happening around here. My question is why someone with your background would be willing to risk everything she'd fought for—unless, of course, she believed she had something to gain from it."

Sophia bit her tongue, but she didn't need to. She had no quick retort to offer. The duchess had just given voice to the questions she should've been asking herself all along. The movie, her goals, the steps she needed to take to achieve them, she'd never let her focus slip before, and yet she'd spent the last two days wrapped up in Vic and her legacy while her own life's work began to unravel at the seams. What could she possibly stand to gain?

The duchess probably suspected she was after their power, money, and access, but she'd never want any of those things unless she'd earned them. And despite all the unsavoury aspects of her past, she would never take them at someone else's expense, much less someone she cared about.

"What's more," the duchess pushed, "I worry that in the time it takes for my daughter to come to her senses, the damage to her reputation will already be done. But, make no mistake, she will come to her senses."

She waited for some sort of reaction Sophia wouldn't give her before going in for the kill. "Victoria will not throw away who she is for you, which is why you are insignificant to me. Deep down you and I both know what Victoria will choose in the end. She has six hundred years of honour and duty bred into her DNA. Do you even know what's in yours?"

Sophia wanted to argue, she wanted to lash out, even punch her in the mouth. Sophia wasn't the type of woman who stood silently while someone, anyone, treated her like the trailer trash she'd been born. But the righteous anger that had been her constant companion for more than a decade failed her now. She felt nothing as the duchess's last barb landed, not because she was right about Sophia, but rather, because of the truth in what she'd said about Victoria.

Vic would choose the right thing eventually. She would sacrifice herself for the people, for the land, for the collective future of the entire area. She couldn't do anything else, and even if she tried to, it would destroy her slowly. Sophia's chest ached at the thought of Vic surrendering any part of who she was because of her.

She finally glanced up to see a curiously soft expression on the duchess's normally stony features.

"What?"

"Oh," the duchess said softly. "I didn't know."

"Didn't know what? That I already understood how this all would end?"

"No." She frowned. "I suspected you were smart enough to read the writing on the wall, but from your expression and your body language I now suspect I may have underestimated you in other areas."

Sophia raised her eyebrows.

"I thought you were like the others."

"Others?"

"Sorry, dear," she said in a wry tone. "You aren't the first woman to turn my daughter's head. I saw it in her before she ever saw it in herself. I was naive enough to believe a sense of decorum and a companionate marriage would take the edge off, but I was wrong."

Sophia had to ease back onto the settee at this confusing turn of events.

"I know what you must think of me, but I am not too small to admit when I'm wrong. It simply doesn't happen often where people are concerned." The corner of the duchess's mouth turned up only briefly. "I've correctly judged every other woman who has caught my daughter's eye in the years since her divorce. Every one of them has been unsuited to the type of partnership she needs, either seeking attention, money, or an utterly frivolous life. When I did my research on you, I had little trouble seeing the similarities."

"Similarities between me and women who sought attention and power?" Sophia scoffed. "Whatever gave you that idea?"

The duchess smiled again, but this time it carried a hint of sadness. "I hadn't ever considered the possibility that someone like you might actually develop genuine feelings for my daughter."

"And?"

"And I enjoy this considerably less now. I wish very much that this conversation could be different now." She sighed. "But I also suspect you understand how little anything you or I may feel changes the realities of our current situation."

Sophia nodded slowly, every part of her body rebelling against the idea of agreeing with this woman.

"You may make her happy for a time, and whether you believe me or not, as a mother it pains me to deny my daughter any modicum of even temporary happiness, but it would be temporary, and she would pay too heavy a price. The price that nearly broke her last time she paid it." The duchess gave a little shiver, and for the first time Sophia considered the possibility she might actually care about something other than her precious image. "By the time Vic's regrets would begin to surface and the realisation of what she'd sacrificed set in, it would be too late to salvage her already tenuous birthright. Seven centuries laid low. What could you possibly offer her in return?"

Sophia shook her head. She didn't know if she had no answer, or if her answer was simply, *Nothing*.

The duchess apparently recognised her victory but showed little satisfaction in it as she stood back. "I am sorry. I misjudged you and the feelings you clearly have for Victoria. I would rather have a different reality, but in the absence of that I would've at least liked to have handled this conversation differently. Had I known sooner, I think I would have."

"Sure." Sophia's voice sounded a little strangled. "We could've become real friends."

"I won't be so patronising as to suggest such a thing, or even try to part amicably, but I will leave you to your thoughts by saying, I trust you to do right by my daughter, and that is the highest compliment I have left to give."

Mercifully, she didn't wait for Sophia to decide if she was capable of a magnanimous response before leaving. And for her part, Sophia managed to keep her jaw clenched until the door closed, because she suspected that if she opened her mouth, she might still tell this woman to fuck off.

She didn't want that. She didn't want to drag any of this out or hurt any more people, not even the Wicked Witch of Northland. She wasn't quite ready to think of her in any more generous terms even if she had revealed herself as motivated by something other than pure malice.

In the end she'd still hurt them, or at least she'd hurt Vic. Sophia, on the other hand, had caused her current predicament herself. The worst part now was having to stew in her own knowledge that the duchess was right, not just about who she was and what she ultimately had to offer Vic, but also what she had to do about it now.

Chapter Fourteen

Vic was exhausted in every possible way. Physically, she'd been on the go ever since her conversation with her father. She'd put out a hundred fires since then, but his voice still echoed in her brain nearly twelve hours later, which of course contributed to her mental exhaustion. And as for her emotional state, she couldn't even remember when that had been thrown off kilter. Certainly, matters of her heart had gone off the rails in the last couple days, but she suspected she'd been doomed from the moment Sophia commanded her to unhand the sword.

She smiled at the memory in spite of her current state of mind. The smile only widened as she pushed open the door to her private quarters and found Sophia sitting on her settee.

"I've never been more chuffed to see anyone in my life."

Sophia's own smile was more tired and weary. "Chuffed? That's a good emotion, right?"

"Very," Vic confirmed, leaning down to kiss her quickly.

Sophia slipped an arm around her waist and tried to pull her down next to her.

It took every functioning muscle in Vic's aching body to resist. "If I sit, I won't get back up, and I need a drink for whatever recap of the day is bound to happen next."

She shed her suitcoat on her way to the drink cart and unbuttoned the cuffs on her dress shirt. "Shall I pour us each a double?"

"No."

The flat tone in which Sophia delivered the word made the hair on the back of Vic's neck stand on end. "No to the double? Haven't you eaten yet? I had half a salad at the office. I could order something up for you from the kitchen, or maybe we could draw a bath and then—"

"Vic."

The way Sophia said her name told her everything she needed to know about where this was going and how much she would enjoy the conversation.

"Very well. None for you, a double for me." She took a deep breath and tried to steady herself, but her fingers trembled as she poured the gin. Then, forcing her expression to remain neutral, she joined Sophia on the settee. "I get the sense you have something on your mind. Please allow me to ease it. Whom shall I guillotine?"

Sophia shook her head. "I'm afraid it's not something you can fix, at least not with a mere beheading."

"Why don't you at least let me try?"

Sophia stared at their fingers for a moment before lifting her eyes and saying, "It's over."

"What?" she croaked.

"We have to end this. Tonight."

"Hmm." Vic bit her lip to keep from yelping at the pain those words shot through her. "I am forced to disagree with you. I know this morning brought some unique complications, but—"

"It's more than this morning."

"A complex couple of days then."

"We both knew this time would come."

"No." She choked on the word. "Maybe. Not yet."

The sympathy in Sophia's eyes made this harder.

"Things will settle down," Vic said in the most level-headed tone she could muster. "I actually had a very helpful conversation with my father today, and then I went to the office to handle a few things."

"And by 'things' you mean 'the fallout from me daring to travel openly throughout your dukedom'?"

"Not that. Well, not entirely that." Vic tried to cling to the positives despite the rising tide of panic inside her. "I actually spent much of the evening trying to reschedule the young filmmakers' group that was supposed to observe the filming this week."

"Who you had to reschedule because we aren't filming, and we aren't filming because everything's falling apart around us, and the press—"

"The press has nothing on us," Victoria cut back in. "A few opportunities arose for me to question some trusted contacts in a natural way, and they all maintained no one has connected us."

"No one has connected us *yet*," Sophia corrected, "but by the time they do, it'll be too late."

"We'll deal with them when the time comes."

"*We* won't," Sophia said with the same calm finality that made Vic's stomach churn. "I won't have to deal with any of it, or at least not anywhere near the bulk of it. You will bear all the pressure, all the risk, all the burden, and all the loss. I can't accept that."

"You bear no responsibility for my life or my choices."

"You're half right. I bear no responsibility, and that's the way I wanted it, but I misunderstood so many things at the start." Sophia gave her hand a little squeeze. "I didn't know then what I know now. I was just playing around at first, teasing, and then I got too swept up in you to think."

"Too swept up in me to think about my title, my job, my family?" Vic's heart couldn't decide whether to soar or shatter. She'd waited her whole life to have a woman be interested in her for who she'd become, not who she'd been born.

"I know you never lied to me about what you had at stake here, and I should've listened. A part of me did listen. Even from our first night together I wanted to understand you, but I had no frame of reference. Nothing in my own experience helped me feel the full gravity until last night." She sighed. "It doesn't even matter what I think or understand. What matters is that I refuse to be the thing standing between you and your people."

A bitter laugh bubbled up before she could stop it. "Why not? My people would thank you for the service. Half of them don't want a duke or duchess at all, and the other half don't want me."

"You don't know that. Hell, they don't even know that because they don't know you. The bulk of them have never been given a chance to see who you really are. They never saw the woman you were in the pub last night when those lifeboats went out, and they've never met the person you were this morning, the one who refused to lie to them or hide from them even when you had every right to."

"They want someone who wouldn't have any occasion to hide or lie in the first place. They need someone who doesn't—"

Sophia waved her off. "People rarely know what they need."

Vic stared at her, searching those dark eyes and wondering if that comment was delivered in the abstract or if it had been meant to apply to one of them. While she didn't pretend to know what Sophia wanted or needed, right now she was certain she both wanted and needed Sophia beside her.

"Don't look at me like that," Sophia pleaded softly.

"Like what?"

"Like I matter."

Vic squeezed her hand. "You matter to me."

Sophia looked away. "You've got to stop doing that."

"Doing what?"

"Being so perfect, so maddeningly good."

She laughed.

"I'm serious." Sophia rose, breaking all contact between them. "I've poked and prodded and scratched trying to find your dark side, and it's just not there. I teased you and froze you out, revved you up and exhausted you. I endangered the life you've fought for, but even at your worst, you are fundamentally good."

"I believe most people are. I'm sure you are."

"I am not," Sophia snapped. "In my heart I know I've done bad things, things that would make you cringe."

"I'm sorry about how I reacted to your films."

Sophia snorted. "The things I've done onscreen don't even

232

scratch the surface of the things I've done in my real life. The people I've walked away from. The deals I've made. The actions I've ignored or buried."

"You did what you had to for your career, your dreams."

"Exactly. Not the greater good, but for myself and my career. And those things have taken a toll on me and on my moral compass." The anguish in Sophia's voice stirred a similar emotion in Vic. "I didn't even believe people like you still existed."

"I can imagine how hard—"

"No, you can't." Anger flashed in Sophia's eyes this time. "You can't imagine the choices I've made because you've never been forced to imagine them. And I resent that. I resent the fact that you've been able to remain fundamentally good, and pure, and pristine in your impeccable chivalry when I have been forced time and time again to choose between demons. I resent it even now when I'm trying desperately to choose something better this time."

"You don't have to choose."

"I do, and I can." Sophia's voice cracked. "For the first time in my life I'm finally in a position to choose something good, something selfless and honourable and long lasting."

A heavy sense of dread settled in Vic's stomach. "What does that choice entail?"

"I can save you." Sophia balled her hands into two tight fists as if bracing for a fight. "I know how it feels to have your dreams used against you. What it's like to live with shame and resentment always swirling deep inside you even when you refuse to apologise for the choices you made. I know what it's like to have the thing you want most, the thing you've fought hardest for become the thing that haunts you in the night."

Vic stood, wanting nothing more than to comfort the hurt she heard in that refrain, but Sophia shook her head sharply.

"Someday you would feel the same way about me that I feel about the compromises I've made."

"I don't know what you mean."

"Good. I don't want you to ever know. I don't want to change you."

"Nor would I change you."

Sophia made a noise somewhere between a scoff and a sob. Vic reached for her again, only for Sophia to step back. "I'm never going to have an easy past to reconcile. I'll never have a pure bloodline. I'm never going to be quiet and demure on social topics. I'll never be an asset in your quest to secure your dukedom."

Vic threw up her hands. "I don't care about the blasted dukedom! The title, the castle, the bloody responsibility, none of it means as much to me as you. I'll renounce the whole lot of it. I don't want it anymore."

"Yes, you do," Sophia shot back, "and I wouldn't love you if you didn't."

Vic froze. "What?"

"'I couldn't love you, dear, so much if you loved not honour more.'" Sophia's shoulders sagged. "That's what you said last night, and it's true. I couldn't love you enough to walk away if you weren't as honourable as you are."

"Love?" The word stuck in her throat the same way it stuck in her chest.

"Yes. I didn't mean to, but I do." Sophia sank back onto the settee. "But I am always going to put you at risk, and I won't do that to someone I love. I have to leave."

Vic eased down beside her and took her hand once more. "Please don't."

"I have to go. I can't change."

"Then don't change," she begged. "I don't want you to. If you did, I'd love you less, too."

"Vic, stop. Please don't say any more."

"I have to be honest. It goes hand in hand with being honourable." She sounded frantic now more than romantic, but all the words rushed out. "I can't let you go without telling you how much I love everything about you, your passion, your wit, the ability to read people, the way you refuse to back down when you know you're right. I wouldn't change a thing about you. Not for an entire dukedom."

Sophia placed her hand on Vic's cheek. "We're a terrible fit."

"We're not. Or maybe we are by other people's standards, but not ours. Not by mine. You're exactly what I've dreamed of." She kissed Sophia softly on the mouth. "I want you, just as you are, right here, right now, but also forever."

Sophia kissed her this time, a little deeper.

"Please," Vic begged. "Please stay with me forever."

Sophia shook her head. "I can't."

They kissed again, and Sophia softened slightly against her.

"Then stay tonight?" Vic asked. "Can't I keep you like this, like nothing's changed, for one more night?"

Sophia hesitated, and Vic used the moment to kiss her eyelids, her temple, her forehead.

"Please," she murmured against her ear.

Sophia nodded slowly.

Vic's heart ached so badly she might have pressed a hand to her chest where her fingers still intertwined with Sophia's. She pulled her up, pulled her close, and kissed her again, then walked them back toward the bedroom.

The acquiescence and the quiet peace that followed seemed so tenuous, they dared not shatter it by talking. As they caressed and clung to one another in turn, slowly removing clothes and kissing their way into bed, she understood she'd won not a victory but merely a stay of execution. Still, as they eased into bed, she relished the press of Sophia's warm body and shallow breathing beside her.

In the final moments of exhaustion before she surrendered to sleep, she stared up at the canopy of her four-poster bed. She felt only a twinge of guilt for the lie she'd told to buy them this last night. It had only been a little one, hadn't it? She didn't want to change virtually anything about Sophia . . . except for her last name.

Try as she might to steel her heart against the crushing inevitability of breaking, she couldn't help but drift off to sleep thinking that Sophia Penchant did have such a lovely ring to it.

A low hum stirred Sophia from a deep sleep. She fluttered open her eyes to see the earliest rays of golden light poking through the space between thick, heavy drapes, but she'd been here long enough to recognise the sun rose at a vastly inhumane hour. The buzzing rattled again, and this time she was too awake to pretend she didn't know where it came from.

She followed the sound with one hand and reached out to grab her pants off the floor beside the bed before extracting her phone from the pocket and pulling it back under the warm duvet. She squinted at the notification on her screen, or rather notifications, as in plural, as in multiples that were still rolling in.

She sighed and scrolled back to the beginning, trying to skim enough to get the gist. Something about work, from Talia, then one from hair and makeup, another from production scheduling, four more from Talia. She homed in on those.

Filming back on.

Intimacy coordinator arrived.

Brian's back on board. No explanations.

What the hell? Mixed emotions fought to bubble to the surface: happiness, a sense of direction, relief, but they were all dulled by an overarching sense of confusion. She typed back to Talia, *What changed?*

No idea, came the quick response, followed by, *I haven't spoken to him, and neither did anyone at the studio.*

She shook her head. This didn't compute. Maybe he sobered up and realised he'd made a mistake, but that would require some reflection and remorse on his part. She'd yet to see anything to suggest he was capable of either.

Her phone vibrated again. *Just got to the set, and someone said Brian was inside the castle last night. Did you see him?*

She shook her head, not for Talia's benefit. *I was a little pre-occupied.*

Whoever got a hold of him did a good job. Maybe Vic?

She finally glanced at the sleeping form beside her, and her heart nearly broke again.

Vic lay on her stomach, her face turned toward Sophia and one elegant hand resting lightly on her pillow. Her long blond locks fanned down across bare shoulders before disappearing under the covers. She wore such a peaceful expression it made her seem younger, and the soft part of her lips appeared almost angelic. Sophia had never seen anything more torturously beautiful.

Forgetting about her phone and the world it connected her to for a moment, she eased her head back down to the bed and simply watched the woman beside her. She wanted to imprint this image on her memory so she could study it like a painting in the days and weeks to come. She could have soaked in the sight of her for hours if not for another message.

Did you talk to Vic about him? Talia texted.

No. She shot back the shortest reply. They'd had more important topics to discuss last night, and she resented the reminder of them now.

Either way, we're back on. The new schedule is ambitious, but if we pull it off, we'll wrap principal filming in a week.

She set the phone down. A week. One more week here. And apparently, she'd be working night and day. There would be no other way to meet the deadline. Not a minute to rest or think or daydream.

She turned her attention back to Vic's sleeping form. A week. She couldn't help but suspect someone meant it to go that way, perhaps the same someone who'd called Brian to the castle. The duchess offered the obvious explanation for both the return to work and the accelerated time frame, which also made Sophia's stomach churn with all the wider implications about what twisted role she may have played in the work stoppage to begin with. It wouldn't be hard to yank Brian's chain. A little seed of doubt planted here, an appeal to his ego there, and suddenly he'd be sensitive to suggestions and insecure about his authority. Sophia didn't know if she should feel enraged or impressed.

Ultimately, she didn't care. A part of her actually felt mildly appreciative. Without a few days off she might have never gotten the chance to fully understand the woman beside her, and without the reminder of how tenuous her own job was, she might have been tempted to drag things out. Now she knew for certain she couldn't do so any longer, not if either of them were to survive.

With that thought, she inched forward on the bed. Placing her own hand atop Vic's, she woke her with a soft kiss.

Blue eyes flitted open under long lashes as a slow smile tugged at lovely lips.

"I have to go to work," she whispered. "You don't have to get up yet."

Vic's smooth brow creased, and Sophia nearly hated herself for wrecking such a serene canvas. Still, she'd have to do more damage than that to extract herself now.

"Brian caved. We've got a full schedule. We have to catch up, and that means I have to go."

Vic sat up slowly. "He caved? Why? I mean, good, but on what terms?"

"I don't know."

"Okay." She stretched. "I'll get ready. We'll go together."

"No." Sophia mustered something akin to firmness in her tone. "I'd rather you didn't."

Vic frowned. "May I ask why?"

"Things are better now. I suspect his hissy fit was never about you and me to begin with, at least not in the way we understood, but I don't think your presence will be productive as we try to right the ship, not for Brian or for me."

"But if you don't know the terms, how do you know he'll accept your autonomy?"

"We've got an intimacy coordinator now, so I think he'll behave, but even if he doesn't, that's for me to deal with, not you."

"I want to help."

"I don't want you to," she said flatly. "I've dealt with a thousand Brians, and I'll deal with a hundred more until it's my name on the back of the director's chair because that's my job, and I want to get back to work."

Vic sighed. "You know I have the ultimate faith in you. You belong in the director's chair right now."

"I know." Sophia kissed her quickly. "And I appreciate your faith in me, but you're not a film producer."

"Most women would've been impressed by the titles I hold instead of the one I don't, but you're not most women, and I adore that about you." Vic flashed her one of those knee-weakening smiles. "So, I propose we both focus on our own jobs today. We'll see how everything goes, and then we can talk more in depth over dinner tonight."

Sophia tensed. This was it. She'd been dreading this moment so much she had put it off for one more night, but she couldn't avoid it indefinitely, and the longer she lingered, the harder it would be on them both. She had to do the right thing now, or she didn't trust herself to do it at all.

Vic must've read her mood, or maybe her body language. "What's wrong?"

"I'm not coming back to the castle tonight. I didn't even plan on staying last night. I already had all my things moved back to the inn before you got off work."

"Without talking to me?"

Sophia laughed a quick shot of a laugh. "I did try to talk to you, and see where it got us. I will always end up in your bed every time I let you get close to me."

"Would that be so bad?"

"Yes." Her voice rose. "It would be bad on so many levels, and we hashed them all out last night. Nothing's changed. Not my past, not your family, not who either of us are at our core. And now we've both got jobs to get back to."

"But you're not leaving yet. We have more time. We can do our jobs together."

"I can't." Sophia pushed herself to the edge of the bed. "I can't do my job when you're this close. It's too hard and only delays the inevitable."

"So what? Because we have to say goodbye in a week, we might as well ignore each other until then?"

"I know it's not ideal." Sophia slipped back into her pants from the night before. "We'll probably cross paths at some point in the coming days, and maybe even after that. We're going to have to be strong, which means we can't let ourselves be alone together again."

"Never?"

A piece of her heart cracked at the sadness in Vic's voice.

"We already had our one more night," Sophia pleaded. "One more night that was already tacked onto borrowed time. How many more can we take before one of us breaks? I don't want to do that to you."

"Nor I to you, but—"

"Then let's not hurt each other any more than we have to. Can't we be strong enough to make a clean break?"

Vic bit her lip so hard the red turned to white, but she nodded.

She would. Vic would always do the right thing. Her mother said it plainly yesterday, and Sophia had known it all along. No matter how much she wanted to lash out or scream or burn down the whole place, Vic would always choose honour. Now, if only she could do the same.

She pulled on her shirt roughly and stepped back toward the bed, not coming close enough to rest on the shared surface but reaching for Vic's hand against her better judgement. "I am never going to forget you."

Vic nodded again, tears filling her eyes.

"I mean it. I'm going to be obsessed with you for the rest of my life. You will always be the one who got away, and I'll probably internet stalk you as long as I live." She managed a half smile. "And when I Google you, I better see you doing well."

Vic sucked in a deep breath. "I cannot promise to do well without you beside me."

"Hush," Sophia commanded. "I won't be happy if you don't. I'll be utterly gutted if I give you up and you don't repay me by thriving. I need to see pictures of you christening lifeboats and read articles about you signing land conservation deals. You owe that to me and to you and to the people who depend on you. I want to follow your work as you bring new life to this area, bring a new kind of compassion to this dukedom, because you have to make it yours."

Her voice cracked, but she pushed on. "You have to fight for your birthright and the future you deserve. You have to do it all, and you have to do it on your terms, and you have to refuse to let anyone else tell you how. You have everything you need inside of you, and I'll never forgive you for conforming to someone else's idea of who you were born to be."

"That's an awful lot of pressure to put on someone you're walking out on," Vic said, more than a small measure of frustration in her voice. "What do you owe me in this deal? What future do you owe yourself?"

Of course, she would make this about Sophia.

Of course, she'd push for them to be equals, even in this moment.

"I'll survive. It's what I do. I'll throw myself into work and turn the torture into creative drive. I've shown that kind of resolve for much less compelling reasons. I have no reason to believe I cannot do the same now with the love of my life at stake."

"The love of your life?" The tears spilled from Vic's eyes.

Sophia leaned down and gently kissed them away. "Yes. Don't ever doubt that. No matter what I do between now and then, when I win my Oscar for best director, that's what I'm going to call you. I'll hold up my little gold statue and say, 'I dedicate this to the love of my life. You know who you are.' And that will send the press into a tizzy."

Vic sniffed. "You're a promotional genius. Are you sure I can't hire you to do my publicity?"

Sophia kissed her forehead. "You can't afford me."

"I'm very rich."

Sophia tilted her head back to look her in the eye. "Yes, you are, in so many ways. And don't ever forget it."

She stepped back into her shoes and started painfully toward the door.

"But what if it doesn't go the way you plan?" Vic's voice trembled.

Sophia stopped, but she didn't have the strength to turn around.

"What if I don't win the case for my title? What if you don't get the director's chair? What if we do this and we find out we really did need each other after all?"

Sophia shook her head. She couldn't even engage those thoughts, not now, not ever. They would break her and haunt her and drag her down. It wasn't that she didn't share Vic's fear. She'd been through too much not to consider failure a possibility, but she couldn't let herself wonder what that might mean for Vic. Instead, she gathered the frail threads of resolve and cut the remaining cords between them.

"We'll either do this for ourselves and for each other, or we'll both go under, but I won't ever be the one to pull you down." She turned and took in the sight of Vic sitting up, bold and beautiful, if broken, in her canopy bed.

Then she walked away.

Chapter Fifteen

Vic dressed herself as best she could in slacks and a polo she hoped came across as business casual instead of revealing the truth that she'd grabbed clothes at random since she could barely see through her own tears. She wanted nothing more than to stay in bed, hide under the covers, and curse the fates for this fresh round of hell, but what was the American phrase Sophia used when describing her ability to sneak out of the castle undetected? Something about this not being her first rodeo? She supposed the same held true for grief, unfortunately. She'd had entirely too much practice burying her own pain in order to focus on the details of her obligations.

Still, her vast and varied experience didn't keep her from slinking down the servants' stairway and keeping her head low as she skulked across the courtyard to the business area of the estate. Her staff either read her mood or were too busy cleaning up the messes of the day before to pay her any mind as she barricaded herself in her private office.

The effort exhausted her. She rested her head, face down, on her desk and just listened to the sounds outside her door. A phone rang, muffled voices conversed, somewhere a chair squeaked. She tried to anchor herself to anything other than the dull throb in her chest, but her mind wandered. Where was Sophia now? Wardrobe? On set? Filming?

She shook her head. She didn't need to know. It was probably better if she didn't, but as her mind drifted back to their last conversation, she suspected Sophia wouldn't be the only one watching from afar. She would probably always do the same, and she would not have the mercy that came from having to make a conscious effort. Sophia would be on every screen and billboard when the movie premiered. Would each one feel like a knife to her chest? And for how long? Could time heal all wounds if circumstance kept ripping them open again?

The castle would undoubtedly publicise their connection to the film. People in the tourism office were designing mock-ups of new brochures or adverts featuring Sophia's likeness right now. They would no doubt make their way to her desk eventually, the desk she was currently pressing her face into in an attempt to brace herself against something stable.

She tried to focus once more on the moment, on the tangible, her ear seeking out sounds beyond her inner turmoil. There were new voices outside her door now, and she lifted her head to try to follow the conversation.

"No, we contacted everyone yesterday. The shadow-study program was cancelled due to complications with the filming schedule." It was Archie's voice. Archie, Brogan's brother. Archie who'd shown up early and sounded the alarm the day before.

The day before? One day's difference between waking up warmer and happier than she'd ever been.

"But we didn't get the message, sir. And we took the first train up from York, and we've been sat outside the gates for hours waiting to see the set," an unfamiliar voice responded. "We won't be a bother. Can't we take a look around?"

"I'm afraid not, lad." Archie sounded apologetic. "It's a closed set, lots of expensive equipment and moving parts, and the crew is bustling about so much today there'd be no one to keep an eye on you."

"We're not some numpties who'll go around knocking things over. We're full-time film students. If we learn what we need to learn, we'll be running a set like this in a couple of years."

"And I sure hope you are." Archie didn't budge. "I wish you all the best in your endeavour."

"You could help us with our endeavour," the student pushed, and Vic smiled a bit at his tenacity. It reminded her of Sophia, which sent another hot lance of pain through her core. Sophia, who had pushed and pushed and pushed to get what she wanted, both in her career and her life, only to walk away so Vic could have what she needed in hers.

She jumped up from the desk as if it had caught fire and swung open her office door.

Archie jumped back and stood nearly at attention, but the group of students merely regarded her curiously. There were six of them, all young, dressed smartly in slacks and light sweaters with school emblems.

"We didn't mean to disturb you, Your La—"

She held up her hand and he fell silent mid-word.

"No worries, Mr. McKay. I couldn't help overhearing, and I think if these aspiring filmmakers can come all the way up here, the least we can do is give them a little tour."

"Right." Archie nodded. "I could ring the summer staff office."

"No. I'll do it."

"You'll make the call?"

"No. I'll give the tour."

He stared at her with a mix of confusion and concern, and she couldn't help but notice the uncanny resemblance to his sister's thoughtful expression.

"We'd really appreciate it, Miss," the lead student offered. "We promise not to be a bother. I know you're probably busy doing . . . whatever it is you do around here."

Archie cleared his throat nervously, but Vic managed her first little smile at the realisation the students had no idea who she was. After everything she'd been through in the last couple days, or years, or well, her entire adult life, she wanted to hold onto as many natural interactions as she could.

Shooting Archie a conspiratorial expression, she said, "I'll be back in a while, Mr. McKay. If that's all right with you, of course."

Archie straightened his shoulders. "Very well."

Then she nodded for the students to follow her.

"Thank you," another student said as he held the door. "We really appreciate this."

"You may want to reserve your thanks." Vic lead them across the still-empty courtyard. "I assume the cast and crew are out at the stables today, but I can at least give you a peek at one of the indoor sets."

"That's fine," another student said, a young woman this time. "We're techies. We're more excited about the equipment than the actors."

"Speak for yourself, Helena," the first young man teased. "I may be at uni to study the cameras, but I wouldn't mind studying Sophia LeBlanc while I'm at it."

Helena elbowed him in the ribs, but Vic felt the blow, and her breath caught at the idea of running into Sophia. Intellectually she knew the prospect fell in the realm of probability, but she wasn't ready yet. She didn't trust herself not to show her raw emotions plainly on her face, or worse, crumple and grovel in front of everyone.

"Has it been exciting having them all here, Miss?" another girl asked.

"That's a bit of an understatement."

"How big is the crew?"

"Roughly a hundred people on site. Another hundred around the area doing things like scouting, props, transportation and the like."

"Wow," a fair-haired boy who hadn't spoken yet marvelled. "Two hundred odd jobs all around the movies . . . in Northland."

The way he said the last word caught her ear as they entered the castle and started up the main stairs. "Is that a bit of Geordie I hear in your accent?"

He blushed. "Aye, Miss. Born and raised in Tynemouth. I only left to go to uni."

"You'll be coming back after graduation, then?"

He shook his head, a hint of sadness in his eyes. "Not likely. I'll probably have to stay south."

"You might be able to head north," Helena offered. "We sometimes can find work in Edinburgh."

He shrugged. "That'd be a little closer to home at least."

"Oliver's a mama's boy," one of the other guys teased.

She pushed open the large double doors to the formal living room, and all the banter fell silent. Awe filled every face around her as their eyes went wide, and a couple jaws dropped.

Then everyone spoke at once as they sprinted to various parts of the room to examine the equipment.

"Oh my god."

"Check out the way they rigged the lights."

"Look at how they laid the tracks on this incline."

"I want to pick up that boom so bad."

"I can't believe they left this stuff sitting out."

"It's in a castle. Who's going to break in?"

"You mean other than us?"

"We're not going to touch anything."

"Yeah, 'cause we know these cameras are worth more than our lives," Helena said, then turned back to Vic. "Don't worry. We know better than to touch, no matter how much we feel compelled to do so."

"Someday," Oliver whispered reverently. "Someday."

"This little window nook would be so delicious if you could get the right angle on someone." Helena examined the spot where Sophia sat on the first day Victoria observed filming. If she closed her eyes, she could still see her there, the late afternoon sun shining on her regal features and a smouldering glint in her eyes.

"Yeah, but it would only be one person at best. There's barely enough room for one of these cameras, much less two people."

"I don't know." Oliver tilted his head to the side. "You could shoot from above or below, but then you wouldn't get a good sense of the window."

"You'd have to start out wide to give the viewers a sense of location in the scene," Vic interjected, merely reciting what she'd heard Sophia explain to Brian. "Then use a Steadicam over the actors' shoulders as a sort of stand-in, with them delivering lines right to the lens. Then the person watching would merge with the character's point of view."

All the students turned to stare at her.

Finally, the leader asked, "Are you one of the film crew?"

She shook her head. "No. I'm . . . well, I work in the castle. I've merely observed several of the shoots."

"Do they have a lot of shoots here?" Oliver asked excitedly, his local accent becoming more pronounced. "I never knew that was an option."

She shook her head. "This is the first, and likely the last time we'll allow filming inside the castle. The logistics are complicated, and my . . . the duke's family prefers to maintain some distance from the whims of popular culture."

His whole body sagged as if she'd tossed him a balloon filled with lead. "Oh. Back to London, then."

The young woman patted his shoulder. "Maybe someday, Ollie."

One of the others glanced out the window. "Yeah, those rolling fields with a castle in the background are perfect for period pieces, both romances and historical battle scenes."

"And did you see the gardens?" the girl asked. "Swoon-worthy for first date scenes."

"What about all the market towns around here with their little nooks and alleys? They're built for shooting mysteries or gritty crime scenes."

"And the seaside," said Vic, as their excitement pricked at her own. "Sailing, naval battles, beach scenes, Viking boats coming ashore."

"Pirates!" another one exclaimed. "Pirates paired with castles. Come on, why aren't we all working on these movies right here, right now?"

The students began to all talk at once again, but in their words,

Vic heard only the echo of Sophia talking to Emma about the filming rights to her next novel. Her words echoed through Vic's memory. *If you filmed in this area, you'd have so much to work with.*

Emma's book, Vic's home, that's how the whole thing had started. The fit had seemed natural from day one, and yet she'd never given any real thought to the project as anything more than a one-off experience. She had never met anyone like these students, the future filmmakers who faced a choice of chasing their dreams or staying in the place they loved and called home. She was self-aware enough to realise why their dilemma might hit her especially hard this morning, but awareness did little to undercut her connection with them. She felt the connection to so many of her people, a deep love for the land and a fading hope for the future of the region. She'd spent her whole life balanced between those two forces. It kept her up at night and bore down on her shoulders so heavily today, she nearly collapsed under the weight of it.

And yet here these young people stood, flush with ideas and excitement she'd never considered. They weren't stumbling or gritting their teeth. Where she'd seen only problems, they saw possibilities.

They continued to list projects suited to the area and the roles they dreamed of playing in their productions. One wanted to use drone-mounted cameras, another expressed a passion for sound editing, another saw the possibility of connecting with a local university for interns and extras. Any other day it would've sent her straight back to the office to begin crunching numbers. Even now part of her fought to process the practicalities, but another, bigger, more wounded piece of herself warned against this particular rabbit hole for fear every twist and turn would only lead her back to Sophia.

She edged over to the wall and leaned against the cool wood panelling to steady herself at the thought. Filmmaking was Sophia's realm. She didn't want to move in the same circles as Sophia and still be separate from her. She didn't want to chase someone else's dream in a misguided attempt to stay close to her. How could she ever know if her intentions were pure if they only sprouted in conjunction with the loss of the woman who'd planted them?

A door opened to her right, and James barged in.

"Out," he commanded, and all the students froze. "Out of here right now, you little hoodlums, before I call security and have you rounded up for trespassing."

"Whoa." The most vocal student waved his hands. "We didn't break in. The office woman said we could be here."

"There are no 'office women' allowed in the residence, and if you—"

"James." Vic pushed off the wall and assumed the most professional tone she could muster, which wasn't easy given the anger surging through her, both at his current interruption and the larger role he'd played in her pain. "The last time I checked, I still had the authority to invite guests into my own home."

He froze, and his face hardened as he turned to her. "Your Ladyship. I didn't notice you there."

"Clearly. Add it to the long list of situations you've misread lately. These are film students on an estate-sponsored excursion for the artistic development of Northland's young people. They are the future of this region. They deserve the respect and welcome commensurate with the regard in which I hold them."

"Of course, Your Ladyship," James said with his cold detachment. "I will take my leave."

"Thank you, James, and while you're at it, please inform my parents I request an audience with them at their earliest convenience."

"I'll inform the duke and duchess immediately, but they're off estate today and won't be home until this evening."

"That'll do. I'll dine with them on their return."

"Yes, Your Ladyship." Then with a short bow to her and a curt nod toward the students, he backed out of the room.

She forced a polite smile before turning to face the others, only to be met with shocked expressions.

"Erm." Ollie bowed awkwardly. "Your Ladyship, I would like to apologise for any, or likely many, social faux pas I've committed."

"I don't even know what I'm supposed to do right now," Helena added. "We didn't know you were—"

She waved them off. "I found your lack of formality quite refreshing."

"Really?" Helena asked. "'Cause I can try to curtsey if I'm supposed to, but I'm in trousers. Do you have to wear a skirt to curtsey? I could just pretend."

"Please don't. I sincerely hope you won't change a thing about how you've spoken to me since we met. You've done me a great favour by treating me as you would any other person. Truly, I've enjoyed being part of your casual conversations more than you could possibly imagine this morning."

They all exchanged a few nervous expressions.

"Okay. Whatever you like, Miss."

"Call me Vic."

One of the others laughed. "See, it's things like that what'll leave people not giving you the proper respect. It makes you seem totally cool and chill."

She laughed for the first time all day. "And see, that's how I'd like to seem. Now that you know my secret, it'll all change, unless you promise not to hold my title against me and clam up."

Helena eyed her suspiciously.

"You don't believe me?"

"No, Miss. It's just with you being all down to earth and answering questions about filming makes me think you enjoy this sort of thing, and you obviously have some power to make things happen around here, but then you say there's not going to be any more movies in the area."

She frowned. She'd asked for them to converse freely, but she hadn't been prepared for them to accept her offer quite so easily. "This movie was a one-time offer to a friend who's written the source material and had another friend in a position to connect her to producers and a studio. The estate brokered very little of the specifics. I wouldn't have known where to begin on such matters."

"But you learned some things from the experience, right?

You're in here talking about filming schedules and scripts and angles and Steadicams," one of the boys jumped in.

"And you probably know a lot of businesspeople and government people, and I don't even know who else," Helena said, then caught herself. "Sorry, I didn't mean to overstep."

"No, go on," Vic urged, both honestly interested in what she had to say and eager to continue any conversation with people who treated her like a normal person.

"It's just you have money and power, and if it's not going to be you to make the leap around here, probably nobody ever will."

She nodded slowly, and her voice caught in her throat as she tried to answer.

"Miss?" Oliver asked. "Are you okay?"

"It's not that I don't appreciate how many young people would love for this to become a Hollywood destination, but I'm not the person people seem to believe I am. I'm not actually powerful. I'm, well, I fear I don't have the skills or the knowledge, or maybe the backbone, too . . ." She bit back a sob as she repeated the same thing that she'd told Sophia mere hours earlier. "I'm not a film producer."

She wasn't sure if she swayed or her if voice cracked, but several of the students stepped forward as if afraid they might have to catch her or prop her up.

"No worries," the leader said gently. "We won't fault you for that. None of us are movie moguls either."

A couple of the others laughed nervously. Then one of them added, "Yet."

"Right," Helena said. "Don't mind us, we don't know what we're talking about. We're just learning as we go. That's what we're here for. Should we tell her our secret?"

They all nodded sheepishly, but no one seemed ready to fess up.

"What is it?" she asked the local lad she'd begun to build a steady affinity for.

"Well, Miss." He blushed. "We actually *did* get the message about the observation being cancelled yesterday. We just ignored it on account of wanting to come up here so badly. We figured if

252

we showed up and acted like we were supposed to be here, maybe someone would take pity on us and help us out."

"Help you out, how?"

He shrugged. "I can't say it was a full-fledged plan so much as a hope that if we broke the seal, the rest might fall into place."

"And it did." The leader laughed. "We got our foot in the door, and we got to see a real movie set and meet an aristocrat who maybe someday will remember us kindly whenever she decides she does want to become a movie producer after all."

She sighed again, but this time her lungs felt a little lighter. Instead of being annoyed or put out by their brashness, she found herself inspired by it. When she'd called them the future of the region to James moments earlier, she meant it only as a dressing-down for him, but now as she looked each student in the eye, she couldn't help notice a new emotion stirring in her, little more than a light flutter amid the wreckage of the last few days. She feared any shift in the wrong direction would likely crush the hope completely, but if she did nothing, surely this would die, too, snuffed out like every hope that had come before.

No, she couldn't withstand another loss. Sophia had awakened something in her that wouldn't go back to sleep. She didn't want to fall back into a void, or endless days of colourless obligation. She might not be able to have the life she wanted with the woman she loved, but Sophia had shown her she didn't have to settle for someone else's life, either.

The tiny flutter grew wobbly wings, and she fought the urge to cage it by managing expectations or undercutting its potential. Sophia had implored her to fight for herself with the same fervour she used when fighting for her people. What if she could fight for herself at the same time she fought for her people?

The vision remained hazy and the details vague, but a fragile dream was better than none at all. Like a child learning to walk, she fought twin impulses to cling to something solid and to charge wildly into the unknown. Either way, she wouldn't get where she wanted to go without deciding on a first step, and in a way, she suspected she'd already done so without knowing it.

She smiled, both at her internal reasoning and at the students who still watched her expectantly. "Come on. I'll walk you back to my office where Archie can collect your contact information so we can stay in touch."

"Stay in touch?" the local boy asked. "What for?"

She shrugged. "I'm not sure yet, honestly, but whatever it is, I have a feeling I better take some time to refine it before that meeting with my parents this evening."

"Cut," Brian called in the same monotone he'd used all day.

Sophia and Tommy both relaxed and took a step back.

"Did you get it?" Talia asked as Brian reviewed the small screen in front of him, then shrugged.

"It's not terrible. We can move on."

Talia shot Sophia a worried glance. They'd both come in hoping to find him more agreeable while still braced for the prospect of petulance. Neither of them had considered the possibility of pure listlessness. At first, Sophia worried he had another massive hangover, but as the day wore into late afternoon, she suspected he'd simply given up and intended to phone in the rest of the scenes for the film.

This, of course, left her and Talia in the uncomfortable position of having to direct their director without doing so in a way that would set him off again. She didn't want to make that mistake twice, but she couldn't let him turn in a subpar performance, either. She'd already given up too much in order to make this film great. The thought of exactly what she'd sacrificed to get back to work made her stomach lurch, and it must have shown on her face because Talia stepped closer.

"Are you okay?"

"Yeah." She waved her off. Nothing was okay. She wasn't sure anything would ever fully be okay again, but she hadn't made her choice for her own benefit. For once, she'd put someone else's needs and goals above her own, and she would stay the course, but she had never expected selflessness to feel so terrible. "Can we take five?"

"Sure." Brian looked almost relieved at the suggestion. "I need a smoke."

Once he was outside, Sophia turned to the cameraman. "Can I see the playback?"

He nodded to some other techs, who provided her with a headset and directed her toward an open screen that flickered to life with her likeness.

Her hair and makeup artists had done a glorious job of hiding the red rims and dark circles around her eyes, and Tommy played a convincing bit of awe at the sight of her, but the angles were flat and static, boring, even. She watched them both hit their marks and deliver their lines on cue. Nothing seemed out of place or even off-putting, but neither was it engaging in any way. The whole thing felt a little too on-the-nose, but Brian hadn't actually made any mistakes worth criticising.

"Ugh." She pulled the headset off.

"That good?" Talia asked hopefully.

"It's textbook, comprehensive, well framed, and dry as fuck." Sophia stared up at the rafters and released a heavy breath.

The rafters.

"The rafters," she repeated in her external voice.

Talia followed her line of sight, but apparently not her line of thinking. "Excuse me?"

"Get someone in the rafters with a Steadicam." She looked around until she found her costar and their new intimacy coordinator. "Tommy, Caroline, I want to run something by you."

"Aye," Tommy said. "Someone's got to liven things up."

"I'm listening," Caroline added.

"What if during the kiss, instead of having Tommy push me against the wall, he lowers me to the ground. From there we shoot from above, a more expansive shot, my dress flared out dramatically. He can draw the layers up slowly, but ball it up in his fist as he pushes. Then we can cut back to the shots we got earlier of his hand on my calf to make it clear what's happening, but instead of cutting close again, we use the shot from above to slowly zoom in on my face. We move from the expansive to the intimate just as I showcase surrender."

Tommy fanned himself with the script. "Sounds amazing."

Caroline nodded seriously as she seemed to walk through the mental steps the framing would require. Then she grinned. "It's similar choreography, only worked from a different position. No new risks, and bloody beautiful."

Caroline had been a breath of fresh air on set all day. She was young and enthusiastic as well as empathetic. Perhaps if she'd been around the whole time, none of them would still be standing in this stable right now.

"Sounds like you've got a real eye for the artistic," Caroline continued, "and since we've already shot the skin-to-skin contact, the main question to consider here is your comfort level with him balling up the skirt, and the limits of how far you'd like him to pull it up."

She nodded, thankful for the consideration. She'd been so set on the shot she hadn't stopped to think about the physical impact or exposure on her own body. She chose not to examine those priorities too closely, not now, not when she was already fighting to hold other emotions at bay.

Instead, she turned back to Tommy. "Same ground rules as when we shot the skin-to-skin earlier. You remember?"

He nodded seriously. "Of course. I know I've done my fair share of joking, but you've been amazing here today. On my honour, I respect your boundaries."

She smiled faintly. "Thank you."

"The shot is exactly the mix of drama and romance we need," Talia agreed, "but who's going to tell Brian?"

All around them shoulders sagged.

"Will he really not allow you to reshoot?" Caroline asked with an adorably naive expression. "Won't he want to make the most of the shot, no matter who came up with it?"

"No," Sophia sighed, "but he will if I make him think it was his idea."

Talia grimaced apologetically but made no move to dissuade her.

So, steeling her nerves and gritting her teeth, Sophia slipped back into character, not the one she'd been hired to play, but the one she'd learned to play over years of working with petty egos and perverts. For the first time in a long time, her stomach roiled at the switch, but she managed to inject a bit more saccharine into her voice as she called, "Brian, would you mind sharing your artistic expertise with us for a moment?"

He sauntered back into the stable, a suspicious glint in his eyes. "What now?"

"It's nothing major. I was just telling the others that as much as it pains me to admit, you may've been right about the need for a more creative angle on this scene."

He furrowed his brow. "It does come across a little flat, but that's what you wanted."

That hadn't been at all what she wanted. In fact, she'd suggested something much more complex, but she swallowed the retort and stepped closer. "I know, and I'd like to make it up to you. Would you like to get some shots from the rafters, you know, a full panorama of me on my back, to weave together with the shots you already got?"

"The rafters?" He raised his gaze as if realizing they weren't talking about the same thing at all. His mind had likely returned to his wretched suggestion of the up-skirt shot.

She rushed to reel him back in. "Exactly the kind of bold cut you were always asking for, right? If you really wanted, I'd even be willing to redo the shots where you zoom in on my face, but from that angle, your more creative one."

He frowned, then nodded slowly. "I didn't want to push it, what with all the hard feelings, but I do think we need something more dramatic here. If you don't mind going back to my angle, let's get someone harnessed up and in the rafters."

A collective whoosh of relief went through the onlookers, and then everyone sprang into action. Sophia had little time to feel any satisfaction at how well she'd played her part, but that also meant she barely felt the sting of how quick he'd been to attribute her idea to his own genius.

It didn't matter. They all had a job to do, and once again, she would sacrifice her pride, her vision, her artistic integrity for the good of the project, only this time her sense of unease didn't fade when he finally called "cut" and the burn of burying herself behind some lesser man wasn't soothed even by seeing the infinitely improved footage.

She still felt mildly nauseated as they broke for the day and she piled into the transport van with Talia and Caroline to head back toward hair and makeup.

"Name your price," Talia said as soon as the van doors shut after their last meeting of the day.

"What?"

"You saved our asses out there," Talia said earnestly. "Don't think I don't know it, and don't think I don't realise how much that cost you personally. What do you want? A bottle of single-malt whiskey? A Louis Vuitton purse? Hell, you want a Rolls-Royce? I can't afford one, but I'll steal one for you."

She shook her head. "The shot is the only reward that would make grovelling worthwhile."

"It's a brilliant shot." Talia gave her hand a squeeze. "It'll make the previews for sure, and the publicity kit, and I wouldn't be surprised if the photography stills end up on the poster. It could be iconic."

"Iconic," she muttered, and let her head loll back on the seat. It wasn't that she didn't agree with Talia's assessment, but when people referenced that shot, they'd always credit Brian. He would build his career on the back of her image and imagination while once again she'd only be seen for her body.

"I get the feeling I missed a lot before I got here," Caroline finally said, "like, not only half the filming, but a whole lot of emotional work as well."

Sophia snorted softly. Emotional work might be an understatement for what she'd survived in the last few weeks. More like emotional wreckage.

"But, what I'm not able to figure out is why you aren't running this whole set, Sophia. Or rather, why no one can speak openly about how you actually *are* running the whole set."

"You want the short version?" Talia asked, then answered anyway. "Patriarchy."

Caroline grunted. "Now, that I'm familiar with. Wouldn't it be great if we could run the world, or at least the movie business, without all the egotistical assholes?"

"That'd be living the dream," Talia mused, "and I even found the perfect project."

Caroline perked up. "What is it?"

"Emma Volant's next book. I got a sneak peek at the rough draft last night, and it's got the potential to be an even bigger hit than this one. Easier to shoot without all the period costuming, cheaper too, but every bit as beautiful. She's not even done with it yet, and I offered to buy the rights off her."

Sophia shook her head. "Not so fast. *I* offered to buy the rights off her."

"You want to do the screenplay?" Talia asked incredulously.

"No, I want to direct."

Caroline laughed. "I don't even know what it's about, but with you two and Emma Volant, I want to be the intimacy coordinator."

"It's a contemporary romance, and you're hired," Talia said. "If we're indulging fantasies, Addie's hired to do costumes, and Lila Wilder's doing the score."

"Wait," Caroline said excitedly, "if it's a romance and Sophia's directing, who's going to be the female lead?"

Sophia's and Talia's eyes met, and they both said, "Cobie Galloway."

"I love her! You've got a writer, a director, a star, the start of a creative team," she said as they pulled onto the street leading into Penchant Castle. "And if it's an Emma Volant book, I bet you've already got a connection to some perfect places to film."

Sophia's chest tightened as she stared up at the battlements and towers up ahead, then turned away only to see the expanse of green fields in the distance. She could follow the picturesque landscape all the way to the sea, and it wouldn't change a thing. All of it led right back to Vic. The one place she absolutely could not go, not even in her dreams. "We have a lot of little pieces, but none of the big ones."

"All of the knowledge and none of the money or the clout," Talia agreed. "You can't produce a movie worth making without a producer, and none of the big studios are going to hand a blank check to a first-time director and the writer's best friend."

"But you two aren't nobodies. You've had big careers with big hits," Caroline pushed.

"We could certainly get something low-budget," Talia admitted. "We could have our way with an art-house piece."

"If only we would dream smaller and know our place," Sophia added over the bile rising in her throat.

"Or maybe you need a sugar daddy," Caroline offered, then snorted in disgust.

"Or a rich actual daddy," Talia offered. "That's how Brian got his start. Lord knows, he didn't establish himself on talent. It's all in his last name."

"Yeah, well I've got none of those things attached to me or my name. No daddies of any kind." Sophia made a little gagging noise.

"Sorry." Caroline grimaced. "I didn't mean to be heteronormative. It's just, you only ever hear about men doing those things. It's always so-and-so and sons on the business marquees. It's always men who get jobs for their mistresses. You never hear of rich women pulling those strings, do you?"

Talia shrugged. "Maybe they have higher moral standards."

"And isn't that some shite?" Caroline laughed as the van came to a stop inside the castle gate. "I long for the day when a sugar mama who actually believes in a project is as valid a funding source as good old-fashioned nepotism."

The intimacy coordinator was still chuckling at her own joke as she hopped out, but Sophia made no move to leave as Talia met her gaze and arched an eyebrow.

Her ribs tightened like a clamp around her heart and lungs as all the implication of that questioning stare and the conversation that had preceded it pressed down on her chest. Every old impulse screamed with the desire to run back toward the castle, to say she'd been wrong, that they could have everything they ever wanted, if only Vic would give up her birthright and they would both sacrifice every ideal they held true.

At another point in her life, the choice wouldn't have just been easy, it would've been downright enjoyable, but she simply wasn't the woman she'd been even a few weeks ago. She had neither the words nor the will to explain the transformation, and she suspected it might haunt her for the rest of her life. But knowing those things did little to lessen the sense of permanence descending around her.

Finally, she shook her head.

Apparently, the fates weren't just cruel, they were downright masochistic.

Chapter Sixteen

Vic jogged up the main staircase, her sensible heels clacking against the stone stairs and her own feet with equal sharpness. Her whole body ached, and her vision had begun to blur hours ago, but her mind hummed with a thrilling rush of possibilities. She couldn't remember the last time she'd felt such a pleasurable sense of anticipation about anything other than Sophia.

She pulled up short just outside of the dining room and struggled to catch her breath more than a single flight of stairs warranted. Sophia had never been far from her thoughts all afternoon, but until this moment she'd been able to keep the pain in her periphery. Now she braced herself for the onslaught she would undoubtedly have to face head on.

Lifting her chin and squaring her shoulders, she pushed open the heavy doors to see both her parents sitting in their usual spots at one end of the long table. They were still dressed in their business clothes, adding an air of formality to an already ostentatious setting, but her father at least smiled at her entrance.

"Sorry, love, we started without you."

"Yes, you're fashionably late," her mother added, without much inflection to indicate her mood.

Vic fought down the urge to apologise. "I lost track of time at the office."

Her father chuckled. "I'm not sure I've ever lost track of mealtimes in favour of land acquisitions."

"Actually, I wasn't working on acquisitions today, or land at all, at least not in the conventional sense." Her face warmed as the words poured out of her, and she had to shed her suit jacket. She tossed it over the high back of her chair, earning a distasteful expression from her mother, but she didn't wilt or change course. Before this was over, a misplaced article of clothing would feel downright dainty.

"I spent most of my day doing research. On the film industry at large and movie producing, specifically."

Her parents exchanged an undecipherable look, and her mother set down her silverware neatly before saying, "I thought Ms. LeBlanc's film was in its final stages. Producers are usually secured before filming, not days before their location contracts end."

Warning bells pinged in the back of Vic's mind. "I didn't know you paid attention to the movie business, much less the specifics of this one's contractual status."

The duchess pursed her lips before affecting a more neutral expression. "I pay attention to everything involving my home and family. It's part of my role as lady of the house . . . and as a mother."

The low thrum of warning in the timbre of her voice made the hair on Vic's arms stand on end, but she had to stay the course, or she'd never make it through this. "Actually, that kind of responsibility is exactly why I wanted to speak with you both tonight."

"Yes. James mentioned something about a meeting with local filmmakers," her father cut back in. "Why not sit down and tell us about it?"

She started to ease into the chair, but her muscles twitched, and she hopped back up, opting to pace instead. She was too wound up on a combination of nerves and excitement to hold still. "Yes, the filmmakers and James, so much has happened since then. First of all, James is horrible and it's time for him to retire with dignity before I sack him myself."

"Victoria!" her mother scolded, "James has been—"

"A snooty little spy for too long." Vic held up her hand to forestall further argument. "But in this case, he needled me into articulating something I should've said to him years ago, and in defending the young filmmakers against him, I finally saw a stark contrast between the type of attitudes and people who want to drag us back and the kind that can move us forward. His disdain for the future also forced me to choose a side, and I came down firmly in favour of the future."

"That sounds rather exciting," her father said.

"Exciting or heretical?" her mother asked, "since you're standing inside an eight-hundred-year-old estate?"

"I see the irony clearly," Vic admitted. "Every power I hold was handed down from those who came before. It's not easy to think about the future when your entire world is based on the past, but none of it was the past when it was built. Each Duke of Northland built his legacy in his own times. Some did so better than others, but from the Wars of the Roses to the Industrial Revolution, this family stayed in a position of privilege by taking bold steps to meet the needs and opportunities of their age."

"Well said." Her father urged her on. "What opportunity do you want to seize?"

"Actually, I may have already grabbed it." She inhaled a deep breath, and when she exhaled, the words also poured out in a rush. "I bought the production rights to Emma Volant's next movie. Rather, it's a book, or it will be a book soon, and when it is, I intend to turn it into a movie, here in Northland, on our shores and with our people."

Both parents stared at her, his expression bemused and hers appalled, but she'd apparently stunned them into silence. She charged on, giving voice to the myriad of thoughts that warred within as she'd poured over facts and figures as well as risk assessments. "We don't currently have all the infrastructure, but as I mentioned, perhaps ineloquently, the book isn't finished, much less published. We have months if not a year before we could begin filming. In the meantime, I intend to leave the land office in Archie's very capable hands so I may spend more time in London and possibly Los Angeles."

"Of course." Her mother scoffed.

"We'll woo some established artists and technical experts away from the city by offering them the type of locations they cannot replicate on sound stages and with a cost of living large metro areas cannot possibly offer. We'll partner with local universities for visual and sound technologies to keep investment figures low until we know if we can make it work. The first film will call for a modest budget, and strong ties to a local artist will foster a sense of community even as we may have to outsource some higher end jobs until more locals gain the type of experience necessary to staff an undertaking of this magnitude."

"Let me guess, you intend to lean heavily on the liaisons you've amassed during the current filming schedule? Perhaps pull from your new *personal* contacts?" Her mother put her emphasis right where Vic had expected her to.

Her face burned, and she opened her mouth to refute the thinly veiled accusation, but she couldn't bring herself to deny the charge completely. Nothing she'd done had its foundation in a desire to keep Sophia close, but it would be a lie to say the spirit of the endeavour wasn't inspired by the passion Sophia sparked in her. How could she explain that even if she lost the woman herself, she was unwilling to lose the way she'd made her feel, her sense of purpose and drive, the desire to blaze her own trail and create something meaningful of her own?

In her inability to convey the substance or strength of the need consuming her, she left herself open to a more direct attack.

"Movies! My god, I should've known this woman addled your brain with visions of Hollywood." Her mother shook her head and levelled her most disappointed stare at her. "Honestly, even after all your past escapades I still believed you too sensible to get swept up in flights of fancy, fits of passion, or gross indulgence. I've always known you were prone to impulsiveness, but this sort of California thinking will—"

"I'm not thinking of California," Vic parried as the reprimand missed its mark. "Or Hollywood. I'm thinking of Northland, first and last."

She turned to her father, whose expression had grown pensive.

"I want to convert the old servants' quarters into headquarters for local filming, both on the estate and beyond. I've already been in contact with several studios in London, all exploratory of course, but we have the castle, fields and forests, elaborate gardens, and dramatic seascapes. With the right incentives we could attract a wide array of films, and best of all we wouldn't have to develop our conservation areas in order to provide good modern jobs. We wouldn't have to export our young people, either."

He nodded slowly. "You make a compelling, if unrefined, argument."

"Edward?" Her mother raised her voice. "Don't indulge her. You've always been entirely too permissive with the girls, and I've adored you for it, but she's not a child anymore. She's well past the time when she should be finding her place."

"I am finding my place. For the first time, I am finding myself, both as a person and a public servant."

"Absolutely not." The duchess shook her head. "Do not bring your position into this. Movies, increased press scrutiny, flash-in-the pan pop culture, none of this offers any dignified return on the reputation you'll squander. It's vulgar and common. Mark my words, you'll lose the dukedom if you follow this path."

"Then *I* will lose it." Vic exploded with a vehemence she hadn't even felt building in her. Or maybe she'd failed to notice its presence because it had always been simmering inside her. "It's my birthright or it isn't. It's my title or it's not, but either way, the operative words are *I*, *me*, and *mine*. They don't belong to some phantom of my lineage or fictional character. And they don't belong to you. I'm the one who will rise or fall, and I mean to do it on my terms."

Her mother sat back, her expression cool, but her complexion had lost some of its colour. "I see Ms. LeBlanc's brash American individualism has also infected your sensibilities, but pray, tell me, while you assert your own divine right, what of the people who depend on you to be there for them?"

"I *will* be there for them in the ways they actually deserve,

266

with or without the title, because the title means nothing if I can't use it in meaningful ways. I'd rather lose it while building a better future than keep it by upholding the status quo." Her voice may have held a hint of pleading, but it no longer wavered on this point. She'd already sacrificed more than most could imagine for the people she served, and she stood firm in her certainty that she'd continue to do so. Nothing else could ever exact the toll she'd paid this morning. "I want to make a real, tangible difference for my people."

"They won't see that. They'll see you only as frivolous and attention-seeking. They won't understand or care about your motives."

"I disagree. I won't infantilise them by pretending they're incapable of comprehending a shifting world or social order, and I won't lock myself in a tower above them. I'll be forthcoming about the fights ahead, and I'll approach each new challenge beside them."

She turned to her father before adding, "I will find my own style, like each Penchant who came before me. I'll win them over one by one if I have to, and in return I trust they'll share my goals, indeed, my hopes for this whole region."

Her mother gave a sharp, humourless laugh. "Commoners don't care about the hopes and dreams of the nobility."

"Maybe that's because our goals have never aligned closely enough with theirs," she snapped back, then reined in her voice. She didn't want to fight. She desperately wanted them to understand, to share her vision. "I know you've always tried to maintain a place of poise and dignity by staying above the fray, and maybe that was the right thing for you and your time, but I'm a different person, and mine is a different time. I want to let the people in. I want to know them, and I want them to know me. The movies are merely the beginning."

"I won't listen to any more of this rash nonsense." Her mother pushed back from the table.

"I will," a softer voice said.

Both of them turned to her father.

"I would very much like to hear more."

Her chest constricted at his earnest faith in her. She swallowed a lump of emotion and tried to match his tone. "The economic impact has tremendous potential, and not merely on a per-film basis. The locations of popular movies could see a considerable uptick in tourism as well. Consider what *Downton Abbey* did for Highclere Castle or what *Harry Potter* did for Alnwick. Did you know that even the series *Gentleman Jack* more than quadrupled visitors to Shibden Hall? Those places are all every bit as remote as Penchant Castle, and I dare say, not as beautiful."

The corner of his mouth twitched up. "I won't quarrel with any of your points, and I admit I find your idea more than a little intriguing. However, you didn't merely research a proposal. You apparently signed a contract. The speed and magnitude of that decision seems more than a bit rash."

He turned to nod to his wife. "Like your mother, I do wonder at this rapid transformation and the new sense of urgency around you. She believes we owe it to the influence of Ms. LeBlanc, while I've reserved judgement until I hear from you on the subject."

She hung her head and let her shoulders fall. This was the bottom line, what it all came down to, even for him. Not the new dreams themselves, but who sparked them. To lend credibility to a future she desired, she'd have to deny the person who finally made her feel as though she deserved to dream.

She couldn't do it. Or perhaps she simply wouldn't do it. No future could burn brightly enough to dim the light Sophia brought to her life, and to deny that would cost a pound of flesh she remained unwilling to pay.

Her heart ached so badly she could barely draw a full breath, but she lifted her chin and met his eyes. "I promise, Sophia never once asked me for any of this, or even hinted she wanted it. If you must know, she said the opposite. She's under the impression that I have a moral duty to my family and my people. She believes I would cease to be me without that calling, and she left me this morning even after I offered to renounce my claim to the title."

Her mother gave a little gasp, and her father's brow creased deeply.

"So, no. I'm not doing this for her. I'm doing it without her, not by my choice, but by hers." Her voice cracked, as even her vocal cords rebelled at the wrongness of the trade she'd made. "My economic ideas and outlook are mine alone, but while we're on the subject of Sophia, I must admit you're not wrong to believe she played a role in my transformation. Without her faith in me, I would've never had the courage to give these ideas voice."

"Helping someone find their voice is no small contribution," her father mused.

"Nor is the extent of her effect on me. She taught me a great deal about myself in a short time, like how to trust in my instincts, how to stand up for what I know is right, and never apologise for doing what I believe best." She released another shuddering breath and tried to find her footing on more solid ground. Even the idea of Sophia gave her strength to go on when every fibre of her being ached to unravel. "Most importantly, Sophia reminded me how useless it would be to fight for a title unless I intended to use it for something meaningful, and that's what I intend to do, now and for as long I am in a position to do so."

"Alone?" her father asked softly, but the single word was enough to knock her back.

She clenched her teeth against the sadness clawing at her stomach lining, but she couldn't say the word. Her body refused to accept the truth she'd tried to force into her brain.

"No," her mother said, flatly.

Her father put his hand on the table. "We've all got a lot to digest."

"No," her mother reiterated, this time placing her hand gently atop his. "This is too big an undertaking. I've never made apologies for pushing you toward a safer path, Victoria. Perhaps I haven't always done so gracefully, but that's all I ever wanted for you, an easier road, one of less resistance, one where I could protect you from what I feared lay ahead, but you seem insistent on blazing a newer, more fraught trail."

She clenched her jaw against the disappointment she heard there, but she wouldn't apologise for who she was anymore.

"However, if there is no swaying you from this endeavour to revolutionise local industry and tourism and fight a lifetime of legal battles"—her mother paused as if giving her one more chance to abandon ship, then sighed—"then you must brace yourself for the challenges that will accompany your quest, and the best way to do so is with a strong partner beside you, one who is savvy and tenacious, and who understands what you have at stake as well as the sacrifices you may have to make."

The words were like a knife between her shoulder blades. She fought the urge to writhe away from the sharpness of them. How could this be happening? How could her own mother give voice to that particular insecurity? She felt herself sinking back into murky waters of doubt with their strong undercurrent of despair. She turned helplessly toward her father, hoping he'd buoy her once more.

"Did you really offer to renounce your title for Ms. LeBlanc?" he asked, his tone grave and wounded.

She nodded, numbly.

Her parents exchanged another cryptic glance.

"And yet Ms. LeBlanc inspired you to find your voice even as she sacrificed herself for you?"

She swallowed a whimper at the piercing summary.

Her father nodded resolutely. "Then I'm afraid your mother and I are of one mind on this. You have our full faith to execute your first foray into movie producing, but I believe it would be a fool's errand to do so without first righting this wrong with Ms. LeBlanc."

"What?"

"A voice will do you no good if you lose your heart in the process," he said seriously.

"Your father's right." Her mother's tone suggested she didn't enjoy the pronouncement. "When you make a mistake, you have to right it. It sounds like we've both made rather sizable mistakes in the last few days, but the bottom line is that you finally found someone who sees you clearly, who understands you deeply, and who loves you enough to sacrifice their own desires so you can step fully into your destiny. And instead of clinging to her in the face of challenge—"

"I let her walk away," Vic concluded.

All the gears in her head began to whirl again. She'd tried all day to make them turn in tandem, but until this moment she'd been working with only half of her heart. She couldn't trade Sophia for her future any more than she could trade her future for Sophia. The two could not be separated. She'd been an idiot to think she could change that.

"Oh, lord. I let her walk away." She pushed her hands through her hair roughly as she began to pace again. "She said it couldn't work, and I bloody well agreed with her. I thanked her. I said goodbye. I bought a movie on my own. I don't know a thing about movies. I could lose her and everything else."

"Darling," her mother cut in, the corners of her mouth turned up in something akin to genuine emotion for the first time in ages. "She's not in Siberia. She's across the street."

She stared at her mother as if seeing her for the first time. Cool, practical, detached, and yet ever pragmatic.

"Take her a present," her father offered good-naturedly.

"And comb your hair," her mother added. "You've mussed it all up. For the love of god, Victoria, if this is the path you've chosen, please do it well."

"And think about what you want to say to her," her father piped in.

"Yes," her mother agreed, "you tend to run on when you're improvising speeches."

"But, be yourself." Her dad grinned.

"Indeed." Her mother's tone softened. "Because, apparently, she loves you very much."

Vic opened her mouth to…do what? To argue? To question? She didn't know, and it didn't matter, because the only sound she could produce was a sob.

Grief, joy, confusion, fear, relief. She couldn't sort any of them as a lifetime of prestigious pressure crumbled around her. When the shards and shrapnel of the life she'd worked so hard to reconcile settled to dust at her feet, one thought, one impulse rose to the forefront of her mind with a clarity she'd only craved—until now.

She had to get Sophia back.

Chapter Seventeen

Sophia lay on her hotel bed staring up at the exposed beams of the ceiling and listening to the rhythmic buzz of her cell phone on the table. Someone had been calling for at least ten minutes, but she didn't recognise the number, and she didn't want to speak to anyone anyway.

Rolling onto her side, she let out a heavy sigh and allowed her vision to focus on her suitcase in the corner. She visually traced the outline of her luggage tags, examining any tangible detail she could to keep her mind from replaying a million conversations she didn't want to relive.

Morose didn't even begin to cover her current mindset. Each time she let her thoughts wander for even a few seconds, she could hear her own voice dripping with accommodation as she sacrificed her vision to Brian's vanity. Then, when she'd exhausted her annoyance, inevitably Talia and Caroline's voices would auto-play their reminders that no matter how good she got, or what creative force she wielded, genius bore little correlation to power. All the things she'd done to try to move ahead would likely be used against her in perpetuity, while others were applauded for never being forced into similar choices in the first place.

That, of course, led her back to Vic and the conversation Sophia most wanted to forget. The others brought anger or resentment. The echoes of Vic's pure pleading proved harder to compartmentalise.

All day long, every time the pain nipped at her or the depression shrouded her like a fog, she strove to stay firm in the knowledge that she'd done the right thing, but here, alone with the ghosts of unhappy endings, she had a harder time forcing herself to swallow that jagged pill.

There was no use asking why the world worked the way it did, but she still couldn't fathom why loving Vic should cost either of them so much when others got rewarded for so little. And now she'd circled right back to Caroline's comments about sugar mamas who believe in something being as valid as nepotism. She didn't want either, really. She wanted to be seen for who she was and appreciated for what she had to offer, without either of those things being weaponised against Vic. On the surface, that didn't seem like too much to ask, and yet nothing that had happened since she arrived here had ever been what it seemed on the surface.

She flopped onto her back once more, but as she did, the sound of metal clinking caught her ear.

Afraid she'd lost some piece of costume jewellery in the comforter, she sat up and glanced around for an errant earring or bracelet she'd inadvertently brought home from the set. Only, she'd changed into yoga pants and a hotel robe the first chance she got.

The sound clinked again, and she widened her search, scanning the room for things like pull chains, or even a radiator. Then there came two more taps in close succession, this time obviously from her window.

She hopped up. Peeking through the curtains, she stopped short at the sight of Vic holding a bottle of gin in one hand and something she clearly intended to throw in the other.

"No, no, no," she muttered even as her heart rate accelerated. She couldn't do this. She couldn't see her. Not now. She wasn't strong enough. God, was this how Vic had felt when their position had been reversed? Had her heart pounded a bass beat to the shrill warning bells ringing inside her head? If so, Vic was infinitely braver than Sophia ever gave her credit for, but then again, of course she was.

Sophia wanted to cower behind her curtains, and she might have done so if some movement farther to the right hadn't caught her eye. There, a few doorways down and to Victoria's back, a small cluster of tourists stood, watching and whispering. Or perhaps they weren't tourists at all, maybe they were some of those nosy journalists who'd wrecked their morning in Amberwick.

"Shit." She hadn't walked away to protect the greatest woman she'd ever known only to have her compromised after the fact.

In one swift movement, she threw open the window sash in time for Vic to release her next throw. A small bit of silver flew up and hit her in the chest. Her reflexes took hold, and she caught the thing in her hand.

"Whoops," Victoria said, then squinting up at her, grinned sheepishly. "Hello."

She shook her head, trying to keep the utter charm of the greeting from taking hold of her senses. "What are you doing?"

"I needed to talk to you, and you wouldn't answer your phone."

"So, you decided to throw things at me?"

"I learned from the best."

"I threw pebbles." She tried to keep the humour from her voice as she glanced down to see a one-pound coin in the palm of her hand. "Not money. Who throws money?"

Victoria shrugged and did a terrible job of hiding a grin. "I'm very rich."

Sophia laughed in spite of herself. This was not going well for her resolve.

"Ask me how rich I am."

She shook her head and shot a glance toward the tourists, one of whom seemed to be moving her phone into a perfect position to capture them on video. "You have to go."

"Not until you ask me how rich I am."

She nodded toward the others. "We can't do this here."

"Then call off your security detail and we'll do it in there."

She pursed her lips. She couldn't let this woman within arm's reach. She understood her own limitations, and yet she got the

275

sense she wouldn't get rid of Vic any other way. She glanced at the camera one more time. In the end, she could lose Vic and fail to protect her all at once. Fear made the decision for her. "Fine. I'll message security."

Vic wasted no time, jogging toward the door.

Sophia tapped off a quick text to the studio man sitting at the front desk and tried to steel herself for Vic's arrival. She snugged the robe a little tighter over her chest and waist. She did her best to summon an expression of dignified exasperation, but she must have failed miserably because Vic's smile flashed full and radiant as soon as she opened the door.

"You shouldn't be here," Sophia said, instead of grabbing her and dragging her straight to the bed.

"That's not your line," Vic said as she strolled into the room as though she owned it, which, for all Sophia knew, she might.

"Right, you came up here for me to ask you how rich you are, but honestly it would be truer to the scene for me to ask, 'Are you drunk?'"

Vic held up the bottle of gin in her hand. "Not yet, but we can start working on the celebration as soon as you give me a proper lead-in to the explanation."

"Celebration? I'm not feeling jubilant today." It stung to see Vic so bright-eyed and bouncy, given that she'd been moping and contemplating the vast unfairness of the world. Still, the longer this went on, the more it would hurt to say goodbye again, so she sighed and surrendered. "Never mind. I'll bite. How rich are you?"

Vic pressed her lips together for an anticipatory beat, then said, "Rich enough to become a movie producer, apparently."

Sophia cocked her head to the side and started to protest, but she wasn't even sure exactly what she was arguing with, so she closed her mouth again.

"Remember this morning, I said I couldn't give you the director's chair you deserved because I wasn't a movie producer?"

The snippet of conversation came back to her. "What did you do?"

"I bought the movie rights to Emma's next book." Vic beamed proudly. Sophia felt like she'd poured molten lead into her stomach.

"You what?"

"I became a movie producer, or I started becoming one. More people will be involved with the money and contracts. I'll obviously need a full creative team of writers, costume designers, a tech crew, a cast, and of course, a director, which is what we're celebrating with this gin, because if I'm going to produce my first movie, I don't see any reason why it shouldn't also be your first directing job." She held out the bottle of gin. "Do you have any glasses in here?"

"Are you fucking insane?" Sophia exploded.

Vic grimaced. "We can drink from the bottle."

Sophia snatched the gin from her hand and tossed it on the bed. "I can't believe you—how could you think—how dare you just throw your money at my dreams? Do you know how long I worked and sacrificed and swallowed my pride to get a job offer like that, and you burst in here and throw it around like a punch line?"

Sophia fought the urge to dissolve into a wild scream. "You're acting like those men who reap what they've never sown. How could you think I'd take something like this as some little bauble? After everything I was ready to sacrifice to keep you safe, to show you how much I value your values. Do you really think I'd accept something I haven't earned just because you packaged it up with a bow on top and—"

"Whoa, whoa, whoa." Vic reached out to her, but Sophia slapped her hand away.

"I didn't mean to sound cavalier," Vic said frantically. "God, my father was right. I should've thought this through. I should've probably thought the whole thing through a little more, but I sort of fell apart without you today."

"So, you bought a movie? Do you know how absurd that is?"

"Yes. And technically I bought a book, but yes."

"You spent—I don't even want to know how much—on a project the magnitude of which you cannot even begin to understand, to try to what? Undercut everything I said this morning?"

"No."

"Self-sabotage your entire future?"

"No!"

"To give your parents heart attacks?"

"I know it probably appears that way, but I swear on all things holy, I did this for me, and for the future of my people, for a modern Northland, and for a chance at a title worth saving." She sighed. "I did it because you gave me the courage to dream."

Sophia snorted. "And you just happened to choose the same dream as me?"

"Except it's not." Vic stepped forward again, the earnestness in her voice knocking a hole in Sophia's anger. "Yes, the dreams are related. They can and should work in tandem, but for me this isn't about a movie. It's about giving jobs, ones that aren't tied to ancient titles or land grants, jobs that could outlast me. It's about a new turn for an old legacy. It's about making my birthright my own, and it's your fault."

"My fault?"

"You said you'd never forgive me if I caved to someone else's vision of who I'm supposed to be. And you were right."

Sophia gritted her teeth against both the compliment and the pleading behind it.

"Yes, I made the decision quickly, but I didn't do it without a vision, and I didn't do it to get you back. I'm building a legacy now, a future full of hope, a life I can be proud of, whether or not I ever secure the title to go with it."

Sophia couldn't bring herself to argue with the passion pouring out of Vic. She was commanding and compelling, and her optimism might well have been physically contagious, because even though her brain rebelled against the image Vic was building, Sophia couldn't put a damper on the fire building at her own core.

"I'm sorry I didn't lead with a better business presentation," Vic continued, "but I've been over everything in my head all day, and I wanted to skip to the part where I give you your due credit before I also tell you how wrong you were on other counts."

"Wrong?" Sophia's anger threatened to surge again. "Seriously, you're going to come at me with some half-cocked plan to merge your dream with mine, damn the details or my own desires, and then you decide to mention how wrong I've been?"

"I didn't want to put it that way."

"Oh no, please enlighten me, Your Ladyship."

Vic wrung her hands and bit her lip for a second. "I didn't want to bring it up this way, but nothing about this conversation has gone quite as I hoped, which is on par for nearly every serious conversation we've ever had. I'm getting used to the direct approach, so I'll say bluntly that you were wrong when you decided that walking away was best for me."

Sophia pressed her lips together.

"Right, I get that you're not used to hearing you're wrong, because you aren't very often, but I won't apologise for saying so. You are wrong to think you're not right for me or that you don't fit into my future. You're wrong to think letting me go was noble. It's not. It's cowardice. It's the path of least resistance. More importantly, though, you told me not to let other people tell me who I'm supposed to be, and that includes you."

Sophia's shoulders fell. "You know that's not what I meant."

"No, I don't. I didn't get to protest. I didn't get to argue or have my own say. You made a unilateral decision about what was best for me, but I've had enough of other people telling me what I need."

Her heart ached at the accusation. Is that really what she'd done? She'd never intended to become one more person who pushed Vic again, another well-meaning master to twist her into knots and make her question her own judgement.

"I don't want another protector," Vic continued. "I want a partner."

Sophia took the step closer this time. "I can't let you throw away your responsibilities for me."

"I don't intend to. I mean to share them with you."

"I'm too much of a liability. My past—"

"I don't want your past. I want your future."

"You can't separate the two. Your mother was right about me."

279

Vic smiled broadly once more.

"What?"

She took the last step, the one that put them close enough to share the same breath. "My mother told me to come get you back."

"Now I know you're drunk." Sophia tried to push her away, but Vic caught her hands and pulled their bodies flush.

"I'm serious. About all of this. I told my parents what I intended to do, and I'm going to tell you the same thing. I plan to make movies in Northland. I'm going to provide for my people. I'm going to modernise and build something lasting of my own, whether I hold onto the title or not. I'm going to do it with you or without you, but it would be better with you. We can be better together."

She wanted to resist this. She didn't believe in fairy tales. She didn't ever wish for a white knight to ride in and save her. "I can't let you hand me your life on a platter. I know what people will say if I get my first director's job from a rich lover. I couldn't live with myself if they said those things about you, too."

"I won't lie." Vic's blue eyes brimmed with sincerity. "Some people will say horrible things, neither of us are new to that. They don't know us, but you know me. You see me more clearly than I've ever seen myself. You had faith in me that I never had in myself. Please let me offer you the same."

The walls she'd worked so hard to build around herself began to crumble. Why did Vic have to be so damned perfect? It was unrealistic to think a mere mortal could resist logic laced with such genuine emotion.

"I need you beside me," Vic pleaded. "I need you in my life. I need you in my future, and god knows, I'm going to need you on this movie. Why does that need matter less if I'm also in love with you?"

"I wanted to earn it. I worked so hard to try to earn it."

"And you have!" Vic said passionately. "You have earned it so much more than men like Brian have. You have earned it with the work you've done. You've earned it with your talent and the vision you've cultivated over years of paying your dues fruitlessly. You've earned it more than I earned my title, and yet you pushed me to make the most of my opportunities. Why can't I do the same for you?"

She shook her head against the idea that they could really be the same.

"Sophia, you earned this opportunity a million times over, and you will continue to do so, probably every day for the rest of our lives."

Sophia rested her forehead on Vic's shoulder and balled the front of her shirt in her fist. She couldn't argue with that logic. She had earned her shot behind the camera, but did she deserve everything that seemed to come with it now? "This wasn't how any of this was supposed to go. I was never one of those girls who dreamed of living in a castle. I never wanted to be anyone's princess. I never wanted anyone to hand me anything on a silver platter."

Vic laughed. "That's not what's happening. Okay, maybe the castle part is real because I do want you to live with me forever, but the rest of it isn't going to be an easy road, love. You think the men you've been working with are idiots. Wait until you come to work with me."

She smiled in spite of herself.

"I mean it. I know literally nothing about filming or production or producing. You'll have to work harder than you've ever worked in your life, and then when you go home at night, I make no promises about you getting any rest then, either. In the end I'll depend on you every bit as much as you depend on me, and that's why this is going to work."

She sank into Vic's embrace. Of course, she would emphasise their equality. She'd never once made Sophia feel less than. Even when they'd sparred, even when they'd disagreed, even when Sophia broke her heart, Vic always treated her as an equal even though she had every right not to. Suddenly it all seemed so clear, what their lives could be, what they could accomplish, how many lives they could shape for the better, together.

Hope filled her senses like a deep breath laden with the scent of Vic's perfume. No more grovelling, no more wasted compromises, no more lonely self-reliance, all of it replaced by love.

Vic hooked her finger under Sophia's chin, gently urging it up until their eyes met. "This morning you said you'd never be the one to pull me down, but now I'm asking for more. I am here asking you to go a step further, to be the one who lifts me up, who holds me accountable, who makes me better, and I'm asking you to let me be the person who does those things for you."

Sophia stared deeply into her eyes, not even sure how she could respond to such a perfect request from such a perfect woman. Were there even words to adequately promise such a thing? If there were, she didn't know them, so she did the only thing she knew would be right and pressed her lips to Vic's.

They kissed like they'd been apart for years rather than hours, but maybe they had been, maybe they'd never been like this before, because Sophia had never experienced such toe-curling completion until this moment.

She could have gladly stayed like that for the entirety of the future they'd just agreed to if Vic hadn't pulled back entirely too soon.

"Wait," she said, her grin unbridled and her eyes dancing with joy, "that's a yes, right?"

Sophia threw back her head and laughed, unable to believe it herself. "Yes!"

Epilogue

One Year Later

Vic stood at the desk of her sitting room and rubbed her forehead as she tried to internalise the elaborate schedule her new personal assistant had dropped off with her croissant and morning tea. "Whose idea was it to plan a wedding and film a movie at the same time?"

"That would be you." Sophia frowned at her own elaborate itinerary as she sipped that wretchedly strong American coffee she insisted on drinking black. "Though I strongly suspect your mother had a great deal to say about the wedding date since she's not fond of us living in sin."

"What?" Vic feigned offence. "I can't believe you'd suggest I'm anything less than a full adult capable of making my own decisions after everything I've learned and executed over the last year."

Sophia laughed. "It's okay, I'm still a little frightened of her myself, and when she begins talking about the gardens and what will be in bloom at any given moment, she gets an almost maniacal glint in her eye."

"Yes, now I remember why we agreed to an August wedding, abject terror laced with a strong desire to get a ring on your finger before the full reality of what you're marrying into really sinks in."

The corners of Sophia's mouth curled up slightly. "At least she's also terrifying people on our behalf these days."

"True," Vic agreed as she stuffed half a croissant in her mouth and thought of her mother's demeanour lately. She hadn't had a personality change. She'd simply gone from using her meddling, intrusive, and underhanded ways to try to keep them apart to applying all those same attributes toward trying to make their relationship official, and therefore easier to promote. She'd accepted nothing short of a by-the-book public courtship period, followed by a short engagement and a full onslaught of wedding publicity that she intended to spin as part of a larger PR campaign to rebrand them as the face of modern nobility. "Then again, maybe she's still exacting her revenge in the form of wedding-planning-themed torture."

"Fair." Sophia stood up and fastened the buttons on the cuff of her silk shirt.

Vic stemmed a surge of attraction. She'd grown used to them over their time together but never grew immune. They came any time of day, in any company, and could be triggered by even the most mundane moments or movements. If Sophia stretched herself awake in the morning, Vic wanted to kiss her. If Sophia practiced pouring the perfect gin and tonic, Vic had the urge to kiss her. If Sophia stood in the courtyard behind a camera dolly with her face turned toward the sun and her hands on her hips, Vic could hardly contain the desire to kiss her.

She surrendered to the impulse now, slipping her arm around Sophia's waist and putting her into a lip lock before she could even process, much less protest.

Then again, nothing about Sophia's reaction suggested she had any inclination to protest. She melted into Vic with a supple sexiness that raised the temperature in the room several degrees. Sophia's lips parted, welcoming Vic deeper. The now familiar press of their bodies warmed her even as a cool bit of morning air hit her exposed midriff. It took her another hazy second or two to realise that part of her body hadn't been bare a moment earlier, but Sophia must have tugged her top loose as her hands began to wander.

She groaned as she took Sophia's bottom lip between her teeth. They were going to be late . . . again. It wasn't that she wanted to show up completely dishevelled and frantic every morning, but she also didn't want to miss any chance to kiss this woman, or to miss an opportunity to let those kisses devolve into the type of activity that made them both lose track of time.

A sharp knock on the door jolted them apart, and her entire body sagged in frustration even as her mind realised the interruption might be for the best.

She jammed the hem of her shirt into the waist of her trousers and granted permission for the knocker to enter.

"Good morning, Your Ladyship," Jane said brightly before turning to Sophia. "Ma'am, the duchess wondered if you had time to approve a few sketches of floral arrangements this morning."

Sophia grimaced adorably. "We already approved all the flowers for the ceremony."

"Yes," Jane admitted, knowing enough to look mildly chagrined as she held out a folder full of drawing paper. "These are for the processional route and the back of the carriage, of course."

"Of course. How could I have forgotten those?"

Vic heard the laughter in Sophia's voice and stepped in to accept the parcel for her. "We don't have a shred of time to spare at the moment, but I promise to review the proposals on our way to the set this morning."

"May I inform the duchess you'll have an answer for her when you meet tonight to go over the canapés for the rehearsal dinner?"

"Yes. Thank you, Jane."

Jane smiled brightly. "Thank you, ma'am, and I hope you have the most wonderful day of movie making."

Then she backed out the door with a little bow.

"When it comes to her timing, she's no less maddening than James," Vic said as the door closed behind her. "But she's much nicer about it."

Sophia shook her head, though her eyes held nothing but affection.

"What, you miss James? I'm sure he'd come back from his long overdue retirement if you asked nicely."

Sophia snorted softly. "No, I still owe you for pressing the issue on that one. I much prefer Jane, and I think your mother is warming to her as well. My mystification was in response to the idea of having to choose flowers for the back of the carriage on my wedding processional. Or the idea of lady's maids interrupting my morning make-out sessions. Or even the casual way she mentioned our plans to taste canapés with the duke and duchess after work this evening? Oh, and by the way, my work is directing a major Hollywood star in a movie produced by my heiress-fiancée. How is this my life?"

"Well, if you hadn't proven so adept at juggling it all, it might not have been," Vic teased. "You've only yourself to blame, but I'm afraid you're indispensable now, which reminds me, we're late for work."

"Shite," Sophia muttered as she pushed some papers into a folder, tucked it under her arm, and snagged the coffee on her way toward the door.

She turned and caught Vic trying unsuccessfully to smother a grin.

"What are you laughing at?"

"Nothing." She collected a few of her own things. "I merely enjoy how you've begun swearing in British. Maybe we should have put that in your application for citizenship. I know my father's put in a few calls to hurry the paperwork along. Perhaps next time he speaks to someone, he could mention that you said, 'bugger it all' to one of the sound technicians yesterday, or did you think I didn't hear that?"

"Very funny. Maybe you should get to work before I start second-guessing the whole dual citizenship thing in the first place."

Vic took the point and headed for the door, but that didn't keep her from sniggering quietly on their way down the stairs.

As they reached the courtyard, she spied Charlie waiting beside the Land Rover. He wore his usual cheery expression as he opened one door for Sophia, then jogged around to the other side and opened one for Vic. They'd told him a hundred times he needn't do so, but he seemed to find it amusing, and he claimed undying gratitude that they let him cruise around in the Rover as opposed to having to borrow Archie's car to run errands.

Charlie certainly knew every pothole and dip in the road between the castle and Amberwick, and he dodged them deftly, allowing her and Sophia to converse or work on the ride, but she did still miss being behind the wheel herself.

She must have sighed, or perhaps Sophia could read her ennui by now because she reached over and twirled a strand of Vic's hair on her index finger before giving it a playful tug. "You know what you said about me making myself indispensable earlier?"

"Yes?"

"The same goes for you needing a driver."

"How so?"

"If you hadn't proven yourself so adept at working on the road, people might not expect you to do so."

She wasn't sure if she should accept the compliment or feel indignant that she'd done this to herself. Lord knows, she'd never intended to be the kind of person who conducted phone meetings from the back of her car or on a train or a plane for that matter, but she'd certainly had ample opportunity to practice those skills over the last few months. "I'm glad I've gotten better at commanding people's attention, but never meant for someone else to chart my course while I did."

"And you haven't," Sophia said quickly. "You gave directions other people are following, and that goes well beyond basic GPS. You've made yourself indispensable to this entire production. You could've chosen to become a chauffeur. Instead you became a producer."

"It's never too late to change my mind though, right?"

Sophia laughed a little harder than the comment warranted. "Oh no, it really is. The chauffeur ship has sailed for you."

"When?"

"The moment you showed the entire estate office how well-suited you are to securing artist grants and economic development funds from the government."

"I suppose there's that." She shrugged, but the work had been nothing to scoff at. Perhaps unsurprisingly, movie producing had proven much more complex than she'd realised when she'd made the rash decision to buy Emma's production rights. The early days had all become a blur in her mind now. She'd had to learn fast, and by "learn" she meant cut deals, make pitches, and call in favours from more than a few personal connections. Even thinking back on it now, her shoulders began to tighten with the fear that she'd missed some minuscule detail or forgotten one of the millions of filing deadlines. And even if things were all sorted for their full production funds, as she'd double-checked a hundred times a day, post-production costs were another matter entirely.

She pinched the bridge of her nose to stem the stress starting to throb there.

Sophia did one better by kissing her cheek softly, then moving back to nip at her earlobe before whispering, "You've done everything anyone could ever ask of a producer, including surrounding yourself with an amazing team of people. Trust us not to let you down."

Her smile returned, both at that thought and at the view spread out before them as they made the wide, arcing curve toward the tiny village of Amberwick. Her heart swelled at the distant sight of people moving busily down on the beach. Not just any people, her people. Their friends and colleagues were already assembling for work, and though she couldn't make out individual faces among the crowd yet, she knew them all the same. Some had been in her circle of trust for years. Others were new to her life but no less valuable to their shared future. "They are good people, are they not?"

"The best," Sophia confirmed as Charlie turned onto a sandy road leading to a beach lot. "And you're good with them."

She nodded absently, her excitement growing as she started to mentally review all her goals for the day ahead.

"I mean it." Sophia's voice took on a serious note that drew Vic's attention back to her. "The people want to follow you. That's my favourite part of seeing you in your new role. I love watching you work with your people and seeing how much they believe in you as a leader."

"They believe in our vision."

"They believe in the vision *you* shared with them," Sophia emphasised as the car come to a stop.

Vic didn't have any quick comebacks as emotion threatened to overtake her, so she merely opted for one more kiss before they stepped out into a glorious coastal scene.

The tide was out, revealing a smooth expanse of sand before endless ocean. Overhead, high white wisps of cloud offered occasional breaks in a blue canvas, as if Mother Nature had chosen this moment to flaunt the gifts she'd bestowed on Northland.

"Nice of you to join us, Your Ladyship," Brogan called, earning her a little elbow nudge from Emma and a laugh from Talia. "These two have been rewriting your movie in your absence."

"Not the whole thing," Emma said, "a few tweaks here and there."

"We're waiting for Sophia's input before we give the amendments to Cobie."

"Where is our leading lady?" Sophia asked as she joined them.

"I got a text saying Cobie's out of hair and makeup and should be here any moment."

"So long as Esther and Diane don't waylay her along the route again," Sophia muttered.

"It'll be fine," Vic said confidently. "I gave Reggie ten quid to be Cobie's bodyguard and handler between the Raven and the beach."

"You didn't." Brogan groaned, no doubt thinking about how serious her teenage niece could be when given a task that came with any sort of gravitas. Still, everyone on set found the kid utterly charming, and what was the point of having the power to choose her own staff if Vic couldn't build up some of Northland's finest along the way?

On that note, she scanned the beach for another one of her new charges. She spotted Ollie, the student filmmaker. He stood down the shore a little farther with a Steadicam strapped to his chest.

"He was the first one here this morning," Brogan said as she followed Vic's gaze. "I know his parents live down the coast, but he's here so much these days, we talked about offering him my old room at Charlie's."

"Just don't take his edge off," Sophia said, a hint of warmth in her voice. "He's the hungriest of all the students we have on the project, and I like him that way. I may even turn him into an assistant director someday if he grows into the title."

"Speaking of titles," Emma cut back in, "any word from your government contact on how the wedding might affect the title?"

"The wedding won't change much that we can tell," Vic acknowledged, but the subject didn't inspire the same tension in her as it had in the past. Of course, she still felt a little prick of indignation at the injustice of women having unequal rights of inheritance, but the conflict felt more general and academic than it ever had. "I honestly haven't given it much thought lately."

They all eyed her as if finding that hard to believe.

She turned to scan the beaches a bit before surveying her local crew and the faces of her friends once more. "There will still be a legal fight someday, but it doesn't hang like a guillotine blade above my neck at the moment. It turns out that when I love the work I do and the people I'm working with, it's easier to take pride in who I am right now instead of worrying about who I may or may not be down the road."

"Hear, hear." Brogan clapped a hand on her shoulder. "And what's more, you seem to have made the right call again, because here come Reg and Cobie."

They all watched the star and her young handler stride up the well-worn path from the village to their part of the beach.

"I got her here straightaway," Reg declared proudly.

Vic tousled the kid's red hair and said, "You've earned yourself a regular appointment, unless Ms. Galloway objects."

"Not at all," Cobie said amiably. "I couldn't ask for better company on my short commute. But if I'd known the rest of the crew was just milling around down here, I would've stayed in bed with a beautiful pop star."

"Ms. Wilder will have to wait," Sophia cut in quickly. "Tell her to order us some scones because we're going to keep you busy for as long as we've got good natural light today."

And just like that, everyone jumped into their jobs. Vic stood back and watched all the principal players work. Talia and Emma scribbled on scripts, techs tested mics over the soft sounds of the sea, camera operators bustled about carrying an array of equipment Vic still hadn't learned the specific names for yet. And there, in the centre of it all, Sophia stood, hands on hips, hair stirring softly on the breeze, surveying the scene like a general preparing to orchestrate an invasion.

She was as commanding as she was beautiful, and when she raised her voice to call out instructions, everyone stopped to stare. For all the talk about Vic's vision, she knew which of them would play the bigger part in sharing that vision with the world, and she couldn't have been prouder.

She'd meant what she'd said about the title earlier. She slept well at night knowing they were using every ounce of their collective creativity to make something meaningful that would last, even if the title didn't.

Then again, sleeping next to Sophia every night was a blessing, no matter how they'd spent the day.

"Places everyone," Sophia called. "I want the big, sweeping scenic shots before the tide shifts. Clear the scene. Everybody but Cobie off my beach."

Everywhere people hustled to get out of the way, and Vic took her place behind her fiancée as Cobie jogged down the shore several metres.

"She's perfect for the part," Emma said as they watched her go. Then turning to Sophia, she added, "Then again, you could've been, too."

"No way," Sophia said without glancing up from a monitor she was studying.

"Be honest, though," Talia nudged. "Now that you've been on both sides of the camera, do you miss being in front of the lens?"

Sophia finally looked up, her dark eyes deep and serious. "Not at all. I know a lot of people would think that the stardom was a lot to give up, but in return I got everything I've ever really wanted, and a few things I'd never even dared to dream of."

Vic smiled, contentedly. She couldn't have said it better herself.

About the Author

Rachel Spangler never set out to be a *New York Times*-reviewed author. They were just so poor during seven years of college that they had to come up with creative forms of cheap entertainment. The debut novel, *Learning Curve,* was born out of one such attempt. Since writing is more fun than a real job and so much cheaper than therapy, they continued to type away, leading to the publication of *The Long Way Home, LoveLife, Spanish Heart, Does She Love You, Timeless, Heart of the Game, Perfect Pairing, Close to Home, Edge of Glory, In Development, Love All, Full English, Spanish Surrender, Straight Up, Modern English, Fire and Ice* and *Straight Up.* Now a four-time Lambda Literary Award finalist, an IPPY, Goldie, and Rainbow Award winner, and the recipient of the 2018 Alice B. Reader medal, Rachel plans to continue writing as long as anyone, anywhere, will keep reading.

In 2018 Spangler joined the ranks of Bywater Books content editing team. They now hold the title of senior romance editor for the company and love having the opportunity to mentor young authors.

Rachel lives in Western New York with wife Susan and son Jackson. The Spangler family spends the long winters curling and skiing. In the summer, they love to travel and watch their beloved St. Louis Cardinals. Regardless of the season, Rachel always makes time for a good romance, whether reading it, writing it, or living it.

For more information, please visit Rachel online at www.rachelspangler.com or on Instagram, Facebook, Twitter, or Tumblr.

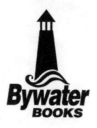

Bywater BOOKS

At Bywater Books we love good books about lesbians just like you do, and we're committed to bringing the best of contemporary lesbian writing to our avid readers. Our editorial team is dedicated to finding and developing outstanding writers who create books you won't want to put down.

We sponsor the Bywater Prize for Fiction to help with this quest. Each prizewinner receives $1,000 and publication of their novel. We have already discovered amazing writers like Jill Malone, Sally Bellerose, and Hilary Sloin through the Bywater Prize. Which exciting new writer will we find next?

For more information about Bywater Books and the annual Bywater Prize for Fiction, please visit our website.

www.bywaterbooks.com